# SONGS FOR CLARA

*To Mom -*

*Whose love of classical music moved me,*
*and love of God changed me.*

# CONTENTS

# CHAPTER 1

The vacant house at 181 Augustine Street wasn't haunted in the conventional sense, but it held its share of ghosts. I wondered which ones awaited me, the prodigal son returning, with no expectant father to greet him.

I parked my blue '79 Horizon halfway up the sloped drive. The foursquare house resembled most of the homes on the tree-lined street: two stories plus an attic, clapboard siding, enclosed front porch, small yard, detached garage. A typical middle-class 1930's-built home in a typical middle-class neighborhood. No fancy lawn ornaments or pristine landscaping. Families lived quiet lives here, simple and uncomplicated, but rarely easy. It was a place where neighbors talked across chain-link fences or on breezy front porches. Where kids walked to school, moms stayed home, and dads rode the bus to work. Where Dad and Mom had raised me and my older sister, in this now vacant, ghostly house.

Vacant, but far from empty.

I wrestled a red Honda lawn mower from the car's trunk, and wheeled it to the top of the drive. A gruff voice called out behind me.

"Frankie Stephens, that you?"

I froze upon hearing that name. My sister Fanny was practically the only person who called me that since I was seven, when I had announced that "Frankie is for babies, and I am NOT a baby!"

At the bottom of the drive stood a frail, elderly gentleman, wearing a white t-shirt and plaid shorts, and holding a leash tethered to the world's ugliest dog. It was some short-haired, miniature, tailless breed. A Tribble with teeth.

"Hey, Mr. Jacoby," I said. "Sure is."

Merle Jacoby lived half-a-dozen homes down the street. Seeing that he was still alive came as a bit of a surprise, as he had seemed ancient even when I was a kid.

I met him at the bottom of the drive, in the cool shade of an elm. It was only nine-thirty, but the heat and humidity were already on the rise this August Saturday morning. With a cigar firmly clamped between clenched teeth, he gave what I assumed was supposed to be a smile. His dog strained at the leash, eager to either gnaw my ankle or harmlessly sniff it. Jacoby reeled the dog back, bent down and scooped it up, cradling it in the crook of his arm. We shook hands; it was like grabbing a warm, raw pork tenderloin. He stood at least a foot shorter than me.

"This is Boris," he said. "Say hello to Frankie, Boris."

Boris did nothing. I considered extending my hand for him to smell but decided against it. I preferred not to get bitten.

"You still in Rochester?" he asked.

"I'm out in Spencerport, teaching middle school band."

"And how's your dad?" he asked. "Still kicking?"

"Somewhat. Slowing down now."

"Still at that retirement place? Which one? Mellowood?"

I nodded. The way Jacoby said *still*, he made it sound like we had committed a crime moving Dad to Mellowood Assisted Living.

Jacoby tapped his cigar, sending ash onto the walk, as the shadow of a sneer crossed his face. "Glad no one's put me in a home," he said.

"Yeah, well, I'm kinda busy," I said, thinking that this conversation was heading to a place I didn't want to go. "Gotta cut the lawn, gather some stuff, fix one or two things. Just in and out."

"You selling the place?"

I sighed and nodded. "Realtor comes out Tuesday."

Jacoby blew out a large cloud of smoke, and grimaced. "Neighborhood keeps changing. Folks moving out or dying."

Our eyes met, and he quickly looked towards the house. He must have read my thoughts, because his mouth twitched ever so slightly.

"Well, the good folks, anyway. Folks you like seem to go long before the folks you don't like. Ever notice?"

"Yeah. Ironic."

He cleared his throat and turned to spit a wad of yellow phlegm towards the street. "Your parents, they were good folks. Your mother, God rest her soul," at which he crossed himself, "was one of the kindest people I knew. Your dad - he cared. Back when you were little...how old are you now?"

"Twenty-seven."

"You were a tyke then. Your folks threw great parties, before things changed in the late 60's." He spat out "late 60's" with the same disgust as he had his phlegm, as if the words curdled his tongue.

"Your folks would have music friends over, bringing their instruments, playing jazz and big band numbers right there in your home. Your dad was great on the piano. And your mom...boy, could Louise sing! And play! The duets with your dad. And cook!"

He took a thoughtful puff on his cigar, and from his expression, it seemed those bygone songs were playing in his head. He cast a soulful glance up at the house.

"I remember. They told me stories, and I knew their friends."

"Of course you remember!" he said. "You played piano a few times yourself! This tall, you were." He held his hand at belt height.

I winced at his recollection. "Listen, I really gotta mow the..."

"I enjoyed those parties," he interrupted, oblivious to my comment. "I went a few times. Stopped going when talk became political. Never understood why some folks thought

3

those changes did the country good. Thank God Reagan's fixing all that." Another puff on the cigar. "Anyway, I remember those parties everytime I walk by."

Boris squirmed to be let down. Jacoby lowered him, and he skittered towards the elm to relieve himself.

"Tell your dad I said hello?" he asked.

"Sure," I said.

"I wonder if he remembers me. He's got dementia, right?"

I shook my head. "Alzheimer's Disease."

He hmphed, closing his eyes. "Dementia, Alzheimer's. Same thing. He still play?"

Not wanting to argue the nuances between the two, I ignored his statement and merely shrugged. "Mellowood has a piano, but I doubt he's played it."

"That's a shame. He was good."

I nodded. This had become tedious. "Better than good, actually. Listen, it was nice chatting, but," and I jerked a thumb over my shoulder, "things to do."

"Right. Let's go, Boris." We shook hands, and he shuffled on his way while I tromped up the drive.

Jacoby called out. "Don't sell to punks, okay? This is a nice neighborhood."

I waved a final goodbye, turned, and rolled my eyes. Jacoby would complain if Jesus, Billy Graham, and even Ronald Reagan himself moved into his neighborhood.

I slowly climbed the wooden steps and entered the screened front porch. I opened the storm door and took a deep breath before unlocking the heavy leaded-glass paned door. I hadn't been here since Dad moved into Mellowood in February: six months ago. His memory had been worsening from week to week. Frequent nighttime calls to my sister Fanny, scared because Mom was missing - even though she had been dead for eight years. He'd gotten lost driving home from the grocery store several times. One evening he'd turned the water on to fill the bathtub, forgotten about it, and caused thousands of dollars of water damage. The final straw had been when he left the gas stove on one morning. Fanny had made an unscheduled visit, smelled the gas, and aired out the house before it exploded, or before Dad asphyxiated. Shortly afterward, following countless arguments with Fanny and his doctors, he'd relented. Fanny had finally convinced him to move.

"Mom would want you to do this," she said, "because she loves you."

And that was that.

Now the house was going to be sold. Fanny had power of attorney and handled 99% of the preparations. I was here to contribute my one. Several boxes in the attic needed to be brought down, and a few small repairs needed to be done. I told Fanny I'd mow the lawn this one last time; the realtor would have to make future arrangements. I had no intention to ever step foot in the place again.

The deadbolt snapped back, and I stepped into a small vestibule. The air smelled stuffy and stale. I crossed through the empty living room, through a double-wide doorway into the dining room, its parquet floor recently waxed. Inside, a doorway on the left connected to the kitchen. A pair of sliding pocket doors formed most of the dining room's back wall. The doors were closed, and behind it was Dad's piano room, his conservatory, added on after he and Mom had moved in.

I crossed the room and slowly slid the door panels open, one to each side. The room was empty, sunlight streaming through the large bay window centered in the back wall. Memories flashed by, of birthdays and holidays, of lessons and recitals, of the parties Jacoby mentioned. In my mind's eye, I saw the old baby grand, pearly black and spotless, its end tucked into the right hand corner. I pictured its cover held up by the top board prop, a Tiffany lamp standing on the left-hand music shelf, and sheaves of composition pages atop the music rack. Spectral shapes of Dad playing while Mom sang along, standing next to him, or of them sitting side by side playing a duet, shimmered for the briefest of seconds, before I blinked them away.

The walls were bare now, once covered with Dad's degrees and commendations from the Prescott Conservatory of Musical Studies, photos of the various ensembles he had belonged to, awards for numerous compositions, and the one Gold Record from when he had been the pianist for a 1940's big band. Years of sunshine had bleached the paint around them, leaving darker rectangles behind. I remembered where each item had hung, and how they had never changed or been added to.

This was where Dad had taught Fanny and me how to play. She'd endured seven years of lessons, while I had lasted all of two. Which is why she now had the piano, while I played trumpet and taught middle school band.

Too many memories were associated with this room, most of which were unpleasant. I slid the doors closed, but the images invading my peace of mind remained.

*Maybe this was a mistake. Did I think today would be different, just because Dad's not here?*

I stepped into the kitchen, and opened the windows above the sink, facing the backyard. A breeze, still cool from the morning, brushed my face, and caused a sheet of paper on the counter next to the sink to flutter. I snatched it as it floated to the floor. It was a bullet point to do list.

"*Frank* –

> *Check Dad's AC unit*
> *Check bulbs (replacements in basement)*
> *Fix garage downspout*
> *Dig out post*
> *Love, Fanny*"

So much for just in and out. I crumpled the note and stuffed it in my pocket.

* * *

Checking lights was the second-to-last chore on the list, and I saved my bedroom for last. The stained wood floor didn't show where my furniture had once stood, but I recalled everything exactly: a desk in the far corner, next to a window facing the neighbor's house; my twin bed across from the doorway, beneath the window facing the backyard; a long six-drawer bureau to the right of the doorway; a narrow bookcase jammed into the farthest corner. The closet door, next to where the bed had been, stood shut.

I peered through the rear window. Immediately below me was the flat roof of the conservatory. How many times had I climbed onto that roof, shimmied down the trellis, and played with neighborhood friends after dark? Hundreds? Thousands?

Our backyard abutted that of Tommy Vickers, a childhood classmate. My best friend until he had been killed in a car accident when in the fifth grade. Tommy had been a middle child, between two sisters, Brenda and Jessica. Brenda and my sister Fanny had been best friends, too, and still were. Jessica and I had become great friends after Tommy's death, despite a four-year age difference. In a way, I had become her new big brother, while she became my new best friend.

The Vickers had moved to the suburbs seven or eight years ago. They were good people, who had suffered more than any parent ought to. Tommy's funeral had been the hardest thing I ever sat through. Even Dad had cried.

I stood back from the window, looking at the space where my bed used to stand. A memory surfaced: the evening after Tommy's funeral, me lying on the bed, Mom seated next to me, her hand gently stroking my hair.

*"I didn't cry during Tommy's funeral."*

*"What do you think that means?"*

*I shrugged. "Dad cried, and he wasn't even Tommy's friend."*

*Mom smiled sadly. "There are different kinds of sadness."*

*"There are?"*

*She nodded. "Many kinds."*

"What kind does Dad have?"

"Compassion. He cried for Mr. Vickers."

I chewed my lip a little, not quite understanding. But then, Dad was always hard to understand.

"What kind is mine?"

She thought a bit before answering. "Remembrance, of the fun times you and Tommy shared. That's why you aren't crying now."

"I've been sad before, and I've cried. A lot."

She brushed a stray hair off my forehead. "I know, my love. Someday you'll think of Tommy again, and crying will be the right thing. When that happens, remember what I always tell you."

"All shall be well, and all manner of things shall be well."

Mom smiled at me.

"Mom, are you sad too?"

"Oh yes," and her smile faded.

"What kind?"

She looked out the window, towards Tommy's house, then back to me. "The kind that reminds you of every sadness."

My bedroom may have been a sanctuary for most of my childhood, but like the conservatory, unhappy memories lingered here. I quickly checked the bedroom and closet lights, then departed for the attic steps.

The unfinished attic was all studs, beams, and trusses. Kraft-paper backed fiberglass insulation was jammed between every joist. Three bare bulbs hung from cords along the length of the room, a silver extension chain dangling from each. I pulled each chain, and each light glowed to life.

Our attic had seemed much bigger growing up, filled with stacks of cartons, luggage, old-fashioned trunks, odd wooden crates, and unused furniture. Getting lost in the maze of columns, stacks and haphazard piles had seemed easy then. Dad and Mom had been known for their hospitality and musical prowess, not their storage efficiency.

The attic now stood nearly empty. Fanny, with her husband Mike and some parish teenagers needing community service hours, had hauled out almost everything. Fanny kept some things, but most of it had been either donated or thrown away. All that remained were eight corrugated boxes wedged in a corner, far from the steps, as if they hoped not to be discovered. None of them were marked. Fanny had probably thought I'd be interested in keeping whatever was in them. I doubted it.

The boxes were identical, maybe two feet long and a foot in width and depth, musty and age worn. I grabbed two of them at once – they only weighed about twenty pounds each - and headed to the steps. Within five minutes, all eight were stacked next to the Horizon.

Returning inside, I closed the kitchen window and made sure the other doors were locked. I took one final look in the piano room, half-hoping for some twinge of nostalgia, or forgotten happy memory. None came.

The doors' glass panels rattled as I slid them shut, resonating with an air of finality. I locked the front door and let the porch door slam behind.

I loaded the cartons into the car, and as I was about to close the passenger side door, I stopped. Eight unmarked boxes, containing who knows what, and I hadn't opened any of them? Not one? Well, it was pretty hot, and I was sweaty and hungry, and my apartment was nice and cool, there was beer in the fridge, and....

*C'mon. You can look in one.*

Temptation won. I peeled back the brittle, yellowed cellophane tape of the carton on the front seat. I unfolded the flaps, unsure of what to expect, recalling stories of recluses who hid millions of dollars in their homes, which were discovered upon their death, bequeathed to nobody. Dad wasn't a recluse, but he had his share of odd moments and idiosyncrasies. Squirreling away wealth would be a nice idiosyncrasy to have. Still, I doubted these boxes contained stacks of bills, rare coins, or anything of great value. I wouldn't be so lucky.

The carton held letter-sized manila envelopes, organized like files in a drawer. I removed two, recognizing Dad's impeccable calligraphy along the top edge. One was marked *Performance Reviews 1951*, the other *Performance Reviews 1952* with *Prescott Conservatory* written beneath. I replaced them and fingered through the rest. About half were identified as performance reviews, while the rest were marked *Student Audition Reports*, organized by type and year.

*Thirty-five-year-old employment records. Thanks, Fanny.*

I was about to close the box when something caught my eye. About a third of the envelopes stood an inch or so taller than the others, all at one end of the carton, even though the envelopes were all the same size. My interest piqued, I removed half of the envelopes, setting them atop the nearby carton.

A thick manila envelope lay flat across the bottom. Prying it loose, I pulled it out. It was unmarked.

I unwound the red string looped between the two circlets, peeled back the flap, and slowly extracted the contents.

It was a collection of music scores, held together by two large tan rubber bands. The handwriting was unmistakable. Dad had written these. The topmost score was titled *Waltz, Opus 1 No. 1*, for piano. The ink had faded a bit, but the music remained readable. Turning the packet over in my hands, I estimated that it contained no more than ten songs.

Along the spine ran a one-inch-wide strip of white paper, crisp with age, held in place by the rubber bands. Upon it were the words FOR CLARA.

I blinked several times.

*Who the hell was Clara?*

# CHAPTER 2

A flurry of thoughts raced through my mind while I drove back to my apartment, all centered on one thing:

Was Dad a cheater?

The implications these songs represented overwhelmed me. My face felt flushed, as the thought of Dad being unfaithful to Mom cycled over and over. When had it happened? Before Fanny and I were born, or during Mom's fight with breast cancer? I was too stunned to think straight. I'd have to show them to Fanny. She wouldn't be happy about them, but what was I supposed to do? Keep them a secret from her, like Dad did from Mom?

*First things first. Get home, get them inside, and look them over.*

I pulled into my parking space behind my duplex. A flight of exterior steps led to the upper floor of a white, two-story, 19th century home converted into an upstairs-downstairs rental property. It wasn't anything fancy – the entry door opened into the living room, with a kitchenette and dining area to the left, and two bedrooms sandwiching a bathroom to the right. A picture window next to the door faced east, while the bedroom windows faced the Erie Canal to the north. The location suited me perfectly: it was close to the village center, and a ten-minute walk to the middle school.

It took me ten minutes to lug the cartons to the spare bedroom. I had left the envelope holding Clara's songs on top of the box, and now I took it with me into the kitchen. A pair of Genesee Twelve Horse Ales and a carryout container of

Chicken Pad Thai awaited me in the fridge, all of it well earned. I grabbed them and wolfed the food down, and drained a beer, barely tasting either.

The newly found songs commanded my attention. Who could this Clara woman have been? Obviously it wasn't a reference to Mom, whose name was Louise Frieda Lasinen. Could she have been a friend? Neither Dad nor Mom had ever mentioned anyone named Clara. They had a small circle of close friends, mostly teachers and musicians from Prescott, some neighbors, and people from the local Catholic parish. They'd hosted the parties Jacoby had spoken of, but those had ended nearly twenty years ago. They had stopped entertaining by 1970, except for family events and an occasional dinner with Dad's coworkers. There was no Clara among them, nor in the extended family. Had she been a former student? A fellow teacher, or other coworker? A love child? Or just some random name he'd picked out of the blue?

Or he had had an affair, and these songs were a testimony to it, or a memorialization of it. A gift never given.

Perhaps the answer lay hidden in one of the other cartons. Whoever she was, Dad had obviously considered her important enough to keep her songs for 35 years, hidden away in the attic. Packed to be nearly impossible to find, which meant...

*...he didn't hide them merely from everybody. He hid them from Mom.*

I uncapped the second beer, took a long draught, and set it down, then carefully took out the scores. One of the rubber bands snapped into several brittle pieces while removing it. The other remained intact, but had lost its elasticity, remaining elongated and shapeless. The topmost song, the Waltz, was five pages long, the score paper-clipped together. Beneath that was *Romance, Opus 2, No. 1*, written in G major, followed by a second Romance, written in C major, both for the piano.

Two Romances? More evidence that these songs were a dedication. I recalled Dad having written numerous pieces dedicated to Mom throughout their marriage: birthday Humoresques; a Romance for their twenty-fifth anniversary; a quartet in memoriam, performed shortly after she died. And others.

Except Mom hadn't been the inspiration for these pieces. He wouldn't have hidden them if she had. Her birthday Humoresques were kept in the piano bench, not in an old cardboard box, stashed away in the attic.

The initial shock had waned, courtesy of the beer and a sated appetite, no doubt. The swirling thoughts settled down, allowing me to better process this. On the one hand, Dad being unfaithful seemed impossible. His marriage to Mom had lasted twenty-seven years, until breast cancer killed her in 1978. He'd always seemed devoted to her. He hadn't dated anybody since her death.

The box held records and papers from the period between 1951 and 1956. Assuming the songs had been there all that time, it could mean he'd cheated on Mom before either Fanny or myself were born. Fanny was born in '56, me three years later. If that were the case, Clara could be dead by now. Or moved away. Maybe the affair had ended amicably, and they'd decided to let bygones be bygones. The affair had been over and done with long before I had come around, and Dad certainly wouldn't have discussed it with me. Would Fanny have known? And would she have told me if she had?

On the other hand, the songs weren't absolute proof Dad had cheated. Maybe he had written them for a girlfriend before he'd met Mom. They had first met at Prescott in 1949, when she started her master's degree, which she never completed. Mom dropped out the following year, and they married in 1951. So it was possible he could have had a serious relationship beforehand, and written songs for this Clara person just as he'd written songs for Mom.

I looked through the remaining pieces: a waltz, four romances, a humoresque, a sonata and two duets for violin and piano. The titles simply listed style, opus, and number. The letters 'IS' appeared in the lower left-hand corner on each piece's first page. Ivan Stephens, Dad's initials. No dates, though, or other notation.

I repacked the scores and glanced towards the spare bedroom. Maybe the other cartons held answers. Half-empty beer bottle in hand, I navigated past the couch, passing the stereo unit that stood against the wall. While walking by, I saw the message light on my answering machine flashing with a single, repeating, red pulse: one message. Probably Fanny.

"Hey, it's Fanny. Listen, if you bring the mower back tonight, you can stay for dinner, say around 6? Mike's burning burgers. Call if you can't make it. Bye."

I erased the message and glanced at my watch - 4:15. I didn't have enough time to look through every box, but maybe enough time for one.

I unstacked the cartons, arranged them side by side, and pried loose a corner of the cellophane tape from one of them. Several layers covered the flap seam, meaning it had been opened and resealed multiple times. The tape peeled away easily. Small, rectangular, white boxes, the kind Christmas cards are sold in, were packed inside. They were arranged in three stacks, with the year written across the covers, in faded blue ink, in Mom's unmistakable flowing handwriting. I pulled out a number of the boxes, and selected the one marked '1959.'

It held a collection of black-and-white photographs, ones I had never seen before. The topmost one was of Fanny, three years old at the time, wearing a light-colored snowsuit, lying in a snowbank. It looked like she was trying to make a snow angel, arms and legs spread outward. I cracked a bit of a grin as I turned the photo over. The date stamp on the back read 'Jan 59.' The photographs seemed to be arranged chronologically: more winter photos, then some from Easter, celebrating with cousins, Mom wearing a flamboyant bonnet, clearly pregnant. There were some photos of the Rochester Lilac Festival and the Maplewood Rose Garden. Then, several pictures of her and Dad holding me, as a baby. The remaining photos centered on me - with my parents and Fanny, my Baptism, a trip to the Catskills with the cousins, some Thanksgiving shots with extended family, then Christmas.

A former girlfriend had once asked me why we didn't have any photo albums. I said I wasn't even sure we owned a camera. That made her laugh, saying everyone in Rochester owned a Prescott camera! It was practically a law. Prescott Camera & Film was as synonymous with Rochester as General Motors was with Detroit, or Disney with Orlando.

"Then we're outlaws," I had joked.

There had been an artfully arranged gallery of framed photos upon the dining room wall, centered around their wedding portrait. Most had been family portraits, though some were from Dad's performances or milestone events. He had always told guests the story behind each one, such as the time he'd played with Benny Goodman's band, or the time he'd been a last-minute replacement conductor of the Rochester Philharmonic Orchestra. Those photos were as clear in my mind as the blue August sky outside my window. New ones had been added on occasion – mine and Fanny's high school graduation portraits, and Fanny and Mike's wedding portrait, too. But those were professional portraits, not spontaneous shots.

I wondered why these had been relegated to the attic, labeled and organized, packed up and forgotten. Maybe only certain memories were allowed to be displayed. Still, Mom had saved all these photos, all these years. I wondered if Dad had known about them.

I looked at the remaining six cartons, and decided to open them all. One contained another collection of white boxes, while the rest were full of mustard-yellow manila envelopes, arranged like file folders, the same as the first. I flipped through them, the envelopes identified by year and a brief description. Composition notes, student evaluations, course work. Each box contained five- or six-years' worth of work, all the way up till 1980, the year he retired. No secret envelopes tucked underneath, and nothing looked out of place. If Clara's identity were contained therein, finding it would require inspecting every envelope.

Searching every envelope would take weeks, if not longer. First things first: tell Fanny about the songs tonight and get her opinion. Then, visit Dad tomorrow. He probably wouldn't – or couldn't - be helpful, but I had to ask. They were his, after all. Whether or not he wanted to explain them, to me of all people. . .well, that was altogether different.

There was no sense begging tomorrow's problems today. I downed the rest of my Twelve Horse and went to take a shower.

* * *

I knocked on the glass storm door, and pulled it open without waiting for an answer. I held the manila envelope in one hand, and a Wegmans grocery bag in the other.

"Favorite uncle is here!"

A female voice called out: "Only come in if you have beer!"

Seconds later, Fanny emerged from the kitchen, stepping into the great room while wiping her hands on a dish towel. As she approached, I stopped and simply stared. She was thin and stood several inches shorter than me, about 5'6", with teased, big brunette hair, expressive brown eyes, and a round, pretty face.

"What?" she asked, noticing my expression. "Do I have something on my face?"

I shook my head, smiling. "No. It's just that you're a dead ringer for Mom."

Fanny looked confused. "I would certainly hope so, since she was, you know, our mom." We exchanged hugs, and she moved back a step. "Why the sudden shock?"

"One of those boxes was full of old photographs," I told her. "Like, 1950's old. You and Mom could've been twins."

I followed her through the great room into the kitchen. Dolls sat upon one of the couches in a perfect row, straight and organized by size. I stepped over a scattered pile of Lego bricks. Pushed into the left corner of the room stood Dad's baby grand, a pair of children's lesson books opened upon the rack. Seeing it didn't always evoke the best of memories, but it was a beautiful instrument, and Fanny took care of it as well as Dad had. She was an accomplished player in her own right, and it seemed she was carrying on the tradition with her kids.

Fanny motioned towards my hand. "Is that what's in the envelope? Pictures?"

"No, I left those at home. I'll bring them next time. This," I said, waggling the envelope, "is far more interesting."

"Oooh, I like interesting."

"You might not like it as much as you think. Where are Mike and the monkeys?"

She hesitated before answering, her left eyebrow slightly arched. I had a good idea what she was thinking, but said nothing.

"Mike's grilling, Justin and Rachel are on the swings. They'll be happy to see you." She reached out a hand. "Whatcha bring?"

"The usual," I said, handing her the bag with the beer in it. She snatched it away, her smirk telling me she had meant the envelope. I leaned against the island that separated the kitchen workspace from the dining nook. A plate of hamburger buns stood next to a glass serving bowl, filled with a fresh garden salad. An oval wooden dining table sat bathed in sunlight, which shone through the sliding glass door wall and windows encasing the nook. Mike, wreathed in grey smoke, stood at the grill, his back to the house. Farther back, Justin and Rachel swung side by side on the playset, each arc rising as high as possible.

"Great, we're low on beer." She put the six-pack in the fridge, keeping three bottles back. Handing me one, she asked,

"How'd it go at the house?"

"Fine." I unscrewed the cap and took a swig.

"AC working?"

"Was until I turned it off."

"Light bulbs? Downspout? Took out the clothesline thingy?"

"Yes, yes, and yes, the thingy is out. Done being anal yet?"

"Shut up."

"At least we've established I took the boxes."

"I purposefully left you the unmarked ones."

"I know you did. Take the good stuff and leave me the crap."

Fanny smiled. "So show me the crap you found."

"See for yourself," and I gave her the envelope.

She unwound the string, and pulled out the compositions. I had replaced the old rubber bands with a large black paper clamp. The label 'For Clara' was tucked underneath, sticking out like a tongue. As Fanny read the label, her facial expression changed from anticipation to surprise.

She looked at me dumbfounded. "Who's Clara?"

"Dad's lover?" I replied. "I don't know. I was hoping you'd have an idea or two."

Fanny shot me a hard glance, removed the clamp, and scanned the scores. "All Dad's?"

"Yep. Nine of them."

Just then, Mike came in from outside, the kids in tow. Mike was 6'4" and broad shouldered, with short cropped blond hair and a trim mustache. He had played college football until a knee injury ended his career. Now he was an account executive for a local auto parts manufacturer. He carried a platter of hamburgers, a few covered with melted American cheese, the rest plain. Upon seeing me, Justin and Rachel tore past Mike and hugged me at the same time. Justin was eight, already four feet tall and shaping up to be as tall as Mike. The jury was still out on six-year-old Rachel, as her head barely reached my waistline.

"Uncle Frank!" they shouted.

I placed my beer on the counter and wrapped an arm around each of them. "Hey monkeys! How are ya!"

Mike placed the platter on the table. "Hey Frank, what's up?"

"Not much, just hanging out until school starts," I answered. I handed him a beer. "For the chef."

He smirked. "Yeah, flipping burgers is so difficult. Thanks."

"Uncle Frank?" Rachel asked.

"Yeah Rache?"

"I have piano lessons now."

I glanced into the family room, towards the piano. "Those your books? Are you having fun?"

She nodded enthusiastically. "Uh huh! Can I play a song for you?"

Fanny chimed in. "After dinner, okay? Both of you, wash your hands before we eat please."

They ran to the washroom. Fanny put down the scores and carried the salad, some dressings, and a couple condiments to the table. I grabbed her beer and set it at her place. Her expression had shifted from surprise to something more serious. She was thinking about my 'Dad's lover?' remark, I was sure of it, and it wasn't sitting well.

"Still dating Jessica?" Mike asked. He air-quoted *dating*.

"Off and on," I said.

"More on than off I hope," Mike said. "Wink wink nudge nudge," he added, with a mock British accent.

"Michael!" Fanny exclaimed, smacking him upon the shoulder. "You're talking about Brenda's little sister!"

"KnowhutImean, guv'ner?" I laughed, continuing a well-worn Monty Python routine. "Say no more, say no more."

Mike laughed just as the kids returned. After saying grace and taking our seats, Fanny said to Mike, "Frank completed those chores and took those cartons from the attic today."

"Find any rare stocks or bearer bonds?" he asked while

handing me the platter of burgers.

I smiled. "I wish. Two had old photos, and the rest had Dad's Prescott school stuff. I haven't looked through them with a fine-tooth comb or anything, but I don't expect any secret windfall." As I slid a burger patty onto my plate, I added, "Oh, and I found an envelope containing some unpublished compositions, labeled as 'For Clara.'

Justin piped up. "Who's Clara?"

Fanny shushed him. "We don't know yet." She tonged some salad onto his plate. "Right?" she added, turning her eyes on me.

Her tone had turned hard, and her eyes narrowed slightly. I got the feeling she hadn't wanted me to bring up the subject.

*Too late now.*

"I have no idea," I answered, as I layered a slice of tomato and several pickle chips upon my burger. "Yet."

"Unpublished?" Mike asked. "They might be more valuable than you think."

Mike's observation laid down a detour around the subject, but I was determined to drive straight ahead. "Maybe, but what's more interesting to me is that these were written for a *woman* named *Clara.*"

"Okaaaay..."

He wasn't getting it. Fanny took over, ticking names off her fingers.

"Mom's name was Louise Frieda Lasinen. Dad's mom's name was Anastasia Eva. Then there are Aunt Jane and Aunt Alice." Those were Dad's brothers' wives. "And Mom's side has never left Finland, except to come for her funeral, and she was an only child. So what Frank is trying to say is that Dad wrote these songs on behalf of somebody else."

I stopped chewing. That wasn't what I was trying to say, at all.

"Okay. Then what's the big deal?" Mike asked.

I needed to state my case, but in a way so the kids

wouldn't think badly of their grandfather. Clearing my throat, I said in Pig Latin: "It eans-may at-thay he uzz-way aving-hay an air-affay ith-way a oman-way amed-nay ara-Clay!"

Justin cocked his head. "What?" he asked. I ignored him.

Mike closed his eyes, translating. I loved Mike as a brother, I really did. Sometimes I wondered, though, if a violent concussion had ended his football career, and not a screwed-up ACL.

As I took a bite of my hamburger, I gave Fanny a sideways glance. Mike sat between us, making me safe from any under-the-table kick to the shin. She was shooting me looks capable of melting my face like those Nazi guys in *Raiders of the Lost Ark*.

Mike reopened his eyes and shook his head. "Not necessarily. Think about it. Do you really think The Police's song *Roxanne* was about a prosti—I mean, a girl named Roxanne? Or *Sweet Caroline* was about a girl named Caroline?"

"Actually, Mike, both songs are about..." I started, but Fanny interrupted.

"What's your point, Michael?"

Her posture changed abruptly with her question: her back was straight, her shoulders squared up, her jaw set firm. Addressing him by his formal name meant she was ginning up for a fight. I'd experienced her anger countless times as a kid, painfully learning that the safest course of action when she got this way, was a rapid, strategic retreat. Some arguments had turned to blows, and I always got the worst of it. It had taught me to choose my battles wisely.

"My point is, just because he called them 'For Clara,' doesn't mean they *weren't* written for your mom. Maybe that was her nickname."

Mike made a good point, except he had no way of knowing that they had been buried underneath old work records. A fact I had no intention of disclosing. At least not yet.

Fanny seemed to relax a bit, but not much. Her shoulders dropped an inch as she shook her head. "No, Dad's pet name for

Mom was Elise."

"Why?"

"Beethoven's *Fur Elise*," I answered. "It was her favorite piece."

"Dad gave everyone nicknames," Fanny said. "I never heard him call anyone Clara."

Mike looked at me. "What was your nickname?"

"He used to call me Felix."

"Felix the Cat?"

"No, Felix Mendelssohn," I said. "Dad loved Mendelssohn. Fanny was named after the eldest daughter, and he wanted to name me Felix. Mom said no, so the compromise was Frank."

"So how did they agree on Frank?"

"Franz Schubert, Dad's second favorite composer," Fanny said. "But Franz sounded pretentious."

"Dad's nicknames were related to classical music," I said. "It was his quirk."

"One of many," Fanny added.

"What's my nickname, Mommy?" Rachel asked.

"Monkeyface," I said before Fanny could answer. "You're Monkeyface, and Justin is Monkeybutt."

"Heyyy!" Justin complained, while Rachel laughed and pointed at him, saying "MonkeybuttMonkeybuttMonkeybutt!"

"Thank you so much, Uncle Frank," Fanny said, her tone sharp with annoyance. She snatched Rachel's hand. "That's enough of that. Finish your salad."

Mike had headed to the fridge during the name-calling and returned with the remaining beers. "Then Clara is someone else's nickname."

I saw Fanny tense up again while he handed her a beer.

"Who in classical music was named Clara?" he asked, offering me the last one.

Fanny's and my eyes locked. "Oh my," she breathed.

"Clara Schumann!" we said simultaneously.

# CHAPTER 3

D inner ended abruptly after Fanny and I reached the same conclusion. Rachel resumed taunting Justin with a refrain of "monkeybutts", who responded with a punch to her arm. Fanny shot me the hairiest eyeball in the history of the world. Mike ushered them to their upstairs bedrooms for time-outs amidst tears, quick apologies, and reprimands. I cleared the table and started loading the dishwasher in reparation, while Mike put away the leftovers upon his return.

"Now, as the musically challenged adult here, would one of you please tell me who Clara Schumann is?"

I dumped a handful of silverware in the utensil caddy. "Clara was a mid-nineteenth century German pianist and composer, who was married to Robert Schumann, also a famous composer."

I glanced at Fanny, now leaning forward in her chair, nibbling at her lower lip. She seemed eager to talk, so I gestured for her to take up the explanation. She had minored in Music History, after all.

Fanny continued. "In the early 1850's, Robert and Clara met Johannes Brahms. Brahms wasn't very well-known yet; his career had just gotten started. He was about twenty years old, a virtuoso pianist, and budding composer. A mutual friend arranged for him to perform for them. Suffice it to say, he wowed them."

"I take it they had pull in their day?" Mike asked as he returned to the table and sat down next to Fanny.

"They did. They were quite the celebrity couple and they had considerable influence. Robert called Brahms a genius, and published an editorial praising him. He considered him a great hope for the future of music. Long and short of it, all three became close friends. Almost too close, really, as Johannes fell head over heels in love with Clara. It was kinda mutual, despite an age difference of fifteen years. Clara loved Brahms, but only as a dear friend, and nothing more. She was devoted to Robert until the end."

Mike nodded. "But they had an affair anyway?"

"No, no, not at all," Fanny said. "Nothing of the sort. Totally platonic. That's what makes it so beautiful, yet so tragic. Brahms had such a profound respect for Schumann that he'd never do anything improper. But he loved Clara, deeply. They corresponded with each other for decades; their letters were published about thirty years after their deaths. I have the books around here somewhere. When Robert admitted himself into an asylum in 1854, Brahms moved into an upstairs apartment in their home to help.

"All this while Clara was pregnant with her eighth child. You can imagine the scandal it caused in Düsseldorf, and among their contemporaries. Yet they remained completely chaste. Brahms took time off from his own work to help the family. This guy was as stand up as they come, right? Then, Robert died in 1856, and the prevailing thought was that Clara and Brahms would marry. They traveled to Switzerland together, perhaps to do just that. But they didn't."

"Why not?" Mike asked.

Fanny shrugged. "No one knows. After that trip, Brahms returned to Hamburg, and Clara resumed her touring career. They remained friends until her death in the mid 1890's. But his love for her never waned. And neither did her admiration and love for him. In fact, she played his *Variations on a Theme by Haydn* in her final concert. To me, that's love."

"Seems to me, then, that Dad loved another woman from afar," I said. "An unrequited passion."

I had finished loading the dishwasher, and remained on that side of the kitchen. Fanny's eyes narrowed, her gaze fixed firmly on me.

"At least we hope so, for Mom's sake," I continued. "But maybe there's a stash of love letters in one of the cartons you have? A modern-day Clara and Johannes? Maybe Dad can shed some light on it when I ask him tomorrow."

I saw Fanny immediately stiffen. "You wouldn't."

"Sure, why not?"

"Dad is sick," Fanny said, her voice clipped and measured. "He's in no condition to be confronted with this."

"Look at it this way, Fan," I said. "If I ask him about Clara tomorrow, he'll have forgotten all about it by Monday."

Shot fired. I locked eyes with Fanny. If looks could kill, then she would have just committed murder. I didn't care. The way I saw it, Dad had cheated on Mom, and I deserved answers, whether Fanny liked it or not.

Mike stood up. "I think I'll go see if Rachel is feeling better."

As he walked by, he grimaced at me, as if to say *You brought this on yourself, dude,* then left us to face each other from across the kitchen. Fanny's arms were crossed, and her mouth twitched. I prepared to stand my ground.

"You are such a jerk," she spat, her mouth small and controlled. "How can you be so cruel to Daddy?"

I spread my hands in defense. "I'm not the one who wrote the songs. Your question should be, how could Dad have been so cruel to Mom?"

Fanny glowered at me, her nostrils flaring. "That's not what I'm talking about. You've hardly visited Dad, and now you plan to shove these songs in his face? For what? To shame him? To cause him pain?"

"No, of course not!"

"Then why? To prove that he . . . he might have been unfaithful to Mom? You want him to feel guilty about something that's none of your damn business!"

"You're being ridiculous! I want nothing of the sort. And it is my business! I found them!"

"Or are you trying to get back at him, some sort of revenge?" She was on a roll now, not pausing to argue my objection. "One last fight in the ring, for old time's sake, kicking him while he's down?"

"What? Fanny, I'm not a psychopath!"

"Then why, Frankie? He didn't cheat on Mom!"

"You can't possibly know that."

She quickly blinked, glancing at the manila envelope pushed to one corner of the countertop.

"I just know."

I took a deep breath. "Listen. I'm not out on some crusade against Dad. Finding these songs was a coincidence! He's the one who tagged them, he's the one who wrote them for another woman, he's the one who hid them. Has it occurred to you that maybe seeing these songs might make him happy? He saved them, after all. If these songs were a source of pain and sadness, I think he would have destroyed them a long time ago."

Fanny turned her head towards the window, the side of her fist pressed against her mouth. I recognized the behavior - she nibbled on her finger when she didn't want to cry. I moved to the table, slid into the chair next to her and put my hand around her shoulder. She flinched at first, but quickly relented and leaned against me.

"I can't stand it, Frankie," she said, sobbing. "He's wasting away every day. Every day he's getting worse." She sniffled a bit, and wiped her eyes. "I go there twice a week, and sometimes, he...sometimes he doesn't even recognize me."

I gave a little squeeze. "I'm not the one being cruel to Dad. Alzheimer's is."

I felt her nod against my shoulder. "Both of you are, but yeah."

"You gotta believe me, Fan - this Clara business has nothing to do with the past, with the stuff that happened between us."

"Then why ask him?"

"Because I want to know," I answered, "and he's the only person I can ask. They're his songs."

"You really think he had an affair?"

My heart said yes as my head tossed out all sorts of objections. The jury hadn't reached a verdict, so I simply said: "I don't know. I don't *want* it to be true, but..."

Fanny pulled away and blew her nose on a paper napkin.

"You never got along with Daddy, ever." I opened my mouth to respond, but she waved at me to stop. "I'm not arguing with you about that right now. I just want you to promise me you won't use these songs against him."

"I promise. It was never my intent in the first place."

"Then what is? I highly doubt he'll remember anything about them, but in the rare chance he does, what will you do with the information?"

I scratched the back of my neck. "I don't know, actually. I only found them four hours ago."

"Then let me help you. If Dad doesn't remember, you'll..." She trailed off, flourishing her hand to encourage me to complete her sentence.

"Throttle him until he coughs up an answer?"

She smacked me hard across the chest. "Ass!"

"Ow! Just kidding! If he doesn't remember, I'll drop it."

"And if he does remember, you will..."

"Consider my options." I arched an eyebrow as her back quickly straightened again. "What?"

"What do you mean, consider your options?"

I shrugged my shoulders. "It depends on his answer."

"No, Frank. You're going to drop it because your curiosity will have been satisfied!"

I shook my head. "I can't promise that. What if he remembers, and asks me to find her?" Fanny opened her mouth to reply, but instead clamped it shut, slumped a bit in her seat, and looked at her lap. "If he remembers, what if he asks me to throw them away? Or publish them? If he remembers Clara, there's no way of knowing how he will react."

Fanny looked up at me. "He won't remember."

She stood up, took our empty beer bottles to the sink, and rinsed them out in silence. Mike returned at that moment, carrying Rachel. Her face had sunken into a deep pout.

"Mommy, I'm sorry for calling Justin names," she whimpered. "Can my time out be over?"

Fanny looked up at Mike, who nodded slightly. She took her from Mike's arms.

"Of course, sweetie. Gimme a hug. Hey, whaddya say you play your song for Uncle Frank?"

I bolted upright. "Oh yeah! That's why I came! To hear you play!"

Not the least bit true, but seeing the big smile crease her cherubic face made the white lie worthwhile.

Rachel scampered into the family room, followed closely by Fanny. She turned on the Tiffany lamp that stood upon the music shelf, to the left of the stand, just as it always used to. The light illuminated the ivory keys magically and made the black keys shine. Rachel dragged the bench out from beneath the keyboard, moved some Legos out of the way, and clambered onto it. Her feet dangled above the floor.

Mike and I sat down at opposite ends of the couch that faced the piano. Fanny arranged a songbook while Rachel carefully positioned her fingers onto the keys.

Justin's plaintive voice called from upstairs. "Can I come down now?"

Mike turned sideways to face the stairway, and shouted back, "Fifteen more minutes!"

"Is this C position, Mommy?" she asked.

"Sure is," Fanny told her, and then joined us on the couch, nestling next to Mike.

I leaned over and whispered, "Are you teaching her?"

"Seriously? If there's one thing our childhood taught me, it's that children are better off if parents pay for lessons."

A middle C chimed, as Rachel began to play *Twinkle, Twinkle Little Star*. She softly sang the lyrics beneath the melody, striking the keys with determined precision, the tempo firm and steady as each note resounded with equal volume. Upon playing the final note, she twirled around on the black bench and smiled hugely as her three-person audience applauded.

"Did I do okay, Mommy?" Rachel asked as she came over to receive a congratulatory hug.

"You played wonderfully!" Fanny said, enfolding her in her arms. Rachel climbed onto her lap.

"Is Justin taking lessons?" I asked.

Fanny nodded. "Reluctantly. He complains like you used to, but with way less drama."

Mike peered around his wife. "You took lessons from your dad, too?"

I playfully socked Fanny in the arm. "You never told him the tales of my infamous piano years? For shame, sister, for shame."

"Not my story to tell," Fanny said, smacking me in return. "Or maybe I tried to forget."

"Hey! No hitting!" Rachel scolded us, and Fanny waggled a finger at me in fake admonishment.

"Am I about to learn a dark family secret?" Mike asked.

"No, not really. Dad taught me for two years," I told Mike. "Then he fired me."

Fanny let out a hearty laugh. "More like Dad *fought* you for two years, until Mom put an end to the battle."

"Really?" Mike asked.

"Oh my gosh, the arguments! Dad yelling at Frank, Frank yelling back, Mom yelling at the two of them. During lessons! As a six-year-old! I'm surprised Mom let it go on for as long as it did!"

"In my defense, the yelling didn't start until I turned seven, and I yelled the least. Because I knew I was right."

"And Dad yelled the most, because you were both equally stubborn."

"Wait a minute," Mike said. "Your dad taught at Prescott,

wrote music, performed all over. And *you* were right?"

I shrugged, arms extended, palms upturned. "What can I say?"

"They should have named you Wolfgang. A prodigy who argued with his father all the time. It would have been more fitting," Fanny said, then turned to Mike. "Dad would teach him something simple, like *Oh Susanna*. He'd play it perfectly, and then follow up with four variations. Dad would get so mad."

"If you're that good, then why are you stuck teaching middle school band?" Mike asked.

"Who says I'm stuck? Summers off, lots of holidays, cute teachers. Some of them, at least."

Fanny struggled to contain herself, her lips pursed, attention focused on Rachel. She wanted to say a lot more, of that I knew. My career choice had been hotly discussed many times, and neither of us wanted to revive that old argument.

"Wink wink nudge nudge," Mike said quickly. That earned a look from Fanny. Before she could speak, he added, "I'd like to hear you play one of your dad's songs."

His request caught me off-guard, an unexpected diversion, and I took advantage of it. "What do you think, Fan?" I asked.

Fanny glanced at me, an eyebrow arched as if to say, 'Get real.' But something else showed in her gaze - a look of longing, perhaps? Whether hoping I'd say yes, or praying I'd say no, I couldn't tell.

"I've heard a lot of your dad's music, so I'm sure these are just as good. Besides," Mike said, "if you're a prodigy, it should be as simple as riding a bike, right?"

"Well, I don't know," I said slowly, scratching my chin. "It's been an awfully long time since I've played..."

"Oh," Mike said, his voice laced with disappointment.

"You own a keyboard," Fanny said. "Stop the false humility and pick a short one."

A small smile appeared on her face as she rested her chin on top of Rachel's head, still held close in her lap. I returned a similar smile and patted her on the leg. I could never fool her.

"Okay. I'll pick one out."

I returned to the kitchen and grabbed the songs. Thumbing through the collection, I selected a three-page piece, a waltz titled *Romance in D, Opus 8 No. 4*.

"How's it look?" Fanny asked as I came back.

"Beautiful," I answered. Tender, wistful, yearning - Dad pulled out every stop. *Andante con passione*. Moderately, with passion. Neither fast nor slow, but a lilting, walking tempo. His dynamic markings created subtlety, and the melody ebbed and flowed with effective anticipation. *Legato* passages begged for evocative phrasing, which culminated just shy of a forceful *forte*, and then descended into equal portions of contentment and longing, like the quick brush of lips between lovers, or the lingering touch of gentle fingertips...

"Frank, we can't hear what's playing in your head, you know," Fanny said. "You have to sit down and plunk the keys."

I blinked a few times, shaken out of my reverie, and I gave her a sheepish grin. Fanny was right, though. The song sounded in my head as clear as if it were being played on the stereo or live in a concert hall. I could hear exactly how Dad had intended it to sound.

I sat down and arranged the three sheets side by side on the stand. After testing the pedals and stretching my fingers, I looked back at my audience.

"Forgive any mistakes," I said.

"Shut up already, and just play," Fanny said.

My fingers floated above the keys for a second, then dropped down, and started playing. The first time in ten years on this piano, but it felt as if no time at all had passed. The action, the pitch, the response - all as I remembered. Each emotion poured into this piece was brought to life through the hammers striking the strings, the strings touched by the pads, the pedals lifting and lowering the dampener bar, the melody reverberating throughout the room.

My eyes darted between the score and keyboard

throughout my performance. And then, it concluded in a coda with the slightest *ritardando*, a delicate release of a feathery *arpeggio* lingering just enough to gently pierce the soul. My fingers settled upon the keyboard as the last echo died away, and I realized I had been holding my breath during the final eight measures. I had played it perfectly.

I turned to face Fanny; one of her hands covered her mouth, the other clasped Mike's hand. Her eyes were moist and quivering. Rachel's head tilted to one side, as if she were lost in a daydream. Mike leaned his head over so that it just touched Fanny's.

No one said a word.

Finally, I spoke. "Well?"

Fanny closed her eyes, lowered her hand. "Oh, how he loved that woman," she said softly, and then seemed to catch herself.

"Your talent is wasted on those band kids," Mike added.

I shook my head. "No, this is all Dad. I only played it the way he wrote it."

Mike opened his mouth, probably to make a comment regarding my ability, but I wasn't in the mood to hear another person explain how I wasn't living up to my potential. Preferring to savor the experience of the music, I cut him off.

"Don't. Okay? Just don't."

Fanny slid Rachel onto Mike's lap, and crossed over to the piano. I stood up, and she hugged me. I returned her embrace, and she whispered, "Thank you."

I pulled away a bit, a quizzical look on my face. A tear trickled down her cheeks.

"For what?"

"For bringing back a part of Dad that's been missing for a long time." She freed a hand to brush away the tears. "And Mike is right. I won't argue with you, but he is absolutely, totally right."

I broke from her hug and gathered the sheet music. "If I agree with you, we'll all be wrong. Except for the not arguing part. That I wholeheartedly agree with."

"When are you planning to visit Dad tomorrow?" she asked, returning to the kitchen. I shot a quick glance at Mike, who was now focusing on Rachel.

I sensed a confrontation brewing, and followed her. "Ummm...two thirty?"

"Remember how to get there?" she asked. "It's been a while since your last visit."

I squinted at her. "It's on a two-lane road off a four-lane road, about a quarter mile from yes, I know how to get there."

"Just checking."

"You know, I may not be the fastest car on the track, but I get the feeling you're showing me the door."

"You might not be fast, but you can read road signs."

"Care to tell me why?"

She closed her eyes and held a breath. "Are you blind? I'm a wreck. I've been one for months, getting the home ready to sell, and now these songs . . . As beautiful as that sounded, and as happy I am to have heard it, it's just . . . I worry what they might mean. It turns the screws even tighter."

"You could have just said so."

"I just did. It's not my fault you didn't hear me the first time."

I put the songs back into the envelope. "As visits go, this one ranks as a pretty good one. Almost an hour, hardly a fight."

Fanny bit down on her lip. "I'm trying extremely hard to keep it together, and you're not helping. I know I'm not being the most gracious of hostesses, but I'm doing the best I can. Thanks for coming, thanks for the beers, thanks for getting the house ready."

She looked up at the ceiling, blinking away stray tears, her arms folded, fists tucked under her biceps. Whatever control she had left, those scrawny tan arms were the only things maintaining it. I gave a short sigh and considered hugging her but decided not to. She felt hemmed in enough.

"Do you want me to call you after seeing Dad?" I asked.

She nodded, still avoiding eye contact. "I might see you though. I bring him communion after the 1:00 Mass."

"Okay, great. Thanks for dinner."

I avoided Mike on the way out. He may have been used to these sibling spats, but I didn't feel like any handshakes or Monty Python quips. I called out from the foyer, "Good burgers, Mike. Thanks for everything."

"Good seeing you," he called back. His tone sounded somber, and tired. "Take care."

"Wait!" Rachel called. "Don't leave yet! I wanted to show you my dolls!"

I heard a thump of tiny feet hitting the floor, and she ran towards me. She wore the cutest pout, looking as if she were about to stomp her foot.

"I'm sorry, monkeyface. Maybe next time. And keep practicing."

I heard Justin call out his good-bye from behind his bedroom door. I squatted down to Rachel's level.

"Tell Justin that Uncle Frank says he has to treat you better. Will you do that?"

"I already *do* tell him that," she said.

"You keep on telling him." I stood back up.

"Do I have to be nice to him too? Mommy says I have to."

"Of course you do! Listen to your mom, she's usually right."

My face collapsed into a scowl the minute I stepped outside. Fanny and her freaking moods.

# CHAPTER 4

It was nearly eight o'clock when I pulled into my parking space. Low clouds and the setting sun combined to paint red and orange streaks above the horizon, as a half-moon crested above the Erie Canal. A faint breeze whispered through the trees lining the canal, gently rustling the leaves.

I kicked off my sandals upon entering the apartment, tossed the compositions on the table, and saw the answering machine message light flashing. Three messages this time. Crossing the room, I tapped the Play button.

"Yo, it's Ned. Me and the guys are going to O'Shea's, like around 10, in case you're not doing nothing. Bring along that chick you're dating. Later."

Ned Kerrigan and I had been friends since grade school, and *the guys* were Don Morton and Joey Haynes, also longtime friends. They had formed a garage band called Toehead after high school graduation, and occasionally played gigs at local bars. From time to time I hung out at Joey's house while they jammed, but never seemed to find time to catch a show.

I smirked at the 'that chick' comment. He knew Jessica and I weren't dating, but it didn't stop him from saying so.

The machine beeped, then recited the time stamp in a mechanical male voice with weird articulation: "Saturday, 6:18 PM. Next message."

"Hey you, Jessica. Haven't seen you in like ages. Maybe we could get together tonight? Catch a movie? Call me back, okay? Bye!"

Speak of the devil. She often called when she had nothing else to do, as if to say, 'hey I'm bored so maybe Frank will take me out.' It never went beyond two friends having a good time, and I liked it that way.

The last message was rather unexpected.

"Frank, Fanny. Listen, I'm sorry for how I acted. You probably don't blame me, but I wanted to apologize anyway. These past months have been really, really hard, and...uh...usually your jokes and being a jerk doesn't bother me, but for some reason, tonight, you just...Again, I'm sorry. I have a lot on my mind, you can't even believe. And now these songs...um, yeah. I'll see you at Mellowood tomorrow. Okay, talk later."

I cracked a wry grin. Even in her apologies, Fanny managed to slip in a dig. And she was right, I didn't blame her. The songs blindsided us both, and they clearly impacted her more deeply than me. Still, I wouldn't be dissuaded from finding Clara's identity.

I deleted the messages, and dialed Jessica. After a few rings, the other end picked up.

"Hello?" A sweet and perky voice - almost too perky for its own good - answered.

"Hey Jessica!"

"Hey you! Miss me?" She truly sounded glad to hear from me.

"With every bullet so far."

"Huh?"

I smiled. "Never mind. Sure, I've missed you. What's it been, two weeks?"

"More like three. And you never call."

"Well, I'm calling now, so you can't say never. Listen, I'm meeting the guys at O'Shea's. You wanna come?"

"Which guys?"

"You remember Ned? Big guy, no shame? Him, Don, and Joey."

"Oh! Ned, he's super funny! And I like O'Shea's."

"Live music tonight, so yeah, should be fun. Get you at 9:45?"

"Sounds perfect! I'll be ready. Thanks, Frank! You're so

sweet!"

"K. Bye."

With an hour to kill, I decided to go through the envelopes in the carton that held Clara's songs. Maybe I could discover more things to show Dad tomorrow; maybe they could jog the old man's memory.

I dragged the carton into the living room and piled the envelopes onto the floor next to the coffee table. While driving home from Fanny's, I had come up with a plan: briefly inspect each envelope's contents, and sort them into groups. I really didn't care about any of it, except to find any clues of Clara's identity. A letter, a hastily scribbled note, a picture, something – *anything* – pointing me towards her.

Sitting down against the couch, I grabbed the top envelope, *Composition Notes 1954*. It contained a collection of music sheets and notepaper. The sheets were half filled with an assortment of chord progressions, phrases, and bits of melody. Remarks and annotations were scribbled in blue and red ink between staffs and in the margins. The notes were written in black.

A title caught my eye as I leafed through the pages: *The Auguries*. Dad wrote this as a kind of experiment, a quartet written in dodecaphony, or twelve-tone technique. I hated this piece. It was a brooding, jarring, atonal exercise of musical bedlam. As I flipped through the score, a page from a stenographer pad slipped free and landed in my lap. Dad's handwriting scrawled across it. Several sentences stood out: *Hard to play, and harder to listen to. Igor's recommendations on measures 36-42, while interesting, proves he drinks too much. Like I've always said, Schoenberg is overrated.* I chuckled. Dad never kept his opinion to himself. His outspokenness about composers and forms of music often caused arguments, consequences be damned.

*He was never shy about his opinions regarding me, either.*

I suddenly realized: if Dad saved old scores, notes, and edits, then he likely also would've saved Clara's rough drafts.

He didn't compose like Mozart, who wrote his scores in a single, clean, perfect draft. Dad tweaked, teased, pulled, and stretched his songs like taffy, until he reached the perfect consistency. He'd lived through a time of musical experimentation and change, when modernism swelled, when jazz grew in prominence, when swing was king, when rock n' roll hit the scene. Nothing was static, everything was fluid. Dad's contemporaries included Copland, Stravinsky, and Bernstein. His fame had lagged behind theirs, but he had reached a level of moderate success. He had earned respect within the field.

I replaced the pages in their envelope and looked at my watch - 9:00. I had barely enough time to change and pick Jessica up. Clara's songs would have to wait.

\* \* \*

Forty-five minutes later, I pulled up in front of Jessica's house and tooted the horn. She lived with two girlfriends in a two-story bungalow in Charlotte, a village nestled between Rochester and the Lake Ontario shoreline. Their home faced Ontario Beach Park, where the Genesee River emptied into the lake. Scores of people milled about the park, or stood about the iconic merry-go-round, its lights flashing and calliope filling the night air. A long line of customers at the Abbott's Frozen Custard stand stretched down Lake Avenue towards the park, around the corner onto Beach Avenue.

A door slam caught my attention, and I turned to see Jessica coming down her porch steps. She wore a tight white mini skirt, a pink tee covered by a white, stringy, fishnet top. Her clothes accentuated her deep, bronze tan. Silver bangles hung at her wrists and matching large hoop earrings dazzled in the streetlamp light. Her blond hair, big and poufy, hardly moved as she walked, held in place with some concoction of mousse and hairspray. She stepped carefully as she approached the car – she was wearing dangerous looking high heels. Jessica's smile was ever present, yet sincere. I stretched across the passenger seat to open her door, and she smoothly slid inside.

"Hey you!" she said. The headliner compressed her hair slightly. Leaning over, she planted a kiss on my cheek. She smelled like hyacinths.

"You look great," I told her. "As always."

"Thank you!" she said. "I like your look! So Miami Vice!"

I had changed into a pair of white slacks and a pastel turquoise t-shirt, and a pair of pale canvas boat shoes. All I needed to complete the ensemble was the white jacket.

I pulled away from the curb, after waiting for a teenage couple to cross the street, hand in hand. Jessica ran her fingers through my hair.

"I don't like this Judd Nelson thing you have going. Stop by the boutique and I'll fix you up."

"Sure, before school starts" I told her. "How's business?"

"Ugh," she said, rolling her eyes. "You wouldn't believe the things people *do* to their hair!"

I cast a sideways glance at her, as she complained about the 'strange and weird styles people want nowadays,' how 'nobody wants a normal look.' It went on for fifteen minutes.

"The thing I don't get," Jessica continued, "is the heavy-metal punk look, you know? Mohawks, spiked hair, dye jobs? Putting all that gunk in their hair is, like, so unhealthy. Bad for the follicles."

"You don't say," I said, wondering how much hairspray she used to keep hair virtually immobile.

She spent the next twenty minutes updating me on housemates Pam and Janice, and their boyfriend problems. I half listened. Today had been long and tiring in more ways than one.

"But at least they have boyfriends," Jessica concluded with a sigh, heavy enough to ensure I'd notice.

I gave a short chuckle. I knew the direction this conversation would take. It was a topic of discussion a few times a year, usually after her dates with other guys. We'd been friends since her brother's death. We'd been paired up in Fanny's bridal party, and I had been her 'date' at her sister Brenda's wedding five years ago. I had taken her to her Senior Ball. Since my college graduation, we'd hung out semi-regularly, but I regarded her more as my kid sister than anything. She liked flirting with me, which I found flattering, but I never considered crossing that line.

"Jessica, what we have is better. We hang out, have a good time, and things are uncomplicated. That's nice, too, isn't it?"

"I suppose." She sounded unconvinced, wrinkling her lips into a frown. "I just think having a boyfriend would be kinda nice, too."

I reached over and patted her thigh. "Someday you'll find Mr. Right, I just know it. And he'll be the luckiest guy in the world."

We were almost at O'Shea's, located near Silver Stadium, where the minor league baseball team played. The bar was popular with fans, but with the team on a road trip this weekend, parking would be easy. I found an open spot on a side street off Norton Street.

"I hope Ned's already here," I told Jessica while helping her from the car. "Place tends to fill up fast."

"Can I hold your arm?" she asked. "These shoes are awful to walk in."

She locked her arm inside mine, and we took the sidewalk towards Norton Street. Kenny Rogers' *Lucille* wafted from the bar, and I could hear patrons' voices joining the band in singing the chorus.

We climbed the short steps and squeezed past the bouncer just inside the open door. The bar ran the room's length to the right, the wall behind it stocked with every liquor imaginable. The band played on a small stage set in the back, flanked by banks of amps and speakers. Round tables jammed the floor, each one fully occupied. A haze of cigarette smoke hung in the air like a gray gauzy blanket. Neon signs for beers and rock n' roll bands covered the walls, along with pictures of smiling redhead Irish girls, bedecked in strategically placed four leaf clovers, or holding frosted beer mugs at chest level. Servers carried pitchers of beer and platters of potato skins and chicken wings from the kitchen and bar, returning with trays of empty glasses and drained pitchers.

Scanning the room, I saw a fat, sandy-haired, clean-shaven man frantically waving his arm, seated at a table close to the stage. I leaned down to speak in Jessica's ear.

"I see Ned! C'mon!"

I grabbed her hand and carefully led her through the maze of tables and chairs. Several guys checked Jessica out as we passed, their glassy-eyed gazes noticeably looking her up and down. I squeezed her hand a little tighter.

We reached Ned. Two chairs were tipped forward against the table, waiting for us. Five other people were seated around: Don, Joey, Ned's girlfriend Denise, and two girls I didn't recognize. Ned righted the two chairs.

"Frank!" he exclaimed, clapping me on the back, nearly making me stumble. Ned shouted to be heard over the band.

"Keg Again!" I called him, smacking him in return. The nickname had nothing to do with his size, but instead with the fact that he always seemed to have a beer in his hand.

"It was tough, holding onto these chairs!" he said. "Five more minutes, and whoosh! Waitress was taking 'em upstairs!" He dramatically waved his arm as he shouted.

"Then I'd just sit on your lap!" I told him, sitting to his right.

"Her, yes!" he said, pointing to Jessica, smiling. "You? No way!"

She smiled back, and sat next to me, to the left of Don's date. They exchanged polite smiles.

"Don, Joey," I said to the guys, nodding.

They raised their mugs in greeting. Their dates smiled at me, saying nothing. I gave Denise a short wave, which she returned. She and Ned had dated throughout high school, and had recently moved in together. I liked Denise - it took a special girl to handle Ned's craziness and extroverted personality.

Introductions were shouted around: Don with Natalie, Joey with Linda. Natalie was a petite brunette, a little mousy looking, and wore a pink Izod top and white hair band. Linda looked like she had stepped off the set of *Desperately Seeking Susan* - teased blonde hair trussed up with a black bow, leather jacket, multiple gold necklaces and a tight, strapless black top.

A couple pitchers of beer stood on the table, along with half a pepperoni pizza on a stand. Ned emptied one of the pitchers into two mugs, and handed them to me. I passed one to Jessica.

The band had concluded *Lucille*, and the guitarist immediately segued into the recognizable intro of *Ramblin' Man*, accompanied by the pianist. A chorus of cheers and whistles went up. Don and Joey sang along with their dates, while Ned drained his mug. Denise looked a little bored. We struggled to talk over the music, and I hoped the band would break soon. A waitress swooped in, leaving a fresh pitcher of beer. Jessica poked me in the arm and pointed to the pizza. I reached across the table and grabbed us each a slice.

A few songs later, the song ended to raucous cheers and applause. The lead singer lifted his guitar over his shoulder and placed it in its rest.

"Y'all are awesome," he said, as his bandmates began leaving the stage. "So hang tight, and we'll be back in twenty minutes."

They headed to the bar as a classic Marshall Tucker tune started playing over the house speakers. Conversation and laughter filled in the gaps.

Ned turned to me. "Good to see you, man."

"Good to see you, too. What's up?"

He shrugged and finished off his beer. "Nothing. Work all day, jam and drink all night."

Ned worked the midnight shift at Prescott Camera & Film as a receiving clerk, and Joey and Don worked with him. The four of us remained friends after our time at Aquinas Institute high school. I was the only one who went to college, but we continued to stay in touch, and hung out a lot during the summers.

Don pointed at me and said to Natalie: "You and Frank have something in common. His dad taught at Prescott Conservatory."

"Really?" she asked, leaning forward. She sounded genuinely interested; her eyes brightened a bit as she spoke.

"Yeah, Ivan Stephens."

*Ivan the cheater.*

"He's your dad? I attended in '81 and '82, studying piano."

"Dad retired in 1980," I told her.

"I know, but I learned a couple of his pieces. His *Nocturne in B minor*, and *Escalade*. What a fun piece."

She piqued my interest. The nocturne was especially difficult, while *Escalade,* a jazz piece that had been commissioned by Benny Goodman's band, was extremely fun to play.

"Small world," I said. "You must be good to be able to play those two."

Natalie blushed a little. "I bet you're rather good yourself."

Joey spoke up before I could respond. "First rate trumpet," he told her. "Better than Chuck Mangione."

Joey and I had played in marching band and wind ensemble together, me as first chair, him in percussion. I rolled my eyes at the comparison, but it clearly impressed Natalie.

"Did you know him?" she asked.

"Oh gosh no! He's twenty years older. He took my dad's composition class, though, in the late fifties."

"I bet you know a lot of famous musicians," Linda said. Her voice was lower than I expected.

"No, not really," I told her. "My dad, though, knew a lot. Leonard Bernstein, Aaron Copland, Igor Stravinsky, to name a few."

A look of confusion crossed her face. "Who are they?" she asked.

Natalie answered. "They're composers."

"Oh, like John Williams!" she exclaimed, at which I spat out my mouthful of beer, splattering the table and soaking the remains of my pizza.

"What? Don't you like John Williams?"

I wiped my mouth with the back of my hand. "Let me put it this way. Ever hear of the Infinite Monkey Theorem?" Linda shook her head. "It basically states that an infinite number of monkeys with an infinite number of typewriters given an infinite amount of time would eventually produce the works of Shakespeare. In Williams' case, take three monkeys, a bottle of scotch, and a xylophone, and within a week, voila - Star Wars."

"I love Star Wars!" Linda said, at which she and Joey started singing the main theme.

Natalie folded her arms and glared. "Huh. You probably hate Andrew Lloyd Webber too."

"Wow, it's like you know me," I told her. "Webber writes Broadway pop songs, not opera, and certainly not classical music."

"*Evita* isn't opera?" she asked. "Or *Jesus Christ Superstar*? What about *Cats*?"

I suppressed a laugh. "Technically, *Evita* and *Cats* are musicals. *Superstar* is a rock opera if rock opera is a thing. My rule of thumb is, if Casey Kasem plays your music, then it isn't opera."

Jessica spoke up. "I liked *Cats*. I thought it was cute."

"Yeah, me too," Ned chimed in, "And who doesn't like *Memories,* right?" With that, he stood up and jumped up on stage, and grabbed the microphone.

"You know, it's called *Memory*, not *Memories*..." I started to say, but Ned's boisterous, booming voice suddenly filled the bar.

"May I have everyone's attention please?" All conversation ceased, and the bartender lowered the music. "Folks, I'd like to make a dedication. This next song is for a dear, dear friend of mine," he said, "my good friend, Frank Stephens, who thinks *Cats* is lame." He motioned towards me as he mentioned my name. "If you know the words, please, join in."

He cleared his throat and began to sing. Ned was great as Toehead's lead singer. His acting skills, though, needed work to say the least. He extended an arm towards an invisible sun, wringing passion out of every word. He paced with deliberate steps back and forth across the stage. Denise looked as if she wanted to turn invisible, covering her face with her hand. Joey and Don were beside themselves with laughter. Linda and Natalie raised their voices in unison, while Jessica smiled. I looked around, and to a person, all were riveted on this overweight, mostly drunk man. Several patrons had joined in, while a few laughed behind their hands, or pointed.

He belted out the second verse with even greater gusto. Jessica joined in now, as did additional patrons. Several put their arms around others' shoulders, swaying to the tempo. I busied myself by refilling my mug.

By the time he started the third verse, many in the bar had joined in, including a couple servers. The bouncer sang along, too, his head bobbing in rhythm. I noticed the band members starting to make their way to the stage.

To my chagrin, rather than ending the embarrassing spectacle, they joined in. The lead singer draped his arm over Ned's enormous shoulder and shared the mic. The remaining members gathered around a microphone stand behind them. What started out as Ned's solo had become a choral ensemble.

They held the final note for fifteen seconds in perfect five-part harmony, while everyone wildly applauded in a standing ovation. The band shook Ned's hand, sharing laughs and smacking him on the back. Everybody at the table clapped - even Denise - and I raised my mug to Ned with humble appreciation. I turned to Jessica, who wrapped her arms around my neck, and kissed me deeply. The smoke, the beer, the singing, the hyacinths…all a bit heady. I didn't know why she'd kissed me, but it felt nice. She pulled away, a broad smile creasing her face, as Ned leapt off the stage.

His face was slick with sweat, and his shirt was soaked to

the skin. He gave me a short jab to the shoulder.

"See? Everyone loves that song. I think you owe Andrew Woyd Lebber an apology."

"I think I owe you another beer," I said, and I raised an empty pitcher to signal our server for a fresh round.

# CHAPTER 5

It was around 1 AM when we left O'Shea's, after the second band completed their set. We all sang too much, drank too much, and Natalie and I argued too much. She was like a junkyard dog after a ham bone, bristling that I held low opinions of composers and music she liked. Don tried to get her to back down, but the more she drank, the more argumentative she became. Almost everyone tossed in an occasional comment, and Ned reduced us to tears with timely inappropriate jokes. Natalie made Don take her home between sets, without wishing me good night, and Joey and Linda left shortly thereafter.

After the band's encore, Denise and Jessica went to use the ladies' room. When they were out of earshot, Ned leaned my way.

"Natalie doesn't like you," he said. His voice was slurred and hoarse.

"Well thanks, Captain Obvious. I hadn't noticed."

"Don't let her bother ya," he said, waving a lazy hand. "She's probably a one and done."

I downed the last of my beer. "I don't have time to give her opinion of me a second thought. Besides, it reminded me of arguments I used to have with my dad."

"Oh yeah," Ned said. "How is your dad doing?"

I squeezed my eyes shut. I wanted to avoid talking about him, but seeing as I had mentioned him, I had only myself to blame. Don had nearly ruined things earlier, bringing him up to Natalie, but Ned's impromptu stage performance had put a quick end to any lengthy conservation. Afterward, Natalie and

I had argued on the relationship between popularity and talent, and whether society wielded significant influence in promoting bad talent. Or something like that. I had kept my dad out of it, while she'd focused on the contributions of Webber, and the brilliance of Williams. To be fair, I had provoked her. A little. It had entertained me, in any case.

"I'm gonna see him…" I glanced at my watch. It was technically Sunday. "…later today. He's the same."

"Well, tell him I said hi."

I nodded, doubtful that Dad would even remember me, no less a former high school classmate whose claim to fame was having been an All-State defensive lineman in 1977.

The girls soon returned, and we left a half hour later. I hugged Denise and made sure she had Ned's keys. She then proceeded to smack Ned on the back; the length of his goodbye hug with Jessica had exceeded her tolerance level.

"Geez Louise, Ned, let her breathe!"

Jessica giggled as Ned let go, and Denise grabbed him by the hand, pulling him away.

"Sorry, babe," he told her. "For a second there I thought I was hugging an angel."

"That was a second? You were one second from *meeting* an angel! Let's go, ya big drunk."

We exchanged goodbyes again, and watched them go arm-in-arm into the nearby parking lot, Ned pleading playfully for forgiveness, Denise responding with empty threats.

"I don't understand why they don't just get married, and make it official," I said. "They already act married."

"Prolly cos iss what their parents 'spect of 'em." Jessica's words rolled from one into the next. I gave her a thoughtful look.

"Come on, Aristotle," I said, seeing her stagger even while standing still. "Let's get you home."

Jessica fell asleep within five minutes after getting in the car, and was still sleeping when we reached her home. I lifted her out, and carried her up the walk. One arm was draped over my shoulder, her face nuzzled against my chest. As I climbed the steps, Pam opened the door. She looked like a grown-up Annie, with tight red curls, and wore a faded blue *Wham!* t-shirt reaching just past her hips. She must've been waiting. She made that face girls make when they see something adorable – doe-eyed, a little pouty, the head tilted just so - and let me pass. I carried Jessica up to her bedroom, tenderly lowered her onto the bed, removed her high heels, and covered her with the sheet. As I softly closed the door, Pam came up behind me in the hallway.

"You're not staying?" she whispered. She looked genuinely shocked.

"No!" I replied, with a level of indignance I hadn't intended. Her question had caught me off guard. She wasn't ignorant of mine and Jessica's friendship.

"No need to get so defensive!" she shot back in a hard tone, turning and heading towards her room. "Lock up, wouldja?" she added over her shoulder.

* * *

Nine hours later, I rolled out of bed as bright sunlight streamed through my bedroom window blinds. I smelled of smoke and cheap beer, and my head chimed like a bell tower. I sat there for several minutes as my equilibrium caught up. I inhaled deeply; the faintest sweet aroma of hyacinths seemed to linger beneath the other odors, but it might have been my imagination.

With a stretch and a yawn, I shuffled out of the bedroom. The pile of manila envelopes on the floor and Clara's songs on the table awaited me. I started a pot of coffee, and then jumped in the shower, washing away the smoke and the beer and the sweat and the hyacinths. After a quick shave and gargle of Scope, I put on a polo shirt and shorts, and poured myself a University of Buffalo mug full of coffee. I was ready.

I had an hour before heading out to Mellowood. Not enough time to read every one of Clara's songs, a task that would require several uninterrupted hours, to do it properly. I supposed I could *play* them. My keyboard in the second bedroom, sitting under the window, stood waiting. No, that would also have to wait. Besides, the ringing in my head demanded attention, not competition.

Taking a seat on the couch, I grabbed the *1951 Composition Notes* envelope. For the next forty-five minutes, I read every note and memo, scrutinized each marked-up composition, and studied the unfinished manuscripts. Over two dozen works in total, most for piano, several ensemble pieces, and one for organ. Several of these completed scores had been published; most had not, but some of the unused motifs and fragments had been incorporated into other pieces. Every composer did it. Some ideas worked better than others depending on the music, and were thus recycled. Whether some of these ideas were used in Clara's songs, I had no way of knowing. Not yet.

I poured myself a second cup of coffee. If only there was a better way of doing this. I was convinced Dad had saved his working sheets for Clara's songs. I knew it in my bones. If they weren't here, then where were they? Four possibilities came to mind. One, Fanny had them in the garage. Two, Dad had given them to Clara. Three, the Prescott Conservatory of Musical Studies had them. Or four, they were destroyed.

Fanny might let me look through her boxes. It was a longshot, but I needed to know, if only to determine where they weren't. If Clara had them...well, not knowing her identity made that a moot point. If Prescott had them, who could I possibly ask, and would they let me? And if they were destroyed? That was impossible to know. It'd be trying to prove a negative.

This strategy wouldn't work. The answers weren't in these boxes, they were boxed in Dad's head. Only he could tell me. A small, minute, infinitesimal chance existed, that something in Dad's mind would unlock, and he'd remember. It was the only course of action available.

I downed my coffee, snatched Clara's songs off the table, and fished my keys and wallet from the pants I wore last night. There was still time to hit a drive-thru for lunch and be at Mellowood by one-thirty.

Stepping outside was like stepping into a sauna: warm, humid, and hazy. Perfect conditions for late summer afternoon thunderstorms.

When I hopped in my car, the scent of hyacinths immediately greeted me, making me smile, and I wondered how Jessica was faring.

A Burger King stood around the corner from my apartment on Route 31. Coming around the drive-thru corner, I noticed a 24-hour Kinkos shop immediately next door. As I paid for my meal, I decided an additional stop was in order.

❋ ❋ ❋

Mellowood Assisted Living sat on ten acres upon the banks of the Genesee River in West Henrietta, south of Rochester. It resembled the letter V with the point chopped off: a single-story main building with two wings stretching rearward at forty-five-degree angles. One wing housed independent residents who needed minimal assistance, while the other was for those needing more around-the-clock medical attention and care. Patients like Dad. The two wings framed a central courtyard, landscaped with trees, assorted perennials and annuals, paved walkways, and a smattering of benches. The complex was designed to not look institutional, to look like a home away from home: white siding, bright blue shutters, flower boxes, grey shingles, and a well-manicured lawn.

We chose Mellowood for several reasons: it was close to his regular physicians, the managing company had a solid reputation, their record with state regulators and ethics boards was clean, and it was located halfway between me and Fanny. Either one of us could get here quickly if need be.

Dad had taken a while to get used to living here. As his memory deteriorated, he'd grown more confused about things. Visits had become difficult, and thus shorter and more infrequent. My last visit had been in May. I didn't know how Fanny managed coming here weekly.

I strode beneath the covered walkway towards the entrance, and the glass front doors slid open. The brightly painted foyer was furnished with blue and yellow upholstered couches and chairs to the left. A pair of closed, solid doors led into the facility. The reception desk stood on the right, behind which a gremlin-like woman huddled, her pale green horn-rimmed glasses and wiry blue-gray hair visible just above the counter.

"May I help you?" she said, her voice thin and ghoulish. Her face was stretched and squashed, and her smile resembled a pained grimace. If she was trying to look and sound pleasant, she failed on both counts. Her name tag read *Imogene*. She hadn't been the receptionist when I had last visited.

Stepping to the counter, I said, "I'm here to see Ivan Stephens. I'm his son."

"Sign in," she commanded, sliding a registry book towards me, a black pen attached by a string to the spiral binder. As I signed in, she continued. "And please put on a Visitor sticker. And I need to see a form of identification. Driver's license, passport, or any other photo ID."

I placed the manila envelope on the counter and showed her my driver's license. She glanced at the picture and then back to me. "Okay, it's you."

I considered saying something funny but realized humor would be wasted on Imogene. Instead, I peeled a Visitor sticker off of its backing paper, and stuck it to my shirt.

"You know where to go?" she asked.

"Room 117, north wing."

She adjusted her glasses and pointed to the heavy set of

doors. "Turn right after going through, hit the automatic door button at the end of the hallway, and his room will be on the left beyond the attendants' station."

It was as if she hadn't heard my answer. Then her gaze narrowed.

"Regulations require that all packages be inspected upon arrival." She extended a hand, expecting the manila envelope.

I handed it to her, saying, "It's just some music to show my dad."

Imogene glared up at me, as if I had violated a regulation by explaining what was inside. She pulled the songs halfway out and briefly looked at them, over the top of her frames. Satisfied, she returned the envelope. I heard her press a button with a determined stab, and the heavy doors swung open.

"Enjoy your stay," she grumbled.

I stepped through the doorway, and started the long trek down the wide, brightly lit corridor. Resident rooms lined the hall. Most rooms' doors were shut; I had learned on my visit never to glance into an open room. Some sights I never wanted to witness again, such as the time an elderly woman had angrily refused to wear any clothes. It had been an ugly sight in more ways than one, and I got a full view of her raging, wrinkled nakedness.

A few residents loitered in the hallway, either in wheelchairs, or supported by walkers. I smiled politely passing by; some smiled in return, with toothless or drooly grins. Others barely noticed me. During my last visit, one resident had believed I was his great-grandfather, come to gather his things and return him to his homeland across the ocean. He didn't seem to be out today, and I doubted he would've remembered anyway.

I approached the attendants' station, which was staffed by two women. Neither made eye contact with me as I walked by; one read her People magazine, the other leafed through papers on her desk. Apparently, visitors granted passage by Imogene were considered safe, or beneath notice.

Dad's room was the fourth on the left. I knocked on the door and slowly entered.

"Dad?" I called out, stepping in and closing the door.

The room was simply furnished with a standard hospital bed, two dressers, and three armchairs. A television was suspended from the ceiling in the far corner, angled towards the bed. The window looked out into the courtyard, beyond which a row of pine trees lined the riverbank. Fanny had mounted Dad's wedding portrait and other photos, including his gold record, and above the bed hung the crucifix that once adorned the wall in his and Mom's bedroom.

Dad sat by the window, wearing a short sleeved plaid shirt and a pair of khaki slacks. He was barefoot. His sparse, gray hair was somewhat combed, and he had shaved that morning. A small, fresh scab ran along the curve of his chin, and I detected a light odor of Old Spice. His glasses sat on his lap. He had become skinnier and more frail since May.

He hadn't acknowledged my presence, even after I sat down in the opposite chair. I placed the envelope on the table between us.

"Hey Dad, it's Frank. How you doing?"

No response. I tried a different approach.

"It's Franz, Dad."

Nothing. He continued gazing out the window.

"Frankie? You know...little Frankie?"

Again, nothing. Fanny hadn't exaggerated when she'd said he was worsening. He'd recognized me on my last visit. I sighed, frustrated, and tried a different tack.

"Dad, it's Felix."

He finally turned his head towards me. He squinted and a determined look crossed his face, as if he were trying to place me. He slipped on his glasses. The thick lenses gave him an owlish look. Then, recognition dawned, like a curtain being drawn open, allowing light to dispel darkness. His eyes widened, and a smile appeared at the corners of his mouth.

"Felix," he said softly. "Is it really you?"

I nodded, and he reached forward to grasp my hand. His long fingers still managed a healthy grip.

"I'm so happy you came by. How's Fanny?"

"Good," I answered. "I saw her yesterday."

"I'm so happy to hear that." His thin voice carried the faintest of Russian accents.

"I know it's been a while," I started to say, "and I really ought to visit more often…"

"I've been meaning to ask you," he interrupted.

He glanced furtively around the room, searching as if something had been misplaced. He became agitated.

"Damn!"

"What is it, Dad?"

"Ach, the piano is still out for repairs." He turned to me, and he had become quite serious. "I was hoping you could play your *Venezianisches Gondellied*. I had a question about it."

He began humming the melody, while I slumped in my chair.

*He thinks I'm Felix Mendelssohn.*

# CHAPTER 6

I needed to improvise, and quickly. I had no way of knowing how long he'd believe I was Felix Mendelssohn, that we were living in early 19ᵗʰ century Berlin. I had to join the charade. Felix's dad was named Abraham, and he was a prominent banker. Perhaps I should discuss my other "siblings," Rebeckah and Paul? My mind raced. Dad mentioned *Venezianisches Gondellied* - Venetian Boat Song – composed in 1830. Abraham died in 1835. That gave me a timeframe.

Of course, I could ignore this altogether. I couldn't laugh it off as a case of mistaken identity. That would be unfair. But I could direct the conversation away from Mendelssohn, towards why I came: to discuss Clara's songs.

The problem was that it might not work. Dad might slip back into oblivion, and cease to recognize me as anyone familiar, including his real son. The charade would have to start over.

Dad stopped his light singing, and ran his hand through his hair.

"Ach, what does it matter? The song's been published, and who am I, a mere banker, to debate music with you? Tis my fate - to be the son of a famous father, and the father of a famous son. What bothers me, however, is you continue to use our Jewish surname rather than our new Christian one. Are you ashamed of it? Of me? Of your mother?"

*Oh boy, I'm being forced to play the part.*

I recalled that Abraham had had the entire family baptized, and changed their last name to Bartholdy, to distance themselves from their Jewish heritage.

"No, Father, not at all. It's just that the name Mendelssohn is widely recognized amongst my friends and contemporaries. It's used strictly for business. With family, it's Bartholdy. There is, however, something I must discuss with you. It's why I've come."

"Is it finances again, Felix?" He leaned forward in his chair, sitting on the very edge of the cushion, lowering his voice. "You know I wield significant influence at the bank. If you need additional funds, I can have it arranged. Discreetly."

"No, father, my finances are in good order," I said. "No, what I want to ask you about pertains to the contents of this envelope." I casually picked it up. "I found this yesterday, and not knowing what it could be, looked inside. It's all in your handwriting."

He looked amused. His eyes nearly twinkled. "What is it? May I see?"

He extended his hand to take the envelope. I held back. We'd come to the moment of truth, and I had no idea how he'd react. I became Frank Stephens again.

"It's a collection of songs, Dad. Songs you wrote a long time ago. You called them 'For Clara.' Do you remember?"

He tilted his head a bit, and a thoughtful look crossed his face. He withdrew his hand, and rubbed his chin. Then he smiled, and clasped his hands.

"A joke! You are jesting me, Felix! I am a banker, not a composer!"

I shook my head. "I'm not kidding. You composed music once. See for yourself."

Dad cocked an eyebrow, looked at me askance, then looked down at the envelope, and snatched it out of my hand.

"I do not understand this game you are playing with me," he said, opening the envelope. His fingers shook as he removed the scores. He placed them on his lap, and flipped the sheets one by one, tracing some of the passages with a quivering fingertip.

As he scanned the music, I watched his eyes. They

danced from line to line, from staff to staff. At times they narrowed, as if unsure of what he held in his hands. At other times, they widened, his pupils dilating. Did I detect a glimmer of remembrance, a shine of recognition? His facial expression changed while turning the pages, from his original bemused smile, to a sort of reclaimed youthfulness, a softening of the years that had forged ridges across his brow and hardness in his jaw. For a moment, he resembled the younger Ivan Stephens in the photos which hung about the room. Something rekindled within him, a vibrancy I hadn't seen since Mom died.

"Do you recognize them, Dad?" I asked, leaning a bit closer.

He looked up at me, his eyes shimmering momentarily in the afternoon sunlight. His face twitched, as if forming a smile.

Then all hell broke loose.

Dad flung the scores away. The paper clamp snapped off and struck the wall with a ping. The pages scattered across his bed; several fluttered to the floor. Redness welled up his neck and through his cheeks, as his face contorted with intense rage. He shot out of his chair and took two menacing steps towards me; I clambered backwards, nearly toppling over my chair in the process. Dad wasn't a big man. He was roughly my height, and weighed maybe 160 pounds. He had lost weight since my last visit, but he remained wiry and tough. While enraged, he could inflict untold damage on me. Or himself. His hands were balled into tiny fists of white-knuckled hate. Those hands once possessed power and strength over a keyboard, and I didn't want to know if they still did. His nostrils flared with every heavy breath. His eyes burned with fury. And I retreated into the corner beneath the television.

"I've had enough of your questions!" he roared. "This is nothing but a damn inquisition! I'm no commie sympathizer! Ya got that? I am no damn Red commie sympathizer!!"

The ferocity and intensity shocked me. We had arguments in the past, and our fair share of knock-down drag out verbal spats. This was new and frightening. I feared for my safety. Whatever pleasant memory the songs may have first triggered had been obliterated by something painful, something beyond troublesome. This made no sense.

I knew nothing I said could possibly calm him, but I still felt the need to try.

"Dad!" I said, my hands up in defense. "What did I say? What did I do?"

"Don't play stupid, you little fucker! This inquiry is a sham, a...a...a mockery of justice! I've been unfairly accused, and you know it! You dragged me in here to prove my patriotism. Me - a decorated veteran! And yet here I am, accused of being a sympathizer. You got no fucking integrity. None! And then...and then you drag *her* into this?! I told you countless times, leave *her* the fuck out of this!!"

I caught my breath. Her. *Her*? Holy crap - she's real?

"Who is *her*?" I asked, my voice wavering and weak despite every effort to remain calm.

Dad pointed his finger at me, inches from my face. "Don't you dare play stupid with me! This is not about her, this is not about me, this is about fucking politics! Maybe someone has it out for me, someone here in the school. You've been ginned up by that lunatic in Washington who sees a commie everywhere. I don't give a shit about him or his accusations! I'm a faithful American. It's all in my file, it's all there! I was only two when I came to America!! You...you think I was a commie, as a two year old?"

My head spun. I couldn't believe my ears. Dad never swore like this, and certainly never spoke of commies. Was this a memory, or a psychotic episode? If a true, historical scenario . . . I struggled to take all this in. All I knew was, these were real emotions, released with the fury of a class five hurricane, battering me within the small confines of a twenty by twenty-five nursing home bedroom.

Suddenly, the door flew open, and three aides burst in. Two swooped in to restrain Dad, while the third grabbed me by the arm. Dad struggled to escape their grasp, while I allowed myself to be pulled out of the corner.

"You can't arrest me!" he screamed. "I'm no criminal! I'm a victim of damned politics!"

He struggled with the aides as they wrestled him back into bed.

"I love America! I'm no red! And neither is she!!"

"You gotta get outta here!" the aide urged, a firm grip on my arm. "This might get ugly!"

Dad had lost any capacity of recognizing reality now. His eyes bulged with fear, pupils swimming in a white sea. I imagined that in his mind, he saw me as the judge handing down his sentence, and the aides imagined as the guards authorized to execute it.

As the two aides finally got him lying flat on the bed, I shouted one last question. "What's the woman's name?"

"Sir, you have to leave! Now!" the aide yelled.

One aide produced a syringe, holding Dad's arm down against the mattress with one knee. The other practically laid on top of his legs to keep him from kicking; she held his other arm down at the wrist. He panted and wheezed, groaning while he continued to fight. The veins in his neck bulged as thick as cords. She jabbed the syringe into his arm, and he moaned and slowly lost the strength to resist.

"Clara, I'm so sorry!" he exclaimed, his voice trailing away. His moans turned into sobs, then descended into whimpers.

As the aide pushed me out into the hallway, Dad had become silent. The door closed behind us, and I slumped against the opposite wall, shaky and out of breath.

"What in the name of the almighty Lord happened?" the aide demanded, her hands planted on her hips, a scowl etched upon her face. A nametag hung from her uniform's breast pocket, complete with unflattering picture. Estelle.

I ran a hand through my hair. "I'm...not sure. I showed him songs he composed a long time ago, and after he looked at them, he grew angry. Instantly. I had no idea he'd react like that." Her scowl only deepened. "Honest! I didn't mean to make him go crazy!"

Estelle frowned even more. "I hope not. People in his state are prone to violent episodes, with no warning. Sometimes, family members push and push, to get their loved one to remember something. Anything. Your pops did remember something, son, something unpleasant and best left forgotten. And let me tell you something else. Next time you are told to get out of a room, you get out. I did that for your own safety. You could've gotten hurt!"

I took a deep breath and nodded. My heart still pounded like a John Bonham drum solo, and I continued to shake. The images of Dad's rage remained vivid and frightening.

"Are you okay?"

"As okay as can be expected. He didn't hurt me if that's what you mean." I motioned towards Dad's room. "What are they doing?"

"They sedated him, and are restraining him."

"To his bed? With straps and stuff?" I asked.

Estelle nodded. "For his own safety. They're checking his vitals, too. He'll wake in about an hour, and if we're all lucky, he won't remember any of this. I'll get a nurse to stay until he comes to, just in case."

"Listen, I'm very sorry about this," I said. "I really had no idea. If I had known…"

"Right, if you had known, you wouldn't have asked. I hear it all the time. You ain't the first, you won't be the last. It's distressing as all hell. I get that. Bad enough his mind is shutting down or tricking him into thinking things that aren't true. Seeing all this, in addition to everything else, makes it a whole lot worse."

"If you're trying to make me feel better, it isn't working," I said. "I'd rather just forget this happened."

"I'm sure you would," Estelle said. "But a report's gotta be filed, and you're the witness. So you can't forget or leave just yet. Go wait in the lobby while we make sure everything is settled down."

I glanced down the hallway, towards the double doors. No residents loitered in the corridor, and all their doors were shut. They must've been moved during Dad's episode.

"Yeah, okay," I said, standing up.

My shirt stuck to my back, slick with perspiration. I hadn't realized how much I had been sweating. My face felt clammy as well. We headed down the corridor together.

"I'll let you out," Estelle said, stepping inside the aide station, and pressing the automatic button hidden beneath the counter. "Someone will come get you in a few minutes."

* * *

Less than five minutes later, one of the two aides who had restrained Dad – a matronly woman named Donna – entered the lobby, her face still flushed.

Donna led me into an office off the main hallway, one I had passed earlier. A couple framed motivational posters hung on the walls. I took a seat while she sat behind the desk in a leather swivel chair. A clipboard holding a blank form lay in the middle of the desk. Donna spent the next ten minutes asking questions about the incident, which I answered in perfect detail. She completed the form, moving from question to question. When I responded to the last one, she put her pen down.

"Mr. Stephens," she said, "thank you for your cooperation. This is a formality, you understand, a requirement of Mellowood Managed Care, to document every incident."

Donna spoke with a gentle, almost maternal tone. I wouldn't have been shocked if she'd offered me a glass of milk and some chocolate chip cookies. I felt myself becoming calmer as she talked.

"So, I'm free to go?"

"Yes, though you may want to wait a week or two before

coming back. Perhaps after Labor Day, just to give your father a little time?"

"If you think that's best," I told her. My mind said, *not a problem.*

"Oh yes. Usually, after incidents such as these, creating space helps the healing process. A precaution, that's all. It would be beneficial for you, too, don't you think?"

A thought popped into my head. "What about other family members? Or friends? Are they prohibited from seeing him?"

"Generally speaking, no," she said. "If he had been injured, or hurt you, or if we felt that he was dangerous, we'd recommend supervised visits. It's too early to tell with your father's situation, given that he's been sedated. We'll know more once his doctor has had a chance to evaluate him."

A second thought. "Just out of curiosity, and then I'll get out of your hair, I promise. Who else has visited my dad?"

Donna smiled tenderly. "Mr. Stephens, I'm afraid I don't know, and even if I did, I'd be prohibited by law from telling you. Privacy, you understand."

"Sure, I understand."

"I'm very sorry for what happened today," Donna said, her eyes soft and compassionate. She extended her hand, and I shook it. "Your father is in excellent care, I hope you realize."

"Yeah, I'm sorry too. Goodbye."

With that, I returned to the lobby. Call it curiosity, call it nosiness, call it obstinacy - I needed to know if Dad had other visitors. I wondered if any of his former coworkers or friends ever visited.

Perhaps a female friend.

The law might prevent Donna and Mellowood Managed Care from telling me what I wanted to know, but it didn't prevent me from trying to find out, guardzillas or no.

As I approached the counter, Imogene lowered her Reader's Digest magazine, and squinted as I took the registry pen in hand. The date, name, and arrival and departure times needed to be filled out. The receptionist wrote down the patient's room number rather than their name, providing a degree of privacy. I glanced at my watch: ten after two.

As I wrote that down, I said to Imogene, "I think my keys fell out of my pocket while I was in Donna's office. Would you be so kind to slip back there and get them?" I gave her the friendliest, most sincere smile I could muster. Her lip curled into a sneer, and she snorted a perturbed sigh.

"I suppose," she said, her voice laced with complaint.

She placed her magazine down, pushed herself out of her chair, and shuffled through the rear door of her conclave. As soon as she disappeared, I dashed to the couch, dropped my keys behind a cushion, and returned to the counter. I leafed quickly through the book, looking for entries marked 'Room 117N.' Fanny's name appeared on every Sunday, and other random days throughout the week. I passed through July, June, and into May, noticing my previous entry. Since April, and no one had come besides me and Fanny. In March, though, I found two other entries. Two other people had visited Dad, and I recognized both. Neither was female.

The reception nook door started opening, so I quickly returned the visitor registry to today's page, and assumed a relaxed stance, leaning against the counter. Imogene stomped back to her chair, glowering at me.

"No keys," she grunted.

"Really?" I tried to sound shocked. "Gosh, I had them when I left Dad's room."

I tapped the counter, and made a thoughtful face. "Maybe they fell into the couch!"

I walked over, and after a few seconds of a feigned search, produced them.

"Here they are!"

Imogene shook her head disapprovingly. "Maybe you should have checked there first."

"The funny thing about finding lost stuff is, it's always in the last place you look," I said.

She grunted, clearly disgusted. "That's not funny." She sat down and resumed reading her magazine.

Upon leaving the lobby, I saw thick, heavy, black clouds building in the west. The breeze had picked up, too, as the trees around the parking lot swayed and rustled. I got in my car, looked down at Dad's scores sitting on the passenger seat, and was glad for my foresight. I couldn't have predicted Dad's reaction, but fortunately he had hurled a set of copies across his room.

Driving home, I brooded over Dad's visceral, powerful reaction. His repeated references to 'red commies,' 'commie sympathizers,' and defense of his patriotism all flabbergasted me. What was he talking about? I knew my grandparents had immigrated from Russia when he was two; Dad had said our last name used to be Stepanov, but Grandpa had changed it shortly after they'd arrived. They had died before I was born, but my two uncles were still alive. Pietr lived in suburban Rochester, and Viktor moved to Pennsylvania in the early 1960's. I also knew Dad had served in the Navy during World War II, having gained citizenship when he turned eighteen. The Prescott Conservatory of Musical Studies had hired him in 1947, and he mentioned 'school' a couple times - what other school could he be talking about? What went on back then?

What had shaken me most was his mention of Clara's name. His final sentence suggested that she was real. He had cared for her and defended her. He had loved her, with undeniable passion. My instinct had been right. Whether he had been unfaithful to Mom, I still didn't know.

When I reached my apartment, the clouds had thickened and grown more menacing, and strong gusts accompanied the steady breeze. The storm approached quickly. A flash of lightning streaked across the western sky, followed by a rumble of distant thunder. With Clara's songs in one hand, and my half-finished Coke in the other, I scaled the stairs two at a time. No sooner had I stepped inside than the first heavy drops of rain started to fall.

Tossing the songs onto the table, I noticed my answering machine light flashing. One message.

"Frank, I'm about to leave Mellowood and come by you. They wouldn't let me see Daddy. What the hell did you do?"

# CHAPTER 7

Fanny must have arrived minutes after I left. I imagined her arguing with Imogene, getting into it with Donna or Estelle - perhaps both - then demanding to use their phone.

My day hadn't shaped up as hoped, and it wouldn't be improving anytime soon.

Music was what I needed right now, something precise and methodical, to uncomplicate things. I turned on my stereo and pulled Glenn Gould's recording of Bach's Partitas from its place in my album collection.

I blew the dust off the disc and placed it on the turntable. The needle touched down, and seconds later, *Partita No. 1 in B-Flat Major* began. As the music began, I sat down on the couch, and recalled the names of the two men who had visited Dad.

Pietr Stephens and Jim Gregory.

Pietr was Dad's older brother. Creating a pretense to visit him and Aunt Jane would be simple. They lived about half an hour away, and while I doubted they knew anything about Clara, they could shed light on Dad's past. Dad had only spoken of his youth in broad generalizations. Honestly, I hadn't cared all that much anyway at the time. Things were suddenly different.

Jim Gregory was Dad's former co-worker, and probably the closest thing he had to a best friend. Gregory taught piano, theory, and composition.

I remembered him from Dad and Mom's parties, as well as the occasional dinner or visit, and the jam sessions. Then, as the saying goes, life had gotten in the way. I began to wonder if the parties and jam sessions had stopped because of other reasons than busyness and other obligations. As far as I knew, he still taught at Prescott. It wouldn't hurt to ask for his opinion.

A flash of lightning illuminated the room, followed immediately by a cracking thunderclap, shaking me to attention. I watched the rain, thick as paint, lash at the windows. The trees were barely visible, indiscernible shapes being whipped by the wind. Another burst of light lit up the area, attended by another blast of thunder. It sounded as if the sky had been torn in two, ripped from one end to the other, before erupting into an explosion.

*This weather won't help Fanny's mood, that's for sure.*

The Partita ended, and the Sinfonia movement of *Partita No. 2 in C minor* came next. The introduction's drama and pathos mirrored the weather - intense, with unexpected crashes of blocked and rolled chords, sudden powerful trills, and a somewhat jarring melody.

Another rumble of thunder rolled outside, further away now. The storm was moving out quickly; the wind had died down, and the rain had let up a little.

Just then, a series of rapid knocks came from the door. I looked up to see Fanny peering inside; her hair drenched, her expression a combination of exasperation and anger.

*Here we go.*

"Hey, nice day for a duck, huh?" I said, holding the door as she dashed in. She carried a plastic Wegmans bag in one hand, her purse in the other.

"Shut up, Frank," she snapped. "And get me a towel."

Water streamed down her face, mostly rainwater, but I could tell she had been crying.

"Sure." As I returned with a towel, I said "Do you want dry clothes? Maybe some sweats and a t-shirt?"

She snatched the towel away and vigorously dried her hair. "I guess so."

Kicking off her sandals, she followed me to the bedroom,

dripping water as she went. I pulled a pair of black sweats and a grey t-shirt from my dresser. Fanny muttered a lackluster 'thanks' as I tossed them on the bed, and closed the door behind me.

While she changed, I turned Bach off, went to the kitchen, and poured two glasses of water. Fanny exited my room wearing my clothes. She dropped her purse and grocery bag on the couch, and I presented her with a glass as she walked up.

"Really?" she asked. "I've had enough water for one day."

I jerked my head towards the fridge. "Out of pop and beer."

Her shoulders sagged an inch. "Fine," and she took it from me.

And immediately placed it on the counter, and slapped me across the face. Hard. My head whipped from the impact.

"You asshole! What's the big idea of going there at one thirty, when yesterday, you told me you'd be going at two thirty?"

I rubbed my face where she'd slapped me. My cheek stung, and felt warm to the touch. I worked my jaw back and forth.

"Is that why you're mad?" I asked. "Because you showed up fifteen minutes early thinking you'd get there first, and saw I already left?"

Fanny blinked several times, opened her mouth to say something, and waggled her finger at me. Then she clamped her mouth shut and looked away.

"You're mad because your little plan backfired."

She whirled back to face me. "No, Frank, I'm mad because what I feared would happen, did happen! You showed him those songs, and he went ballistic. You have no idea how upset it made me, to show up and be told 'No visitors, sorry!' He's sedated and strapped to his bed, because you did the one thing I didn't want you to! You pushed him, didn't you."

She didn't ask. She declared it.

"You weren't there," I told her.

"What is that supposed to mean? Maybe if I were, maybe if we visited him together, this wouldn't have happened. But you had to go early, to avoid me, right? Is that what you did?"

"What? No! You asked what time I'd be going. You could have suggested then and there that we go together."

"Frank, what I told you was, I might see you there! I visit Daddy every Sunday after 1:00 Mass!! Every freaking Sunday!" she shouted, smacking her palm on the counter with each word. "Don't tell me you forgot, because I know you, and I know you don't ever forget."

Tears welled up, and would soon be spilling down her cheeks.

"You did what you wanted, without consideration for anybody else."

She swiped away the tears with the back of her hand before they could escape.

My shoulders slumped, and I cast my eyes downward. She was right; I remembered her saying that. It just hadn't seemed important at the time.

"Every Sunday, I drop Mike and the kids off at the house after church," she continued, her voice getting louder, "then bring Daddy Holy Communion! Every Sunday. And today," her voice having ascended to its peak, "I couldn't!"

I closed my eyes and winced.

"I didn't think you needed to be told, but I guess you did."

I forced myself to look her in the eyes, as difficult as it proved to be. "I'm sorry, but you gotta believe me, I wasn't trying to trick you, or upset you, and I certainly wasn't trying to hurt Dad. Was I thoughtless? Yes. But I wasn't being malicious."

"Sometimes I wish you were. Then I'd know for sure you actually think about others." She left the kitchen, sobbing in uneven waves. Through her tears, she said, "Do you own any Kleenex, or am I stuck using toilet paper again?"

"Errr," I said, a sheepish look on my face. The last time she'd visited, she had suffered a sneezing outbreak due to an allergy, and I hadn't had a single box.

"Well, on the plus side, it's Charmin," I called after her as she stepped into the bathroom.

The roll holder rattled as she unwound it, followed by several nasal honks. I sat down in the chair, and put our glasses on the coffee table. She emerged a moment or two later, a fresh roll in her hand.

"Kleenex, pop, and beer," she said. "If not for you, then for me."

"Sure." I motioned to the Wegmans bag. "Whatcha bring?"

Fanny sat down next to her things, and shook her head. "Not now." She took a deep breath, and exhaled slowly. "All the way here, I thought, I knew something bad would happen. I just knew it. When you said you were going to show him the songs, remember what I said? And now look. Daddy's tied to his bed, and they tranquilized him."

"I know. I witnessed it."

"When I looked at the registry, I thought, that little shit, Saturday ended on a weird note, so he's avoiding me. I thought, thanks a lot Frank, way to pile on."

"Unintentionally, I swear."

"That's a piss poor defense." She blew her nose. "But that's how my mind is working nowadays. I either blow everything out of proportion, or assume the worst. You don't realize how hard this is for me.

"Keep reminding me and eventually I will."

"Ever since Mom died..." she paused, placing a hand on her chest. "Daddy calls me Louise, every visit. He thinks I'm her. Then yesterday, you tell me I look just like Mom. I know you didn't know, but it...Frankie, it's just so hard. And now I'm dealing with the realtor and the bank and...Mike's a huge help, but he can only do so much. And now this."

She unwound several sheets of toilet paper as she spoke, then blew her nose again.

"Maybe the best thing is go home, try to relax and..."

"Not until you tell me what happened. Every detail."

I described how Dad had believed I was Mendelssohn the composer, and that he was Abraham. That elicited a sob-choked smile.

"What did you do?"

"I played along as best I could. He first asked, how's Fanny, so naturally I thought he meant you. Then I figured out what he meant. We chatted a little, and I worked the conversation to where I asked about the songs. I handed them to him, and . . . it was strange, Fanny. As he looked through them, for a few seconds I swore he remembered. His face, it looked like years melted away. He became young again. It was surreal."

"I wish I could have seen."

"Yeah, me too. But then..."

Fanny leaned forward. "What?"

"I asked if he recognized them, and he immediately changed. Raving mad."

I recounted Dad's transformation, and his tirade, verbatim. Fanny covered her mouth during my recounting, her eyes wide with shock. She leaned back, slowly shaking her head, as I described everything in perfect detail, up to when the aides had barged in, subdued him, and forced me out.

"Poor Daddy," Fanny said softly. She dabbed her eyes with a fresh tear-off of toilet paper. "I knew something like this would happen."

She kept saying that. I took a sip of water. "I'm shaking again just talking about it."

"When I got there, the receptionist said no visitors today, that there had been an incident. I demanded to be told what happened, and I raised so much hell she fetched the head nurse. When she stepped away, I saw your name in the registry, and that's when I became really upset."

She reached for the bag, and pulled out the scores.

"She gave me these. I explained to her I was Dad's power of attorney, so then she showed me the report. She repeatedly apologized, and at my insistence, let me use her phone to call you. It's good I showed up after all, otherwise you'd never have gotten these back."

"Those are copies. The originals are on the kitchen table."

"So you thought Dad would react badly."

"I had no idea what would happen. Why take any chances? What if he wanted them? I'd never be able to convince him to return them."

"So now what?" Fanny asked.

"Well, what do you make of this commie sympathizer stuff? You're the history buff."

"Isn't it obvious? It's all about McCarthyism. The second Red Scare."

"But I thought that only involved Hollywood."

"A lot of the accusations and blacklisting focused on Hollywood," Fanny said, "but some musicians and composers were involved. A booklet published in 1950 called *Red Channels* listed over 150 people accused of being associated with subversive groups. Aaron Copland and Leonard Bernstein were included."

"Really?"

"Yeah, I know, right? Copland only wrote a tone poem on Abraham Lincoln, the kind of thing an unpatriotic person would do," she said, rolling her eyes. "Sure, Copland embraced progressivism, but he also publicly denounced Stalin and communism. People were spooked, and suspicion ran high. The start of the Cold War. People were guilty until proven innocent. A lot of careers were ruined and destroyed."

"Was Dad listed in the *Red Channels*?"

Fanny shook her head. "No. As far as I know, he didn't make anybody's list anywhere. But it sounds like there may have been a witch hunt of sorts at Prescott. *If* Dad's episode was an actual memory, and not because of his Alzheimer's."

Her emphasis on 'If' hadn't gone unnoticed.

"Seemed real enough to me."

"Seemed real to Dad, too, but it's almost impossible to

know for sure. Unless there's proof an inquiry actually happened, then Dad may have imagined all of it."

I remained unconvinced. "It wasn't fake."

"Based on what? Where's your proof?"

"The proof must be at Prescott. Dad was a victim of McCarthyism, and Clara's involved in some way."

Fanny sighed. "Frank, you're getting carried away."

"Maybe one of Dad's old friends knows about it," I said, ignoring her. "At the very least, they can verify whether it's true. Did Dad or Mom ever talk about this to you?"

"What? Of course not!"

"Just thought I'd ask," I said. "You guys were always pretty close."

"Closer than you, maybe, but that's not saying much," she replied. "Dad never spoke about being investigated. And I'm sure Mom didn't know. Again, that's assuming Dad was even investigated to begin with."

"Well, if it's true, someone somewhere knows about it. And I'm going to pursue it."

"But why? After all these years, what's the point?"

"He mentioned Clara's name, remember? And maybe his reputation needs to be restored. Perhaps put some things to rest."

"You think Dad's name has been sullied? Everybody at Prescott respected him. Remember his retirement party? Hundreds of people attended. I don't think Dad's reputation needs rehabilitating. Which means one of two things. Either the charges were dropped, and his file expunged, or it never happened."

"There's a third possibility."

"Pretty sure there are only two."

"Maybe he threw himself on his sword. For Clara."

"That makes no sense!" Fanny said. "If Daddy had admitted to being a sympathizer, he would have been fired, blacklisted, and unemployable! None of which happened!"

Her answer made sense, but Dad had said something

which made me think otherwise. *Maybe someone has it out for me, someone here in the school.* "Dad believed someone at Prescott wanted to hurt him, as well as Clara. To protect Clara - if he loved her as much as those songs indicate I could see him making a sacrifice for her."

"But Prescott didn't fire him," Fanny said, emphasizing each word. "You're forgetting that part. During the Red Scare, people lost their livelihoods merely for being suspected. Burden of proof was unnecessary." She shook her head. "You need to understand something. Things Dad says now can't necessarily be accepted as fact. He thought you were Felix Mendelssohn, which you're not. He thought the school accused him of being a communist. Doesn't mean it happened."

"I get all that. I just . . . I can't explain it. But I'm going to find out."

"How?"

"Do you remember Jim Gregory?"

"Sure," Fanny said, nodding. "He used to come to the house back in the fifties and sixties."

"He visited Dad shortly after he moved in."

"How do you know? That's confidential. Did Dad tell you?"

"I used the Jedi mind trick on the lobby goblin. It doesn't matter," I added as she shot me a look and straightened up in her seat. "Point is, I intend to ask him about it."

Fanny put her head in her hands. "Oh Frank, you haven't changed a bit. An idea forms in your head, and you won't let it go. You're so stubborn."

"Thank you."

"It wasn't a compliment," she retorted, looking up. "That stubbornness caused your problems with Dad, and with Mom."

The conversation shifted in an unwanted direction. "Don't change the subject."

"I'm not. You are the subject. This stuff about Clara's songs, and the Red Scare thing - if it's even true - is not about Dad. It's about you."

"What do you mean? Twenty-four hours ago, I schlepped a bunch of boxes out of the attic, as a favor to you, and uncovered previously unknown history about Dad. Songs for another woman. Possible communist scandal. I didn't search for any of this. How does that make it about me?"

"You have to just let it go," Fanny said.

"You're not remotely curious? About Clara, or about any of this?" I indicated the stack of manila envelopes on the floor. "And the other boxes? Not in the slightest?"

"I don't have the energy to be curious. Please, let it go."

"Why, because it's upsetting you?"

Her back straightened more. "No, because you're trying to prove to yourself that all those arguments weren't your fault. It's too late for that. Dad, for all intents and purposes, is gone."

I held my breath for I don't know how long, feeling my blood pressure rise. Through clenched teeth, I said: "Fanny, I really think you should leave."

Her jaw flinched, and her cheek muscles twitched. "We are all we have, Frank. It's only you and me. Please, don't let this come between us. Let it go."

"Keep my clothes, just get your stuff and leave."

Fanny waited a beat, then stood up. "Think about what I said. You're gonna do what you want. You always have. But consider your motives, and be honest with yourself."

She picked up the bag off the couch, and held it out towards me.

"I brought this for you, too. Thought you might find it interesting, given the songs and the conversation yesterday at dinner."

I took it from her. Inside was a medium-sized paperback, entitled *Letters of Clara Schumann and Johannes Brahms, 1853-1896, Volume II*. Beneath the title were illustrated images of a male hand and a female hand, one holding an envelope, the other resting on some papers. An ink well was placed between them.

"It seems stupid and pointless giving it to you now, but whatever," she said. "I couldn't find volume one."

I looked up to thank her, but she'd walked into my bedroom. When she came back out, I tossed the book on the couch and handed her the empty bag.

"For your stuff," I told her. She stuffed her wet clothes into it, while I stood up and followed her to the door.

"Think about what I said?" Fanny asked, placing her hand on my chest. "I need you, okay? Mike is doing his best, but I really need you. We need each other. It's just us. Do you understand?"

I counted to five, taking slow and measured breaths, and managed a short smile.

"I do. But you need to understand something, too. I have to find out what this is about. I need to know what's true and what's not. I gotta answer these questions. At least try to. I haven't thought of my motivations, beyond figuring out how to solve this. Do you understand?"

Fanny nodded quickly, patting me on the chest. "I do. I think I do anyway. Maybe I was a bit...blunt. It's been a hell of an afternoon."

"I know."

Sadness tugged at the corners of her mouth despite a faint smile. "Come by for dinner later this week?"

"We'll see." With that, we hugged, and she left.

The rain had stopped.

After watching her drive away, I replaced the needle on *Partita No. 3 in A minor*. As the first movement began, I laid down on the couch and tried to let the music calm me down.

# CHAPTER 8

F anny's visit gave me a headache in more ways than one. My jaw felt tender from her slap, my eyes stung from a dull pressure in my skull, and her comments echoed between my ears. I sighed heavily, and squeezed my eyes shut to push back the pain and aggravation. Listening to Bach and Gould had offered no relief. Normally, music made everything right. Not today, though. Three partitas in, and the funk remained. I lifted the arm from the record, and shut off the stereo. While I was sliding the disc into its sleeve, a childhood memory involving Gould arose.

Prescott's president had invited him to the school in February of 1968, to lecture on theory and technique. Gould lived conveniently close by in Toronto. Dad had been excited to meet the young pianist, to discuss the things musical geniuses tend to discuss. Dad wanted to introduce him to me - he always made the effort to introduce Fanny and me to the virtuosos and masters when they visited Prescott. I hadn't cared much, being nine. Meeting a sports star would have been more interesting than meeting a pianist who had sat on a funny looking chair and hummed as he played.

The day before Gould's visit, a strong lake-effect blizzard had hit, blanketing western New York with several feet of snow, and shutting down the US-Canada border crossings. The lectures had been cancelled.

*"So much snow."* Dad, standing at the piano, looked through the conservatory windows. His voice was thick with disappointment.

*"Weatherman predicts a total of two feet,"* Mom said from

the kitchen. The aroma of chocolate chip cookies wafted into the dining room. She came in and put a plate of two warm cookies on the table where I was seated, surrounded by school assignments. "You were looking forward to meeting Glenn so much, too. I'm sorry, Ivan."

He idly waved his hand as he joined us. "Eh, I'll have other chances. Frankie, though…he's missing out."

I looked up at him, already two bites into the fresh cookie. Missing out? It's a snow day! How could I possibly be missing out? As soon as I finished my homework, Tommy and I were going to build the biggest snow fort ever.

"Da, if you had met Mr. Gould, you'd understand it's the piano you should be playing, as you were meant to."

"Ivan, must you…"

Dad interrupted her. "Instead of wasting your talent on that inelegant trumpet."

So. That had been his plan all along.

Mom gave Dad the same expression I always got for teasing Fanny. She was good at hiding her anger, but we knew she was angry all the same.

"Thanks for the cookie, Mom," I told her, eliciting a smile as she looked down at me. "I think I'll practice before going outside."

Homework and snow forts could wait. Pushing away from the table, I stood and left the room. Mom wouldn't chide Dad until she heard my door shut.

"He's doing that on purpose, Elise," Dad said.

I grinned the entire way to my room.

It was said that Gould had a photographic memory and perfect sight-reading skills, able to play a piece perfectly after only one reading. I knew the feeling. The memory was as real now as when it happened; every word, inflection, facial expression, taste, and aroma. I suddenly missed Mom's baking.

Gould's visit had never been rescheduled. After his death in 1982, Dad had remarked to Fanny that the world had lost a genius with no suitable one to replace him. He'd known I was sitting within earshot, and I'd known he meant me. I had thought, let it go, you douche.

After slipping the record into its spot in my alphabetically arranged collection, I decided the best way to clear my mind would be a bike ride. A quick change of clothes, pump up the Schwinn's tires, and head on out.

I wheeled my bike out the door onto the landing. The storms had left clear, blue skies in their wake. The oppressive humidity was gone, and a light breeze rustled the trees. Perfect weather for a long ride on the Canalway Trail.

A couple hours later, I returned home, braking to a stop at the staircase. The ride had been the perfect antidote for what was plaguing me. My mind felt clearer, and while my questions still lacked answers, the sense of being overwhelmed by them was gone. I looked forward to a quick shower, dinner at a village restaurant, and a little TV before bed.

I carried my Schwinn into my apartment, and wheeled it into the corner of my bedroom. My peace was threatened by the answering machine's blinking red light. I resisted with every ounce of willpower, determined not to listen to it, and burst this bubble of tranquility. The message could wait until tomorrow, after a good night's sleep.

I heaved a vanquished sigh. Not knowing would be worse than knowing. Maybe Fanny had called to apologize again. Or Jessica had left a message thanking me for last night. Who else would call on a Sunday evening?

Giving in, I pressed Play.

"Ummm, Frank? Uh, hi, this is Natalie from last night. Natalie Johnson? I was with Don? Listen, I'm just calling to... well, I'm not really sure why I'm calling, but...actually, um, I wanted to apologize for last night. I hope you don't remember how rude I was, arguing with you. I mean, I had just met you. I should have been more considerate. I suppose I could blame the beer and the loud music, but that's a lame cop-out. You don't have to call back, but if you want to, my number is 555-6541 bye!"

I didn't even hear the time stamp, her voice echoing in

my head. It sounded different than it had at O'Shea's; almost pleasant, much less strident.

I shuffled into the bathroom to shower, my mind blown by the message. All during my shower, I wondered how many times she had started to dial, and then hung up. I wondered why she felt compelled to apologize. It wasn't necessary. To me, it had been a fun back and forth on a topic in which we held opposite opinions. In fact, I had goaded her, taking slight advantage of her drunkenness, getting her more and more worked up.

I wondered longest about why she wanted me to return her call. There was more to her call than soothing a guilty conscience. That was probably a pretense. Was it safe to presume she and Don weren't dating? Had that been a blind date? The last time we'd all hung out, at a baseball game in mid-July, he hadn't mentioned her. Maybe her interest was solely due to my connection with Dad. A hope to have a vicarious brush with celebrity. Of course, if I told her Dad had Alzheimer's, her interest might vanish. Maybe she wanted to tell her friends with musically incorrect opinions she knew the son of a local composer.

*Was she hoping I'd call her back?*

I shut off the water and stood an extra moment in the steam. Regardless of her reasons, I had no intention of calling her back. Most likely she was embarrassed about her behavior, and had been taught by her stern, frigid mother - so I imagined - to always apologize when making a bad first impression. She was probably kicking herself right now for leaving the message.

I stepped out of the shower and wrapped a towel around my waist. Before going to the bedroom to dress, I returned to the answering machine. Its message indicator light glowed a solid red. My index finger hovered above the 'Erase Message' button, as I contemplated. Maybe I should save the message for a day or two, just in case. No harm in that, right?

I quickly dressed and walked into town. Natalie's message had me craving for a beer or three.

\* \* \*

By my third Genny Light, I concluded that more drinking wasn't going to lead to less thinking about Natalie. Halfway through the fourth beer, I realized our musical tastes were far too dissimilar for there to ever be any semblance of common ground. I made that point clearly to Connie, my regular waitress at Grandpa Sam's Italian Restaurant. She was in her forties, and she wore a pink and white uniform, her white waist pouch covered in marinara sauce stains and a smear of blueberry.

"Now is Natalie the one you come in with sometimes? She's super pretty," Connie said, wiping her hands on a towel she produced from her pouch, and pulling out a chair to chat.

I waved my hand. "No, no, that's Jessica. I met Natalie last night. At O'Shea's."

"Ohhh," Connie said, nodding. "And what kind of music does she like?"

"Apparently nothing older than herself," I said. "I mean, she likes *Cats*! *Cats*! Can you believe that? People with style or taste don't like *Cats*."

Connie twisted her towel a little. "I liked *Cats*. I thought it was cute."

"Oh. Well, what I meant was, this girl should know better. She's classically trained, you know?" I drank the rest of my beer, searching for the right words. "Stuff like that is like vaudeville, right? Entertainment for the masses. You know what I mean."

"Well, as my mom used to say," Connie said, smiling, "there's no accounting for taste."

"Quite right," I said, nodding. "On no account does Natalie have any taste. She tried to convince me that John Williams is more accessible than Hector Berlioz! Can you believe that?" I held open my left hand, saying, "Berlioz," and then held open my right hand. "Versus Williams." Mimicking a scale, I raised my left hand and lowered my right. "There's no comparison!"

"Didn't Williams compose *ET*? I thought that music was wonderful."

I dropped both hands into my lap and sighed.

"If you ask me," Connie said, "she sounds like a nice girl." She glanced at her watch, and placed my bill on the table. "Here's the damage, Frank. It was nice chatting."

"Connie, she is not a nice girl! She called me a music snob. She is argumentative and has all the wrong opinions. In fact, I don't even know why I'm talking to you about her."

"Well," she said in a sweet, cooing voice, "that's either due to the four beers, or you like her. You decide which one. Good night, Frank."

Connie walked off, my place setting and beer bottle in her hands. I folded my arms and leaned back.

*Like her? Gag me with a spoon! Definitely the four beers.*

I paid my bill and left.

Grandpa Sam's stood on Union Street, on the south side of the canal, four blocks from my apartment. The evening was cool, with a hint of a breeze, and the western sky was a coalescing swath of reds, oranges, and yellows. Several pedestrians strolled about, and the low rumbles of canal boat motors competed with the crickets and evening songbirds. It took me five minutes to reach my apartment, and Natalie occupied my thoughts during each one. Why was I letting her bother me so much? It was her stupid message. She could've let things be, and kept her fake apology all to herself.

I tromped into my apartment, daring to look at the answering machine. No blinking light. Taking a seat on the couch, I surveyed the stack of envelopes sitting on the coffee table. I wasn't in the mood to look through them, and I was too tired to look at the songs. All I wanted was minimal mental activity for the rest of the evening. Watching TV would help.

As I swung my legs up onto the couch to lay back, facing the television, something jabbed me between the shoulders, and I quickly sat upright. I reached behind me, and felt for whatever it was.

It was the book Fanny had loaned me. The front cover was slightly ragged, the upper corner dog eared. I thumbed through it, noticing Fanny had highlighted or circled numerous passages, and written notes in the margins.

This second volume included letters written from 1877 through the summer of 1896, the year of Clara's death. The last few letters were ones Brahms had written to the eldest Schumann child, Marie, who had been Clara's caretaker in her last years. There were long gaps of time between many of the letters, and places where the correspondence was mostly from Clara. I recalled learning in one of my college courses that Brahms had returned most of the letters Clara had written, asking her to destroy them. She had burned quite a few before Marie insisted she stop.

Many of the letters dealt with the publication of Robert's music, and Clara's dealings with publishers and revisers. She'd relied heavily on Brahms' advice, and their collaboration proved successful. Many of Brahms' letters spoke of pieces he had included for Clara's enjoyment, and her replies to him regarding those pieces were heartfelt and touching. She wrote of the joy his music brought her, and of her admiration of his style and skill.

Too bad Fanny hadn't found the first volume of letters. In 1877, Clara was already in her late fifties, Brahms in his early forties. At this stage, their relationship was one of maturity and mutual admiration. It was still love, but one that glowed rather than burned. Comparing the letters' styles from the 1850's, started several years prior to her husband's death, to these later ones would have been interesting.

The letters spoke of the disappointment in not being able to coordinate visits, or how their travels would mean being far from home, or delays in seeing each other. Both used discreet and proper language, but their care and love for each other was evident. Their adieus ran the gamut from 'I am Your Clara,' to 'Your heartily devoted Johannes,' and from 'Your old friend, Clara,' to 'Affectionate greetings, JOH.'

Flipping through, I came across Brahms' letter in which he responded to the news of the death of her son Felix, only twenty-five at the time. He wrote:

*"Every letter I have received from you lately has prepared me for the sad news which has come today. But when I held this one in my hand, I felt sure of what it contained and as I opened it all my thoughts were with you. One would imagine that at such a moment one ought to feel relieved and uplifted. But I have never found it so. All the memories of the good things I have had in the past and the thoughts of all the good things I may yet hope for and expect, crowded in upon my mind. At the moment, I only feel with double force what I felt before.*

*"It is a good thing Fate cannot assail me many more times. I very much fear that I should not bear it very well...I wish I could be with you. For no matter how long I may sit with paper and pen before me, I should find things so much easier if I could sit in silence beside you.*

*"Yours affectionately, Johannes."*

His breadth of compassion impressed me; but then again, he poured total and complete emotions into each of his compositions.

The last words in his final letter, written to Marie six weeks after Clara Schumann's death, were moving.

*"I must thank you most heartily for your kind offer to send me some memento of her - but I want nothing. Men are wont to desire some outward token of remembrance, and the smallest trifle would suffice for me, - but I possess the most beautiful of all!"*

He'd possessed her love, and his memories of her. I was sure that was what he had meant. How long and hard he must have mourned her death! Perhaps every day, given that he died the following year. Maybe life had become too lonely for him. I tried to imagine Dad loving his own Clara that much. Had his love glowed all those years, even while he was married to Mom? Or had it turned to ash, packed away and forgotten?

Perhaps Clara would be able to tell me, once I found her.

# CHAPTER 9

Monday morning arrived with streams of sunshine, and a chorus of sparrows in the nearby trees. I had dozed off while reading, woken up in the middle of the night, then dragged myself off the couch and shambled to bed. I hadn't bothered to change my clothes.

I rolled over and faced the window. The sky was brilliant blue, streaked with high wispy white clouds. Other noises became recognizable, above the sparrows' chirps and whistles: traffic on Union Street; the beeping of a delivery truck as it backed into a loading dock; indeterminate voices of chatting neighbors down the street; the occasional dog, probably on the Canalway, enjoying a morning walk with its owner.

My leisurely weekday mornings were disappearing, as school was set to resume in three weeks. There were mandatory teacher meetings at the end of next week, then new school year preparations: finalizing lesson plans, setting up the band room, checking instruments, reviewing class lists. I was looking forward to returning, despite the fact it meant the end of summer.

The phone rang, shaking me from my thoughts. I staggered to my feet and reached the phone before the answering machine picked up.

"Hello?"

"Rise and shine, Franklin!"

I pulled the handset away from my ear. Ned's thunderous voice first thing in the morning was an unpleasant wake-up call.

"Listen dude, me and the guys are gonna hit House of Guitars this morning. Want in?"

I had planned on reading Clara's songs more closely today, and playing them on my keyboard. Perhaps I would look through more boxes, or call Gregory and arrange a meeting. But if I hung out with the guys, I could swing by the Prescott Conservatory afterward, and maybe head over to the main branch of the library afterwards - do a little research - hey, and maybe ask Don if he's serious with Natalie...

I shook my head. *Where the hell did that come from?*

"Dude, did you hear me?"

"Um, yeah," I stammered. "Sure. When do you want to meet?"

"It opens at ten, so I guess at ten."

"I'll be there."

We hung up. Talking to Ned had flipped my thoughts over to Natalie. Not where I wanted my thoughts to go, not this early in the morning.

Just after ten, I pulled into the House of Guitars parking lot, Rochester's go-to place for rock instruments and record albums. Two brothers had bought the former Irondequoit Grange Hall in the 1960's, and converted the two-story home into a store. It had expanded over the years, with a warehouse added onto the back for its extensive record and tape inventory. Their selection easily dwarfed the shopping mall record stores and national chains.

Big name acts visited the store when their tours stopped in Rochester, which added to its reputation as the world's largest guitar store. Every local act bought their gear here. Ned and the guys came here weekly for new releases, the occasional equipment purchase, and to hang out. I joined them every so often, mainly to scavenge through the classical music section, and to occasionally accompany their impromptu jam sessions, goofing off on the electronic keyboards.

Climbing the steps to the front door, I entered and squeezed past haphazardly placed stacks of unboxed merchandise, and headed to the drums section in the back. I found Joey sitting at a silver and black Pearl kit, twirling a drumstick in each hand.

"What's up, man." I motioned to the drum set. "Your next kit?"

"I wish!" he said with a laugh. "I doubt I can even afford one cymbal," he added, as he struck it. He quickly grabbed it to silence the reverberations.

"Where are Don and Ned?"

Joey pointed up with a drumstick. "Guess."

Guitar floor, practice rooms.

"Where else?" I said, smiling. "Catch ya later."

I made my way to the flight of steps leading to the second floor. Numerous guitars were mounted to the walls, in protective clear cases, autographed by famous musicians such as Paul McCartney, Jimi Hendrix, and Jimmy Page. Signed photos of rock stars standing with the House owners and staff hung in virtually every open space.

The upstairs contained every guitar make on the market. Five aisles in total, ceiling-high shelving running from one end to the other. Countless amps covered the rear wall. In the far corner stood three sound-proof chambers with large plexiglass windows, where customers could try out guitars. I headed that way.

They were in the furthest room. Ned was tuning a red Fender Stratocaster, while Don was strumming a glossy black Rickenbacker bass. Ned had already broken out in a sweat. Both were amped up, and I felt vibrations through the plexiglass. I tapped the window a few times before they heard me, and Don shot me a thumbs up while Ned opened the door.

"Dude," he said, letting me come in, "we're totally shredding *Tom Sawyer*. Bring up a keyboard and let's jam!"

I laughed, stepping inside. "Not this time, you shred without me. Just letting you know I'm here. You know where to find me."

"Not the classical section," Ned groaned. "Geez, Frank,

it's like you're an old man. Believe me, girls don't go for Choppin or Botch. You need songs written this decade, at least." Ned teased me about my taste in music every chance he got.

"Or in the past century," Don added. "That old stuff is useless for a mixtape, you know."

"No kidding!" Ned said. "You need gnarly artists for a mixtape, like Lionel Richie. Or Air Supply."

"Don't forget Spandau Ballet," Don added. "Their song *True*? Perfection. And Chris Deburgh's new one too."

"Totally righteous!" Ned said, smacking Don in the shoulder. "*Lady in Red*. That song is awesome."

"Dudes, what are you talking about? Mixtapes? I haven't made one since freshman year in college," I said.

"Yeah, and it shows," Ned said. "We all talked about this on the way here; you'd improve your chances with Jessica if you did a mixtape. How do you think I landed Denise? Mixtape, man! Worth every hour I spent recording that thing. Now, song order is key. It's a progression, y'know? You can't start too heavy or too mushy, otherwise you ruin the mood. Let it build up, and up, and up, and bam!" He spread his arms like a conductor. "Enter the power ballad!"

Before I could set them straight about Jessica, Don slapped me on the arm. "I got *Lady in Red* if you want to borrow it. Start with that one."

"Yeah, perfect mixtapes are a mystical blend of art and science," Ned said. "Use the right power ballad, and you got her."

Don chimed in. "Every mixtape needs one - the newer the better. The element of surprise, y'know? I can give you a list of suggestions. What do you think?"

"I think it's disturbing you guys listened to *Lady in Red*."

Ned and Don looked at each other, surprise on their faces.

"Of course we've listened to it!" Ned exclaimed. "Research, dude. Love songs have the ability to turn off the part of a girl's brain that tells her to keep her clothes on. Didn't college teach you anything about music? You *majored* in music, and you never learned this?"

"Higher ed failed you, man," Don said, shaking his head solemnly.

Looking at Don, I asked, "Did your mixtape work on Natalie?"

He snorted, and played a quick riff on the bass. "Never got that far. In fact, thanks to you, I didn't get anywhere with her."

"Thanks to me? What did I do?"

"The entire way back to her place, she kept going on and on about how much of a jerk you were. About how you hate John Williams, and made fun of her opinions. She wouldn't shut up. Totally shot down any chance. I might move on."

"Nice going, Frank," Ned said. "You ruined Don's chances, and you weren't even there."

"Sorry, dude," I said. "In any case, I'm past my prime on mixtapes. You guys work on your Rush, and I'll go check out *Chopin* and *Bach*." I emphasized their correct pronunciation in Ned's direction. "Come get me when you head out."

They were laughing as the door clicked shut behind me. I looked through the window, and after getting their attention, flipped them both birds, mouthing the words 'In stereo.' They returned the favor, still laughing.

"Mixtapes," I muttered, at the same time thinking that maybe Natalie's phone call might have been more than a simple apology after all.

Half an hour later, we were leaving the store.

"So what'd you buy?" Ned asked me.

"Murray Perahia's *Beethoven's Piano Concerti 3 and 4.* Released earlier this year."

"Who the heck is Mary Pariah? You buy any *normal* music?"

I rolled my eyes. "Eat my shorts. That *is* normal music. But because I knew you'd be a dork, I also bought Peter Gabriel's *So.*"

"Bodacious album," Joey said. "Has a bunch of great songs. Some cool percussion."

"I'm shocked!" Ned said. "You bought music written by a living person!"

We reached our cars, having parked next to each other. Joey unlocked his truck and tossed his bag behind the driver's seat.

"Wanna grab some lunch with us?"

"I gotta motor," I answered, shaking my head.

"Hot date?" Ned asked, smiling.

I cast a glance at my Horizon's passenger seat. The manila envelope of Clara's songs lay on the upholstery.

"Not exactly. Something came up."

Ned, Don, and Joey shouted in unison: "That's what she said!"

"Later, dudes," I said laughing, as I climbed into my car.

* * *

The Prescott Conservatory of Musical Studies was a ten-minute drive from the House of Guitars, directly south on Hudson Avenue. Hudson terminated at North Ave, and I angled right, entering downtown. I then turned onto Main Street, and drove past the Prescott Theatre, part of the school complex.

The school stood four floors tall, having been built in the early 1920's. Its architectural style typified those times: gray sandstone blocks, series of carved ionic columns, tall windows capped with ornate stonework arches. Across the street from the school stood an eight-story building called the Tower, connected by an enclosed pedestrian bridge. The faculty's offices were located in the Tower, which represented my best chance for finding Gregory.

I parked behind the school, and grabbed the envelope while getting out. Bringing the scores seemed sensible, despite the fact that the main reason for my visit centered on the inquiry. Certainly, Gregory would appreciate seeing Dad's unpublished, never performed works, as his friend and former coworker. At the very least, the scores could be used as an ice-breaker, to keep the conversation focused on Dad.

Plus, he might have some idea of Clara's identity. If she had been Dad's mistress, it was possible Gregory knew of her.

The reception area stood mostly empty. A few students lingered in a small group, while others stood by the bank of elevators along the side wall. A directory hung on the wall be-tween two of the elevators; Gregory had a fourth-floor office. As a set of doors opened for passengers going up, I stepped inside.

"Four please," I said to a female student standing close to the operating panel. She held a flute case and several music books.

The fourth floor was the first stop. I got my bearings, and headed to Gregory's office. I hoped he was available. He played and taught piano, like Dad. They had played duets whenever he and his wife came to visit. I hadn't seen him in years; I won-dered if he'd remember me.

A brass nameplate on his closed office door read "Prof. James T. Gregory." I knocked, and from within, came a gruff reply.

"It's unlocked."

I let myself in. A window faced the office doorway; its blinds were open, allowing the late morning sunshine in. A light brown maple Steinway upright piano stood against the left-hand wall, music books stacked on its cover, a small desk lamp squeezed to one side. Framed diplomas, photographs, and awards covered the walls. A large wooden desk stood op-posite the piano.

Gregory sat at his desk, writing on a legal pad, and he didn't look up to greet me. He seemed larger and grayer than when I saw him last. His wire-framed glasses were too small for his head, which was a mass of cheeks, jowls, and double-chins. His hands resembled paws with stubby fingers. It amazed me he could play so well with such small, short fingers.

"Take a seat right there," he said, jabbing his pen towards a chair stacked high with textbooks, next to the piano, without looking up. "I'll be with you in a second."

I carefully placed the books on the floor as he had instructed, turned the chair around, and sat down. The manila envelope of Dad's songs lay across my lap. He finally put down his pen, and swiveled around to face me.

"Now," he said, "how may I help you? Are you a new grad student?"

"No, Mr. Gregory," I said. "I'm Frank Stephens, Ivan's son."

His eyes widened a bit, and I detected a bit of a twinkle when I mentioned Dad's name.

"Frank Stephens, how have you been?" he asked, smiling.

He extended his chubby hand, and I shook it. His grip was powerful and enthusiastic.

"Can't complain."

"Haven't seen you since...wow, how long has it been?"

"Probably my mother's funeral," I told him.

The shine in his face seemed to fade. "I think you're right. So sad, about your mother. Taken too soon." He cleared his throat and adjusted his glasses. "So what brings you here?"

I took a deep breath. "A couple things, actually. I saw my dad at Mellowood yesterday, and I found out you visited him in March. I wanted to come by and say thank you. I'm sure it meant a lot to him."

"It was the least I could do. We've been friends for a long time, lots of great memories. How has he been?"

I considered a moment before responding. "He's regressed a lot. Has trouble recognizing me and Fanny."

He shook his head. Removing his glasses, he pulled a handkerchief from his pocket and used it to wipe them. "What a shame. An absolute shame. I'm so sorry to hear that."

"Thanks," I said. "Not much can be done about it, but we still go and see him."

"We used to have so much fun," Gregory said. "Your dad was…is a good man, Frank. Talented beyond description." He replaced his glasses. "He talked about you quite often."

"Really?" I didn't think I wanted to hear about this.

"When you were a boy, he used to boast, 'Frankie will be the next Mozart, you just wait.' I'd smile and say to myself, ah, Ivan's playing the part of the proud papa. Some dads say their son will be the next Jack Nicklaus, or Bobby Orr, or Joe Namath. It's a natural desire, right?"

I shrugged. "I don't have any kids, so I can't say."

Gregory leaned forward and tapped me on the knee. "You'd be shocked at how many parents came in with their sons and daughters, and tell me, our child is a prodigy. Please be their teacher, please work with them. I have them play for me, demonstrate their ability, and ninety-nine times out of hundred…no, nine hundred ninety-nine times out of a thousand, I have to tell them, your son or daughter is no prodigy. They may have some skill, but they aren't prodigies. They'd get upset, as if I had stabbed them in the heart, or didn't know what I was talking about. And yet they'd come to me, seeking my opinion! Your dad had as many of these experiences as I did.

"But then I thought, Ivan knows what makes a prodigy. He wouldn't have said that about you if it weren't true. The next time he boasted, 'My boy is Mendelssohn's second coming,' I said 'Let me confirm that.' He smiled, and agreed."

He leaned back in his chair, and interlocked his cigar-like fingers. "So that Saturday evening, my wife and I came over. You might have been five at the time. This tall," he said, holding his hand three feet off the floor, "your feet couldn't even reach the pedals. Your dad asked, 'Did you bring music?' I had brought something simple, Schumann's *Album for the Very Young*. You were very young, so it seemed appropriate. Do you recall this at all?"

I closed my eyes, remembering this perfectly, and angry at myself for letting the conversation go down this path.

"No, I really don't," I lied.

"Well, I remember it as clear as yesterday. Ivan suggested I pick any song,  so I chose *The Happy Farmer*. He placed the book on the tray, and said, 'Felix, please play this for our guests.' He always called you Felix, didn't he?"

I nodded. As recently as yesterday.

"So you played the song. Flawlessly. You scaled down the larger chords to fit your hands, but yes, a flawless performance. I looked at Ivan and said, 'He is exceptionally good, but a prodigy? You exaggerate!' He smiled, raised an eyebrow, and shook his head. 'He's not done yet.' Ivan looked at you and gave you a little nod."

Gregory pulled his chair forward, closer to me. He poked me with a stubby index finger, on the knee.

"And what did you do next, but play three variations on that piece!" He pulled away again. "No music. No mistakes. As easy for you as if you were throwing a ball or running in the yard. I looked at Ivan and said, 'You are right.' I've never forgotten that experience."

My cheeks and neck felt warm, and I shifted in the wooden chair. I hadn't forgotten either.

A pall of disappointment creased Gregory's face. "Ivan wouldn't let me teach you, though. He wanted to instruct you, and we disagreed over that. A few years later, he told me you stopped playing."

"My mother stepped in," I told him. "Too many arguments."

"Similar temperaments," he said, nodding. "It's more common than you might think. Ivan told me you took up the trumpet. After you switched, we attended your parents' parties, but didn't see you around."

I stared at my lap. This visit was becoming uncomfortable.

"Yeah, he sent me to my room. Dad called me a disgrace to the family."

Gregory adjusted his glasses and cleared his throat. "I am sorry to hear that. If it means anything, I always believed you were a phenomenal talent. So what are you doing now?"

"I teach band at Spencerport Junior High."

Gregory looked at his hands, his face clouded and unreadable. "Well," he finally said after a long three seconds, "at least your talent isn't being completely wasted."

I shifted in my chair some more, crumpling the envelope. My eyes narrowed, focused on Gregory's scuffed up brown slip-on loafers. If I were to look him in the eyes, I didn't know what I'd have said, but it wouldn't have been polite.

He must've sensed my rising anger. He cleared his throat a second time, somewhat uneasily.

"Well, you said you came here for a couple reasons, right? Certainly not to listen to an old man reminisce. I imagine you're curious about what your dad and I spoke of during my visit. We had a short, difficult conversation. I could tell his memory was slipping. He struggled to recall times and places and people." He motioned to the envelope gripped in my hands. "Is that something you'd like to show me?"

I took a deep breath and released it slowly.

"It's some of Dad's music," I said, hoping my tone didn't come across as too abrupt. "I came across them the other day.. They've never been published. I wondered if you might recognize them."

I handed him the envelope, noticing clear, pinched impressions from my fingertips. Gregory placed his glasses on his desk as he pulled out the photocopied set of scores. The songs were clipped together, and I had left the 'For Clara' tag in my car. I didn't want his memory influenced in any way.

Gregory flipped through the songs, in silence. After a few minutes, he looked up at me, an excited look on his face.

"I have never seen these before," he said. "Ivan, on occasion, asked my opinion on particular compositions. Not these.

I see, though, that these are photocopies. His notations were in blue or red, never black."

"The originals are back in my apartment."

He nodded. "And no notation or indication when they were written? Pity. These seem less mature than his works from the past few decades, and yet, these possess a somewhat greater depth. They seem beautiful. Would you object to me playing one?"

"Not at all," I said.

Gregory replaced his glasses, wheeled over to the piano bench, and half-slid, half-hobbled onto it. He pried the waltz out from under the clip, placed it on the music tray, positioned his hands on the keyboard, and began to play. The tune sounded exactly the way I'd heard it in my head when I'd read the first handful of measures on Saturday. The song brimmed with light, grace, and charm. Gregory played it with style, without mistakes.

He stopped midway through the first page, and placed his hands on his lap. He seemed moved. Blinking quickly, he put it back in the envelope, and handed it to me.

"Thank you for indulging me."

"It sounded great," I told him. "The style is so unlike his other compositions. Freer, in a way."

"If I were to guess, these were written for your mother. Waltzes, romances, a fantasy...not sure about those duets, though. Your mother didn't play violin. She was a vocalist."

"She played a little piano, too. Did Dad know any violinists?"

"Well, numerous violin professors taught here, and there had been several resident performers. I'm sure he knew plenty from his own performing days."

"Was he particularly close to any of them?" I asked.

"Not that I can recall," he answered. His eyes narrowed. "Are you implying your father may have written these for someone else?"

I shrugged my shoulders. "They've been in an unmarked

carton for over thirty years. For all I know, they're dedicated to a woman he knew before he married Mom."

Gregory pursed his lips. "I don't recall anyone."

"They met here, right?"

"Exactly right. She arrived from Finland in 1949 and enrolled in the graduate program, left school in 1950, and they married in 1951." He patted his right leg. "Listen, my knee seizes something fierce if I sit too long. Can you accompany me over to Madeleine Hall, or do you have other commitments?"

"I have time. There's something else I'd like to ask if you don't mind."

"As long as you can keep up," he said, a chuckle in his voice.

# CHAPTER 10

**M**adeleine Hall occupied the main building's entire second floor. Clusters of chairs and sofas, encircling low tables, stood scattered throughout this grand gallery. Students and visitors sat at several of them, chatting among themselves. Tall windows filled the exterior walls, spaced every four feet, allowing bright sunlight in. Portraits of past school presidents and distinguished faculty hung upon the walls.

Ornate mahogany double doors stood at each end, and a side entrance led to elevators and the covered pedestrian bridge that connected to the Tower. Gregory and I entered the hall from the side entrance. Most of the way, he complained about his arthritis, and said he was considering knee replacement surgery in the spring.

"Barely any cartilage left," he told me. "Bone on bone. Even hurts when sitting at the piano."

As we walked past the elevators, I saw a poster advertising a concert - "Great Music From The Movies" – scheduled for the upcoming weekend.

*Great movie music? An oxymoron!*

Gregory limped to the far side of the room, across a tiled central aisle, and over to a pair of Queen Anne chairs set between two windows. Gregory slowly sat down in one chair with a breath of relief, and I took the other one. He waved and smiled at someone behind me; I turned and saw two people halfway across the room, waving back.

"Two students of mine," he said to me.

A thought occurred to me. "Do you remember your

former students?"

"A fair amount," he said. "Particularly the talented ones. Why do you ask?"

"This might sound funny, but I met a girl the other night who attended Prescott a few years ago. A piano student named Natalie Johnson?"

Gregory tapped his chin with his finger. "Sounds familiar. Yes, as a matter of fact, I do remember her. Showed promise, but had to drop out."

"Oh?"

"Something tragic, I believe. A death in the family." He nodded. "Yes, that was it. Her parents were killed in a car accident. She had younger siblings to take care of."

Natalie had suddenly become more of a real person.

"When she learned Ivan was my dad, she mentioned she had learned two of his pieces. Just a wild guess you taught her. I figured you included his songs in your lesson plan."

Gregory smiled. "It's a small world."

I rubbed the back of my neck. Perhaps a segue had presented itself.

"I'm learning that every day. Which kinda leads me to the other thing I wanted to ask you about." He nodded, so I continued. "It might sound a little weird."

"Weird in what way?"

"Well, you started at Prescott before 1950, right?"

"I was a student in the late 30's and joined the faculty in 1947."

"So you and my dad began at the same time."

"Within months. We were classmates before that, before the war."

"Here's the thing. During my visit with him yesterday, he became...confused. He went on and on about being brought before an inquiry, on charges of being a communist sympathizer. Shocked the heck out of me. We're talking about McCarthyism, right?"

Gregory's face grew serious. He folded his arms and nodded.

"My sister thinks he imagined it, the Alzheimer's messing with his brain. I think so too. But I need to know for sure. Did anything like that happen here, that you know about?"

He took a few moments before answering. His mouth was working, as if it had gone dry and he was trying to moisten it, pursing his lips, and flexing his cheeks. He then leaned in close, his elbows on his knees. I leaned forward as well.

"If you ask me," he said, his voice low, almost a whisper, "the times we're living in now, with that doddering actor in the White House, we're closer to nuclear annihilation now than we ever were back then. The fool probably sleeps with the launch button under his pillow. I know, that's neither here nor there, but that whole Red Scare business was utter and absolute bull."

"So it was true?"

Gregory nodded. "Yes, and suspicion was cast on Ivan."

"Just him? No one else?"

"Not as far as I know," Gregory said, shaking his head. "Because of his heritage, you see. He became a citizen when he turned eighteen, but you know how some people can be."

"So what happened?"

He paused. "This stays between us, and doesn't leave this room. Is that understood?"

"Sure thing."

Gregory swallowed and continued. "An inquiry was called in April 1950. It lasted a couple days, and then the decision was handed down."

"Were you a witness?"

"I abstained, at great risk. If you weren't willing to denounce, you were thought to be a sympathizer. Silence was consent, you see. But I and three other faculty members banded together, refused to testify, and the board relented."

"So what was the decision?"

"That's the curious thing. I had heard the inquiry declared him guilty, and he was going to be fired. But, at the eleventh hour, as they say, the charge was dropped, and he was permitted to keep his position. It was all very strange."

"What happened?"

Gregory spread his hands. "No one knew. Your father refused to discuss it, ever. To this day, I still don't know."

I recalled Dad repeating, 'keep her out of this.' If Dad had agreed to plead guilty on Clara's behalf, then his being fired and subsequently blacklisted would have been the logical result. But if the charges were dropped, as Gregory said they were, and Dad kept his position - which he obviously did, for thirty years - then why did the inquiry change its ruling? Had Clara sacrificed her career for Dad?

"Surely rumors and speculations floated around," I said.

"Here and there," Gregory said. "But the school was adamant about keeping the inquiry quiet. I'm sure everyone involved, including your father, was sworn to secrecy. You have to remember, Frank. Since its founding, Prescott has been the leading school of music in America. It's internationally famous. People from all the world over come here to study, work, and teach. It was in their best interest not to draw attention to what would have been a miscarriage of justice."

"But if Dad had been blacklisted, it would have been made public."

"Such is how things go. An exposé when it's a benefit, a cover-up when it's an embarrassment."

"Do you think the charge was dropped because it was bogus?"

Gregory shrugged. "Personally, I think the inquiry was a sham, and your father was singled out to be the Judas goat. The school never put out an official statement, and your father never spoke of it. It was as if it had never happened." He removed his glasses. "I'm not surprised you were never told. If Ivan didn't speak to his closest friends, he wouldn't have told family either. I can imagine how much of a shock this must be to you."

"Shock is one word to describe it," I said. "You're sure he

was the only person brought before the inquiry?"

"I was asked to only testify at your father's," Gregory said. "If there were others, they were covered up as well. I'm sorry to be the one who told you about this, but now you know Ivan's illness wasn't responsible for yesterday's episode. And now you have a clearer understanding of why your father eventually changed his name."

I was nodding as he spoke, but when he finished, my head froze, and my mouth went slack. What seemed like minutes was only several seconds before I closed my mouth and stared at him.

"Wait. . .what?"

* * *

*Dad changed our name from Stepanov to Stephens?? Not Grandpa??*

I was still stunned. Gregory and I had said our goodbyes fifteen minutes ago, after several apologies on his part. He'd presumed I had already known. He returned to his office, and I returned to my car. I had tossed the songs onto the passenger seat, and sat there.

Gregory had said he didn't know why. Though generous and hospitable, Dad had been jealous of his privacy. I could picture his close friends asking him, and the school administration demanding an explanation, while he stood his ground, refusing to satisfy them.

After the inquiry, perhaps he'd felt he needed to sound more American. During a time when all things Russian were distrusted, any connection had been considered suspicious. But he had become a US citizen in 1934. He had served in the US Navy during World War II, until he was honorably discharged due to an injury. He had nothing to prove to anybody.

And yet, he had lied to us. He had told us years ago that Grandpa had changed our name shortly after having immigrated to America. Why had he lied?

*Asking Dad would be pointless. Besides, I can't visit him for some time.*

But there was one person I could ask: Uncle Pietr. He might be able to give an explanation. The last time I'd seen Uncle Pietr and Aunt Jane had been Christmas, at Fanny's house. Visits had been frequent and regular when Mom was still alive. When she died, though, it seemed the center of the family had fallen out. I had just started my freshman year of college when breast cancer took her. She had been diagnosed in April of 1978, and had died by the end of October. Only fifty-two years old. Fanny had been pregnant with Justin when they found the cancer, and he'd been born in September. We were happy she'd gotten to meet him and hold him, but it had nonetheless been heartbreaking.

Since the funeral, Fanny had become Dad's lifeline. I'd returned to the University of Buffalo the day after, and spent my summers there. Living in the house with Dad would have been ugly. I had gone home for holiday breaks, and the short stays had been barely endurable. After graduating in 1982, I'd gotten my job and moved into my apartment, and since then, gone to the house on the rarest of occasions.

Memories rushed by, and for the first time in a long while, I missed Mom. How much easier this would all be if she were still around.

I quickly caught myself. Easier for whom?

When this started, all I wanted to know was Clara's identity. But now it seemed the question had become 'Who is Dad?'

\* \* \*

It was two-thirty when I made it back home, a Wegmans grocery bag in each hand. Clouds had rolled across the sky: another round of storms was imminent. The intermittent drops became a steady downpour seconds after I made it back inside.

Two messages on the answering machine awaited me.

After putting away the food, I broke open the case of Genny Cream Ale and removed a bottle. I had a feeling I was going to need it.

"Hey you! Thanks for being so nice Saturday. I can't remember the last time I passed out like that! I felt cruddy all day yesterday, and I'm totally dragging at work. Anyway, call me at the salon, okay? You need that haircut, mister! Byeeee!"

Hearing Jessica's voice made me smile. I ran a hand through my hair, a little surprised at how long it had gotten.

"Hi Frank. Hey, I spoke with Dad's doctor, and I'm going to see him tomorrow. Um, come over Thursday for dinner, okay? Okay. Love you."

Fanny sounded tired, which wasn't a surprise. No jokes or kidding around. She was still upset, and that wasn't a surprise either.

Before I could hit the 'Erase' button, the machine blurted, "Saved messages. First saved message."

And Natalie's message replayed in its entirety.

Hearing it again caused a different reaction. Now that I knew something about her past, about her parents' death, it seemed wrong to dismiss her out of hand. I wasn't sure why I was starting to care, or even if that's what this feeling was. Perhaps she intrigued me.

Or maybe I was overthinking things.

A sudden flash of lightning lit up the room, followed by a deafening crash of thunder. The rain came down in sheets, lashing hard against the window, relentlessly pelting the roof.

I picked up the receiver to call Uncle Pietr. No dial tone. The message light on the answering machine had gone dark.

Perfect time for a power outage. I slammed down the receiver back into its cradle, and sat down on the couch. The storm made it feel more like dusk than midafternoon, the apartment illuminated in half-light. The same stacks of envelopes covered the coffee table, and Fanny's book still rested on top.

I picked up the book, and recalled Fanny having said that people had expected Schumann and Brahms to marry, but that they hadn't. I wondered why. They'd admired and respected each other, and they'd loved each other as friends. What had stopped them? Had it been their age difference? Had such a thing been frowned upon then? Brahms had ended up a lifelong bachelor. Maybe they'd sworn an oath to never marry; Clara had remained a widow until she died.

I wondered if Dad and Clara had been planning on getting married. Maybe they, too, had decided that remaining friends was the better option. If so, how long afterward had he met Mom? Maybe Uncle Pietr knew something about that. Dad and Mom's relationship details had never interested me. Until now.

Unanswerable questions, nagging doubts, unknown histories, countless theories. Every question seemed to spawn three more. I knew that the only way to answer them would be to find Clara.

Just then, the kitchen lights blazed to life, the refrigerator rattled and hummed, and my answering machine beeped. It had only been a brown-out. It was time to invite myself to Uncle Pietr's for dinner.

# CHAPTER 11

The drive to my uncle's house in Pittsford the next evening took nearly thirty minutes, battling rush hour traffic on the 590 Expressway. I exited via Monroe Avenue, and reached their neighborhood moments later. Stately elms and maples lined the road, and the homes – or estates, to be more accurate - stood back from the road. Privacy hedges lined the frontage, many with wrought iron gates closing off the drives. I wondered if the hedges were meant to keep outsiders from seeing the homes, or to spare the homeowners from seeing a car like mine pass by.

After several turns through the neighborhood, I reached Uncle Pietr's home. His backyard abutted the private Oak Hill Country Club; the family were members.

I pulled into the maroon and brown brick paved driveway. Their colonial house stood atop a small rise, guarded by evergreen shrubs and numerous flowery plants. Halfway up the rise, the driveway split; straight ahead was a large, detached garage, slightly beyond the home. The garage was larger than Dad's entire house. To the right, the driveway formed a loop past the main entrance.

After parking in front of the house, I got out, carrying a bouquet of flowers for Aunt Jane, and a bottle of expensive-looking merlot for Uncle Pietr. It was probably the brand their chef cooked with, but I didn't want to arrive empty-handed.

The door opened seconds after I rang the bell. Uncle Pietr stood there, smiling, a glass of wine in his thick, meaty hand. He resembled my dad in several ways - the high forehead, the brushed back hair, flat nose, bushy eyebrows. But he stood several inches shorter, and carried a lot more weight. And he was as strong as they come.

"Ah, Frank!" he said, a slight accent in his voice. "So good to see you! Come in, come in!"

He ushered me into the foyer. My tennis shoes squeaked on the Italian marble floor, while his leather loafers click-click-clicked with every step. A huge crystal chandelier, hanging from the vaulted ceiling, bathed the entranceway with glittering light.

"It's good to see you, too," I said, offering him the merlot. "For you."

He took it and read the label, his smile growing wider. "Ah, my favorite! How did you know?"

He clapped me on the shoulder as I stepped into the main living room. I was sure that it wasn't his favorite label; he was simply being polite. That was just his way.

"Jane!" he called out. "Jane, Frank is here!"

The great room was three times larger than my apartment. The far wall was all glass, showcasing the backyard: a brick patio that ringed a kidney-shaped built-in swimming pool; a manicured lawn, lush and green; evergreens standing like sentries near the garage and far corner of the yard; tall arborvitae clustered along the back-property line. An ornate black iron fence separated their yard from the golf course.

"Frank!" a voice behind me called. I turned and looked up, seeing Aunt Jane standing at the railing of the second story hallway. She descended the curved staircase, and approached with arms outstretched for an embrace. She was seventy, but surgery and hair color made her look fifteen years younger.

Her smile was contagious and genuine. "It was so nice of you to call yesterday! Oh, and you brought me flowers! How sweet! I'll have Whitney put these in water right away!" She turned and shouted out. "Whitney! Would you please come into the great room?" She turned back to me. "So how have you been?"

"I've been . . .okay," I said.

"And Fanny? Are she and her family doing well?"

"They're all fine. Fanny's going crazy getting the house ready to be put on the market, and she's counting the days until the kids go back to school."

"We never see you in August," Pietr said. "Christmas, Thanksgiving, big things. This is unexpected."

Just then, Whitney, Aunt Jane's personal assistant, entered the room. "Whitney, dear, please take these and have them put on the table for dinner."

"Yes, Mrs. Stephens. Good evening, Mr. Stephens, sir," Whitney said, taking the flowers from Aunt Jane's outstretched hand. At first, I thought she was addressing my uncle, until I noticed she was looking at me.

"Oh, hi Whitney. Nice to see you."

"Likewise. We don't normally see you in August." She then departed the way she'd come, without waiting for my response.

"Sit down, Frank," Pietr said. "Look, Jane, he brought my favorite wine."

"How very nice of you," Jane said. "You should have given it to Whitney. Now I have to call her back!"

Pietr waved his hand at her. "I can carry my own bottle of wine, dear, thank you. Sit down, and let's catch up while dinner is prepared."

Pietr and Jane sat down on a black leather sofa, while I dropped into an overstuffed floral armchair, facing the expansive window and the view beyond.

"Is this about Ivan?" Jane asked.

"How's he been?" Pietr asked. "It's been too long since I've seen him."

"Dad's getting worse, actually. You saw him in March, right?"

Pietr nodded. "He struggled to recall things, his memory jumbled. Kept confusing me with Viktor."

"He hardly recognizes Fanny or me now. This past Sunday, he confused me for Felix Mendelssohn."

"How tragic," Jane said. "Isn't that tragic, Pietr?" She placed her hand on his thigh. He patted it gently.

"This disease makes one feel so helpless," Pietr said. "We still know so little about Alzheimer's, about dementia and memory loss. Effective treatments are a long way off, much less a cure. I feel your frustration." His shoulders lowered a bit, and then he narrowed his eyes at me. "Yet there's more to your visit than just updating us on his condition. That could have been done over the phone. You sounded...urgent."

Taking a deep breath, I told them of the music I had found, and my curiosity about Clara's identity. I described Dad's violent episode, and about the inquiry at Prescott. Uncle Pietr's eyes widened, and his posture stiffened. Aunt Jane shot him occasional quick glances as I spoke.

"I've learned more about Dad's life in the past forty-eight hours than in the previous twenty-five years," I concluded. "The more I learn, the more questions come up."

"So you're hoping I have answers?" Pietr asked, to which I nodded. "And what if those answers make matters worse?"

I spread my hands out. "Worse for whom? Mom is dead, and Dad's memory is deteriorating by the day."

"His memory may be collapsing, but his reputation is still intact, nyet? And your mother...she was deeply loved. Not to mention," Pietr continued, "it may be worse for Clara."

Jane's hand flew to her cheek. "I can't believe that Ivan would have been unfaithful to Louise. They were so devoted to each other!"

"It's possible the songs were written before he met Mom," I said, to make her feel more at ease than anything else. I planned on keeping my suspicions to myself.

"You found something Ivan wanted to remain hidden," Uncle Pietr said. "These are his secrets you're looking into. I'm not suggesting you simply lay them aside as if they'd never been found. Just tread carefully. I know you and Ivan weren't especially close, so I have to ask: What is your motive? Are you looking to prove a point, or are you simply satisfying a curiosity?"

I inhaled sharply, then let out my breath through flared nostrils. "I'm not out to prove anything. My dad made his choices in life, just like me. Yeah, our relationship sucked, by every definition. But I did find the songs, for better or worse. And I think I deserve to know who he wrote them for, which hopefully will help me better understand why he made the choices he did."

He waited several seconds before responding. "I loved your parents very much, and it's important for me to know you aren't intentionally trying to harm them."

"That's the furthest thing from my mind."

"Good. Now – what do you wish to know?"

I took a deep breath to clear my head. "Okay. First of all, did Dad date anybody before meeting Mom? A girl from high school maybe, or someone at Prescott?"

Uncle Pietr closed his eyes and stroked his chin. "Not that I was aware of. Ivan kept to himself growing up. He preferred his piano and composing to girls and dating. We corresponded very little once I went to university, and when the war started, he served in the Pacific, while Viktor and I fought in Europe. After the war, I returned to John Hopkins, and Ivan returned here. He always kept his personal life very private. In fact, his engagement announcement surprised me completely! I remember teasing him, asking if he had dated a girl only because someone stole his piano, and he had nothing else to do."

"What did Dad say?"

"Oh, I don't recall now. But he loved Louise. Their age difference baffled some people, but it didn't bother them."

Pietr leaned forward, his elbows on his knees, fingers meshed. His demeanor and tone shifted.

"This story of Ivan sympathizing with communists, and an inquiry. It is too incredible to believe."

"Dad never spoke about it?"

"Ivan never said a word. Not one." Pietr ran his hand through his hair.

"A very private person, you understand," Jane said, caressing Pietr's back.

"Our father never mentioned it either," he added. He didn't seem to have heard Jane's statement.

My curiosity piqued. "What do you mean? What does he have to do with it?"

"Your grandfather? What do you know about him?"

"Not much," I said, shrugging. "However, Professor Gregory told me that Dad changed our name, and not Grandpa. That wasn't the story we were told."

Uncle Pietr seemed genuinely surprised. "Ivan told you and Fanny that? I never knew."

"So it's true? Dad changed our name?"

"Most certainly! Father died a Stepanov." Pietr shook his head. "I'm beginning to wonder what other tales Ivan might have told you about Father."

"He hardly spoke of him," I said. "I know he and Grandma immigrated after World War One, he got a job at Prescott Camera and Film, and died of a heart attack, I think. Mom never spoke about him either."

"Louise never spoke about him, because Louise never met him."

I sat up a little straighter. "Really?"

Jane nodded solemnly as Pietr took a deep breath, and exhaled slowly. He seemed to age as he spoke.

"Father and Ivan's relationship started to worsen in the spring of 1950. About the time of this inquiry you mentioned, actually. By the following fall, it was utterly destroyed. Naturally, we assumed - that is, Viktor, your aunt Jane and I – that Louise was the reason for it. She was Roman Catholic, you understand, and we were Russian Orthodox. Ivan converted just before their marriage, which infuriated Father, and he disowned him. Then, when Ivan changed his name to Stephens..."

Pietr made a noise like an explosion, raising his hands upwards and outwards.

"Wow, I never knew."

He went and poured himself a glass of wine from a decanter standing atop a nearby butler table. Sunlight refracted through the glass cast sparkling red flickers upon the picture-frame covered wall.

"I think it broke Mother's heart," he said, his voice wavering a little. "She died two months after they wed, and Father followed two years later." He took a long draught. "They never reconciled, despite Viktor and me imploring them to make amends, several times, but their stubbornness and pride prevailed. Nothing could be done."

As Pietr returned to his seat, I asked, "You didn't know for sure the reason for their falling out?"

"It was never discussed. However, your news of this inquiry has sowed some doubts."

"I don't understand. Why would they have fought over the inquiry? That would mean Grandpa knew about it, but how could he? Dad kept it a secret from everybody."

Pietr placed his glass down on the coffee table. With hands folded as if in prayer, he pressed them against his lips and stared at me for several seconds. Finally he spoke.

"There is much you do not know, Frank, about your father, and about your grandfather. About dignity and integrity. Those things, in this country, are uncommon compared to where we came from. As wonderful as America is, it lacks a . . . how do I put it? Formality? A sense of family honor? It is hard to put into words. Here, emphasis is put on individualism, independence, status. Perhaps it is because America is a land of immigrants, of opportunity, of making one's own way. Who's to say, huh?"

I didn't know where Uncle Pietr was going, so I remained silent.

"But my family, back in Russia, we were what you might call nobility. There were . . . customs, formalities, a way of living. Traditions. Do you understand what I am talking about?"

I shook my head.

"My family immigrated to America in 1918. Viktor was

five, I was four, Ivan was two. The Bolshevik Revolution began in 1917. You learned about it in school, da?"

"Yes."

"The Stepanov family was not Bolshevik, Frank. Our family were landowners, upper class you might say, influential in our town. Father was a learned man, a gifted chemist, and loyal to Tsar Nicholas. Mother was well-educated in the arts. Our lineage could be traced back through dozens of generations. The revolutionaries soon suspected us, and other families like ours. Father knew we were in danger, and through the efforts of brave friends in America, and allies in the motherland, we escaped. Our family was one of the fortunate few."

"So we're kinda like royalty?"

Pietr gave a slight shake of his head. "That's not what I'm saying. My point, Frank, is that your grandparents opposed the revolution. They became targets, and we barely escaped with our lives. We wouldn't be sitting here today if it hadn't been for your grandfather's courage and the help of good Americans. I would be dead, Ivan would be dead, and you would never have been born. Which is why this inquiry story is so fantastic. It borders on the ludicrous. Father would have been offended to the utmost, one of his children accused of being communist."

"So did he believe Dad, or the inquiry?" I asked.

"Oh, Ivan, I'm sure!" Pietr exclaimed. "I have no doubt. And I suspect the school attempted to keep the whole affair secret from Father."

"But the inquiry was kept secret from everyone. What made grandpa so important?"

Pietr heaved a sigh, followed by finishing off his glass of wine. "Who did Father work for when he came to America? You said so yourself."

"Prescott Camera."

Pietr nodded. "Father's expertise was photography. But he had been no mere employee." He leaned forward again. "William Prescott personally hired him. The company's founder, eh? Prescott helped our family escape the revolution.

115

And Prescott made Father an officer of the company. Vice-president. Do you now see?"

Realization dawned on me.

"How do you think America would have responded if the son of a vice-president of one of the world's largest companies had been declared a communist? Who happened to teach in the university founded by that company's president?"

# CHAPTER 12

We didn't discuss Dad during dinner. By silent assent, our conversation centered on other topics. 'Other topics,' meaning 'whatever Aunt Jane wished to talk about.' She dominated the conversation, giving me the up-to-the-minute news on my cousins' lives (mostly wonderful, of course), what their spouses were doing (incredibly successful, don't you know), as well as the exploits of their seven grandchildren. Uncle Pietr interjected with occasional corrections and minimized Aunt Jane's exaggerations. I nodded, or responded when necessary, but my mind was still reeling from the family history lesson.

At one point, Aunt Jane placed her fork down on the china plate with a distinctive clink, and cleared her throat.

"Frank, have you heard anything I've said?"

Something – an out-of-place answer, or perhaps my facial expression - had given her the impression that my mind was preoccupied. Which it was. But I had never stopped paying attention.

"Mm-hmm," I said, nodding. "Artur and Molly are moving to Boston because he's been accepted into Harvard's grad school to get his MBA, and they're worried about their kids adjusting to the upcoming move. Elena and Kevin are expecting their third kid next spring, and are considering remodeling the house so that she can work from home. Pete Jr. and Kim are building a new home in Henrietta, on 15 acres, so that Kim can raise horses. And Natasha and John had a huge argument last week, and you suspect they're seeing a therapist, but you're not sure and you're debating whether or not you should talk to them about it."

Jane put her hand over her mouth. "I . . . I said all that?" Aghast, she looked to Pietr for support.

Pietr nodded, and shrugged. "My love, once you get going . . .," he trailed off, taking up his wine glass. "Frank's listening skills are better than yours, it seems."

Jane's face tightened as she turned a pale shade of pink, and she snatched up her fork. "No matter. Everyone knows they're having problems." She stabbed a Brussels sprout. "And if they're going to a therapist, it's a good thing, right?"

Pietr and I agreed with her, while exchanging a quick glance and subtle smile.

❋ ❋ ❋

After dinner, Uncle Pietr suggested going out on the patio for drinks. Aunt Jane declined to join us, having stated quite emphatically she had *important* phone calls to make regarding an *important* upcoming charity event, of which she was one of the co-chairs, doing *important* work.

"Which event, Aunt Jane?" She was involved in multiple charity organizations, and she spoke often of them.

"Pietr's hospital's Christmas fundraiser for New York Right to Life," she had said. "Remember? It's the event Louise helped me run until she died."

I remembered. It had been one of Mom's passions.

"A bit early to be thinking about Christmas, isn't it?" I asked.

"Frank, it's almost the end of August! I'm in charge of entertainment, and you wouldn't believe how much advance notice these entertainers require," Aunt Jane said. "It's appalling, simply appalling! You'd think they'd be so happy to participate, out of compassion and concern. Can you believe they expect to be compensated? Appalling. Anyway, the gala is scheduled for December 6. Shall I reserve a ticket for you? They're only

$500."

I coughed out of shock. Five hundred dollars was a week's salary. Before taxes. "That's outside my budget, Aunt Jane."

"Nonsense! If you start saving now, a little each week. . ." she said. She wasn't begging - not exactly – but her voice held a plaintive tone.

"A little less guilt, my love," Uncle Pietr chimed in.

He had returned from the alcove, a cigar sticking out of his shirt breast pocket, a snifter in each hand, containing about an inch's worth of copper-colored cognac.

"Frank's not one of your children," he added.

She either didn't hear him, or simply ignored him.

"Please think about it, Frank dear. There will be music, dancing, wonderful food, and again, it's for an excellent cause."

Tears seemed to well up in her eyes in an instant, and her mouth quivered with emotion.

"Sure, I'll think about it," I said, giving her a peck on the cheek. She smiled and patted my cheek softly in return.

"It's black tie, so you'll need a tuxedo."

With that, she turned and left the dining room to make her phone calls, calling out for Whitney. I followed Uncle Pietr through the French doors out onto the patio. We headed to a pair of padded chairs arranged at a round table speared by a wooden umbrella pole. The water in the pool sparkled in the late sunlight, and swallows chased insects and each other through the trees.

I sat on a blue-and-yellow cushioned chair while Uncle Pietr, after setting down our glasses, adjusted the umbrella so we'd be seated in its shadow. He let out a chortle as he sat down.

"What your aunt lacks in subtlety, she makes up for in heart."

Uncle Pietr lit up his cigar with short, sharp puffs, then shook out the match with several hard flicks of his wrist. Aromatic grey smoke curled around and above his head.

"Your mind churned like an auger during dinner, Frank."

I chuckled. "Yeah?"

"Behind your eyes. Like a giant drill bit, mining through memories, facts, and preconceived notions." As he spoke, his index fingers revolved around each other, like toothless gears spinning on off-set axes. He leaned forwards, aromatic tendrils of cigar smoke twirling towards me. "Ivan used to look that way, when he was working things out."

I looked the other way, away from the wafting smoke. My temples felt taut and cramped; the feeling wasn't so much like burrowing, as it was the tightening of a screw. Raising the snifter to my lips, I sipped the cognac slowly. Hints of vanilla and caramel teased my taste buds, and it went down as smooth as a Schumann sonatina. The screw loosened ever so slightly.

I heard Uncle Pietr draw deep on his cigar, after which he said: "*Yabloko ot yabloni nedaleko padayet.*"

My jaw clenched. The last time I heard that Russian expression was when I was a high schooler. Mom taught herself just enough Russian to be somewhat fluent - *To keep your father on his toes,* she'd say - while I picked up the more interesting words from my cousins.

"Mom used to say that to me all the time," I said, turning back towards Pietr.

"So you know what it means."

"The apple doesn't fall far from the apple tree," I answered. "She rarely meant it as a compliment."

"Eh, you were a child then. If she said it today, it'd be intended as such." Pietr tapped cigar ashes into a crystal ashtray. "Much goes on up here," he said, tapping his head with a thick finger. "Ivan, much went on up here, too. Songs, music, schooling. I recall many times during meals, he'd sit silently with this look - *your* look - upon his face. Always - always! - Ivan's mind worked out problems, and yet he still paid attention to what was being said."

Uncle Pietr smiled, letting out a low, soft laugh, as if tickled by a fond memory. "Viktor and I, we tried tripping Ivan up, knowing Father would get cross at him for not paying attention. But we couldn't. How Ivan could focus on more than one thing at a time. . ." Uncle Pietr took a long sip of cognac. "It is sad seeing how he has become. But seeing you," he said, pointing his cigar at me, "seeing you brings him back to me."

Uncle Pietr set his glass down on the table, and dabbed his eye with a knuckle.

"A stray ash. . . from my cigar."

I swirled the cognac in my glass. It reflected the sunlight with a copper glow, a repeating flash keeping cadence to a silent melody. A miniature beacon, like a lighthouse. I silently counted the beats between each flash - flash, two, three. Flash, two, three. Flash, two, three. A waltz rhythm.

The *Romance* I had played for Fanny was a waltz. I was conducting Clara's waltz with a snifter of cognac.

"Perhaps," Uncle Pietr started to say, then paused. He gave a tedious sigh. "Perhaps I will visit Ivan this weekend. Yes. It has been too long." He reached over and grabbed my forearm. "I'm grateful you came today."

*Fine. Whatever. I didn't come to lay a guilt trip on you, Uncle Pete.*

What did he expect me to say? 'Dad would be happy to see you?'

*Dad would never know you were there.*

The conversation was veering in a direction I had neither intended nor desired.

"Uncle Pietr," I said, watching the eddying cognac settle, having concluded Clara's waltz, "I get why Dad changed his name. I'm curious why you changed yours."

He heaved a sigh and considered his drink before answering, but left it on the table.

"Not for any sensational reasons, but for professional ones. Mostly. After Father died in 1953, I changed our name to Stephens. The McCarthy hearings, the accusations, the witch hunts – these frightened many of us. What a spectacle! Naturally, Jane and I became concerned. Not only for our young family - most of your cousins were just starting school, you see -

but for my career. It seemed prudent, nyet?"

I couldn't disagree with that.

"You must realize, Frank, that after the Bolshevik Revolution and Civil War, more than two million Russians fled the country, with tens of thousands coming to America. Our family, and those like us, were known as the Whites. White Russians, opposed to the Red communists, see? But thirty years later, who can remember this? People heard a Russian accent in those days, and thought, aha! A communist! Deport him! Send him back to Russia! And sadly, many were."

He picked up his glass, and made what looked to me to be a toast - a nearly imperceptible acknowledgment to long lost friends and compatriots. He went on.

"Colleagues in New York City and Chicago, for instance, were hounded unjustly, and some were kicked out. They've remained in Russia ever since, unable to return. Perhaps with this talk of *glasnost* and *perestroika* . . ." He waved a hand idly. "I didn't want it to happen to me."

"So you changed your name."

"Da. And denounced my heritage."

"Why?"

"To prove my loyalty, I suppose. For some people, having fought alongside their sons and brothers in Europe wasn't enough."

His eyes shone with a deepening darkness in the umbrella's shadow.

"I love America, but I don't love all Americans."

I remembered Dad's outburst, his fury about needing to prove his patriotism. A sudden thought struck me, and anxiety began to swell.

"Do you think it's possible Clara, assuming she was Russian, was deported?"

"Who's to say, eh? If Ivan's memory can be trusted - if this Clara was involved in the inquiry, it's possible. Very possible." He tapped more ashes off his cigar. "Perhaps they . . . what is it called? They struck a deal?"

"What do you mean?"

"The school wrongly accuses Ivan of being a communist. Father finds out, and through his influence at Prescott, pressures the school to end the inquiry on Ivan's behalf, and in return, Clara is deported, and everyone involved is sworn to secrecy. As if the entire affair never happened."

"So Dad blamed Grandpa for protecting him and his family, which ended his relationship with Clara?"

"Da, I think that's plausible."

I mulled it over. Something still didn't add up.

"It doesn't explain why Dad was accused in the first place. There must have been *some* reason to accuse him, right? And the school administration had to have known Grandpa was a White Russian. That he denounced Communism?"

"I did say they wrongly accused him."

"But why? Did someone have it out for him? Did he have enemies?"

"A rival? A jilted lover?" Uncle Pietr's frame shook with laughter. "Your father had neither interest nor time to jilt any women, lovers or no."

"I have nine compositions in my apartment that suggest otherwise."

He stopped laughing. "*Touché*," he said, with a tip of his cigar.

I finished my cognac. "You know what's frustrating, Uncle Pietr? The one person who can tell me about Clara, is the same person who doesn't know who I am anymore."

"Da, that is frustrating."

I ticked off on my fingers. "Grandpa's dead. Mom's dead. Fanny knows nothing. You didn't know about the inquiry. Dad's coworker didn't know about Clara. I'm sure nobody at the school would willingly talk about the inquiry, provided anyone there knows about it, and I bet most of the people involved are dead. I've got nothing."

"You have the songs. What do they tell you about Clara?"

His question caught me off-guard. I blinked several

times.

"Your father was a brilliant musician and composer. Jane and I attended many of his concerts, and were amazed. Mesmerized. His music told stories. Your father used notes, measures, and melodies the way authors use words, sentences, and paragraphs. Now, I haven't heard these songs he wrote for Clara, but I'm willing to bet a story is woven into those songs. If you listen to them, perhaps you'd learn who Clara was."

I recalled Fanny's remark after hearing the waltz: *Oh how he loved that woman.* Maybe he was right. Maybe the songs were not merely Dad's feelings about Clara, but were about Clara herself. A ballet, or a tone poem. Like a Shakespearean sonnet put to music. If true, I'd still not know what I wanted to know. It'd be like admiring the Mona Lisa - you knew it was a woman, but you'd never discover who she was.

"That still wouldn't be the same as learning her identity," I told him.

He gave a slight shrug. "But it could be enough, nyet? Perhaps you'd also learn who Ivan was."

"I have a pretty good idea of who Dad was," I reminded him. "Finding these songs doesn't change that."

"Didn't you say before dinner that you've learned more about your father in the past forty-eight hours, than in your entire life? And didn't you also say you might come to a better understanding of the reasons for his choices?"

"Maybe what I should've said was, learning those things doesn't change the past. Things done don't become undone, and things said don't become unsaid. Lies don't become truths. If I end up learning the reasons behind his choices, then perhaps the best I can hope for is that I learn how to avoid making the same mistakes with my own children someday."

Uncle Pietr crossed his arms, pursed his lips, hmphed, and leaned back in his chair. He looked straight at me, and with barely moving his mouth, slowly said:

"If that's the best you can hope for, then for their sake, I hope you don't have any future children."

He spoke with calm deliberation, which meant he was either disappointed or angry. Probably equal measures of both.

I cast him a sideways glance. He resumed smoking his cigar, and watched a golfer search for his ball, just beyond the iron fence. The cigar's ashes pulsed red like a warning beacon, and smoke billowed about his head. I tried making sense of what he said. Long ago I had vowed to treat my kids completely opposite of how Dad had treated me. Things I was discovering about his past wouldn't change my mind, would they?

As I was about to ask him what he meant, he turned to me and spoke.

"Frank," he said, "do you know how I came to have all this?" He indicated the house and the golf course with a few gestures. "Country club membership, the nice cars, personal chef?"

I clamped my mouth shut and spread my hands. A quizzical look spread across my face, and I shook my head.

"Hard work and a successful practice?"

"Da, that explains some of it," he said, nodding. "But not all. When you were young, were you jealous of your cousins, that they lived here? Did you ever ask your parents how come they got to live in a big, fancy house, while you and Fanny didn't?"

"I guess so? Maybe? What are you . . . ?"

He motioned me to stop. "And how did they answer?"

Childhood memories surfaced, to the times our families had celebrated holidays together, driving home after a Christmas gift exchange, or an Independence Day barbecue complete with fireworks. As early as I could remember, I had loved coming here because it seemed luxurious and exotic compared to our home. I knew I'd asked once or twice. Fanny probably had too. I recalled the two-week vacations spent at Uncle Viktor's Pennsylvania huge dairy farm, when we were in grade school. I remember thinking how awesome it was.

"Mom probably said it was sinful to be envious of other people's good fortune, and to be grateful for what we had.

Dad would have said it was none of our business. What's your point, Uncle Pietr?"

"Those sound like the answers they would have given. Your father, though, he knew why, and would never say. Your mother knew, I'm sure, but was too polite to pry. And of course, it wasn't my place to explain anything, especially since you never asked me. But I'm sure that, as you got older, you remained curious: how come my cousins are so wealthy?"

"It was none of my business, so I never asked."

He tapped his forefinger against his lips a couple times before continuing. "I did very well for myself in my practice, that much is true, but not well enough for all this. Did Ivan ever tell you where he grew up? Where our family lived?"

"He told us he grew up outside downtown Rochester, and that his childhood home had burned down in the 50's."

"You know where the William Prescott Museum is?"

I nodded. Everyone in Rochester knew. He was the city's most famous son.

"We lived half a block away, at 27 Barrington Street. And the house is still there."

I swallowed, hard. That's where *Old Money* once lived. Before suburbia.

"Your grandfather died a wealthy man, Frank. He had done quite well at Prescott, and they made sure he had been taken care of. But because Ivan had estranged himself, Father cut him out of the will. He received nothing from the estate. It was divided between Viktor and me." He paused a moment, allowing me to absorb this new information. "That's why we, and your cousins, have done so well."

"You inherited it." I took a deep breath and let it out slowly. "So what you're saying is, if Dad hadn't been a jerk to Grandpa, and if Grandpa hadn't been a jerk to Dad, Fanny would be putting a fancy, expensive home on the market this week instead of a crappy, cheap house, and Dad's songs would've been hidden in a fireproof safe in a vault instead of an attic? Is that what you're saying?"

"Nyet! Calm down and let me explain." He crushed the last couple inches of his cigar in the ashtray, grinding it into the glass. "The way Ivan and father ended up, it broke my heart. He was still living at home when this happened. When a family endures what we had endured - forced to flee our home, strangers in a new country, struggling to find our footing - all we had were each other. There was no Russian community here, not like in New York or Chicago. For instance, do you know how many Russian Orthodox churches there were in Rochester in 1918? None. Do you know how many there are today? Still none. Family. All we had was family. We had the ways of the old country to . . . to keep us grounded. Traditions, honor, customs. We brought nothing else with us."

Uncle Pietr shifted in his seat. "That all changed when Ivan left. All these years, I thought he was to blame, for changing his name, and for marrying Louise. Believe me, I made peace with myself, in here," and he tapped his chest, "yet I never spoke of it to Ivan."

"Wait. You said you loved Mom."

A surprised expression spread across his face. "And I did. I never blamed her, but I did blame Ivan, for a time. I convinced myself he had married Louise, not simply because he loved her, but because he knew it would anger Father. She was Roman, remember? And Ivan converted to her faith. But what I could never understand was why Ivan did it."

"You never asked him?"

Pietr shrugged his shoulders. "Such questions weren't asked. It was none of my business, and I certainly wouldn't have spoken to Father about it. And that's what I'm trying to tell you. If Father was angry at Ivan for having married Louise, then it was taken as a given that Father was right, because Father was always right."

"Father knows best," I interjected. I knew that all too well, a thin line I had been expected to toe as a child. A line I had repeatedly crossed.

"That's how it was," Uncle Pietr said. "Who else did we

have to rely on, eh? Russian immigrants, all alone."

"What does this have to do with the inheritance?"

"After Father died, Ivan didn't attend the reading of the will. He knew he had been written out. It would have been beneath him to . . .what's the saying? Spit on his father's grave? Ivan wanted nothing to do with Father. He attended his funeral solely out of love for me and Viktor, and for Mother's memory, but that was all.

"But now I look at their estrangement differently. You weren't the only one thinking things over during dinner, eh?" He repeated the spinning motion with his two index fingers. "The inquiry, and Father's involvement, were the source of their dispute, not Louise. It changes things."

"How?" I asked.

"A man's dignity. You said Ivan was prepared to accept the inquiry's ruling, hmm? Perhaps to protect this Clara person? If so, it was an act of great courage, of supreme sacrifice. To lay down his life for the woman he loved. It was stripped from him when Father intervened, sacrificing Clara instead. A battle between two men's dignity - one for the sake of his name, the other for the sake of his heart."

Uncle Pietr shooed away a fly buzzing around his snifter as he picked it up, and then finished his drink.

"I am speculating, of course. Father is dead, and Ivan can never tell us. But if I'm right, the tragedy here is that Father forced Ivan to accept a choice he had rejected. His choice had been taken away without his consent, and found himself unable - or unwilling - to forgive Father. So, no longer proud to be a Stepanov, he chose to start over as a Stephens. Remaining a Stepanov would have been dishonorable for Ivan, and his becoming a Stephens would have made it dishonorable for Father to give him any inheritance."

"So Grandpa made things worse, without knowing, and it snowballed from there?"

Uncle Pietr nodded. "It would seem so. Ivan chose his dignity, and Father honored that choice. Traditions and customs, eh? Sometimes, though, it's hard to tell the difference between those, and stubbornness and foolish pride."

He leaned closer and poked me in the shoulder with his thick stubby index finger.

"You said the best you could hope for was to avoid making the same mistakes with your own children someday? I tell you, the best you should hope for, is for the ability to understand that not all mistakes are of our own making. Sometimes all we're given are terrible options, which only lead to terrible outcomes."

# CHAPTER 13

We chatted for another forty-five minutes on the patio, while the sun sank below the tree line beyond the golf course. As if on cue, the mosquitoes emerged en masse, so we retreated indoors. It seemed an opportune time to leave.

I waited in the foyer while Uncle Pietr called for Aunt Jane. She descended a minute or so later.

"Has it gotten that late already?" she asked, kissing me on the cheek. "I'm so delighted you came out today. I'll make sure Pietr visits Ivan soon. Won't you, dear?"

Uncle Pietr nodded. "Da. Saturday or Sunday, perhaps." His hand engulfed mine in a warm, firm handshake. "Remember what I told you, Frank."

"Oh? And what was that?" Aunt Jane asked, eyebrow raised in apparent expectation.

"Buy low, sell high," I said, smiling. What was I supposed to tell her?

"Oh, you!" She cast a sidelong glance to Pietr. "You should follow your own advice."

I leaned over to kiss Aunt Jane. "Thanks for an incredible dinner."

"Much too kind." She turned towards Pietr. "I know! Let's have a cookout Labor Day weekend! We'll invite everyone - the kids, Frank, Fanny and her family. It's the last weekend before closing up the pool. It would be so much fun." Her face beamed in the chandelier glow.

Uncle Pietr nodded. "That is a wonderful idea, love. Come early for a round of golf, Frank?"

"I'd like that." I hadn't golfed in years, and I was slightly better than the average hacker, but neither fact would stop me from accepting an invitation for free golf.

"I'll make reservations for Saturday," Pietr said.

"This could be the start of a new tradition!" Jane said.

*Tradition.* I knew what Aunt Jane meant, but that word carried a bitter connotation now. Like a bad take on Tevye's lament from *Fiddler on the Roof.*

After a final round of goodbyes, I stepped outside and quickly shut the door, before any moths and mosquitoes fluttered inside behind me.

*   *   *

We could have been wealthy.

That thought cycled through my mind during the ride home. If not for tradition, dignity, and stubbornness, we would've had a third of Grandpa's estate. I didn't want to admit it to Uncle Pietr, but I *had* wondered, many times, why they lived somewhere fancy, while we muddled by in a middle-class neighborhood with a middle-class lifestyle.

The more I thought about our conversation, the angrier I became. Not about the lost inheritance, but about Dad's unstoppable pride and Grandpa's immovable obstinacy. Uncle Pietr spoke of cultural heritage, but all I saw were two men unwilling to compromise for the good of the family.

Then I remembered what he had told me: *Not all mistakes are of our own making. Sometimes all we're given are terrible options, which only lead to terrible outcomes.* Stuck between the devil and the deep blue sea.

The inquiry had forced Grandpa to get involved, making a difficult decision he felt was best - for him, for the family, for the company he worked for, for their reputation. So out of desperation, he had done what he thought had been right, for the sake of keeping the family intact. He'd ultimately caused the very thing he'd wanted to avoid.

As I crossed the Troup-Howell Bridge spanning the Genesee River, Prescott Center came into view, towering above surrounding buildings. PF&C, spelled out in large block letters mounted near the top of each side, glowed yellow in the night sky. Numerous windows throughout its twenty-two stories were illuminated; either employees were finishing up their work, or janitors were cleaning offices for tomorrow. Until this evening, I'd never known that Grandpa had worked there.

I suddenly realized why we'd never owned a Prescott camera. Dad's contempt had run so deeply, that he'd even refused to buy their products. Prescott Conservatory had paid his salary and supported his work, but he'd made damn sure Prescott Camera & Film got none of his income in return.

Then why stay at the school? Perhaps Clara was the reason. Perhaps he'd stayed as a witness to her memory, so she wouldn't be forgotten by those who tried to ruin his career. Maybe he'd thought that if he remained there, something of her spirit would as well.

*I'll never know if I don't find out who she is. I'll never know unless she's still alive.*

As Prescott Center receded in my side view mirror, I decided nothing more could be gained from pursuing the inquiry. As Gregory had said, the school administration had made everyone swear to secrecy. So even if I discovered who ran the inquiry, they'd deny it ever happened.

Dad had severed his past so decisively that he'd even lied about his house having burned down. I wondered who lived in his childhood home now, and whether they'd let me see it. I wondered if Mom had known. Uncle Pietr had mentioned that she'd never met Dad's parents. Portraits of Pietr and Viktor's families had hung on our dining room wall, but not of the grandparents.

Dad had cut off nearly every connection he had to the first thirty-five years of his life. All in, no bluff, no call back.

*And all for Clara.*

Which brought me back to where it all started: Clara's songs.

I recalled Uncle Pietr's words: *I'm willing to bet a story is woven into those songs. If you listened to them, perhaps you'd learn who Clara was.*

Well, I hadn't listened to them. I'd played only one, and Gregory had played part of a second. I'd *heard* the songs while reading them, but that wasn't the same as listening to them. Much can be learned reading sheet music, but the story comes alive in the playing. One can read a Shakespeare play and understand the plot, and grasp what motivates the characters. But it's in watching the stage production where the story comes to life, with its complications, connotations, and consequences.

Reading Barber's *Adagio for Strings* might move you, but listening to it will change you.

If Clara's story existed in those songs, I needed to play them. No, not merely *play* them, but absorb them, every note, rest, and measure. If those songs told her story, I'd discover it.

Dad bared his soul in every composition, whatever the emotion, whatever mood he intended to convey. I recalled the string quartet he'd written a year after Mom died, titled *Videniya Luizy*: Visions of Louise. It had been his last major composition, his tribute to her memory.

A chamber music group composed of Rochester Philharmonic Orchestra musicians had performed it in October of 1979. Fanny had called me at college several days beforehand, suggesting I attend. Close friends and family members would be there, and my absence would be disgraceful. At first, I'd balked. Supporting Dad had been a low priority item, and encountering him face-to-face ranked even lower. Fanny had said, "If you won't do it for Dad, then do it for Mom instead."

Dad had selected three other songs to accompany his piece. First was Dvořák's *String Quartet, No. 96, Opus 12*, known as the American Quartet. It was simple, joyful, and uplifting, establishing the evening's mood, and I understood Dad's decision to include it: it was Mom personified.

Mendelssohn's *String Quartet, No. 2 in A-minor, Opus 13* had followed. Some considered it a memorial to Beethoven, since it contained themes and allusions similar to Beethoven's later quartets. Its significance didn't go unnoticed: Mendelssohn, Dad's favorite composer, and the piece, a tribute to a deceased friend. The melodies exuded romance and passion, with passages full of tenderness, interspersed with moments of introspection.

The third piece was Jean Sibelius' *Voces intimae.* Intimate Voices. Mom was of Finnish descent, which explained the song's inclusion. Fanny told me later that Dad had studied at the Sibelius Academy in Helsinki in 1947, and that the two composers had become close friends. She also told me he had attended Sibelius's funeral, which had taken place a couple years before I was born.

Finally came Dad's quartet, in four movements. The first, *vivace ma non troppo.* Lively, but not too much. The rush of new love, led by two violins dancing arm in arm, while the cello and viola provided restraint and control. Then, *allegretto con dolcezza.* Moderately quick, with sweetness. All four instruments combined to express the comfort and tenderness of married life. The joy of children was represented by sprightly violins. Beneath it all was a foundation marked by a firm viola, never letting the listener forget the seriousness of life. The cello underscored the other instruments, deep and foreboding, like a harbinger of loss and uncertainty.

The third movement was the intermezzo, *adagio con tenerezza.* Slowly, with tenderness. Dad held nothing back here - heart-wrenching emotion, his sadness on full display. The motifs introduced by the cello in the previous movement became the melody, now played by the viola, soft yet deep. The violins represented tears and sighs of lament. Yet despite overwhelming poignancy, one detected notes of hope - an allusion from the first movement, an intimation from the second. These were melodic representations of the happiness they shared.

The intermezzo wasn't all despair, as slivers of faith shone through the darkness, swelling in strength, culminating with an *accelerando* immediately beginning the final movement. *Allegro con fuoco*. Quickly, with fire. Emotions collided, producing outbursts of uncontained love, fury, and expectation.

This was no naive optimism, as Dad clearly hadn't ignored his grief. Sorrow emanated from every measure, pain from every trill, anger from every chord. Despite the raw pathos, one clearly heard their undying love, and their belief in the promise they'd be reunited. The movement concluded with a glorious, magnificent chord, held for what seemed like an eternity, as if the gates of heaven were opening.

Goosebumps spread across my arms, and a chill ran down my spine. The performance had happened nearly seven years ago, and yet it sounded as clear as if it were playing on the car stereo.

*Dad may have been a douche, but man, could he write.*

# CHAPTER 14

Wednesday morning arrived sooner than expected – probably because I had fallen asleep on the couch. The feeling of being somewhere unexpected caused me to wake and sit up suddenly. Several pages of sheet music slid off my chest onto my lap, and a few fluttered onto the floor. With a disoriented gaze, I blinked several times, rubbed the remaining sleep out of my eyes, then gathered up Clara's songs and placed them on the coffee table.

Upon returning home last night, I had taken to the couch and started reading the songs. I had tried to envision her, her personality, and how she had won Dad's heart and soul. I'd attempted to determine whether Dad had woven a theme among the pieces, or created an emotional blueprint, which would reveal who Clara was based on how she'd made Dad feel.

My back felt stiff, and a crick stung my neck. Stretching, I remembered the two messages waiting for me last night. Jessica had said she had an opening at eleven if I wanted it. The second message, left at 5:45 PM, was from Martha Richards, the Cosgrove Middle School office assistant, asking me to meet with the principal this afternoon. It was odd, I thought, that she'd called so late in the day.

I picked up the phone and called the middle school to confirm my appointment.

* * *

The sun shone brightly in the late morning sky as I pulled out of my parking space, on my way to Jessica's salon,

*A Cut Above.* I recalled the songs I had pored over last night before having fallen asleep: the first waltz, two romances, a ballade, and a duet. The first four pieces were for the piano, each one beautiful and expressive, full of creativity and subtle challenges. The melodies were simple to follow, with fluid transitions and key changes typical of the neoclassical style, and yet he included progressive modulations that seemed out of place. As they played in my head, though, I realized that the unexpected moments were perfect.

I presumed Dad had written them in the 40's, during a time of musical experimentation, even revolution. And yet these songs were clearly influenced by Mendelssohn, Beethoven, and Brahms. An occasional nod to modern styles emerged - a dash of Gershwin here, a sprinkle of Khachaturian there. I detected echoes of Shostakovich as well, which surprised me a little. These allusions consisted of short passages, or chord progressions tucked beneath the melody.

Perhaps Clara had liked the contemporary composers. Perhaps he'd wanted to acknowledge her preferences. A shared secret, or an unexpected surprise. Like the way a poet might hide messages in an ode using an anagram, or include a play on words to profess a secret known only by his intended.

The duet, *Rondo Opus 5 No. 1, allegro*, intrigued me. Quick and cheerful, the piano and violin played off each other in subsequent contrasting themes, alternating between lead and follow, switching the roles of pursuer and pursued. The song evoked images of a game of tag between two children, or two lovers. At times, the violin allowed the piano to capture it, only to be released and then chase the piano. These series of chases returned to the main theme, where both instruments ran hand in hand until a joyous conclusion. An exquisite piece.

Recalling the song sparked a memory from Saturday's conversation with Fanny. Had Dad and Clara written to each other? If so, where might those letters be? Stashed in a carton? Destroyed? I hated thinking that Dad had destroyed them, as Brahms had done with Schumann's letters. Fanny might let me search through the boxes in her garage. Dad hid Clara's songs among his school records, compositions, and student progress reports, so who was to say he hadn't hidden letters with the Christmas decorations?

My head started to throb, as songs, letters, melodies, and notes ricocheted within my mind. I recalled Uncle Pietr's words while on the patio: "*Yabloko ot yabloni nedaleko padayet.*"

The apple doesn't fall far from the apple tree. I was sure Uncle Pietr had been talking about more than just Dad's and mine shared thinking styles and facial expressions. But I didn't want to think about that now, with so much time passed by, and so many words between us. Since Mom died, our relationship had become nothing more than a cold, forced politeness. Family get-togethers had become exercises of avoidance, yet from time to time, old arguments resurfaced.

Fanny had asked me to reconcile on multiple occasions. I had refused every time.

"*Man up and tell Dad you're sorry. It's time to put all this behind you,*" Fanny pleaded.

*It was Rachel's third birthday party. We were alone in the kitchen, preparing dessert and drinks for the guests out on the patio.*

"*He's older, so he should go first.*"

*Fanny pushed a candle through the center of a large pink rose atop Rachel's cake.* "*No, you. Out of respect.*"

"*Respect is a two-lane road, you know,*" *I said.*

"*And neither of you are on it. Frank, this has to stop.*"

*I shrugged.* "*Got anymore orange Fiz? This bottle's gone.*"

*Fanny pointed a candle at me.* "*You're being an ass. If you won't do it for Dad, or even yourself, then please just do it for Mom's sake? It's what she would have liked more than anything.*"

"*Mom liked orange Fiz?*"

*A white-and-pink striped candle hit me squarely between the eyes. Fanny stood straight as a rail, hands clenched.*

"*Nice aim, Fan.*"

*I picked up the candle and handed it to her, seeing that her eyes were narrow and rimmed with anger.*

*"What's it going to take for the two of you to reconcile? An- other tragedy? Mom's death wasn't enough?"*

*I shifted my gaze from her clouded face to the backyard. Dad was seated at the table, with Rachel on his lap.*

*"He has plenty to be sorry for. He only came to my high school concerts when Mom begged him hard enough. Hell, Jessica attended every concert, and my college commencements, and she's not even flesh and blood. Did he? No. All he's ever said is I've wasted my talents, and become a huge disappointment."*

*Fanny's eyes softened a little, but not much. "Well, if you want my opinion..."*

*"I know your opinion and I don't care," I interrupted her. "He's the bigger ass. He's been the adult my entire life. He took my decision to dump piano as a personal attack, and he's treated me like the black sheep of the family ever since. He broke Mom's heart, not me."*

*I grabbed a bottle of root beer and filled the remaining empty cups.*

*"And you're an adult now too," Fanny said, "and all Mom wanted before she..."*

*"Then tell him to be the bigger man, for Mom's sake," I said, pointing towards Dad.*

*"I have. Many times."*

*I filled the last cup, and placed the bottle on the counter. "So we're back where we started. Remind me why we keep arguing about this?"*

*Fanny's shoulders sagged a little, and she gave a weak smile.*

*"Tradition? Hope that one of you will come to your senses?"*

*"Fool's hope."*

*"I hope not."*

*She picked up the cake plate, while I grabbed the platter of drinks. After one more sigh, she turned to me and said,*

*"Know what? We had a breakthrough this time. You called Dad the bigger ass. You finally admitted that you are, in fact, an ass."*

*Before I could respond, Fanny stepped out the door, leaving me to trail behind, the final word lodged in my throat.*

That had been our last argument about me and Dad. Any new fights would have been pointless; just a rehash of the same pleas, interruptions, and standoffs.

Plus I didn't want objects thrown at my face.

\* \* \*

Entrance bells jangled as I walked into *A Cut Above,* and Jessica looked up from the cashier's counter and smiled at me. She had changed her hairstyle from Saturday. She now resembled Markie Post's *Night Court* character Christine Sullivan; her hair was more feathered and layered, with a few loose strands dangling over her forehead.

"Hey you!" she said.

"Hey you back! You changed your hair."

"Yeah, you like it?" she asked, turning her head from side to side. She put down her People magazine and stood up. She wore a waist-length bright blue smock and yellow shorts, with white tennies.

"It looks good on you."

"Aww, you're so sweet," said in the way girls speak when they see a basket full of kittens. "Come on back. You doing okay?"

I followed her towards the wash basins, arranged along the back wall. Three stylist's stations lined each side of the salon, and five of the six were occupied. Jessica's booth stood immediately behind the cashier on the right. Sounds of blowing hair dryers, clipping scissors, and the indistinct murmuring of multiple conversations filled the air.

I didn't know whether to answer her question. The past few days had been anything but normal, so replying "Same ol', same ol'" seemed disingenuous. Telling her about Clara's songs, or any details regarding my dad's past, would be over-sharing.

Describing Dad's episode on Sunday would only upset her. She possessed every quality of a great friend, and we could talk about everything under the sun, but now didn't seem to be the right time to divulge family stuff. She wouldn't understand the implications, for one thing, despite being friends since childhood. She and Brenda had spent a lot of time with me and Fanny, but our parents had hardly associated with each other.

The main reason I hesitated to discuss my discoveries with her, though, was that I felt Fanny should be told before anyone else. Family business needed to stay in the family, and not be broadcast in a hair salon in front of complete strangers.

"Since Saturday night? Sober."

Jessica blushed and looked down at her feet.

"I am so embarrassed," she whispered. She turned on the water while I sat down. As she adjusted the temperature, I settled in, resting my neck against the smooth porcelain scalloped edge.

"I haven't gotten wasted like that in I don't know how long."

"Well, you didn't do anything to embarrass yourself," I told her. Her face seemed to hover over me. "It's not like you took to the stage and serenaded the whole bar or anything."

She flashed a meek smile, and began wetting down my hair with the handheld sprayer.

"That's nice of you to say. And you were a gentleman, carrying me up to my room. But you know," she said, lowering her voice to a whisper, leaning down so her mouth was close to my ear, "you could've stayed."

I swallowed. She smelled of jasmine. "I had plans in the morning," I told her.

She straightened up, and her face left my field of vision. I didn't have to see it to know she felt disappointment. The way she sluggishly tousled my hair under the running water told me that.

"Plans?" she asked, a whiny twinge to her voice.

"I went to visit my dad," I said.

Her demeanor changed, and she ran her fingers through my wet hair with added vigor.

"Aww, that's so nice of you! How's he doing?"

I considered how to answer. When I left on Sunday, he had been sedated and strapped to the bed.

"Well, he won't be going anywhere anytime soon, I can say that much."

"I hope he gets better," Jessica said, turning off the water and grabbing a towel. As she toweled off my neck and blotted most of the water out of my hair, she added, "Okay, let's turn you into cute *About Last Night* Rob Lowe."

"You're the boss," I told her, as we headed to her station.

She fastened a black cape at my neck, and after lowering the chair, she grabbed her scissors and comb, and started. Our eyes met in the mirror's reflection.

"Your friends are so fun," she said. "When Ned got up to sing, I laughed so hard."

"Yeah, he's a riot, all right. Never a dull moment with him."

We chatted for the next ten minutes or so, reminiscing about O'Shea's, talking about my start of school schedule, and exchanging end of summer plans. Some customers left, soon replaced by new ones. A couple stylists talked across an empty chair, one sweeping up hair into a pile. Finally, Jessica stepped around my chair, standing between me and the mirror. Her expression became serious, as if she were choosing her words with care and precision. The jasmine scent distracted me.

"Frank, I've been thinking. A lot."

"About?"

"I want you to be totally honest with me."

I raised my eyebrow just a tick. "Jess, I'm always honest with you. You know that."

"We're not going to go steady, are we? We've been friends for seventeen years. And not once in those seventeen years, have you made a move on me."

With her comb, she teased my hair, then parted it, and

began feathering it between her fingers, trimming the uneven ends. She stopped cutting, and our eyes locked. She reached forward and brushed some hair off my temples.

"Well?" she asked.

"To be fair, you were only six when Tommy died, and much too young to date for most of that time."

She shot me a heavy smirk. "You know what I mean!" She brandished her scissors. "And I know how to use these."

I smiled with as much charm as I could muster. "Just kidding! You wanted me to make a move on you?"

"I'm not saying you would've been successful, but you could've at least tried."

She resumed cutting. I closed my eyes as she trimmed the hair across my forehead. I knew Jessica wanted to take our friendship up a notch. Her spontaneous kiss on Saturday night had been a clear sign of that. And I'd enjoyed it. But that didn't mean I wanted to move our friendship in that direction.

"Jessica, I don't know what to say. I know you really like me, but..."

"Really like you?" she said, interrupting me. "*Really* like you?"

Her voice grew louder, and she smacked the comb and scissors onto the table behind me.

"Frank Stephens, I have been madly in love with you since my Senior Ball. Five years. Five years!! Before you say anything, yes, I know I was only eighteen then. But I knew. You treated me like a princess that night, and since then, you've acted perfectly in every way. From that moment on, I've dropped hints and clues like Scooby Snacks, and you're like... like that Fred guy, who's never eaten a Scooby Snack. Ever! He's never smelled one, licked one, tasted one..."

She practically shouted at me now, her face beautiful and horrible. She waved her hands about her as she spoke, making me grateful the scissors were laid on the table.

"Stop being Fred! Be my Scooby, and eat me!"

The salon fell silent. We turned our heads as one towards

the other stations. Every customer and stylist stared back at us, their mouths agape, their eyes wide with shock. One customer, a punk rocker getting his mohawk colored, flashed me a thumbs up. I felt redness rise up my neck and color my cheeks.

"Eat my...Scooby Snacks," Jessica said feebly, forcing a smile. She turned towards me again, her face crimson, her eyes blinking rapidly. "Whatever. You know what I mean, right?"

"Yeah, I do."

I took a deep breath, exhaled slowly, and grasped her hands. They were shaking.

"Jessica," I started. Before continuing, I scanned the room. All the customers and stylists leaned towards us, intent upon hearing our conversation. I cleared my throat and scowled, and the stylists resumed their work, while the customers quickly sat erect and faced forwards.

Turning back to Jessica, I said, "I'm so flattered. I really am. It's just that..."

"It's just that there's someone else?" she asked. Her eyes became sad and worrisome.

I shook my head. At least I didn't think so. Natalie's face appeared in a blink of an eye, then vanished.

"No, nothing like that. It's just that we're the kind of people who are meant to be friends." And I squeezed her hands and gave her a warm smile.

"Does that mean you don't love me?"

"Of course not! I do love you!"

A collective "Aww!" erupted. Our heads swiveled towards the salon. Everyone had all stopped to eavesdrop again, and each face bore a similar, schmaltzy, punchable expression.

"Really?" I asked, with as much disdain as I could muster. Jessica glared at the stylist next to her. Everybody resumed their cutting and drying and styling and conversing.

After waiting an extra second, I continued. "I love you very much. Like a sister."

Jessica made a face, and her eyes narrowed a bit. "That's not saying much. I've seen how you treat Fanny."

"In all fairness, I treat you better," I replied. "How about this, then. Best friends?"

Jessica's face brightened a little, and she managed a smile, and grabbed the hair trimmer.

"I suppose. You treat me so much better than other guys I've dated. They pull their lame moves and say their stupid pick-up lines, and I know they're just trying to score. But you never acted that way towards me. I guess that's why I love you. You never pursued me the way the other guys did."

"Stupid pick-up lines?" I asked. "Like?"

"Like, 'Are you a parking ticket because you got fine written all over you.' Gag me with a spoon." I saw her roll her eyes in the mirror, and I concealed a wince.

*I may have used that one once.*

"And mixtapes." She made a fake gagging noise. "Guys actually think they work!"

"They don't?"

"Trust me. Girls want to hear her man say 'I love you,' not Lionel Richie or Air Supply. Music sets the mood, but it doesn't make a girl fall in love. You should know, Frank, being a music teacher and all."

"Hans Christen Andersen once said, where words fail, music speaks," I said.

"Not when it comes to mixtapes," she answered.

My haircut concluded with a shampoo, blow dry, and a generous amount of hair gel.

"Whaddya think?" she asked, holding a hand mirror behind my head.

"Like I just stepped off the set of *About Last Night*," I answered.

She had cut a couple inches off the top and sides, and left it long enough in the back to just touch my collar. Several strands fell wayward across my forehead, begging to be swiped away, even though they didn't reach my eyes. I brushed stray hairs from my jeans as I followed her to the cashier's counter.

"Here you go, and keep the change," I said, handing her a

twenty.

"Aw, thanks!" Jessica rang up the sale, then came around the counter to hug me.

"I do love you, you know," she said, her arms around my neck.

"Who doesn't?" I replied with a wink. "Love you too."

I kissed her on the cheek, which she returned.

"Call me, okay?" Jessica asked, pulling out of our hug. "Don't wait three weeks?"

"You got it. Thanks for the haircut."

With a wave and a smile, I turned to go. When I was halfway out of the salon, Mohawk yelled out, "Bye Scooby!!"

The door closed behind me to the sound of laughter.

# CHAPTER 15

I f any other girl had told me "I love you" while comparing me to Scooby Doo, I probably would've been offended. Since it was Jessica, though, I smiled, owing it to her sweet nature, big heart, and tendency to get carried away by the moment. The fact we'd be staying best friends made me glad. Our friendship was a rare and beautiful thing, and I saw no reason to complicate it. She understood, with zero drama, and that was a big relief.

Additional drama was the last thing I needed. I had that in spades with Fanny at the moment. She'd invited me over for dinner tomorrow. At some point, I'd have to tell her what Uncle Pietr told me, as well as Gregory's inquiry confirmation. She deserved to know about Dad changing his name, too. She'd be shocked and angered, and it would probably get ugly.

Or should I wait? She was already stressed out, pulled as tight as a violin string, dealing with Dad's decline and the sale of the house. Could I make it through dinner without talking about it? She didn't know I'd visited with Uncle Pietr, after all. Though she'd find out as soon as Whitney called about the upcoming Labor Day barbecue.

*Best to tell her tomorrow. Get it over and done with.*

Two new messages were waiting for me on the answering machine when I got home.

"Hey, it's Fanny. Just confirming you're still coming for dinner tomorrow. I'm making Zweigle's white hots, nothing fancy. And Mike has to work late. Come around 5. Bye!"

She sounded relaxed. Then the second message played.

"Um, hi Frank. It's Natalie, Natalie Johnson? Um, listen, I was wondering...God, you probably think I'm some sort of weirdo, but...anyway, I have this extra ticket for this Sunday's matinee performance at Prescott? It's the *Great Music of the Movies* concert? I thought maybe you'd like to, um... Listen, call me if you're interested. Or not. I thought it might be, um, fun. 555-6541. Bye."

Natalie??

I dropped onto the arm of the couch, shoulders slumped. Natalie called me again? Asking me out...on a date?? I sat dumbfounded, my mouth hung open. *Music of the Movies*? Was she kidding? Was she pranking me? And what about Don? Don had said she wasn't his type, but he hadn't actually said he wasn't seeing her.

Why this? Why her? Why now?

Still stunned, I stood up and tapped the 'save message' button. I couldn't deal with this now. Maybe later, like tomorrow. Or never. Right now, I needed to get to Cosgrove and meet with the principal.

\* \* \*

I steered my bike into the bus loop and student drop off drive, and coasted to a bike rack stationed near the Cosgrove Middle School's main entrance. After securing my bike to the rack, I unclasped my helmet, and, running a hand through my newly cut hair, entered the building.

Whenever I was asked to describe Cosgrove Middle School, my response was one word: institutional. Cement block walls painted in two tones to match the school colors – blue on the top, yellow on bottom; the school logo and an image of our mascot, which resembled an aggressive Smokey the Bear, on prominent display inside the entrance; neutral linoleum floors; heavy oak classroom doors with an offset narrow windowpane; steel gray lockers set flush into the corridor walls.

Despite the building's decor, I enjoyed teaching here. The staff acted cordial and professional, the administration did the best they could, and the student body. . .well, middle school years were the meat grinder years of public education. The times I helped students through difficult experiences had become too numerous to count over the past four years.

In some ways, the parents were worse. I dreaded parent-teacher conferences. Sure, most parents were reasonable, and were easy to work with. The crazy ones, though? The ones who felt their son or daughter should be first chair flute or trumpet despite not knowing the difference between a quarter note and a quarter pounder? Those parents were the bane of my existence. They confronted me after concerts, or left messages at the main office. Every teacher has to deal with it, and with the advice of more experienced teachers and administrative staff, I had navigated my first year no worse for wear, and was now considered a seasoned vet.

The main office sat off the central hall down from the front entrance. I stepped inside and approached the counter, behind which Martha sat. She was engrossed in a phone conversation while flipping through papers in an open manila file folder.

I set my bike helmet on the ledge and waited for her to finish the call.

"Yes, I understand your frustration," she said, "and I wish it were different, but we're contacting all the parents whose students have been affected by this." She paused, closing her eyes. "Mrs. Smith, you're free to speak with the superintendent about this, but in the meantime, your daughter's schedule needs to be changed, and..." Another pause, and she propped her elbow on her desk and rested her head in her hand. "Like I explained, those courses are no longer being offered, so Brenda will need to select a..."

She paused a third time, now raising her eyes heavenward. Exasperation emanated from her in waves. Martha finally noticed me standing there, and her expression changed from annoyed to slightly guarded. She squeezed out a smile, and covering the mouthpiece, said, "Frank, this call might take a while. Dan's in his office. Head on back."

"Rough day?" I asked.

"Rough week," she replied, at which she uncovered the phone and resumed the conversation with the obstinate, embittered Mrs. Smith. I gave a reassuring smile, grabbed my helmet, and headed towards Principal Dan McCourtney's office.

Dan sat at his desk, swamped with papers, files, and several floppy disks. An IBM terminal stood on top of a monitor stand on the desk's right corner. The credenza behind him held trophies, plaques, and awards the school had earned over the years – these were in addition to the ones on display in the school's common area. Cosgrove consistently scored high in student achievement and academic excellence.

I rapped on the open door, and he looked up from his work.

"Frank. Come on in," Dan said. He rose and extended his hand, and I shook it.

"So what's up?" I asked. "Looks like Martha is fighting a one-woman war out there."

"Yeah, stuff blew up Monday, and the rest of the staff are on vacation this week. Just our luck."

"So what happened?" I asked, settling into one of the cushioned chairs opposite his desk. He sat down at the same time.

He took a deep breath and exhaled loudly, with puffed out cheeks. His face showed dejection, and a bad feeling started to stir in my gut.

"I'll just come right out and say it," he said. "District funding from the state didn't come through as promised, which means we had to make some painful cuts. Everything fell apart last Friday, and state lawmakers tried to come up with a fix over the weekend. Everybody has been forced to scramble. You didn't see this in Sunday's paper? Or on the news?"

I shook my head. I didn't watch the news, and I didn't have a *Democrat & Chronicle* subscription. My mouth turned dry, and I tried to swallow.

"Cuts?"

Dan sighed. "Some of the sports programs, art classes...band..." He raised his eyes to meet mine while saying 'band,' as if to make sure I heard him.

"You cut band?" I asked.

"I'm really sorry, Frank. My hands are tied like you wouldn't believe. State legislature dropped a bomb, and it's blown everything to hell. It pains me to no end to be the one to tell you we don't have a place for you here."

I slumped back in my chair. *I'm being fired?*

"What about seniority? Don't I have seniority?"

He shook his head. "Two other teachers have less seniority than you, and I just let them go this morning. You were next in line."

"Well, what about the grade schools? Or the high school? Can't I be transferred?"

He shook his head again. "They're doing the same thing. Everybody's making cuts, laying off teachers. Now, there's a chance...a small chance, mind you, that Albany does their job, and the district gets the funding restored, but that could take a couple months."

Months? I squeezed my eyes shut and covered my face with my hands. Months??

"Like I said, Frank, I'm truly sorry. You're a great asset at Cosgrove. The students love you, you've done great things with the music program here, you've got an exemplary record. I hate being forced to do this."

I dragged my hands down my face, drawing them together as in prayer, my fingertips at my lips. Dan's news came out of nowhere. This couldn't be happening. Fanny watched the news and read the paper, didn't she? Why hadn't she mentioned anything to me? Then I remembered - Justin and Rachel attended parochial school. Fanny and Mike didn't pay attention to public school issues.

"Martha's got some paperwork you need to sign before you leave," he continued, "and if you have any personal things in the band room, one of the custodians can get you in the room."

"Wait," I said, folding my hands together, fingers interlocked. "Can't I help out with the high school band? I mean, marching band isn't canceled, is it? Mr. Jorgenson isn't out of a job too, is he?"

"He already has an assistant. And no, marching band isn't canceled. Or the wind ensemble. They've got boosters, anyway. But nothing's available. This funding issue is hitting the high school too. Listen, Frank, most likely this is temporary, affecting only this school year. Come next fall, we'll want you back. That is, if you're available."

"Now you're saying this might last a whole year?"

He spread out his hands. "It could. I'm hoping it doesn't, but it very well could. You need to be prepared for that possibility."

"Is this statewide?"

"I've spoken with other principals around Monroe County, and they're in the same boat. Gates-Chili, Brighton, Rush-Henrietta - they're going through the same thing. As far as other counties are concerned, I don't know. To be honest, I haven't had time to make many calls. Martha and I are focused on fixing student schedules."

I rubbed my forehead, trying to make sense of this news. "What about severance? I'm entitled to severance, aren't I?"

"It's all in the packet at Martha's desk," he answered. "Off the top of my head, I'm not sure. Contact your AFT union rep if you have any questions." He stood up. "Frank, I know you weren't expecting this when you came in. I didn't want to tell you over the phone, or mail you a letter. You deserved to be told face to face. I can't tell you how sorry I am that this happened. I wish I could hang on to you. You're a great kid and a well-respected teacher."

I got to my feet. "I just can't believe this. I appreciate you telling me in person, but...holy crap, this totally blows."

Dan extended his hand, and I shook it. "Yeah, it does. Do you need to go to the band room?"

"No, I've got nothing there," I told him. "You'll call me as soon as this gets fixed, right?"

He nodded, and I picked up my bike helmet and left. After signing the paperwork at Martha's desk, I walked down the hallway with my head down and shoulders drooped. Stepping outside, I heaved a somber sigh and slapped on my bike helmet.

Several hours later, I returned to my apartment. The twenty-five-mile bike ride had become forty miles. Passing by the kitchen, I removed the mail sticking halfway out of my waistband, tossed it on the counter, and continued on to my bedroom. The answering machine showed no new messages. Thank. God. A boring evening would be a welcome change.

Twenty minutes later, I was showered and dressed. Before heading to Grandpa Sam's for dinner, I sifted through the mail, and pulled out an envelope from the AFT. I begrudgingly tore it open. The letter, typed out on American Federation of Teachers letterhead and addressed to 'Dear AFT Member,' had been dated Saturday.

"Would have been nice to have gotten this yesterday," I muttered.

The letter confirmed what Dan had said about funding and lay-offs, and included basic instructions on how to apply for unemployment. I stuffed the letter back into the envelope, and tossed it on the counter. The union telling me how to collect unemployment was cold comfort. Help in finding another job would've been more appreciated. The letter mentioned nothing about that.

*Too bad Dad screwed up the inheritance. Some of that cash would be handy right now.*

I wondered if Dad would have helped me, if he and Grandpa

hadn't disowned each other. Would things be different between us, if they hadn't? Would it have mattered?

# CHAPTER 16

Grandpa Sam's didn't look too busy. Connie stood at the podium just inside the restaurant entrance, chatting with the hostess.

"Hey stranger!" she said. "What're you doing here on a Wednesday?"

I shrugged my shoulders. "I got hungry. Can't wait till Sunday."

Connie laughed, her thick belly shaking. "C'mon, I'll sit you in my area."

Half the tables were occupied, and Connie led me to a two-top along the wall. Not my usual spot. As she started clearing away one set of silverware, she looked at me and cocked an eyebrow. "Someone meeting ya?"

"Just me tonight."

"Aw, okay. I'll get your Genny while you look over the menu. Specials are inside."

Connie waddled towards the bar while I scanned the special list. The sausage cacciatore looked good. Half a minute later, Connie returned with my beer, and I gave her my order.

"Good choice," she said while scribbling my order on her pad. "So. Having any more problems with that *Cats* girl?"

I had taken my first sip of beer when she posed the question. The *Cats* girl. She had to bring up Natalie. I licked away the foam from my upper lip before replying.

"No, not really. We haven't spoken to each other since Saturday."

"Hm. Haven't returned her call then."

I chuckled, having forgotten I had told her about her first

message, and I decided not to tell her about the new message from today.

"Hadn't planned on it."

"You sounded pretty confused about her, so I just wondered."

"Nope. Not confused. Not having problems. Just not interested."

Connie made a sad face. "Aw, that's too bad. I'll get your order started, hon, and be right back with a basket of bread sticks for ya."

She moseyed towards the kitchen, stopping at another table on the way to take away the patrons' dishes, while I reacquainted myself with Genny, somewhat perturbed that Natalie had suddenly appeared on the menu.

She had a lot of nerve, asking me to attend that concert. *Music from the Movies.* I tried to remember what the posters hanging around Prescott had looked like. I seemed to recall some Disney characters and Star Wars spaceships. If Star Wars, that meant John Williams, and Natalie knew all too well my opinion of him.

If so, why had she asked? She was up to something, and I couldn't figure it out.

Connie placed a basket of breadsticks, wrapped in a white cloth napkin, on my table, along with a small plate. The fresh-baked aroma, with a hint of olive oil and Parmesan, smelled delicious.

"Here ya go, hon," she said. "Food should be up in a few. Need anything right now?"

"No thanks," I answered.

I pictured Natalie from O'Shea's. Slightly angular and compact face, bright hazel eyes, fair complexion. Her hair wasn't big, like Jessica's had been. She wore it shoulder length, lightly feathered, moderately styled. Like Kate Jackson from *The Scarecrow and Mrs. King.* I replayed our argument in my mind. She'd thought I was a music snob. But it's not snobbery when you're right and you can prove it. I'd told her exactly that.

Maybe Natalie had invited me to prove her point, that I was a snob. If I refused the invitation, then in her mind, she'd be vindicated. But if I accepted her invitation, she'd think I was conceding, and believe she'd won the argument. Natalie was playing mind games with me, I thought - mind games she felt confident she'd win. She was expecting me to turn down her invitation, and in case I did, she'd concocted a rationale to support her theory. She wanted it both ways. This was the sort of game girls like Natalie liked to play - back someone into a corner until their only remaining option was to surrender.

Just then, Connie walked up with my order: slices of homemade Italian sausage, mixed in a simmering tomato-based sauce with green peppers, onions, mushrooms, and diced tomatoes, served on a large plate as deep as a soup bowl. A healthy serving of spaghetti topped with marinara sauce was heaped on a smaller plate.

"Do ya want Parmesan with your noodles, hon?"

Connie always called pasta 'noodles.' She had waited tables at a local German restaurant for sixteen years, before it had closed a couple summers ago. Some habits die hard.

"No thank you, Connie. The food looks delicious."

I stirred the cacciatore with my fork. Steam billowed like intoxicating fumes from a magical brew.

"I'll get you another Genny," she said, and took my empty glass and tottered off towards the bar.

My thoughts returned to Natalie. She was goading me, setting me up in a no-win situation. And she probably assumed I wasn't smart enough to figure out she was trying to trick me. It was so obvious, though! She'd underestimated me, and now I had the upper hand. Girls and the silly games they play. Natalie hardly knew me, yet she thought she had me all figured out.

*Just as I think I have her all figured out.*

"Touché," I whispered, while twirling spaghetti on to my fork.

But why else would she call me twice in one week, inviting me to a concert she *knew* I'd hate? What other reason could there be?

"How is everything, hon? Good?" Connie asked, putting down a fresh beer. I hadn't noticed her approach.

"Better than good. It's phenomenal," I told her.

Connie half-smiled, half-winced, and nodded. "Good, I'm glad. Except you got this...this...," and she waved her hand in a vague circular pattern in front of her face.

"What?" I asked, suddenly concerned. "Is there sauce on my face?"

I dropped my fork, and wiped my lips and chin with my napkin.

"Did I get it?"

"No, not that," Connie said. "It's um..." and she twirled both hands now, clearly at a loss for words.

Maybe I had butter and crumbs on my cheeks. I wiped a second time.

"Gone now?"

"There's no food on your face, hon. You just look all scroonchy." She made a pinched-faced look. "The lines on your forehead were all ridgy, too. I thought maybe something tasted funny."

Scroonchy? Ridgy? I shook my head. "No, everything tastes fantastic. I just have a lot on my mind."

Connie snatched up the empty breadbasket and smiled, but seemed unconvinced. "If you say so. I'll bring ya more breadsticks!"

I realized she had described my thinking face, the same one Uncle Pietr had observed yesterday, when he'd compared me to Dad. With a snort, I resumed my meal, determined to enjoy every bite, regardless of what or who occupied my thoughts.

*But dial it back a bit, dude. Don't scare the staff.*

Responding to Natalie's invitation would require finesse, and I needed help and advice. I considered Fanny for all of one second, but with all the stress in her life, she'd be unreliable. Ned, or Joey, or Don? Definitely not Don. The others would be unhelpful, and probably suggest making a mixtape. This thing with Natalie exceeded their capabilities.

Jessica? Definitely not - asking her about Natalie would be totally unwise, and end up hurting our friendship.

That left my brother-in-law Mike. He might not have been the sharpest tack on the board, but he'd made occasional surprisingly insightful comments before. For one thing, he knew his limitations. If he thought he couldn't help me, he'd say so. Two, he could handle Fanny's short fuse, and that took a lot of skill, which told me he was observant and perceptive. And three, he'd been married to her for nine years. I'd known Fanny my whole life, so I knew living with her could be a huge pain. He must have been doing something right if she hadn't killed him yet. I decided to call him this evening.

Pleased with my decision, I downed the rest of my beer just as Connie walked up.

"Ready for your bill?"

"Yep. And I'm sorry for acting strange earlier. A lot on my mind." I wanted to avoid mentioning Natalie, so I deflected. "Got laid off from the school this afternoon."

Connie's maternal instincts kicked in, and she looked as if she wanted to hug me right then and there. Her frown pulled everything on her face downward.

"Oh I'm so sorry! Ya know, I saw something on the news earlier this week about the schools. Something to do with money, but I never ever imagined that teachers would get laid off! That's terrible! What will you do?"

Hunching my shoulders and spreading my hands, I said:

"Don't know yet. I guess I'll call the private schools, see if they have openings."

Connie sat down on the adjacent chair, and put the dishes down on the table. "Did they say how long before you get called back?"

I shook my head. "They don't know. It's all in Albany's hands."

I told her of my meeting with the principal. The longer I

spoke, the lower her frown drooped.

"I feel so bad," Connie said when I finished, patting me on the hand. "I wish I could help. I really do."

She stood up, and then her frown transformed quickly into a smile.

"You know what, dinner's on me tonight. No, no!" she added, as I opened my mouth to object. "You've been a loyal customer, and I want to help."

"You don't have to."

"I insist."

I felt myself starting to redden. Acts of kindness and generosity made me feel uncomfortable, especially when there was no way for me to reciprocate. I considered refusing more vehemently, but I didn't want to hurt her feelings or embarrass her.

"Well, thanks Connie. It's really nice of you."

Connie's face glowed with satisfaction, and she turned to take the dishes to the kitchen, a bit more bounce to her step than before. I threw a few singles on the table, and left.

* * *

As luck would have it, there was a message on the answering machine when I got home. I didn't think any more people were left in my life who hadn't called in the past several days.

A familiar voice blared through the unit's speaker.

"Dude, it's Ned! Listen, we're jamming at Joey's tomorrow around 1. Stop by and be a pain in the ass. Later!"

*Sure, why not. A fun diversion before heading to Fanny's.*

It was time to call Mike. Taking a deep breath, I dialed their number.

"Hello?" Mike answered.

"Dude, it's Frank!" I replied.

"Hey, what's up? Everything good? Need to talk to

Fanny?"

"Nope. Just hanging out, and figured I'd give Mike-amundo a call."

A short silent moment passed, and when he spoke, his tone had become very matter of fact.

"What do you need, Frank? You only call me Mike-amundo when you need something. Do you need parts for your car again? Remember what I told you last time - getting that rack and pinion was a total fluke."

I grimaced. "I'm cool, Mike. The car's fine."

"Okay. Then what's going on? What do you need?"

"First of all, promise me you won't say anything to Fanny."

"Oh shit. Shitshitshit," he said rapid-fire, and he lowered his voice to a hoarse whisper. "You're in serious trouble, aren't you Frank. You've robbed a bank, or...or...or you've gotten fired, or..."

"Well, now that you mention. . ."

Mike carried on, interrupting me, becoming hysterical. "Or you've...oh my gosh, you've gotten a girl pregnant, haven't you?"

"Mike."

"Aughh!" he squealed. It shocked me to hear him squeal that high. "Jessica! You got her pregnant, didn't you!"

"Mike!"

"How could you do that, Frank? Well, I mean I know how it's done and that you're capable and all, but Frank! How could you-"

"MIKE!"

"WHAT?!?"

"Stop. Shut up for a minute!" I took a deep breath, counted to five, then exhaled. Things had spiraled out of control.

*Career ending knee injury my ass - it had to have been a concussion.*

"Listen to me. Jessica's not pregnant."

"Thank God!" he said, relief washing through the phone like a wave. He let out a long, drawn out breath. "Close call, then, huh?"

"What? No, you idiot! We're not having sex, okay? No one's having sex, no one's pregnant, there's no close call. It's nothing like that, at all!"

"Then why are you getting all worked up?" he asked.

This had been a mistake. I squeezed my eyes shut. "Put Fanny on please."

"Oh my God, you really are in trouble, aren't you?"

"Mike!" I exclaimed. "Fanny! Phone! Now!"

With his voice muffled, Mike called out her name. Several seconds passed, and then I heard the two of them talking, their voices indecipherable. A second later, Fanny took the line.

"Frank? What's going on? Mike says you're in trouble?"

Yep, big mistake. "I'm not in trouble. I only called to ask one simple question. That's it."

"What question? I heard him from all the way upstairs."

"Forget about it."

My mind raced to devise some semblance of a feasible exit strategy. Nothing emerged.

"You sure you're okay?"

Fanny sounded legitimately concerned. She covered the mouthpiece, and I barely heard her ask Mike: "What did he ask you?"

She quickly got back on. "Mike says you didn't ask him anything. How much have you had to drink?"

"I'm not drunk."

I could give her the reason for calling, but that'd be asking for more trouble than I needed. Fanny had enough issues to deal with, and dumping Natalie on her would be like tossing a cinder block to a drowning man. Yet despite knowing that, I felt Natalie's name begin to form in my mouth, my tongue pushing up behind my upper teeth, air pressure building in my diaphragm, lips parting to speak. Her name would escape unless I regained control.

"Nnnnnnever mind," I said, catching myself. "It's not a big deal."

I pushed my hand through my hair. I still needed an excuse for calling. I could tell her about getting fired, but that seemed more appropriate to talk about in person.

"You're such a dork," she said. "Are you still coming to dinner tomorrow?"

"Yeah, I'll be there."

"Well, thank you for the weirdest phone call ever," she said. "By the way, I met with the realtor today, and the house is listed."

The house. Something about the old house. Fanny continued talking about the realtor as I thought quickly. Wheels were turning. Stuff from the house. Boxes. Boxes that Fanny and Mike took from the old house.

"Hey before I go," I said, cutting her off in mid-sentence, "those boxes you have in the garage, from the attic?"

A beat. "That's what this is all about? Boxes?"

"Yeah. Can I look through them tomorrow?"

"Why?" Her question exuded wariness and confusion in equal measures.

I told her my theory that Dad and Clara may have written each other letters, that maybe he stashed them in her boxes, because they weren't in mine. And if I found the letters, I'd know Clara's real identity.

Fanny waited a moment before responding.

"Letters? You think they wrote letters, and Dad saved them? Are you out of your mind? There are over thirty boxes! They're stacked six high!"

"Did you look in them?" I asked.

"What? No!" Now it was her turn to become hysterical. "Mom was sensible. If she marked a box 'Christmas decorations,' she put Christmas decorations in it. If a box was labeled 'Stemware,' it contained - ta da! - stemware! Why? Because normal people pack their crap in a box, then write on the outside of the box the crap they just packed inside! And Mom was normal people!"

"It shouldn't take me long to check them out," I told her.

"Frank, I can't deal with this right now," she said. "You are driving me nuts. But you know what? You want to waste your time and look through each one, knock yourself out. I do not care."

"You sure you don't mind?"

"Don't push me."

"Thanks, Fan. You're the best."

"You know it," she said. "And if I ever find out why you called, I am going to kill you. Future generations will learn of your fate, and tremble with fear."

Her voice oozed menace, with no hint of hyperbole.

"I love you too. See you tomorrow."

"Mm-hmm," and she hung up.

*That could've gone worse.*

# CHAPTER 17

Hanging up, I realized I still didn't know what to do about Natalie. The call had gotten out of hand quickly.

It hadn't been my intention to agitate Fanny. Someday, after she'd settled down, we'd share a laugh about this phone call. Certainly not tomorrow, or the next time we got together, either. But someday. Someday when we were old and gray.

I pressed my palms against my eyes, and drummed my fingers on my scalp. What to do about Natalie. On the one hand, she liked John Williams. On the other hand, she was intelligent in spite of some of her musical tastes. On the *other* other hand, it was a *Music from the Movies* concert. But on the other other *other* hand, it was a free concert. And on the final hand, I'd be walking into her trap. Playing her game.

She'd left her phone number on two separate messages. That had to mean something, right? Could it simply mean she liked me? Is it possible for a girl who thinks John Williams is an exceptional composer, to have pure intentions? Should I risk finding out?

Uncovering my eyes, I glared at the telephone. I had to return her calls. Advice or no advice, from Mike or anybody else, I had to decide whether to accept her invitation.

But not now. There's nothing so important that can't be delayed another day. I'd call her tomorrow. Clara's songs were a bigger priority.

I gathered up the scores from the coffee table and carried them into the second bedroom. Removing the Romance I had played at Fanny's, I sat down at my Casio keyboard, turned it on, and slipped on my headphones. Time to play the remaining eight songs.

An hour later, I played the last notes of the final piece, *Duet for Piano and Violin, Opus 9, No.2*. I felt emotionally spent, yet revitalized at the same time. The feeling reminded me of the adrenaline rush after a tough bike ride, but without the sweat. Basking in the pride of achieving a goal, I looked at the songs on the music rack. Each piece seemed like a chapter in a book, or a stanza of a poem. A clearer picture of Clara began to reveal itself, but it still lacked focus, like a Polaroid photo in the midst of developing.

I took the duet off the rack. *Largo con tenerezza*. Slowly, with tenderness. As with the other compositions, this piece evoked passion and desire. Unlike the other songs, though, the duet contained threads of melancholy and sadness woven into every passage. In a way, this duet seemed to counterbalance the other duet in the collection. The first duet professed joy, freedom, and love with unbridled abandon and delight, while this duet, though mirroring those themes, was wistful and poignant, haunted by an undercurrent of remorse and regret. I heard no recklessness here, only restraint. Every time the melody tried to escape its chains and flee, or become fully realized, a somber realization kept it in check. The heart strained between happiness and sadness.

Throughout the song, motifs and phrases from the other eight pieces emerged, either directly or with slight variations. Dad included them as harmonic support in some places, as bridges between different themes in others, and as recapitulations to the main theme. The insertions were seamless, brilliant even. This piece seemed to express every emotion evoked by his memories of Clara. Not only his, but Clara's as well. This was a duet in every sense of the word.

This had to have been Dad's farewell piece. He'd had nothing left to give.

\* \* \*

The next morning arrived with streaks of sunlight streaming into my bedroom, accompanied by the faint sounds of traffic and chorus of birdsong. It was almost ten, but it felt good to sleep in after an emotional roller coaster of a day.

Under normal circumstances, I would have been waking earlier each morning rather than later, until getting up at 6:30 became routine. But circumstances were no longer normal. With no job, there was no need to set the alarm. I had the freedom to do what I wanted when I wanted, to go where I wanted with whom I wanted, beholden to no one.

Until the severance ran out, anyway. I had total freedom as long as the rent got paid, and the car stayed filled with gas. Sooner or later, I'd have to get a job.

I started a pot of coffee, and decided to gather the two boxes of photos, in preparation for giving them to Fanny. As I crossed the room, I glanced at the telephone, and let out an exasperated grunt. Natalie. I needed to call her this morning.

*You're delaying the inevitable. Call her, and get it over with already.*

Maybe I should eat breakfast before taking a shower. . .

*Stop stalling.*

You know, it might make sense to load the boxes in my car now, rather than after I shower, just in case it's hot and humid. Why get all sweaty . . .

*For God's sake, call her!!*

"Fine, I'll call her!" I shouted, stomping across the apartment. I snatched the handset and punched in Natalie's number.

No busy signal. With every ring, my pulse quickened, and I felt my face turn flush. Midway through the fourth ring, someone picked up.

"Hello?" A female voice, but it sounded younger than Natalie's. Either that, or the intense *thu-thump thu-thump thu-thump* of my heartbeat made it difficult to hear.

"Hi, may I speak with Natalie?"

"This is she."

All the moisture in my mouth evaporated, and I swallowed what felt like a crumpled-up wad of sandpaper. I took a quick sip of coffee. "Oh hi, this is Frank. Frank Stephens."

"Hi!" she said, her voice awash with... surprise? Excitement? I couldn't tell. "You got my messages."

"Um, yeah. How you been?"

"Okay. I'm getting ready to go to work. You?"

"Every day above ground's a good day." My face knotted up into a painful grimace. Way too corny.

Natalie gave a polite laugh. "I've heard that."

"Yeah." I reminded myself to make this a quick call. "So about that concert..."

"Yes! Are you free? I'm so sorry it's such short notice. My friend and I bought season tickets for this concert series, and she had planned to come with me, but she had to bail, because at the time we bought them she didn't know her work schedule, and now she's scheduled to work, and I couldn't think of anyone else to ask." She spoke rapid-fire and without taking a breath.

*The old 'my friend has to work so she can't go' story. Riiiight.*

My heart rate slowed down, and my anxiety dissipated. I needed to play this cool.

"I hate it when that happens. When's the concert?"

"Sunday at 3:30, at the Prescott Theatre. It'd seem weird to go by myself."

I almost asked why none of her siblings took her friend's place. Because there was no *friend*?

"I've got nothing planned."

A slight pause. "But?" she asked.

"But what?"

"Whenever someone says something like 'I've got nothing planned,' it's always followed by a *but*."

"I didn't say but."

"You didn't have to say *but* in order to say *but*. It was implied."

*Mind-reading now?*

"I think you meant to say inferred," I said. "You asked if I was free, to which I answered I had nothing planned. From that you inferred I implied a but."

She didn't immediately respond. "But?"

Again? "But what?"

"You definitely implied a *but* that time."

I wrinkled my nose in irritation. "BUT there was no implied *but* when I said, 'I've got nothing planned.'"

"You're lying, but that's okay. Since you're not doing anything, would you like to go?"

My grip on the phone tightened, and my eyes grew wide. Lying?? She started playing unfairly now, but I had to maintain my composure.

"This is the *Music from the Movies* concert, right?"

"Uh huh."

"I'm not a fan of movie scores."

"I remember you saying that at O'Shea's."

"You knew that, but you still asked? Why?"

I needed to force her hand. This had gone on long enough. Several seconds passed.

"You still there?"

"Yes," she answered. Her tone changed. "I asked you because...well, I thought it would be fun, and maybe we could talk about the concert over dinner afterward."

She sounded more hurt than angry, that I would question her motives. And I might have believed her had she not added The Dinner. She had overplayed her hand.

"I'm not asking you or expecting you to pay for my dinner," she added quickly. "This isn't a date or anything. I really enjoy going to the orchestra, and I haven't anyone else to ask."

Damn skippy I wasn't going to pay for her dinner! Implied *but* or no implied *but*. If we ended up going to dinner. Big if. *Huge* if. And I'd reimburse her for the ticket, too. No way did I want to be indebted to her.

"Never crossed my mind this was a date," I told her, avoiding the bait. "It just seemed strange that you'd ask me.

169

Movie scores and all."

I snorted, pretending as if this had been a misunder-standing on my part.

"Coincidence," Natalie said.

"Coincidence," I echoed, in the best agreeable tone I could produce. "So what do you think? Meet at the theatre at quarter after three?"

"Meet?" she asked. Her voice contained the right amount of surprise that would make a naive person believe she was being sincere. "I thought you might pick me up. They charge for parking, you know."

I hadn't forgotten. Going together made sense, but I still suspected subterfuge. This meant I needed to get the car washed. Natalie was the judging type.

"That's right," I said, playing along. "So where do you live?"

She gave me her address. "It's off of Mt. Hope, near Strong Memorial Hospital. You familiar with the area?"

Mom had been treated for cancer at Strong Memorial. It was more than familiar.

"Yeah, I know it. I'll swing by at three?"

"Sure, that'll give us plenty of time."

"And let's play dinner by ear," I suggested. "Decide that after the concert."

"We can do that." She paused for a moment. "Frank, I ap-preciate you doing this. You're really sweet to help me out. I can only imagine the weird things you thought about getting two messages from me."

*You have no idea.*

"It's no big deal," I said, hoping it sounded earnest. "I'll see you Sunday."

"Great. Good-bye, Frank."

I responded in kind, and we hung up. I sat perched on the arm for a few moments, a single thought rolling through my mind.

*This girl is crazy.*

# CHAPTER 18

Joey lived with his mom and sister on Albemarle Street, two blocks from where I'd grown up. The two-story home, with light blue cladding, stood atop a terrace much like my old house. I pulled into the driveway, parking behind a tan and gold Chevy Impala; band stickers from Aerosmith to ZZ Topp covered the chrome bumper. Ned loved his rock n' roll. Farther up the drive stood Joey's blue GMC pickup.

As I got out of the car, I could hear the muffled strains of pounding drums, wailing guitar, and throbbing bass coming from the backyard. The guys had soundproofed the garage several years ago to cut down on neighbor complaints, turning it into their permanent practice space. Joey's mom probably figured the benefit of maintaining good neighborly relationships far exceeded the convenience of parking in a warm, dry garage.

I waited by the side entry door for them to finish, noticing the glass panes vibrate in tempo with their playing. Thick black acoustical foam covered the inside of the windows. After the song concluded with a flurry of power chords and drum rolls, I let myself in. Joey sat at his kit atop a carpeted platform made of two-by-fours and plywood. Don played his bass to Joey's left, close to the door, while Ned played on his right. Cords for the mikes and instruments snaked across the floor to the various amps. Several opened cans of beer stood upon the drum platform.

Ned saw me first. His black AC/DC t-shirt was soaked through with sweat.

"Dude, what's up?"

High fives were exchanged all around. Don opened a red

and white cooler near the door.

"Want one?" showing a can of Miller Lite. I nodded.

As he tossed me the beer, he asked, "You haven't forgotten, have ya?"

"About?"

"Dude, Van Halen in ten freaking days! At Silver Stadium!" Ned answered, ripping off the opening chords from *You Really Got Me.*

"And Bachman Turner Overdrive!" Don added, mixing it in with the bass line from *Takin' Care of Business.*

"And Kim Mitchell!" Joey yelled out. Ned and Don both stopped playing, and we all faced him.

"Who's Kim Mitchell?" Don asked.

"Opening for BTO and Van Halen! Kim Mitchell, man, she's hot!" Joey said, and he launched into a drum roll.

"Actually, Joey, Kim Mitchell's a dude!" I said.

"A dude? You sure?" he asked, stopping in mid-roll. I nodded back. "Must be thinking of a different Kim Mitchell," he said with a shrug, and he proceeded to finish his roll.

"Have you bought your ticket yet?" Ned asked.

"I planned to, but..." my voice trailed off.

"But what?"

"I got fired yesterday, man. I'm out of a job."

After a chorus of disbeliefs and expletives, I described yesterday's meeting with the principal, the letter I'd gotten from the union, and the likelihood I wouldn't be teaching until the following year.

"Dude, that totally blows," Ned said. "What are you gonna do?"

"I'm not really sure," I answered.

Don snapped his fingers. "I got it! Play keyboards for us!"

"Yeah, do it!" Ned said. "We could use you on some of our Rush covers, dude!"

I held up my hands. "Dudes, I need a job that pays real money. You know, a regular paycheck?"

"Whaddya mean? Rooster's Rockhouse is paying us

$250," Ned said. "That not real enough for you?"

"You're getting that on top of your Prescott paycheck," I pointed out. "It's cool you asked, but I need something more reliable."

"You said you're getting severance, dude," Don said.

Joey rapped out a double flam to get my attention. "So you're gonna turn down an easy fifty or sixty bucks?"

"I've never played in a rock band before."

"So?" Joey scoffed. "Dude, you're totally awesome. Remember that time in high school, in the band room?" He motioned to Don and Ned. "I'm messing with the kit, and he's at the piano. Next thing I know, he's playing ELP's *Karn Evil 9*. Not just the radio single, either - the whole thing. All thirty minutes. From memory."

Ned whistled in admiration.

"Really?" Don asked. "Keith Emerson is like, incredible."

"I didn't play the whole song," I said. "I improvised and cut out the repetitive parts. More like twenty-four minutes."

"Whatever. Point is, you're righteous," Joey said. "Adding a keyboard would be gnarly. Besides, you got that Casio, right?"

"And it's not like you aren't used to crowds," Ned said. "Your brat band plays in front of an audience, right?"

They were pressuring me hard, and my objections weren't cutting it.

Ned put his arm around my shoulder. "Look, Frank, I know when it comes to modern music, you're woefully behind the rest of civilization. It's sad, but it doesn't make you any less of a person. And while it's true Toehead doesn't play covers of Beethoven, Mozart, or Bach, we have been known to play classic rock n' roll."

"I own a rather extensive rock n' roll collection, Ned," I interjected, recognizing his fake condescending tone, and waited for the jab.

"Sure you do, Frank, sure you do. Anyway, what I'm saying is, if you're as good as Joey says you are, I'm sure you'll fit in and do a fantastic job." He patted me a few times on the back.

"We'll set you up behind the amps, though, just in case."

He concluded with a sharp smack, and laughed. Joey and Don joined in with a few chuckles. Right on cue.

"Gee, thanks."

"So you gonna do it?" Don asked. "I'll give you our set, you work on 'em over the weekend, then practice with us all next week."

"C'mon man," Joey added. "You'll be great."

I looked from Joey, to Ned, then to Don, their expressions a combination of hope, optimism, and expectation. I finally turned my gaze to Ned.

"Fine."

They cheered in their own fashion - Joey with a quick flourish across his toms, Don with a fast run across the frets, and Ned with a loud and obnoxious version of *The Spirit of Radio*'s concluding riff.

For the next couple hours, I listened as they ran through their set, worked on transitions between songs, and fine-tuned tempos. Though they were fun-loving guys and amused themselves with bad jokes and obscene humor a lot of the time, when it came time to perform, they maintained high focus and concentration. They took pride in what they did, and Ned's versatile vocal range impressed me.

After finishing a set of three Aerosmith songs, Don grabbed a couple beers out of the cooler, and flipped one to Ned. I sat atop an unused amp, against the insulated garage door.

"You want another one?" he asked me.

I shook my head. "I gotta motor. Dinner at my sister's."

I also wanted to make an unscheduled stop on the way.

"You know," Ned said, "you should invite Jessica. She'd love it. The more the merrier, right?"

"I'll think about it."

"Yeah, well, Denise and Linda will be there, because they're stage help. Don, you bringing Natalie?"

A lump formed in my throat, and I took a moment to retie my shoe, even though the laces hadn't loosened.

"She's not returning my calls," he answered. "We haven't spoken since O'Shea's."

I didn't dare look at him, thinking he'd figure out that Natalie and I were meeting Sunday, simply by looking at my face. I took my time with the shoelace.

"She might be history," he added.

Ned snorted. "Too prim and proper? Dude, that girl will probably end up a nun or something."

"Not the rock 'n roll type, I guess," he replied.

It was time to leave. Don's comments had made me feel weirdly uncomfortable, and I worried about saying something I'd regret.

"Dudes, I gotta go," I said as I stood up.

Ned checked his watch as well. "Crap, it's later than I thought! I gotta get some sleep before work tonight."

Don and Joey grunted in agreement. Joey laid his sticks across one of the toms, and stepped off the platform, while Don started packing his bass in its case.

"Later!" and I left the garage and headed back to my car. I didn't know what I was getting myself into, and I didn't know if playing in their band would work out. One thing I did know, though: it would probably be a hell of a lot of fun.

❋ ❋ ❋

A right off Albemarle Street onto Raines Park, up the hill, then a left hand turn on Augustine led to my old house. All of us had grown up in this neighborhood. As kids, we'd walk to and from school together, and we'd hop on our bikes or hang out at each other's houses during the summers. Joey was the only one who still lived here. Ned had moved in with Denise a couple years ago, closer to the lake, while Don had gotten an apartment in Greece when his dad remarried.

Heading down Augustine, I saw the Rochester Realtor sign planted in my old home's front lawn, a red post supporting a white beam, from which hung their sign. A red and white sign stuck to the beam read 'Open House: Sat/Sun 1-4 PM.' The garbage I'd dragged to the curb on Saturday had been taken away.

The old place, on the market. It seemed a little strange seeing the *For Sale* sign, but it was bound to happen sooner or later. I wondered why Dad hadn't asked me if I wanted the house. Had he asked Fanny? Had she turned it down?

Stopping at the house wasn't the unscheduled visit I had planned, though. Rather, I drove past, and pulled up in front of Merle Jacoby's house, assuming he'd be home. Where would a curmudgeon go on a Thursday afternoon? I bet he was reclining in front of the TV, puffing away on his cigar, Boris upon his lap, both watching *The People's Court*, Judge Wapner presiding.

While driving to Joey's house, I'd recalled something Jacoby had said about my parents. He had told me that he'd enjoyed their small parties, until the 60's, when things had become, in his words, political. I remembered his exact words: *"Never could understand why some people thought those changes were good for the country."* At the time, I hadn't thought anything of it. In fact, I'd wanted the conversation to end so I could get on with my chores. Now, though, I wanted Jacoby to explain what he'd meant.

Hopefully, he'd be willing to talk.

I rang the doorbell, and immediately Boris started yelping and yipping. I heard his tiny paws scratching at the door, eager to defend his master's home. Jacoby yelled at him.

"Settle down, ya stupid mutt! You're not frightening anybody!"

Jacoby's face peeked through the sidelight, and he scowled upon seeing me. He unlocked the dead bolt and opened the door. A screened storm door separated us, and Boris stood on his hind paws to get a better look at me. He let out a low, sustained growl.

"Hey Mr. Jacoby."

"Frankie," he said. "Whaddya want? I'm busy."

I doubted it. He wore a faded New York Yankees tee-shirt which barely covered his gut, checkered shorts, and calf-high white socks. His hair was uncombed, and he held a cigar in one hand and a tumbler full of what looked like scotch in the other.

"I was in the neighborhood, and thought I'd pay you a quick visit."

Jacoby squinted at me. "Pay me a visit? Whatever the hell for? I been living here for over forty years, and you know how many times you visited me? Huh?"

He put the cigar in his mouth, and formed a circle with his thumb and fingers, holding it at eye-level.

"This many times," he snarled through clenched teeth. "So don't piss on my leg and tell me it's raining. Whaddya want?"

So much for pleasantries.

"It's about my dad."

"What about him?" Boris had apparently decided I wasn't a threat after all, and trotted away. Jacoby watched him go, then faced me again, finishing his drink.

I rubbed the back of my neck. Standing here, talking through the screen door, felt awkward.

"Can we talk about this inside?"

"No."

Jacoby placed his empty glass on a table to the right of the door. I glanced quickly around the porch. A couple aluminum lawn chairs with maroon and beige webbing sat off to the side. I jerked a thumb towards them.

"Can we talk out here?" I asked, flashing a friendly smile.

"No," he repeated. He crossed his arms and puffed on his cigar. "I'm fine right here. So what happened, he die or something?"

I blinked twice, taken aback "No! He's fine. I just wanted to ask about something you said on Saturday."

"Then get to the point already."

Okay, he *really* didn't appreciate my visit. "You said you stopped going to my parents' parties because of the political talk. What sort of political talk?"

Jacoby eyes lowered, and he worked the end of his cigar round his mouth. After several seconds, he looked back up at me and took the cigar from his mouth.

"I'm a simple man. I love my God, I love my country, and I try like hell to love my neighbor. I know, I don't do good with that last one. But loving my neighbor doesn't mean having to go to their parties. Your mother was a wonderful lady, God rest her soul," and he blessed himself as the other day, "and your dad was friendly enough. But the times changed, and no way in hell was I gonna change with them."

"My parents? They changed? What did they do?" Distress tinged my voice, and I hoped Jacoby didn't notice.

"They didn't change so much. It wasn't what they did, but what they *didn't* do."

"What do you mean?"

Jacoby tapped the ashes of his cigar into an ashtray sitting next to his empty glass, and scratched his stubble-covered chin.

"Their guests would take over, you know? How can I put it? When talking music, their guests were pretty interesting. When talking politics, they were assholes. Practically communists."

I swallowed. "Did my dad agree with them?"

Jacoby shook his head. "Naw, but he didn't disagree with them either. He would let them argue. Once in a while he'd tell them to shaddup. Castro, Bay of Pigs, Soviet space race, no school prayer, Great Society, military industrial complex, Kennedy." He counted each topic off on his fingers as he said them, each one spoken with obvious contempt. "Though Kennedy, he was okay. Meant well, Catholic man. Shame what happened to him, God rest his soul." He blessed himself a second time.

"Dad didn't care one way or the other?"

He gave a full two-shoulder shrug and took a long pull on his cigar.

"I stopped going, so I can't say for sure. One thing I did

know was that people came because they adored your mother, not just because they liked your father. The parties ended because your mother stopped liking the people."

Jacoby took half a step closer to the screen door, and what looked like a smile broke across his face.

"You used to sit on my lap, when you were this big." His hand hovered a couple feet above the floor. "Didja know that? I'd bounce you on one knee, your sister on the other. When you got a little older, your dad had you play for everybody. You were four, five at the time."

Reminiscence spread from one side of his face to the other, and he looked beyond me, over my shoulder, a faraway look in his eyes. I took a deep breath, felt my joints tighten and my hands began to ball up. I shoved them into my pockets.

*Not another childhood story.*

Jacoby blinked a couple times, as if coming out of a trance. Something that might be considered compassion appeared in his eyes. Or maybe it was the scotch.

"For what it's worth, that bothered me. You were good. Really good, don't get me wrong. The way your dad acted, though. Like the owner of a well-trained pet performing parlor tricks. Everybody acting amazed. Didn't sit right with me." He leaned a little closer. "Didn't sit right with your mom, either, in case you didn't know."

I hadn't known, but it didn't surprise me. It hadn't taken long for Mom to weary of the contentious teacher-student relationship between Dad and me, and she had done her best to endure. But two years of lessons had been more than enough. She'd convinced Dad to stop teaching me, and when that happened, I had no longer been included when they entertained. Thankfully, Mom had supported me when I chose to switch instruments. Dad hadn't cared that I played the trumpet as well as I'd played the piano.

"I kinda figured," I said, "but never knew for sure."

My hands relaxed, grateful that his recollection hadn't been one of glowing praise, but instead one that was more . . .

normal.

"Your mom said to me at the last party I went to, remember it clear as day, both of us in the kitchen. She said, 'These were much more fun when I would sing, and Ivan would play. When they were about songs and music. It feels like there's no room in the world for music anymore.' And she looked sad, she really did."

He crushed the remainder of his cigar. I stood there, hands still inside my pockets. I pictured Mom standing in the kitchen, perhaps preparing a plate of hors d'oeuvres, or stacking dishes at the sink. A flash of wistfulness in her eyes, melancholic over how things had become compared to how they used to be. To how she wished they could have been. I had seen that look in the occasional private moment, when she hadn't known I was there. She'd worn a brave face in public. She had been the patron saint of brave faces.

"So, what used to happen monthly turned into every other month. Then a few times a year. And then, your folks stopped entertaining altogether. Except for the occasional dinner with close friends."

I raised an eyebrow at him, and he flashed a slightly chagrined look before settling into his familiar scowl.

"So I'm a busybody who notices stuff when walking my dog! Every neighborhood has one!"

He looked like he wanted another drink and cigar, and I had to leave. I didn't want to be late to Fanny's.

"Thanks, Mr. Jacoby," I said. "Sorry I stopped by unannounced, but I appreciate it."

He flapped a dismissive hand. "If you had called, I would have let you in."

I caught what might have a flicker of happiness in his eyes, for a split second. Or maybe it was the scotch.

"Next time."

He was still standing at the screen door, watching, as I pulled away.

# CHAPTER 19

T he car clock read 5:14 when I parked in Fanny's driveway. It read 5:23 when I finally decided to get out. I knew the Gospel verse 'with God all things are possible,' but this time I had the feeling that God was shrugging his shoulders with a stumped look on his face, saying 'Sorry, dude, I got nothing. Good luck.'

I knew Fanny was annoyed - saying yesterday's phone call had ended on a bad note would have been like saying the Titanic's maiden voyage took an unexpected detour. Fanny didn't compress her emotions into a cold, hard ball, coat it with apathy, push it deep down into her gut, and consider them dealt with. She'd be giving both barrels tonight, with ample time to reload and reshoot.

And she still didn't know I had dinner with Uncle Pietr. She didn't know about Dad's forfeited inheritance, either. Or that he'd changed his name. She didn't know about his and Grandpa's mutual repudiation. By the time tonight's dinner was over, her reason for having been annoyed with me – a weird phone call where I asked about the boxes in her garage – would seem ridiculous by comparison.

My visit would be unenjoyable, to say the least, regardless of how much attention I paid to tone and inflection, no matter how carefully I minded my non-verbal cues. None of that mattered, not when each word I uttered could trigger an angry reaction.

But that didn't mean I had come unprepared.

On the passenger seat sat a case of 12-Horse Ale, her favorite beer. In the trunk were the two cartons of old family photos. These things would be about as effective as a fire extinguisher in Pompeii, but it was better than nothing.

I walked up to the front door, beer in hand, and after taking a deep breath, rapped on the door, and let myself in.

"Favorite uncle is here!" I announced.

Immediately came the sounds of two chairs scraping upon tile, and rapidly approaching running steps. Justin ran out of the kitchen past the couches and piano, and Rachel came tearing straight behind him.

"Uncle Frank!" they both shouted, and I barely had time to squat down, and let go of the beer. They ran into my open arms, Justin first and then Rachel.

"Hey monkeys!" I said, squeezing tightly. I took one in each arm, grimacing a little at Justin's unexpected weight, and stood up. I clomped with exaggerated Frankenstein steps towards the kitchen, from which came the noise of glass dinnerware being rattled about, followed by a smack of a cupboard door closing.

"What sorts of trouble have you been getting into?" I asked them.

"I've been very good," Rachel said. "I helped Mommy make cookies yesterday."

"You did? Did you help bake them, or help eat them?"

"Both!" she said, with a big grin.

"I've been good too!" Justin chimed in. "I haven't hit Rachel at all this week."

I whistled in mock awe. "Good for you! I know how hard that can be."

I entered the kitchen via the hallway. Fanny stood at the counter next to the sink, her back to me. A stack of four plates sat nearby, along with two plastic glasses and a mishmash of silverware. She turned around, wielding a chef knife in her right hand, a few pieces of diced white onion stuck to the blade.

Fanny's eyes were full of tears, and she wiped them away with her free hand.

"Um, you okay?" I asked.

"Stupid onion," she answered, blinking hard. She sniffled a couple times, and wiped her eyes one more time.

"Let the kids down. They need to set the table."

I closed one eye, and motioned to her knife with a short nod. "Promise you won't throw anything at me?"

"For now." It sounded more like a warning than a promise.

I let Justin and Rachel slip out of my grasp, gently dropping them to the floor.

"Justin, take the plates to the patio table, and Rachel honey, would you carry the cups out please?"

As they set about their chores, I told her I had to get a couple things from my car, and retreated to the front door. After bringing in the two boxes of photos, I removed the carton dated *1956*, snatched the case of beer, and returned to the kitchen. Fanny was washing her hands as I placed the beer and carton of pictures on the counter.

"Want one? They're mostly not cold."

Fanny shook her head. "Take one from the fridge, and I'll have water. What's this?" she asked, picking up the carton.

I wrenched the cap off my beer. "Take a look. It won't bite."

Fanny glowered at me for a second, and then read the cover, after which her gaze lightened a bit. She gasped upon seeing the contents, and flipped through several of the photos before looking back at me. Her eyes were wide, filled with sudden understanding, and I saw tears beginning to well up along her bottom lids.

"Stupid onions," I muttered.

She flung the box lid at me, barely missing me, flying over my left shoulder. A slight smile creased her face; if she had been angry, she wouldn't have missed.

"Shut. Up," Fanny said, grabbing the towel to daub her eyes. "You mentioned there were photos. I forgot. I forgot to ask if you'd bring them with you today. I can have them?"

"Sure! Of course, I'll need to see two forms of ID, and the rest can be yours for only $100, payable in four easy installments of $24.99, including shipping and handling! Call now, operators are standing by!" I took a swig. "I left two full boxes in the vestibule."

At that moment, Justin's voice called out in a panic. "Mom, the grill's on fire!"

"Oh no, the hotdogs! Frank, get them please!"

I quickly circled around the kitchen table, beer in hand, and dashed onto the patio. Greasy gray smoke wafted from underneath the grill's lid, and I could hear the dripping fat crackle and hiss as it struck the flames.

"I hope everyone likes them well done," I murmured while shutting off the propane.

* * *

Fanny and I didn't talk during dinner – she was busy looking through the photos. Justin and Rachel dominated the conversation, recapping the events of the week. The kids ate quickly, then asked to be excused. Fanny nodded, and they dashed off the patio. I watched them scamper through the neighbor's backyard to a nearby friend's house, where several children were playing on a jungle gym.

"These pictures are incredible," Fanny said. "Dad and Mom looked so young."

I leaned over to look. She held a photo of Fanny sitting on Mom's lap, in front of a lit-up Christmas tree, and wearing a shirt that read 'Santa's Little Helper.'

"So did you," I said. "Cuter, too."

"My life was so much better as an only child." She watched me through narrowed eyes, and then rattled off some advantages: "No aggravation, no annoyances, no interruptions..."

"No one to blame, no one to tease," I interjected, mimicking her tone.

"No interruptions," she repeated. "When you go in to get yourself another round, take in the plates please?"

"No one to order around," I added with a smile, then collected the dinner plates, and headed to the kitchen. I returned with two beers.

Fanny cocked an eyebrow. "Planning on staying awhile?"

I jerked my thumb towards the garage. "I presume you still don't care if I look through those cartons?"

She shrugged in a *Whatever* sort of way. "Just don't make a mess."

She had taken my empty beer bottle, and rotated it in place upon the metal contoured table, creating a xylophone-like, strangely melodic, percussive sound.

"I drove by the house on the way here," I said.

"A little out of the way from Spencerport, isn't it?"

I shook my head. "I stopped at Joey Haynes' house beforehand. Remember him?"

"The goofball who thinks he's the second coming of Keith Moon?"

She continued to twirl her bottle, focusing on it rather than on me.

"No, John Bonham. I watched his band practice for a few hours."

Fanny smirked. "Is that the one Ned Kerrigan plays in? What's the name? Toejam?"

"Head. Toehead."

"Dorks," she said, rolling her eyes and taking a drink of water.

"They asked me to join. Play the keyboards."

Fanny did a spit take. Most of the spray missed me, leaving a splatter pattern across the patio.

"Oh my gosh, I'm sorry! Are you serious? Why?"

She cleaned off her chin with the back of her hand, while I wiped my arm with a napkin.

"They have a gig next Friday night at Rooster's, and

they've asked me to play. They're trying to help me, Fanny. See, I've been fired."

She didn't immediately respond. Her incredulous expression remained frozen, mouth slightly open, her eyes locked on mine, waiting for a signal that I had been kidding. It took her three seconds to realize no signal would be coming.

Compassion shone through her eyes. "Aw, crap, Frankie. I'm so sorry. Why?"

I told her everything, while she slowly shook her head.

"I haven't been paying attention to the news. I had no idea. What are you going to do?"

"Besides play keyboards for a garage band and wait for that lucrative recording contract?" I asked. "Not sure. Maybe I'll offer private lessons. Or call the private schools, see if they need someone. My skill set is kinda limited."

Fanny tried hard not to frown. Her eyes seemed down-turned at their corners. She had the look of a mom who just watched her son strike out with the bases loaded in the bottom of the ninth inning.

"Want me to ask Mike if he knows anyone who's hiring? He says the economy's not the greatest right now, but he knows a lot of people."

"If you want. I have some money saved up, but if worse comes to worst, I saw a huge empty cardboard box back on Lake Avenue."

"Stop it Frank, that's not even funny!" She gave me a knowing look, tilted her head just a bit, and dropped her shoulders. "That's why you called last night! To tell him you lost your job, and you wanted his help, but you were too embarrassed to ask. And you didn't want me to know. Right?"

I swallowed and didn't immediately reply. She leaned forward and patted me on the arm.

"It's okay, I understand," she said. "It can be hard to ask for help. It's sort of a thing that happens in our family."

Her concern was reassuring. "So you're not going to kill me? Last night you said future generations would cower in fear upon learning my fate, if you ever found out why I called."

Fanny gave a reassuring smile, and gently squeezed my arm. "I'm granting you clemency, due to the circumstances." Her grip on my arm tightened. "Why, are you lying?"

I winced from the sharp pain of her fingernails digging into my forearm. "Not about being fired. And technically not about the phone call, either."

Fanny released me and leaned back, arms folded across her chest. A tight-lipped, cold-hearted glower replaced her assuring look. "Technically?"

"You assumed I called about having gotten fired, but I never said that." My arm throbbed where she had gripped it. The fingernail marks were visible. "But let the record show I'm voluntarily correcting you of your mistaken assumption."

Her lips pressed tightly together, and her jaw clenched and unclenched. I had to come clean.

"Okay, I called because I wanted Mike's advice about a girl."

Fanny's face turned red, contorted somewhat, and without warning, she burst into a loud, uncontrolled belly laugh. One hand gripped her side, and she bent over far enough for her chest to touch her knees. She even stomped her foot several times. I propped my elbow on the arm of my chair, rested my chin in my hand, and drummed my fingers upon my cheek. Tears streamed down her cheeks, and her laughing subsided to gasping snickers.

"You wanted to ask Mike ... for advice ... about ... girls?"

The raucous laughter returned. I took a long drink of my beer.

Fanny finally took a deep breath, held it for five seconds, then exhaled slowly, composing herself. She wiped the tears from her eyes, grabbed her half-empty glass of water, and drowned her outburst with a long draught.

"I wish you had asked him, just so I could have heard his answer," she said, brushing a few hairs out of her face. "Mike is clueless about girls. Like, Inspector Clouseau level clueless. The mere fact that you think Mike could have helped you tells me you're equally clueless."

I opened my mouth to defend myself, thought better of it, and clamped it shut.

"So what is this about? Problems with Jessica?"

"As a matter of fact, no. It's about this girl Natalie."

A shadow of confusion crossed her face. "Who's Natalie?"

I explained everything; how we had met, described our argument at O'Shea's, how she left two messages on my answering machine, and our conversation this morning. Throughout my presentation, Fanny listened with interest, chin cupped in her hand, her elbow rested on the table. Her eyes seemed to sparkle as I narrated every detail, and a self-satisfied smile crossed her face.

"And so," I concluded, "I'm going with her to this concert Sunday, a concert I don't want to attend, which she knows I don't want to attend, and I know she knows I don't want to attend, but she doesn't know I know she's playing games with me, because I didn't fall for the 'my friend canceled' trick and the 'let's have dinner after' trick, either. And while it looks like I fell for her tricks, she doesn't know I know they were tricks."

I gulped down the last of the beer and placed the bottle down.

"Turns out I didn't need Mike's advice after all."

Fanny slowly rocked her head, still supported in her hand. "I take it all back."

"What?"

"You're not equally clueless. You're astronomically clueless." She sat up straight. "Mike actually could have helped you. Mind games? Tricks? Frank, Natalie likes you. It's so obvious."

Her conclusion confused me. "She likes me? I don't think-"

"Clearly."

"-she likes me," I finished. "She's trying to win an argument."

"Uh huh. Tell you what. Call me after your date, and try to tell me she doesn't like you."

"It's not a date," I reminded her.

"Uh huh. Does this mean you aren't dating Jessica anymore?"

"We were never dating."

"Uh huh. Jessica is head over heels in love with you. Has been for years. Hadn't you noticed?"

I smirked at her. "Yes, thank you, I'd noticed. We talked about that very thing yesterday when she gave me my haircut."

"Looks great. *Oxford Blues*?"

"*About Last Night*."

"So what happened?"

"I said we're the type who remain best friends."

Fanny closed her eyes, raised her eyebrows, and let out a breath. "You told her that?"

"Well, yeah. You know she's always been like a little sister to me."

"You told her *that*??"

I opened my hands in exasperation. "What?"

"You are such an ass. If Jess's heart isn't already broken from you telling her you want to be best friends, it absolutely will be when she learns you're dating this Natalie girl."

She waved away some flies that were buzzing around the condiments and toppings on the table. She stood up and said: "Help me put these away, would you?"

"I'm not dating anybody!" I insisted, snatching the mustard, ketchup, and jar of relish.

Fanny had taken the dish of remaining onions and leftover hotdogs, and I heard her titter while walking away. Following her, I continued my objections.

"You weren't there when we talked, and Jessica completely understood. We hugged, and it was all good. She was, like, totally fine."

"Well of course, doofus! She wouldn't cry in front of you and the other people in the boutique. I bet she cried her eyes out when she got home, and her housemates have been telling her what an ass you are."

An image of Jessica crying and curled up on her bed appeared in my mind, with Pam and Janice sitting alongside, probably saying 'When a guy says they want to be best friends, it means they're probably gay.'

I opened the fridge and put the condiments away, and shook the thought away.

"And Natalie does not like me. Like I said, she's trying to prove her point that I'm a music snob. Nothing more."

"You didn't tell me she called you a music snob," Fanny said. "Oh my gosh, I like her already. When can I meet her?"

I smiled my best *Bite me* smile. "This is why I don't talk to you about my girl issues."

Fanny patted me on the chest. "This is exactly why you *should* talk to me about your girl issues. All these years, and you still think you can solve them without me."

We returned outside. Scattered sunlight shone through the tops of the oak trees at the back of their yard, casting patch-work shadows on the patio.

"You don't understand. She likes John Williams."

"Oh no! A heretic! Burn her at the stake! Tie her to the rack!" She smirked at me. "People can have their own musical tastes, you know. Doesn't make them bad people."

I sat down, slightly miffed at her defending Natalie. "It's the principle."

"Okay, Ivan."

I suddenly didn't want to talk about Natalie anymore. I opened my second beer, and took an angry gulp. The bottle cap rolled across the table, and settled in front of Fanny.

"You really think I've broken Jessica's heart?" I asked.

Fanny gave a little shrug. "I hope not. She was being very vulnerable, saying she loves you. It's a huge risk when we say 'I love you' to a boy, hoping the feeling is mutual. We're offering our heart, asking it to be received, cherished, and protected. If it's rejected, a piece of us dies inside. It's very painful."

"I didn't say I didn't love her. I said the opposite, actually."

"Time will tell," she said. She began pecking at the corner of the bottle label with her thumbnail. "That and a phone call to Brenda tonight after you leave." She smiled and winked.

I pointed at her. "That's why I don't talk to you about my girl issues."

Fanny continued smiling. "Speaking of girl issues . . ."

Waving her off, I said: "I'm saying nothing else about Natalie."

". . . anything new about Clara? Find out who she is yet?"

"No," I said, shaking my head. "I have a couple impressions of who she might be, but not an identity or anything like that."

"What sort of impressions?"

I needed to be careful. Even talking in generalities about Clara could lead to talking in specifics about Dad, and I didn't want to go there just yet.

"I believe he knew her before meeting Mom, he cared about her a lot, and had something to do with the school."

"Really, Einstein?" Fanny said. "You already knew all that. I'm asking about new things."

"I read and played all of the songs, and yeah, she meant a lot to him." My mouth became dry, and I took a quick sip of beer. "I'm fairly certain she played violin, given the two duets, and that their relationship ended in the spring of 1950."

That grabbed her attention, and she sat upright. "That's rather specific. How did you learn that?"

I described my meeting with Gregory. "He confirmed that Dad was accused of being a communist sympathizer, and that an inquiry had taken place in April."

"Holy. Crap." Fanny slouched in her chair.

I nodded solemnly. "I know, right? Dad's episode wasn't imaginary. He really had been investigated."

"But how does Clara tie into it? Did Gregory mention her?"

"No. I showed him Dad's songs, and didn't tell him about

Clara, but I asked if Dad had been particularly close to anyone at Prescott. He said the only woman he knew of was Mom."

"Yes, but she dropped out," she said. "You seem pretty convinced Clara's tied in with the inquiry, though."

"Dad did say her name when he attacked me," I reminded her. "He said 'I'm so sorry Clara' before passing out."

We were headed towards a trail I didn't want to wander down.

Fanny nodded. "I also remember your romantic notions of Dad falling on his sword, making the supreme sacrifice for love. But how did you confirm it?"

"By deduction, I suppose." I ticked off reasons on my fingers. "The songs, Dad's inquiry in '50, he marries Mom in '51, and..."

"And?"

"Well, you said that during the Red Scare, people were fired just for being accused, regardless of innocence or guilt. But Dad kept his job. So Clara lost hers as a compromise or concession."

Fanny made a wry face and looked unconvinced. "Frank, that's not deduction, that's speculation."

"Then how do you explain Dad not getting fired?"

"Cooler heads prevailed?"

A plausible explanation if I hadn't already known that Grandpa had intervened. Fanny couldn't possibly know that, and I didn't want to drop that volume of Stephens Family History on her head. Not if it could be avoided.

Instead, I simply answered, "That's possible."

Fanny stood up, and looked towards the neighbor's yard where Justin and Rachel were playing. Squeals of laughter and sounds of play rang out from the playset. Fanny sat back down and resumed picking at the bottle's label.

"Whoever Clara is," Fanny said, "I highly doubt she was involved with Dad's inquiry. Sure, he mentioned her name during his episode, but just because the inquiry was real, doesn't mean she was connected to it. It is interesting that Dad kept his job, though. That hardly ever happened."

"Well, Bernstein and Copland didn't get fired," I mentioned.

Fanny shook her head. "Their names were on an unofficial list, nothing more. They weren't investigated to the extent that Dad was. Did Gregory say what happened after the inquiry?"

"He said the school swept it under the rug, and everybody involved was sworn to secrecy."

Fanny nodded, her face calm and composed. "That's what I would've done. Bury it and move on."

I scratched the back of my neck. Ironic she should say that. That's what Dad had done regarding his relationship with Grandpa: buried it and moved on. I couldn't tell Fanny that, though. Not now. She seemed convinced that no connection existed between Clara and Dad's inquiry. She didn't press me for more information, so I didn't feel compelled to tell her that Dad changed his name after the inquiry. That he had lied to us about that. I cleared that hurdle. Now I had to broach a more sensitive subject.

"Gregory wasn't the only person I spoke to," I said.

"Someone else from the school?"

"No." I shifted in my seat. "I had dinner with Uncle Pietr and Aunt Jane on Tuesday."

Fanny sat perfectly erect, her shoulders square. "What? Why?"

"Because if Dad knew Clara before having met Mom, and if Clara wasn't connected to Prescott, then I thought maybe Uncle Pietr knew something."

"So you phoned him and said, Hey Uncle Pete, can I come over and ask you about this mystery woman Dad wrote a bunch of songs for?"

"Give me some credit," I told her. "I saw in the Mellowood registry that he had visited Dad earlier in the year, so I told him I'd like to talk to him about it."

"Which he didn't fall for."

"Not really. But he invited me over for dinner anyway."

"Lucky you." Fanny exhaled through flared nostrils. "Let me guess. He had no idea."

I gave a half-hearted shrug. "He had no idea."

"So why are you telling me this, other than to make me upset?"

I leaned forward and looked straight into her eyes. "Because Whitney will be calling you in the next few days, to invite you to a Labor Day weekend barbecue, and I wanted you to hear firsthand I was there on Tuesday, and not from her."

"Hm, let me think," Fanny said, placing her index finger to her lips, and making an inquisitive face. "Is Frank being considerate to his big sister, or just covering his ass? I'll go with the latter." Her expression changed back to an angry scowl.

"Why either or?" I asked. "Can't it be both and?" I had touched a raw nerve.

"Any other surprises I should know about?" she asked, her voice taut as piano wire. She resumed peeling off the label, bit by bit, with renewed vigor. Shreds of the white and green paper lay scattered beneath her chair.

*I have about five. But now isn't the time to talk about them.*

"Just some cousin updates," I told her. "Did you know Artur was accepted into Harvard's grad program? They'll be moving to Bos-"

The bottle cap pegged me on the bridge of my nose. Fanny glowered at me, her eyes dark and dangerous. A vein bulged just beneath her hairline, above her left temple. Her lips were quivering, and I could see her teeth grind behind them.

"You're such a liar!" she spat out, her mouth tight and controlled. "You're not telling me the truth, and you know it!"

# CHAPTER 20

"**W**hat the hell?!"

"Be grateful I didn't throw the bottle."

I didn't want to see our fight escalate into something worse, so I tried to keep my self-control.

"What have I been lying about?"

She folded her arms. "You visited Uncle Pietr to ask why Daddy changed his name! I'm not stupid, Frank!"

That stunned me. Her assertion came out of nowhere. "What? How did you find out about Dad changing our name?"

She took a deep breath and slowly exhaled. "When Dad finally agreed to move to Mellowood, he wanted me to handle his estate. That's when I found out that he changed his last name to Stephens. I've known since March."

"And you didn't tell me?"

"Dad said you didn't need to know."

I slumped back in my chair and closed my eyes. I could get mad at her for not having told me, but what would that accomplish? It wouldn't be worth it. I gave Fanny a hard look.

"So did he tell you why he changed it?"

"Not exactly. I read the Name Change Petition forms he filed with the state, and he indicated 'Career benefits' as the reason. I asked him what that meant, and he replied that if Louis Bernstein could change his first name to Leonard, then Ivan Stepanov could change his last name to Stephens."

This meant she didn't know the real reason. Dad wouldn't have explained why. 'Career benefits' came close to the mark, but still not as accurate as 'I've renounced my dad,' or 'Offended honor.' He'd been carrying his secret for over thirty-five years, and saw no reason to tell anyone else, including his daughter. Doing so would have violated his sense of dignity.

I had one more question to ask. "And did you ask him why he lied to us about Grandpa?"

Her face clouded over, and her eyes grew dark. "Yes."

"What did he say?"

"He just said that young children deserved simple explanations, and the simplest one was that Grandpa had changed our name when they had arrived in America."

"Did you press him on that?"

"He refused to discuss it further, so I let it drop. It didn't seem like a big deal at the time." She noticed the unconvinced look on my face, and quickly added, "You know how Daddy gets once his mind's made up! It's like trying to push over a bridge. Arguing about something that had happened over thirty years ago would've been a waste of time."

She took a deep breath and tried to compose herself.

"Anyway," she continued, "after Dad's episode with you, I wondered if the inquiry had been the reason for his name change. It made sense and the timing fit. It would seem Gregory's story confirms it." She cast her hooded gaze towards me. "It didn't explain why Pietr and Viktor changed theirs too, but I haven't had the opportunity to ask them. But you," she said, waggling her finger at me, "you with your obsession with this Clara. Sure, you visited Pietr to ask if Dad had an old flame, or worshiped a girl from afar, but more importantly, you wanted to know why he changed his name."

"You know I hate the finger pointing thing," I told her.

The waggle increased in intensity. "I know. Answer my question."

I squirmed in my chair. "Yes, I wanted to ask him," I admitted.

Fanny hung her head, looking down at her hands, now folded in her lap.

"You knew, and you waited for me to say it," I said.

She looked back up at me, pain in her eyes. "I made an

educated guess, when you said you visited Uncle Pete, and it turned out I was right. Gregory told you, didn't he? Of course he did. They've been friends for forty years. He probably assumed you already knew. I only found out the truth when I got power of attorney. Never in a million years would that thought have entered my mind. When you weaseled about your reason for visiting Uncle Pete . . . well, the only reason why I care about it now, is that I suspect there's more you're not telling me."

"Fan, I'm sorry. I just wanted to spare you stuff that might get you upset. I had the best intentions."

"You know what they say about best intentions," she said, rubbing her temples in small, tight circles with her fingertips, squeezing her eyes shut. "There's nothing else then?"

Given her current mood, the other things were going to have to wait.

"No. Do you mind if I get started on the boxes in the garage then?"

She gave a couple short shakes of her head. "If Dad and Clara had written to each other, and if he'd saved the letters, you really think they'd be there? Where Mom could have found them?"

"Dad could have hidden them after she died."

Fanny opened her mouth to speak, but no words came forth. She looked at me as if I had grown a set of horns.

"I swear, there are times I think I become dumber hearing you talk."

She stood up from the table again, looking towards the neighbor's yard. Her head angled this way and that, attempting to get a clear look. After a few moments, she sat down, apparently satisfied.

"Hey, you remember those parties Dad and Mom used to throw?" I asked.

"The ones where you performed like an organ grinder's monkey as a warm-up act for Dad and his friends? Where Mom sang like an angel? Where their conversations became so political, I thought I would die? No, I don't remember those at all. Why do you ask?"

"I stopped and saw Ol' Man Jacoby this afternoon, on my way here."

"Merle the Squirrel?" she asked. "Surprised that nosy old man is still alive. What inspired that?"

I suppressed a laugh. That must have been a nickname Fanny used among her friends, because I had never heard it.

"He walked his dog past the house when I was there on Saturday. He told me he used to go to the parties, and said they were enjoyable."

"He enjoyed the food and liquor," Fanny said.

"Why do you think Dad and Mom stopped them?"

Fanny gave a half shrug, and rubbed her arms. "Times changed, and Dad and Mom refused to change with them. They hosted them more and more infrequently, and then just stopped. I think Mom was more disappointed about it than Dad, and I think he had had enough by that time. They stopped because they had become shouting matches about rights, race, and riots. About the 'unjust system' and the 'outlaw American military.'" She lowered the pitch of her voice and made air quotes with each political sentiment. "They were more fun when they consisted of music and Mom's singing."

She'd repeated everything Jacoby had said.

"I could hear all the arguing from my room," I said.

"I'm still confused as to why you went back to talk to Jacoby."

"I needed some closure, I guess."

"With Jacoby?"

"No, of course not! With the house. Does that make sense?"

"Sort of. In a 'My-younger-brother-is-weird' sort of way."

"By the way, you picked out a very attractive *For Sale* sign."

Fanny smirked. "It's the latest in fall fashions. The realtor said the house should sell quickly this close to the start of the school year."

"Once it sells, then what?"

"Realtor gets her cut, and what's left goes to Dad. Mortgage was paid off a few years back. Why?"

I shrugged my shoulders. "You never asked me if I wanted the house."

Fanny folded her arms and leaned back. "A little late to be making your opinion known, don't you think? Besides, Dad made that decision, not me. He never told me to ask you."

"Were you asked?"

"What the hell, Frank? You think Dad should've just given you the house? Is that what you think? Or now that you've lost your job, you think you should be allowed to live there free and clear? Is that why you drove by the house? Were you scoping it out?"

"So he did ask you." It wasn't a question this time.

She snorted once, like a bull facing a matador. "Yes he did, and Mike and I talked about it, but it wouldn't have really worked for our family." Her hand slid down to her abdomen. "When I said no thank you, Dad told me to sell it for whatever I could get."

"My name never came up?"

"No, it did not."

"And you never considered suggesting it to him?"

"Would you have accepted the offer?" she asked. Her breathing became more pronounced, her diaphragm visibly rising and falling.

"That doesn't answer my question, Fanny."

She looked at the sky and scanned the branches, but her eyes seemed incapable of settling on anything other than mine. "I didn't want to have to tell you this, but his specific instructions were, 'Do not ask Frank if he wants the house.' Either it was mine if I wanted it, or it got sold. When I asked Daddy why, he said you wouldn't need a piano room."

That sounded like something Dad would say. Always getting in the final word.

Not today though.

"There's nothing stopping me from buying it," I said.

She tilted her head to one side, knowing I wasn't being entirely serious. "Frank."

"Well, I would have liked to have at least been asked."

"Yeah? Really? And I'm sure Daddy would have liked to have at least been visited, talked to, called, and . . . and . . . and treated with love and respect by his son! The way a dad deserves to be!" She got to her feet. Fanny's chest heaved, and her cheeks were flushed. Every muscle in her arms tensed, her fists tucked tightly underneath her elbows. "When will you ever stop making everything about you, Frank? Are you ever going to let it go?"

"I've earned my bitterness."

"Then I hope you choke on it. I'm going to get the kids."

Fanny whirled away, a force of nature wielding words rather than weather, destructive and wildly unpredictable. Outbursts were part of her personality, but I had to admit, their intensity seemed to increase with each encounter. I hadn't intended to upset her, but like she said, good intentions didn't mean squat.

I couldn't worry about it now. There was work to be done, and I wanted to be gone before Little Miss Whirlwind could make a second pass.

* * *

I had just opened carton number twenty-three when the sound of knuckles knocking against wood caught my attention. Looking up, I saw Mike standing next to the garage door, holding two beers between a couple splayed fingers, a worried smile on his face. The light spilling from the garage formed a rectangle on the driveway, disrupted by Mike's gigantic shadow.

I got to my feet and Mike handed me a beer. "So Fanny's

in the bedroom and doesn't want to talk. You know anything about that?"

"Guilty," I said, raising a hand in admission. "The evening got emotional."

Mike took a swig of his beer. "Been a lot of those here lately," he lamented. "So don't be too hard on yourself."

"I'm not. Things suck all over, dude."

He motioned towards the stacks of cartons. "Fanny told me that's why you called. You coulda asked me, you know. Any luck yet?"

Last night's phone call. I turned around to survey my progress, and to obscure a little bit of embarrassment. Half a dozen boxes remained.

"No. Mom has quite the collection of Depression glass, though, did you know that?"

Mike chuckled. "And barware."

"And Pro-life pins and t-shirts. And holiday decorations. Tell me, does anybody really need three boxes of Easter decorations?" I asked. "I could have sworn the attic had more than this. It seemed packed to the rafters as a kid."

"Fanny said the same thing," Mike said. "Funny how when you're a kid, things always seem bigger."

I nodded while tipping back my bottle. Not everything though. Some things seemed much, much smaller.

"So what happened?" Mike asked, motioning towards the house with his bottle. "She's pretty upset."

I considered how to answer. Both of us deserved blame, but a recap of our conversation without her here to defend herself didn't seem right, and I didn't have time to give Mike a play-by-play. Still, he deserved an answer.

"In a nutshell? Dad."

Mike nodded knowingly. "She's totally stressed out. Between visiting your Dad, putting the home on the market, getting the kids ready for the school year, dealing with the realtor..."

"Fighting with her brother," I added.

"And now these songs you found? It's driving her crazy."

"Really?"

"Yeah. It's really thrown her. It's like," he stopped for a moment, and looked upwards at the rafters. "It's like she's balancing all these glass plates. On sticks. You know how clowns do that trick at the circus?" I nodded. "She's got all these plates spinning on sticks, and she's riding a unicycle, and then," he took another swig, "and then someone tosses her a bowling ball."

"On a stick?"

"What?" He looked at me confused. "Why's the bowling ball on a stick?"

I rolled my eyes under closed lids. "Never mind. But yeah, I know what you mean."

"Let me tell you something," he said. "I've been in the family for more than ten years now, and I've never stuck my nose in anyone's business. You know that, right?"

"Yeah, I do."

"The first time I met your family, it was Thanksgiving. Remember? Fanny brought me home, and we ate at your rich uncle's place. It was really cool. I remember it snowed a lot that November, and your uncle got us on the golf course for some cross-country skiing. Remember?"

"Yeah, I remember you and Fanny getting lost. For like an hour?" I smiled at him.

"Wink wink, nudge nudge," he said, his eyes brightening a little. "Uh, where was I?"

"Thanksgiving, rich uncle's house," I reminded him.

"Oh yeah. Anyway, Mom super impressed me. She made me really feel at home that weekend." He stopped to take a long drink of beer. "But what I remember most is how your dad treated you. I don't know how else to put it, but he was sort of a dick. And I thought, man, how does Frank put up with this? You just sat there and took it."

I started to regret letting Mike tell me something. There were only six more boxes to check, and then I could go home.

But I let him continue.

"I mean, if it were my dad, and he treated me that way, I probably would've decked him."

"There were times I was tempted," I said.

"Your mom, of course, being the coolest, told him to stop, or changed the subject. A couple times that weekend, I heard them argue in their bedroom. I felt kinda bad."

"Well, you should have. You were eavesdropping."

"I felt bad for you, man. I didn't get why your dad just couldn't be happy for you. I didn't understand why playing the trumpet made him so upset. You were awesome."

"Dad didn't like the trumpet because it wasn't the piano."

"Yeah, I understand that now," Mike said.

"Fanny never told you the reason? After all these years?"

He shrugged. "She might have, I don't remember."

That I could believe.

"So I was totally on your side, Frank. The way he treated you was totally uncool. Now, don't get me wrong, I thought your dad was cool, too. I never met a professional musician before, who composed songs and stuff. And he was always nice to me."

"Because you never let him down, and you've taken good care of his baby," I told him.

"Well, sure. But even still, I never liked the way he treated you."

My chest seemed to swell with a little bit of pride. "Well, I appreciate hearing that, Mike, I really do."

"I'm not done."

The pride drained from my chest like stale air from a party balloon.

"After that weekend, I asked Fanny why the two of you didn't get along. She said you were two stubborn mules fighting over a busted bale of old, dry hay. I didn't know exactly what she meant, but I understood the two stubborn mules well enough." He downed the rest of his beer before continuing. "But now that I'm older, and I've been around you guys all these years, I think I've finally figured out what she meant.

"You've been angry with your dad for so long, you act as if he's still fighting over that busted bale of old hay. But it's just you now. He's done fighting."

He regarded his empty bottle for a second, as if considering whether to go after the very last drop. Mike then looked at me.

"And Fanny's not gonna take his place."

Mike looked back towards the house, a concerned look on his face.

"Now, I gotta help her pick up all those plates and sticks, and get them spinning again. Could you stop tossing her bowling balls?"

Despite the fact I'd known Mike for the past ten years, this was only the second time he'd been this open with me. The first time had been when Fanny was pregnant with Justin, and Mike had been nervous about becoming a new dad. For some reason, he'd seemed to think talking with me would calm his nerves. And now tonight. We held several things in common: a disdain for politics, an affinity for Monty Python quotes, and Fanny. Music didn't interest him, and I didn't follow football or auto parts. He'd help me when I had car trouble, and I came over when he needed a second set of muscles around the house. Deep conversations about emotional stuff required subtitles.

"I'll do my best, bro."

He acknowledged me with a salute of his bottle, which I repaid in kind, and he shuffled out of the light. I stood for several minutes after he went inside. Mike was right, and I felt bad that it fell to him to clean up the mess I helped make. He loved Fanny more than life itself, which had endeared him to Dad and Mom from the get-go. He handled her fiery personality better than anybody, including me, which was one of the biggest reasons why Fanny loved him. Though I teased him for being literal-minded and slow on the uptake, I had learned long ago that his gentle giant demeanor masked a reflective nature. He was observant as hell, and despite not always understanding the whys and wherefores in the moment, if called upon, his conclusions were invariably right on the mark.

Tonight was a prime example. Dad had stopped fighting with me years ago; when, exactly? When Mom got diagnosed with cancer? Had he focused all his energy on that battle? After Mom died, had he lacked the will to pick up where we had left off? Or was it because I had cut him out of my life as best I could? Whenever the change happened, I had been too angry and stubborn to notice. Maybe if he had offered an olive branch, a request for a truce, things would be different now. Maybe he'd tried, and I hadn't seen. With him fading away in Mellowood, is it too late?

Mike's comment had been a warning. He'd planted his flag, declaring his wife a neutral territory. He loved Fanny to pieces, and he'd just drawn a line in the sand I had better not cross.

I knew better than to ask if that's what he'd meant, gentle giant or not. Unfortunately, I knew there'd be more bowling balls. Fanny hadn't learned everything yet, and when she eventually did, all the plates and sticks would come crashing down again.

As I resumed my search, one last thought came to light: Fanny had secrets, too. What else did she know, and what else wasn't she telling me?

# CHAPTER 21

It was shortly before three on Sunday afternoon when I turned onto Natalie's street. Her neighborhood bore several resemblances to mine, with homes built in the 50's, but slightly larger and on deeper lots, and better maintained. They sported dormered attics, large front porches, and detached garages in the back. Large oak trees lined the wide street. Several kids raced their banana-seat bikes up the street, skimming past cars parked curbside.

The house had been easy to find, a half block west of Mt. Hope Avenue. The green siding contrasted nicely with its buttercream trim, the house number in black script, mounted above the door of the screened-in porch. Bamboo shades, rolled halfway down, kept out the afternoon sun. The porch looked unoccupied, but I couldn't tell. Natalie might be lurking there, like a sentry poised for an ambush.

I parked in the driveway, checked my hair - definitely *About Last Night* - and straightened my skinny red leather tie before getting out of the car. I may have looked cool and collected on the outside, but a different song and dance played on the inside.

During the drive, I had repeatedly told myself to relax and not get worked up. That this would be no big deal. Except my brain had refused to believe any of it, and kept bringing to mind my conversation with Don and Ned after Friday's practice ended.

"We're going to O'Shea's tomorrow night," Ned said. "Wanna come?"

"I don't think so. It's been a long week," I replied, deciding that going to the bar the night before this thing with Natalie would be unwise.

"Well, if you change your mind..." He left the invitation unfinished, and then elbowed Don. "You gonna ask Natalie?"

"She's not returning my calls," he growled. "I left a message, telling her to meet us, so we'll see."

Ned slapped him on the back. "Dude, you gotta face facts. She just ain't into you."

"A dude's gotta try, right?" he replied. "Until she says no to my face, or calls me back and says beat it, I'm gonna keep trying."

"Didn't you say Natalie wasn't your type?" I asked. I tried to sound nonchalant and disinterested. It wasn't as if I *liked* her, but Fanny had seemed rather convinced that she liked me. Getting the lay of the land was important.

"Maybe not," he said, "but you know how girls are. Always playing hard to get."

"Dude, you should ask her to come to our gig," Ned said. "When she hears how you shred that bass..."

"I plan on it," he answered. "If she ever picks up the phone."

His pursuit of Natalie weighed on my mind. Was she playing games, playing hard to get? Or was it something else? I didn't know why I cared if he liked her, or if she was interested in him, but something stirred inside me, making me feel uncomfortable all the same. I considered making one more comment about her, but decided to just get in my car and drive home.

And now I was sitting in her driveway, past the point of no return. I took a deep breath and slowly exhaled before getting out of the car. It was now or never.

I sauntered down the flagstone path connecting the drive to the front stairs, and coolly climbed them two steps at a time. A noise came from inside the porch; Natalie stepped forward and stood at the screen door. She seemed cuter in some unexpected way. She wore a light blue short sleeved blouse, buttoned up to the neck and squared off with shoulder pads, paired with a gray mid-thigh skirt. Her brunette hair looked like it had last Saturday - brushed back, this time held in place by a blue, gray, and white argyle headband. She flashed a smile that I didn't recall seeing at O'Shea's, and I wondered about its sincerity.

"Hi!" she said, and took a step back from the door. "I'm so glad you agreed to this crazy idea of mine." She gave a soft giggle and half-rolled her eyes.

"Were you afraid I'd bail?" I asked as I let myself onto the porch.

Her smile waned almost imperceptibly, and she cast her eyes to the floor. "Well, no, not exactly. I mean, it is movie music, after all."

Her hands were clasped at her waist, and it seemed she was trying to braid her fingers.

"Would you like to come inside for a drink? I've got New Coke. And we're only fifteen minutes from Prescott, so we've got a little time."

I shrugged. "Sure."

As she led me in, I added, "So, uh, you look nice."

"Thanks!" she replied. She looked back at me, waving her hand above her hair in a loose circular fashion, saying, "So do you. I like the Judd Nelson thing you got going there."

*Judd Nelson???*

She stepped into the foyer. "I thought about wearing a dress, but since we're attending a matinee, a blouse and skirt would be fine. I plan on bringing a sweater in case the AC is blasting cold."

She turned, seeing I hadn't yet followed her in, but remained holding the door.

"Frank? Coming?"

I considered a scathing retort. Can a girl who mistakes Judd Nelson for Rob Lowe be right about anything? Sure, it was probably an honest mistake. But still. If this were an indication of how our afternoon would go…

"Yeah, sorry." I simply said as I stepped inside. "Brain fart."

"I'll be right back," Natalie said, and she took off down a hallway that led to the kitchen.

I stepped into the front room, its elevated ceiling extending clear to the second floor. A stylish dried flower arrangement sat upon a round mahogany table. A wide, open doorway on the right led to the living room.

A staircase started near the kitchen doorway, turning at a landing as it ascended. Bookshelves were built beneath the steps, and each one was completely full. The room's left wall was a solid bookcase, divided into two four-foot sections, and it stood over twelve feet tall. Parked in the corner was a rolling ladder, its upper casters fixed upon a brass rail mounted nine feet above the floor. Paperbacks and hard-cover books jammed every shelf. I stepped to the shelves near the bottom of the steps, and perused the titles and authors. The collection was a mix of classical fiction, histories, autobiographies, and textbooks.

Built-in shelves also lined the wall abutting the porch, filled with sculptures, vases, framed photos, and other knick-knacks. Most of the photos were family portraits, and all but one included her parents. A silver frame held a photo of Natalie and her three siblings: two girls and a young boy. It looked recent.

*Wonder where they are. Did she kick them out before I got here? Am I alone with her?*

"Here you go," she said behind me.

I turned, and took the can she offered, and motioned at the bookshelves.

"Quite the collection. The high ceiling is impressive, too. I didn't think these homes were built in this style."

"Oh, none of it is original," she said, looking around the room. "My parents had this remodeled before they. . ." She broke off her answer, almost without missing a beat, then quickly resumed. "They had this done years ago. They impressed upon us the importance of reading."

I knew she had almost mentioned that her parents were dead, since Gregory told me last week. She didn't want me to know, so I pretended not to notice the quick shift in her answer.

"Did their plan work? Have you read all these?"

Natalie rolled her eyes. "No, not *all* of them. Not yet anyway. I do love to read, though."

"Fiction or nonfiction?"

"Depends on my mood. You?"

The last time I'd read fiction for leisure's sake had been when Fanny recommended *Pet Sematary* four years ago, and I'd hated it. Leisure reading didn't interest me. Before I could respond, Natalie spoke.

"Let me guess. You only read classical literature, because popular fiction sacrifices style, form, and refinement at the altar of crass commercialization, and today's authors pursue profit by appealing to the lowest common denominator."

She smirked quickly before taking a swig of pop. I recognized it as the same 'I'm gonna push all the buttons' smirk Fanny used on occasion.

"I mean, if your taste in music is any indication," she added.

I returned the smirk and said, "If your musical preferences are any indication, then Jackie Collins, Sydney Sheldon, and Barbara Cartwright are your favorite authors."

"Cartland, not Cartwright," she said. "C'mon Frank, if you're going to insult me, at least get your names straight."

"Not surprised you know her name."

"Seriously, though. Do you like to read? Can you read?" The smirk reappeared.

"Right now, I'm reading the second volume of Schumann and Brahms's letters."

Her smirk vanished in an instant. "Seriously? I love those letters!"

"Seriously?" I asked.

"No lie."

She placed her pop can next to the flower arrangement, and crossed to the ladder. She rolled it a few feet out of the corner, locked the floor wheels, and climbed halfway up. Natalie removed two books and handed them to me. She hadn't been kidding: Volumes 1 and 2. The same as Fanny's edition.

"I've read them a few times. They're fascinating, beautiful, and so romantic."

"I'm borrowing the second volume from my sister," I told her.

"You're welcome to borrow Volume 1, if you need it," she said. "Don't mind my chicken-scratches in the margins. They're from when I read it in class."

"You sure?" I asked.

She nodded. "So why are you reading it? It's not exactly mainstream."

My brow creased, and I scratched my neck. Should I tell her about Dad's songs? I barely knew the girl. I still wasn't sure if she was even normal. In fact, accepting the book meant I'd have to see her again, to return it. How involved did I want her in my life, anyway?

"I'm, uh, satisfying a curiosity," I said. "My sister and I were discussing Brahms and Schumann last weekend." That sounded innocuous enough.

I watched as she replaced Volume 2, and scanned the titles and authors of the nearby books: music theory; books on composition, tone, and harmony; composer biographies; instrumentation; books on various instruments. There were books on musical styles: baroque, romantic, chamber music, opera, atonality, symphonic. She had several on the history of jazz, and rock and roll, as well as one on musical cryptograms. All told, she had four complete shelves dedicated to music.

I hadn't expected this. This was far more than a pleasant surprise.

"Are all those music books yours?"

Natalie had descended, pushing the ladder back into the corner.

"Pretty much. A bunch were from Prescott, and others are ones I picked up here and there at used bookstores. My parents were musical, too." She motioned for me to follow her. "If that impresses you, come here."

I tore myself away, and followed her in the living room. A dark blue camelback couch stood against the opposite wall, framed with two deep brown - almost black – identical end tables. A low coffee table matching the end tables sat before the couch, upon a thick rectangular grey rug. Wainscoting wrapped the room; white wallpaper with a blue fleur-de-lis pattern covered the upper half of the walls. A large rectangular mirror hung centered above the couch. The room's formal, impeccable decorations seemed almost anachronistic.

*It's like a shrine, or a testament to her parents, keeping the house the way they did.*

Natalie stopped in front of the coffee table, turned to face me, and like a *Price Is Right* girl showing off a new washer and dryer set, placed her right hand on her hip, and extended her left arm towards the far corner.

A polished, ebony Mason & Hamlin baby grand stood there, similar in size and length to Dad's. Its lid was propped open, and a Schirmer's publication of Beethoven sonatas stood upon the music stand. The brass pedals gleamed, and the white keys reflected in the fall board with a shine. It looked flawless.

"Wow, a Model A," I said. "I am impressed. What year?"

"1931, I believe," Natalie answered. "It belonged to my grandmother. She was the original owner. Would you like me to play you something?"

My watch said ten past three. Frankly, I wanted to hear *myself* play it, but that would have to wait.

"I'd love to, but we better motor if we don't want to be late."

She wrinkled her nose. "So now you want to go to the concert?"

"Not really," I said. "But if I pretend hard enough, you might be convinced."

Natalie smiled, and it seemed earnest. "Maybe afterward, then."

# CHAPTER 22

"How are you managing so far?" Natalie asked me. "Gonna make it?"

The concert had reached its intermission, and we strolled about the upper gallery lobby. The crowd was thin. Several clusters of families milled about in the lobby, the children among them jabbering about the movies from which the music came. I watched two brothers fight a pretend lightsaber battle using rolled up programs.

"Well, I don't know, there's still half a concert to go," I answered, giving her a look of feigned weakness, followed quickly with a grin.

She smirked back. "Doesn't the orchestra sound great? The acoustics here are fantastic."

"They certainly are. But all this is, is the John Williams Spectacular Music Show, with James Horner and Nino Rota singing back-up," I told her. "They've played *Jaws*, *ET*, *Star Wars*, and *Raiders*, a little bit of *Star Trek*, and the *Godfather* theme. Not exactly a night at the opera."

"It's not billed as a night at the opera," she responded. "That's October's concert."

She stopped at the glass-paneled railing overlooking the main lobby, and watched other concert goers gathered below.

My interest perked up. "Ooh! Does your friend have to work that day, too?"

Natalie gave me a sideways glance. "If you're that interested, I'm sure tickets are still available at the box office."

I stood next to her, leaned against the railing, and opened my program.

"Well, at least the second half includes music from Leonard Bernstein. Did you know *West Side Story* was a stage production before being made into a movie? Whatever, I'm not complaining. Ever hear him play *Rhapsody in Blue*?"

"Gershwin wrote that, and yes, I've heard him play it," she answered, crossing her arms. "The question you need to ask yourself is, will you ever get to hear me play it?"

With that, she headed towards the stairs leading to the main lobby.

"Unfortunately, they're also playing the Sherman brothers' stuff from *Mary Poppins*. This would've been better named A Children's Concert."

Her question suddenly registered. Natalie was halfway down the stairs by the time I reached her.

"Hang on a sec! You can play *Rhapsody in Blue*?"

"Wouldn't you like to know."

"As a matter of fact, yeah, I would." We reached the bottom step, and I took her elbow. "I can play it too."

Natalie tilted her head to one side, looked up at me, and batted her eyes. "Well aren't you every sort of special!"

Her tone rang with condescension, underscored with a quick grin that seemed unfriendly, her lips tightly pressed together.

"I'm going to the ladies' room."

I watched, a bit dumbfounded, as she headed towards the restroom.

*What'd I say? What'd I do?*

A patron descending the stairs bumped into me while I stood in front of the stairway. Mumbling an apology, I stepped aside, and leaned against a wall. She had invited me to the concert knowing I disliked this sort of music, and now she seemed annoyed. Did she really expect I wouldn't be a little sarcastic? It wasn't like we were on a date or anything.

And, truth be told, I *was* every sort of special. It only took me a week to learn *Rhapsody in Blue*. I bet it took her a *whole year*!

While I flipped idly through the program, the lights flashed several times, and a soft chime rang through the lobby. I looked up just as Natalie emerged from the restroom.

"Good timing," I said as she met me. She was wringing her hands, in the same way she had when I had arrived at her house. Something was up.

She chewed her bottom lip for a moment and finally said, "You know, if you're not enjoying yourself, we can leave. It's no big deal."

I waved off her suggestion. "And miss out on Bernstein?"

"You sure?"

"Totally. Honestly, it's better than I expected."

She managed a small smile, and we made our way upstairs.

"Besides," I said, "you deserve to get your full money's worth. And don't let me forget to pay you back for your friend's ticket."

"That's nice of you," Natalie replied.

The lights dimmed a second time, and the chime resounded. The auditorium entrances were a little congested as audience members returned to their seats. We shuffled forward, and once inside, descended the ramped aisle to our row. The house lights darkened as we settled into our upholstered seats. As the conductor entered to a round of applause, Natalie poked me in the arm, and leaned close to whisper. The applause had stopped as the conductor stepped onto the podium and taken up his baton.

"You play the trumpet, right?" she asked, to which I nodded. "And the piano?" I nodded again. She raised an eyebrow. "And you really know *Rhapsody in Blue*?" I nodded a third time, after which she faced the stage. I thought I detected an impressed look in her eyes. I nearly whispered, "Learned it in a week, too," but resisted. She seemed normal again, and normal was okay.

The orchestra started playing the Overture from *West Side Story*.

* * *

Not far from the Prescott Theater, a couple blocks down East Main Street, stood George's, a modest diner which catered to locals, students, and concert goers. Since it was one of the few restaurants near downtown which stayed open past five on a Sunday, Natalie suggested walking over for a post-concert cup of coffee. I obliged. The late afternoon sun cast our long shadows ahead of us as we walked. Natalie had removed her sweater, tying it around her waist.

"My treat," I said, holding open the door for her. "Doesn't make it a date or anything."

"No, of course not. Not a date."

"It's just my way of saying thank you for the invite."

"In that case, I might order a slice of pie too," she said.

George's was less than half full, and we were immediately seated in a booth by the front window. Large framed black and white photographs of city landmarks decorated the walls, and brushed aluminum fixtures hung above each table and booth. The sound of muted, indistinguishable conversation and the clatter of plates and silverware filled the air, mixed with the faint aromas of bacon cheeseburgers, French fries, and vanilla milk shakes.

Our waitress approached with two glasses of ice water. We each ordered coffees and pecan pie.

Natalie shook her head. "I still can't believe you think John Williams is a hack. You know he went to Julliard, right?"

"That says it all right there," I answered, loosening my tie, and undoing my collar button. "Lots of hacks came out of Julliard."

Natalie grabbed two creamers from a small white bowl sitting at the end of the table, beneath the window.

"You are such a snob. Just because your father taught at Prescott doesn't mean every other music school and conservatory is second or third rate, you know. Julliard is an excellent school in its own right."

"Prescott has nothing to do with it. Every school's got hacks, a mix of contenders and pretenders, from the students to the faculty."

The waitress returned with our orders. She placed large porcelain mugs on the table, and set the pie plates and forks down.

"Can I get you kids anything else?"

"We're good for now, thanks," I told her.

After the waitress stepped away, Natalie picked up her fork and, shaking it at me for emphasis, said, "Williams is not a hack! He's won numerous Oscars, Emmys, and Golden Globes. He's nominated practically every year, all the while conducting the Boston Pops. And he's composed several symphonic and orchestral works. That's not the resume of a hack."

She looked at the fork in her right hand, and then at the two creamers in her left, and then looked down at her pie.

"I need more hands." She put down the fork, opened the creamers, and poured them into her coffee.

"You sure are passionate about John Williams," I said.

Natalie looked me square in the eye. "I am passionate about a lot of things."

I considered her comment. What did she mean by that? Was she being coy and mysterious? Or just making an insignificant, vague declaration? Did I dare find out?

"Listen," I said, lowering my mug, "let's stop arguing about this. Been there, done that, right? So how about a truce."

"Okay, truce," she said. "It takes a big man to admit when he's lost."

My neck suddenly grew warm. My jaw clenched, and my nostrils flared, at which point Natalie laughed. She dropped her fork and wiped her mouth with a napkin.

"I'm sorry, but the look on your face..."

I stabbed at my pie, glowering at her a little. "You don't fight fair."

"Girls never fight fair. Didn't you know?"

"I know all too well. I have an older sister."

"And I *am* the older sister. It comes with the package."

"Two sisters and a brother, right? I saw your family portraits on the bookshelf."

Natalie nodded. "Pamela's twenty-one, Valerie's eighteen, and Eric is fourteen."

"And what do your folks do?"

She paused a second, and daubed the corners of her mouth with the napkin, all the while focusing on the table between us.

"My parents died, about four years ago."

I had already known this, but telling her I knew, and how I found out, would've been weird.

"I'm sorry, Natalie. I lost my mom to cancer about eight years ago."

Natalie drew a deep breath and raised her gaze to meet mine. Her light brown eyes had turned sad.

"They were killed in a car crash during my second year at Prescott. I had to drop out to take care of my siblings."

She blinked a few times, then looked out the window to watch a couple stroll by, hand in hand.

"Sounds rough," was all I could think of to say.

"Parts of it were. Well, most of it, truthfully. I was nineteen at the time, and I had no other family nearby. An aunt from out of state lived with us for about a year, to help settle things."

She returned her gaze to me, either having lost interest in watching the couple, or they had walked out of sight.

"It took some convincing for the state to allow us kids to stay together, and not get separated, or . . .or whatever."

"How'd you manage? I mean, nineteen?"

"My parents were well off. Dad worked as an exec at Lincoln First Bank, with big life insurance policies on him and Mom. A more than generous wrongful death lawsuit settlement took care of the rest. I was able to pay off the house, the lawyers, tuition, and all the rest. We've managed to stick together through it all. Grew closer, actually. Tragedy does that to families sometimes, y'know?"

*Not all families.*

The waitress returned to refresh our coffees, and we waited while she filled the mugs.

"Will you be ordering anything else?"

Natalie shook her head, and I told her no. The waitress placed our bill on the table near me, and after she left, Natalie continued.

"Pam's studying nursing at Niagara University, with one year to go. Valerie just graduated from high school, and is going to Fredonia this fall. I'm driving her there on Wednesday, in fact. And Eric will be a sophomore. It's been the hardest for him. He struggles at times, and I don't make a particularly good dad. But he plays football at Bishop McQuaid High, and thankfully the coach has taken him under his wing."

"And what about you?"

"I work at a florist across from Strong on Mt. Hope." She gave a weak smile. "It doesn't pay much, but then, I don't need much. I seem to have a knack for floral arrangements and decorating."

"The one on the table in your front room?"

She nodded. "Mine. I'm working there until Eric graduates. After that, I'll return to Prescott and get my degree."

"That's pretty noble of you," I said.

"Well, it's not like I had much of a choice, right? When life hands you a shit sandwich, you either eat it, or go hungry. And since I couldn't exactly send it back to the damn kitchen . . ."

A subsequent shoulder shrug spoke of begrudging acceptance. She ate the last piece of her pie and washed it down with some coffee.

The mild obscenities caught me off guard, as she didn't strike me as the swearing type. I wondered if she still struggled with her parents' death, perhaps with more resentment than she cared to admit.

Then she smiled and her eyes cleared.

"There," she said. "That's the two-minute story of my life. What about you? Don said you teach high school band?"

I shook my head. "Middle school. And I *used* to teach band. Got laid off Wednesday."

"Oh no! What happened?"

"The state assembly couldn't pass a spending plan, so just like that," and I chopped the air with my hand, "my school's program got axed."

"That sucks. I'm so sorry. So what will you do?"

Shrugging, I said, "I'm okay for now. Next school year, I'll be teaching again."

"You have to do something until then, though," Natalie told me.

"My current strategy is to mooch food off my friends and move in with my sister's family once the money runs out."

"Your dad's retired, isn't he? Doesn't he have a room to spare? Maybe you can move in with him," Natalie suggested.

First the job, now my dad. Two subjects I didn't want to discuss. Not that she could have known.

"No, I can't."

"No? I'd think he'd be willing to help you."

I put my elbows on the table, interlocked my fingers and, with my thumbs supporting my chin, I gave Natalie the most serious look I could.

"My dad has Alzheimer's, and has been living in a nursing home since February. He has no clue who I am. At my last visit, he thought I was Felix Mendelssohn. And his house is for sale."

Natalie seemed to shrink and pull away, sinking into the bench cushion. "I...I didn't know. I'm so sorry about your dad. How sad. I've never known anyone with Alzheimer's. It must be incredibly hard to not be recognized by your own father."

I felt like saying that it was no big deal, he barely cared about who I was before he lost his freaking mind. I felt like saying that even if he weren't sick and at Mellowood, I wouldn't move back home even if it were the last house on Earth, and I was offered a million dollars to come back. There were ten more things I felt like saying to her, none of which would have helped, and all of which would make me sound like a jerk.

I stifled those urges, managing a look I hoped could be taken for humility, accentuated with a brave half smile, and a modest shrug of the shoulders.

"It is what it is," I told her.

"I didn't realize you had such a rotten week," Natalie said, leaning forward again. My chin still rested on my hands, and she brought her face closer to mine. "Your dad not recognizing you, losing your job..."

A strange feeling emerged from beneath the conflict and uneasy discomfort roiling in my head. Our conversation produced feelings of anxiety, and yet I sensed a soothing, relaxed feeling too, barely perceptible. Not quite the calm before the storm, but rather, like seeing a thin streak of blue sky far in the distance, near the horizon, while riding out a wild and dangerous storm.

Looking into her eyes, I noticed that they weren't light brown after all, but a vibrant, luminous hazel. Nearly translucent. They were unlike any I'd ever seen.

"...attending a Music from the Movies concert," Natalie continued. She blinked and smiled at me, and it seemed a patch of clear sky split the clouds of an overcast day.

I returned her smile. "The rottenest of weeks," I said.

Natalie glanced at her watch and bolted upright.

"Oh gosh, it's after six. Later than I thought. Can you take me home? I left Eric a note in the kitchen on what to heat up for his dinner when he got home from his friend's house, but you know teenagers. Selective comprehension skills."

She slid off the bench, and I did the same.

"Afraid he's going to starve?" I joked.

"He's probably watching TV, wondering why no one's made dinner. Pam's at Niagara already, and Val's with some friends." She opened her purse. "Want me to pay the tip?"

I shook my head. "I got it," I said, dropping five bucks on the table.

"You sure? I feel bad having you pay for me, being unemployed and all."

"I can manage a whole five bucks," I told her. "As well as paying for your friend's ticket." I held out a twenty. "Will that cover it?"

She almost didn't accept it, both hands clutching her purse. A second passed, and then she fished out a ten, exchanging it for my twenty.

"That's more than fair. Thanks."

We left the restaurant and returned to the parking garage. The sun hung lower now, burning orange and red in the western sky. It was a portent of a beautiful night.

We didn't talk much on the way back. We agreed that the coffee and pecan pie had tasted great. We disagreed on *Amadeus.* She said it was fun, while I said Salieri's portrayal was inaccurate and patently unfair. We both laughed at a car's bumper sticker that read "Disco Still Sucks."

Five minutes later, we were pulling out of the garage onto a side street, then stopping at East Avenue. I flicked on my left-hand turn signal, to head towards downtown and Natalie's house. The traffic cleared, but I hesitated. An idea popped into my head.

*We're so close, it'd be foolish to not go.*

"Lost?" Natalie asked, noticing my indecision.

"No," I answered, and then faced her. "Listen, on a scale of one to ten, with one being Not At All, how important is it that you get home as soon as possible?"

Her eyes narrowed, and she gave me a sideways look. "Why?"

"Scale of one to ten. Tell me."

She shrugged her shoulders, spreading her hands. "I don't know. Six? Four? Five point three?"

"Cool. Then there's time for a quick detour."

I flipped my turn signal, and after waiting for a couple cars to drive by, turned right onto East Avenue.

"Where are you taking me?" Natalie asked. She sounded more curious than suspicious, which reassured me.

I smiled at her. "It's a surprise," I said. "For both of us."

# CHAPTER 23

We hadn't driven more than half a mile before she started guessing our destination. I gripped the steering wheel with anticipation, resisting the urge to tell her. There was no particular reason not to, other than to increase the suspense, and maybe to drive her slightly crazy.

We stopped for a red light at Goodman Avenue. On the right stood a three-story white and sandstone building, behind which crested an olive-green dome, overlooking the building and surrounding parking lot. The setting sun reflected off its windows, blazing copper and bronze.

"You're taking me to the Science Center? But they're closed." She then oohed with enthusiasm. "We're going to the Strasenburgh Planetarium, aren't we!"

"Nope," I told her.

The light turned green, and we drove by the block-long museum and science center complex. Groups of people walked through the main entrance. Large posters hung upon the Science Center walls advertised the evening's show: *The Start of It All: Enter The Big Bang.*

"I love the planetarium. It's been years since I've been there," she said, pouting. "Why won't you tell me where we're going?"

"We're nearly there," I said. "Next street."

I turned right onto Barrington Street. Majestic maple trees towered overhead, their leafy branches forming a canopy that covered the street. The homes on the west side of Barrington cast long shadows, stretching across the lawns, reaching the edge of the street, creating a premature twilight.

"Such beautiful houses," Natalie asked. "And expensive. You know someone in this neighborhood?"

"Not exactly."

Ahead on the right stood an open space, and I swung the Horizon into it, parking in front of a large Tudor style home. The dark brown brick first floor contrasted sharply with the crème-colored second story, framed and crossed with brown wooden trim and beams. Peaked gables rose above the upper story windows. A wide brick chimney towered high above the peak.

A cobblestone path wended its way from the street to a wide set of stone steps beneath a brick arched entrance. Bay windows on each side protruded above low bushes and shrubs.

"This is it," I said, stepping out and hopping the curb.

"This is what?" Natalie asked as she joined me on the sidewalk.

"27 Barrington Street," I told her. "Where my dad grew up."

Natalie's eyes widened as she took in the view. "What? You're kidding!"

"Nope. This is the first time I've seen it."

She turned towards me, her mouth agape. "You mean the first time you've seen it . . . in years? Or the first time you've seen it, ever?"

"Ever."

"That's just crazy," she said. "Your dad never took you on a drive to the old house when you were a kid? Every kid's dad does that. You never visited your grandparents?"

I shook my head. "They died before I was born, and my dad told us his house had burned down. One of my uncles recently told me this is where he grew up."

Natalie folded her arms and exhaled loudly through her nose, like a snort. "That's just so crazy. Why would your dad say that?"

I couldn't answer her, not directly. Fanny didn't know

this part of our family history, as far as I knew, so telling Natalie seemed disrespectful, in a way. Maybe Fanny had learned about this place when she'd assumed power of attorney, and never told me, but I didn't know.

Regardless, Natalie didn't have the right to know why. Showing her the house seemed harmless enough, given that she admired Dad's work. That formed a sort of connection. Disclosing additional details and family squabbles, however, would betray an unspoken trust with my sister.

Shoving my hands in my pockets and shrugging my shoulders, I said, "I have no idea. You know how a lot of composers, musicians, and artsy people can be - strange idiosyncrasies, compulsive issues, eccentric habits. For instance, my dad organized his sheet music by the song's composition year. Put a Mozart ahead of a Bach, and he'd lose it. Anyway, I can't ask my dad why. He doesn't even remember who he is; how would he remember where he grew up?"

Natalie made a face. "It's still crazy."

She wouldn't get an argument from me about that. She also wouldn't get any further explanation.

We continued to look at the house from the sidewalk. The sun had sunk completely behind the house, its features fading more and more into the growing dusk.

"There are no lights," Natalie said.

"What?"

"In the windows. No lights. The house is completely dark."

Not a single light shone from inside. In the gathering gloom, I couldn't see if there were curtains drawn or blinds lowered.

"Maybe no one's home," I suggested.

"The lawn looks like it hasn't been mowed for weeks, too," she added, pointing to the yard.

The grass stood nearly a foot high, and scattered throughout the lawn, yellow dandelions poked their heads above the blades. The landscaping looked unkempt as well.

Tall lilac bushes along both property lines sprouted wild and uneven branches. Overgrown, shapeless yews and boxwoods spread out beneath the bay windows.

"Not the level of lawncare one expects in such a neighborhood," I said.

"Do you think the house is vacant?" Natalie asked. "Abandoned?"

"Or the owners are on vacation somewhere. Or they died in their sleep, and their decaying, rotting corpses are stinking up the house."

"That's gross!" she said with a disgusted look on her face that quickly changed into a grin. "Let's go check!"

She dashed up the driveway, leaving me on the sidewalk.

"Wait! What're you doing? Are you crazy?" I called. It had been *mock* disgust.

I looked up and down Barrington, to see if anybody was about. Seeing no one, I chased after her.

"Shouldn't I get you home? Eric is probably starving!"

Natalie darted around the corner of the house at the end of the drive. I thought I heard an impish laugh as she ran out of sight.

I followed her, stepping onto a flagstone patio. Five tremendous round cement planters stood along the patio's exterior edge, filled with shaggy, dark green arborvitae. Their shadows splayed like spectral fingers of a massive hand upon the patio and rear wall. Two sets of French-style doors opened onto the patio. Natalie stood at the first set, jiggling the handle.

"What are you doing?" I whispered as loudly as I dared. "There could be an alarm! And it's still daylight! What if the people in the house behind see us?"

I looked behind me; a thick ten-foot-high hedge of evergreens ran along the back-property line. I breathed a sigh of relief.

She replied in a similar hushed voice. "Aren't you the least curious to see inside? To see where your dad grew up?"

She moved to the second set of doors. I had been content to look from the street. If the house had looked inhabited, I might have been persuaded to meet the occupants. But I'd never imagined myself doing this.

"A little, yeah," I told her, "but I'd rather not get arrested for trespassing!"

I ran up to her and grasped her wrist just as she grabbed the door handle.

"Don't, please."

She became serious, for a split second, as if considering my plea. Then she batted her eyelashes, and gave that elfin grin.

"If we get caught, I'll tell them you had nothing to do with it."

Using her free hand, she grabbed the handle and turned it. I heard a distinct click. Our eyes widened at the same time. Natalie's mouth transformed into a gaping smile of amazement. She inhaled quickly, and blinked several times.

"Ohmigosh, Frank. It's unlocked!"

"Don't," I told her.

I released her wrist, suddenly feeling odd for having grabbed her. My heartbeat hammered against my ribcage and pounded in my ears.

"Leave it shut, and let's go."

"But now if we get caught, it won't be breaking and entering. It'll just be entering."

Her reasoning didn't convince me, nor did her smile persuade me.

"Here's a thought: let's not do either. This way, if we get caught, we'll only be charged with trespassing."

She tilted her head and raised an eyebrow. "You were the one who said there might be corpses. We could be heroes, and get rewarded by grateful surviving relatives."

"I was only kidding!" I wedged myself between Natalie and the door, preventing her from pulling it open. "What's gotten into you? This is crazy! You have responsibilities. You . . . you have a brother at home, waiting to be fed."

I racked my mind for more reasons to convince her this was a terrible idea.

"The florist needs you to create beautiful arrangements! Your sister needs you to drive her to Fredonia on Wednesday." I placed my hands on her shoulders. "Don't throw your life away! The risk isn't worth it!"

Natalie released the door handle, and her arm fell slack to her side. Her smile vanished, and her bright hazel eyes lost some of their luster. I let go of her shoulders, and we stood in silence for a moment.

She sighed heavily, and spoke. "For the past four years, all I've ever heard is 'You're in charge now, Natalie, time to grow up.' 'Your brother and sisters are relying on you, Natalie, so be responsible.' 'Don't do anything stupid, Natalie, they look up to you.'"

She raised her eyes and looked deep into mine. I saw sadness there, and a flash of resentment.

"You called me noble, in the diner. You have no idea how many times people have told me that. Know what though? I grew up overnight. I was forced to become an adult and parent before I was ready, and I'm sick and tired of being noble."

Her mouth twisted in what looked like frustration. "I'm not asking you to feel sorry for me, or take pity on me. I know there are people in this world who are worse off, and I'm not exempt from having problems. When we complained about stuff, Mom used to say 'And what makes you so special, that you should be exempt from suffering?' But I deserve to do something wild and crazy, just for myself, regardless of the risks, once in a while. Don't I?"

Natalie moved away and sat on the lip of the nearest planter. After making sure the door was closed, I sat next to her.

I understood the suffering part well enough. Dad had been a major source of mine throughout my life, and Mom's battle with cancer had seemed unfair. She'd borne the suffering of ten.

Beyond that, I couldn't relate. Natalie's situation staggered belief. Thrust into the role of raising three people, in the wink of an eye? I couldn't begin to understand that. How much worse it would have been for them if the money hadn't been there. Even with things as they were, financial security provided cold comfort. Nothing could replace the security of a father and mother, and the ability to grow up as any normal nineteen-year-old should.

"I'm sorry for going overboard and being melodramatic," I told her. "I didn't know what else to say."

She gave a sad, sweet smile. "You were fine. I'm the one who needs to apologize. You wanted to share a part of your family history, and I've ruined it for you. I'm grateful, I truly am, and I'm sorry."

*Whaddya know. An apology.*

I smiled back.

"It certainly is a beautiful home," she said.

I looked back at the house, covered in early evening shadows. The vertical blinds in the doorways were turned flat, while dark curtains were drawn across all the windows. A brick and concrete balcony, enclosed by an ornate stone railing, extended from an upstairs room.

"Yes, it is," I agreed. "And under normal circumstances, I'd want to look around inside. I'm intrigued, to be honest. My entire life, I've been told this house no longer existed. To be this close, to be standing in the backyard, is surreal. It's hard to believe."

We sat silently for a few more minutes. Finally, Natalie stood up and smoothed her skirt. "Maybe you should take me home now. Should we lock the door?"

"Good idea." I strode back to the door, turned the tab on the inside doorknob, and pushed the door shut.

We headed back, listening to the crickets chirping from their nestled hiding spots in the lawn. The hum of traffic on East Avenue set a steady, soft background rhythm. Looking up, I noticed a tall, elderly man shuffling towards us on the public sidewalk, carrying a plastic grocery bag in each hand. He stopped at the driveway as we approached.

"Uh oh," Natalie whispered. "The neighborhood watch!" Her comment made me smile.

"G'evening," he said.

He looked to be about eighty. Age spots covered his hands, and his head was a tumbleweed of thin gray hair. He wore an ill-fitting short sleeve brown, tan, and white plaid shirt, tucked into a pair of blue old-man slacks, hiked up to his ribs, and probably a size too short as well.

"Good evening," I said, smiling for good measure.

He jerked a thumb at the house. "You kids moving in?"

Natalie cleared her throat, which sounded more like a stifled laugh, and I shook my head.

"No, we, uh . . ." I tried to think of a plausible explanation as to why we were here. I didn't want to give him the idea we'd been making out behind the house. Or worse. "You see, we were. . ."

Natalie interrupted my stammering.

"My puppy Baxter got away from me! He saw a rabbit, and chased it that way," she said, pointing up the driveway. "We tried catching him, but he squeezed under the bushes into the neighbor's yard. We need to catch him before he gets totally lost."

The man's eyes narrowed a bit, but he nodded, nonetheless.

"You live around here?" I asked.

"In this neighborhood since the mid-twenties," he said, nodding. "Settled here with my wife and her mother. Now this here house was built in 1917, which of course was before I got here, but I knew the family. Quiet Russian folks, I recall, and..."

"Do you know who lives here now?" I asked abruptly. I didn't want a history lesson of the neighborhood, or hear him inadvertently reveal something private about my family.

Natalie tugged at my sleeve. "Frank, we need to get Baxter!" she urged, maintaining the fiction. She cast a desperate look at the old man. Playing along, I patted her hand.

"Nobody right now. Folks moved out three weeks ago or so," he said. "Owner rents it out. Kinda wish he'd clean up the yard."

"Who owns it?" If he knew the owner, I'd know who to ask for permission to look around. Legitimately.

"Far as I recollect, the owner lives in Pennsylvania. Man named Vic Steppenoff."

*　*　*

After tearing ourselves away from the elderly man to 'find' Baxter, I turned the car around to head north. Natalie waved to the old man while my brain raced. As we wound through the downtown streets, eventually reaching Mt. Hope Avenue, one question kept repeating itself. Why hadn't Uncle Pietr told me that Viktor still owned the house?

Maybe he didn't know. Maybe he thought Viktor had sold it. He had to have known Viktor owned it, since it would have been bequeathed to him in the will. So why tell me the address, but not tell me who owned it? What was it with this family and all these damn secrets? It couldn't all be attributed to dignity, old-world customs, and traditions, could it?

"You're pretty quiet," Natalie said. "I hope you're not angry with me."

Her voice pulled me back to the present, and I gave her a friendly smile. "I'm not mad. I mean, the whole breaking and entering thing was unexpected, so yeah, that threw me. I just got a lot on my mind, that's all."

She nodded. "Stuff get stirred up, seeing the house?"

"You could say that."

"It's kinda how life goes," she said. "Nothing ever stays settled. Not for long, at least. Things calm down, and then whoosh! Everything goes crazy. Life gets complicated all over again, and between trying to figure out up from down and right from left, you hope it settles back down to some sort of normal. All the while trying to make sense of what the hell just happened."

I nodded. She had pretty much described my recent life.

"And you feel paralyzed," she continued. "Afraid if you take the wrong step, or say the wrong word, *whoosh!* all over again."

She stared out her window, as we drove by the Mt Hope Cemetery. Beyond the black iron fence stood rows of tombstones, interspersed with small mausoleums and stone statues of angels and crucifixes. Mom was buried there, and I suspected Natalie's parents were, too. The last rays of the sun caught her reflection in the window. Her eyes were dark and full of anguish. It occurred to me that she had just described every moment of her life since her parents' death.

She turned to face me, the worn out, faraway look suddenly replaced with a warm smile, and she placed her hand on my arm.

"For what it's worth, thanks again for going to the concert with me. And for the pie. I had fun. And I appreciate you taking me to your dad's home. I hope I didn't ruin it for you."

"You didn't," I assured her. "I had fun too, in spite not being able to find Baxter."

She gave my arm a gentle squeeze. "Maybe next time."

We crossed Elmwood Avenue, the cemetery now behind us, and drove past the Strong Memorial Hospital complex. On my left was a small strip mall, and I noticed a small floral shop called Flower City Florist nestled between an insurance agency and a local pizzeria.

"That's your florist?" I asked, pointing out my window.

"Yup. I'm there eleven to six, Monday through Friday, and every other Saturday.

The signal at the next intersection turned red. Out of the corner of my eye, I saw Natalie kneading her fingers in her lap, working them over like stiff dough. She attempted to stifle a laugh, but it came out as a series of snorts.

"What's so funny?" I asked.

Natalie placed her hand to her mouth, and the lines around her eyes deepened and seemed to intensify. "I just remembered . . ." she snickered twice, "At O'Shea's. When Ned serenaded you?" Her snickers evolved into chuckles. "He was so funny."

I chuckled along with her. "Yeah, Ned's the life of every party."

"He got the whole bar to sing along." The chuckles had grown into a fit of laughter. "You were so embarrassed." She wiped away a runaway tear.

"It happens more often than I care to admit. Embarrassing me is one of Ned's incredible talents."

"And then when Jessica kissed you, you turned even redder." She wiped both eyes, and dried her fingers with her sweater. Taking a deep breath to calm herself down, she said, "She means a lot to you, doesn't she?"

"Jessica? I guess so. Known her since forever. Been friends a long time."

"Like, serious friends?"

The light turned green.

"Just really good friends. She's like a little sister to me."

"Little sisters kiss their big brothers like that where you come from? There's a word for that, you know."

I let out a laugh. "She drank too much, and got carried away. Nothing more than that."

I shot her a wry look, and paused half a beat. "What about you and Don?"

Natalie rolled her eyes. "So not my type. He's persistent, I'll give him that much. He's left five messages this week. He even called yesterday, asking me to meet him at O'Shea's last night. Said the whole gang would be there. Did you go?"

I turned right onto her street, and shook my head.

"There's something weird about you and your friends," she said.

"What do you mean?"

"It's like that old Sesame Street song, about one thing being different and not really belonging? Three head bangers and a music snob?"

"We grew up in the same neighborhood, attended the same schools. I went on to college, and they didn't."

"Or couldn't?"

I shrugged. "Or whatever. We make each other laugh, and we have fun together. My going off to college didn't change anything. We're best friends. You have best friends, don't you?"

Natalie gave a small smile that looked painful to make, and turned away. "Oh look!" she immediately said. "Valerie's home early."

A tan Buick Riviera sat parked halfway up the driveway between Natalie's house and the neighbors. It looked new.

My question had touched a nerve, clearly. Then again, I resented her insinuation that my friends were somehow beneath me. Ned and the others might be blue collar, middle class average Joe's, but that didn't matter to me. Did it matter to her? Born into a well-to-do family, she'd lacked for nothing her entire life, even before getting the windfall from a wrongful death lawsuit. Private universities, parochial schools, better than average neighborhood; those things had always been part of her life, and she'd made sure her siblings had them in the aftermath of their parents' death. The same privileges, the same opportunities. The possessions and lifestyle were her touchstones, her way of keeping their memory vibrant.

I began to suspect she didn't have much else.

Natalie knew her legacy, had intimate contact with it, and preserved continuity with her history. I had thought I was the same, until recently. Everything I'd thought was true about my family and my heritage had become dismantled: my father's past, his family's life, secrets known and unknown. I was relearning my legacy and history, while she preserved hers. Given the choice, I would have preferred a different journey.

I was sure Natalie felt the same.

Before stepping out of the car, she asked, "Do you have time to come inside?"

For a second, I felt that my judgement of her had been correct. She was just a lonely kid wanting friendship.

"Sure," I answered.

"Good. You can prove you know how to play *Rhapsody in Blue*." She looked like the cat who swallowed the canary.

# CHAPTER 24

The refrain of Bon Jovi's *You Give Love A Bad Name* greeted us as we entered the house. Eric was sprawled out on the couch, eyes glued to the television that stood across from the piano. Jon Bon Jovi and Ritchie Sambora obnoxiously pranced about in the blaring music video. The big hair, the leather pants, the exaggerated expressions – they were all cringe-worthy. An empty white dinner plate lay on the rug, a crumpled cloth napkin draped across it.

"Got your note," Eric grunted. He kept his eyes glued to the TV as we stepped into the living room. "And you're late."

"Eric, this is my friend Frank Stephens. Frank, Eric."

"How's it going, man?"

He barely moved, muttering a gruff 'Hi' in my general direction.

"MTV, huh?" I asked.

He perked up a bit, taking a half second to glance my way. "First single from their new album. Bon Jovi rocks."

A silver Magnavox VHS videocassette player and the cable converter box sat on top of the TV. A haphazard stack of videocassettes stood next to it on the floor, *St Elmo's Fire* on top.

There came a loud click, and the screen went blank. Bon Jovi vanished from sight. Eric quickly sat up, and glowered at Natalie, who held the remote control in her hand.

"Hey! I was watching that!"

"Frank here is the son of a famous composer," she told him, as if that explained everything. "He's going to play something on the piano for me."

Eric's face expressed total indifference. She could have told him my dad had cured cancer, and he wouldn't have cared.

"Whatever," he scowled, peeling himself off the couch. "I'll be in my room."

"Plate!" Natalie reminded him. His scowl deepened as he snatched it off the floor, and then stomped the entire way into the kitchen. I heard some clattering, followed by more stomping through the kitchen, which then led to additional stomping up the stairs.

"He's got big feet," I whispered to Natalie.

"They match his attitude," she said. "He's in the middle of two-a-days for football, so I'm trying to cut him some slack."

An upstairs door slammed shut, after which she motioned towards the piano.

"Right. Time to put your money where your mouth is."

Natalie opened the hinged bench and dug out *Rhapsody in Blue*. I immediately recognized it as the same edition I had used to learn the piece, written for two pianos. She offered it to me while I took a seat on the black, glossy bench.

"No thanks," I said. "Which section would you like me to play, 1st Piano or 2nd Piano?"

1st Piano was for the piano, while 2nd Piano was the arrangement based on the orchestral score.

"You know both?" she asked, her tone half astonishment, and half disbelief.

"What, doesn't everybody?" After a pause of several seconds, I decided, "1st Piano."

She set the open book on the music rack, but I took it down.

"Not necessary," I told her, handing it back. "You hold it while I play, and read along."

Natalie slowly took it from me, and stepped back. I felt her vision drilling into the back of my head.

"In fact, let's make this fun. You pick."

"You mean, pick the measure?" she asked.

"Sure. Give me the page, line, and measure, and that's

where I'll begin."

As I adjusted the bench to a comfortable position, and tested the pedal action, I smiled to myself. I had played this game with college classmates many times.

"Okay, here we go. Page fourteen, line four, second measure."

I set my hands upon the keyboard and closed my eyes, picturing the score in my head. Every note, slur, bar line, staff, accidental, trill, and dynamic marking came into focus, crisp and crystal clear. Pages turned in my mind until I reached the spot Natalie had chosen. My eyes dropped down to the fourth line, then across to the second measure. My hands floated above the keys, fingertips lightly brushing them, adjusting for sharps and flats. My left hand slid farther down the bass clef, my right hand positioned itself for a chromatic scale . . .

"Wait," I announced, eyes snapping open. "That measure's for 2nd Piano. I think you meant page fifteen."

And with that, I made a final adjustment, took a breath, and played. She had chosen a spot near the beginning of the second solo section, a smooth, melodic passage featuring difficult chord progressions and numerous crossovers. Part jazz, part classical, part blues, completely American. My hands traveled up and down the keyboard, striking with precision and certainty, the melody bursting with pathos and emotion, the harmony supportive and ascending. The tempo swelled and ebbed like a summer's breeze, just enough to cool the heat, but not enough to produce a chill.

"Holy crap," Natalie whispered, and I grinned.

After a few more measures, she patted my shoulder. I stopped in the middle of a cross-over arpeggio passage.

"Okay, okay," she said. "Challenge met. I'm duly impressed. A bit show off-y, but still." She placed the score on the rack. "But you studied trumpet in college."

"First chair, with honors," I replied. "I did take piano lessons for a couple years, though. I taught myself this during winter break one year in college."

"A couple years?" Natalie sounded amazed. "I took fifteen years of lessons, and I couldn't do what you just did."

"And I quit before the age of nine." Before she could respond, I quickly added: "Hey, sit down. I've got an idea."

I slid leftward, in front of the lower octaves. She glanced at me warily, then joined me on the bench. I grabbed the score, and opened it to the section I had in mind.

"This is a duet for two pianos, Frank, not one."

"This part we'll play on one piano with two hands. Your left, my right."

I placed the book on the music stand, and pointed to the intended measures.

"Start from that G chord, second position. Join in after I play a couple pick-up measures. Got it?"

Natalie shifted a bit, leaving a few inches between us.

"You have to sit closer for this to work," I said.

"Like this?" Her shoulder gently nudged my arm, and she dropped her hand into position on the keyboard.

"Perfect," I answered, following suit. "Ready?"

As written, the long section required the pianist to cross their right hand over to play the melody in the octave below middle C, while the left hand played a progression of chords directly above it. For our duet, we played the notes as indicated, our hands side by side. In several spots, though, my right hand needed to cross over Natalie's left to play upper octave responses.

It took us several times to perfect, and after each failed attempt, either she would laugh, or I would continue with a quick improvisation. On the sixth try, we played through without a hitch, and played it several times after. Any time my fingertips brushed the top of her hand as I was reaching for the higher keys, I noticed she increased her tempo, and I had to catch up.

Finally, she said, "Y'know, I have a book of duets in the bench, if you'd like to play a couple."

I said yes.

✻ ✻ ✻

My telephone started ringing as soon as I unlocked my apartment door. I answered it halfway through the third ring, knowing that only one person would be calling me at 9:00 on a Sunday evening.

"Frank, it's Fanny."

"Oh. Hey." I wasn't disappointed to hear her voice. Sooner or later we would have spoken; fortunately, she called me first, instead of the other way around. This way I felt surer her anger had died down. If I had called her before she felt ready to talk, the conversation would have been awkward and uncomfortable. Even if I started it with 'I'm sorry for being a jerk.'

"Listen, I visited Dad today, and his doctor wanted me to let you know that you're cleared to see him whenever you want."

"It hasn't been two weeks."

I took a seat on the couch, Natalie's copy of Volume 1 still in my hand. I waited for her to follow up with additional information, or some sort of sarcastic remark. Nothing.

"Did he say why?" I asked, hoping our conversation wouldn't turn into a tedious game of Twenty Questions.

"He said Dad recovered well from last week's episode, and that if you don't show him the songs again, we'd avoid another clusterfuck."

"He didn't say that. I happen to know that's not a medical term."

"That's what he meant," she retorted.

Dad's violent outburst after seeing Clara's songs, and his subsequent attempt to injure me, remained seared in my mind. Being pinned down and strapped to the bed, then sedated, certain he had failed his Clara, was the clear definition of clusterfuck. If that wasn't, I didn't know what was. Dad had the benefit, if it could be called that, of being unable to recall what had happened. Not me.

"How was he today?"

"Same-ish? Saying much less. Still called me Louise, asked about Fanny." She paused. "I tell him what's going on, but in third person. It's weird, really weird. He remembers some things, like kneeling and saying 'Amen' when he receives Holy Communion, but stuff I wish he'd remember, like my name? It's like his brain is a houseful of pitch-black rooms, with every light socket empty, with the electricity shut off."

After another long pause, I said: "Listen, Fan, about the other night..."

"It's okay," she interrupted.

"Really? Cos I can tell you're still kinda angry."

"Alright, it's not okay. Yes, I'm angry with you. I'm angry at a lot of things, at a lot of people. Life's coming at me from every side, angle, and direction."

"I know. Mike spoke to me, and I'm sorry for throwing a bowling ball at you."

Fanny snickered. "He's so cute. He told me what he said."

"He called you a clown."

"That didn't go unnoticed," Fanny said. "This has been hard on him, too. I'm not an easy person to live with, you know."

"You don't say."

"And as if all this wasn't enough..." Her voice trailed off, and after a couple seconds, she whispered: "I found out last week we're pregnant."

I blinked several times. This came out of left field. "Really? Congratulations, Fan! Right? Congrats?"

"I think so? I mean, we weren't trying to get pregnant, but we weren't *not* trying, either. You know what I mean?"

I had no clue what she meant. How does a couple *try* and *not try* to get pregnant, at the same time?

"Not really, but if you say so? Is it when a mommy and a daddy share a special hug, and afterward, a baby grows in..."

"Shut up!" Fanny said. I detected a slight smile in her voice. "I mean, we want a bigger family, and we're open to kids. We just timed it wrong. But with what's going on right now . . ."

"Not the best?"

"It's one more thing, Frankie."

I relaxed. Her calling me 'Frankie' was a sign that her anger had cooled. I reclined into the back cushions, feeling the tension ebb away.

"I'm happy we're having another baby, don't get me wrong," she continued. "But with all this stress - Dad, selling the house, you being unemployed, Clara's songs - it'll be harder to enjoy. I don't know. All shall be well, and all manner of things shall be well."

"Mom used to say that."

"I still do."

Her response gave me pause. I wasn't shocked in hearing it, since Fanny had always been more religious than me. But in that split second, I recalled Mom's faith, and wondered what else it had carried her through beyond just a losing battle with cancer.

"Look at it this way," I said. "Maybe pregnancy will make all that stressful stuff easier to handle."

"Look at you, all wise and smart and stuff," Fanny teased. "Who are you, and what are you doing in my brother's apartment?"

I laughed. "I've always been wise and smart. You just never acknowledge it."

"Wise ass and smart aleck don't count." Fanny suddenly gasped. "Speaking of wise and smart, you had your date with Natalie today! Tell me about it!"

"It wasn't a date," I corrected her. "It was just a thing."

"Ohhhh riiiiight, a thing. Where she set up an elaborate trap involving a fake friend to win an argument, unaware you had a plan to neutralize her trap by fake falling for her trap, plus some 'I know she knows I know, but what she doesn't know I know' gobbledygook, and at the end you fall in love.

That kinda thing?"

"Like I said, not a date," I said, ignoring her synopsis. "A concert followed by pie and coffee at George's, and then we played a little piano at her house."

*Now wasn't the time to tell her about Dad's childhood home.*

"What's the house like?" she asked.

I bolted upright, sucked in my breath. "What?" I asked, trying to mask the nervousness in my voice.

"Natalie's house. What's it like?"

Exhaling with relief, I settled back. "Oh. Nice, I guess. Lots of books, she lives near Strong Memorial, they've got cable, she has a Mason & Hamlin..."

"A grand?" she interjected.

"Model A baby grand from the 30's."

"Ooh, fancy schmancy. She sounds rich. So playing a little piano at her house, was that really about playing the piano, or a euphemism for making out?"

"What?"

"You know. Were you tickling her ivories? Pushing her pedals?"

"Fanny!"

"Playing a duet, four hands, no piano?" She giggled.

"Okay, you can stop now. Nothing happened. Nothing more than a pleasant non-date." I felt myself turning red.

She continued laughing, not listening to anything I said.

"Were you Mozarting her Chopin?"

"What does that even mean??"

"I have no idea, but it sounds so dirty, doesn't it?"

I took a deep breath to regain my composure. "Who knew pregnancy made you so vulgar."

"Pregnancy has nothing to do with it," Fanny said. "I just like embarrassing you."

"Congratulations. You succeeded."

"As expected. I'm glad your date . . ."

"Non-date," I corrected.

"...your *date* with Natalie turned out well. What else did

you do?"

"You know how you lent me Volume 2 of those letters?"

"Yes, be patient. I'm still looking for Volume 1."

"Don't bother," I told her. "Natalie let me borrow her copy."

"Aw, how sweet," Fanny said, her voice heavy with charm. "She clearly adores you and wants to see you again."

I let her remark slide by, and changed the topic. The more I engaged in her teasing, the more likely something I'd later regret would slip out.

"How did the open house go yesterday?"

"The realtor said a dozen people walked through. A couple expressed mild interest, but no one went gaga over it. I don't know about today. I'm hoping someone buys it on the spot. One less stress to deal with." She paused for a moment. "So when will you go see Daddy?"

"You sure you want me to?"

"Yes. Just go and be with him. Watch TV. Sit in silence. It doesn't really matter."

"If it doesn't really matter..."

"He's still your dad," she interjected. "And it makes me feel better knowing that somebody's with him, that he's alone a little bit less. Now, when will you go?"

"I don't know," I told her. "Ned wants to practice every day, the show is Friday night, and then there's the barbecue at Uncle Pietr's on Saturday."

"I'm sure you can spare a couple hours from garage banding," Fanny said. "You probably know the songs better than they do, anyway."

She had a point. "I suppose I can go Wednesday afternoon."

"Good. Oh, and Whitney invited us to the barbecue."

"Told ya."

"I never doubted you about the party," Fanny said. "I only doubted your intentions when you told me. Big difference."

Suddenly, loud, high-pitched, unintelligible shrieking

came over the line, followed by a crash, and what sounded like Rachel crying.

"Oh crap!" Fanny exclaimed. "I gotta run! See you later!" She yelled out Mike's name while hanging up.

"See you Saturday," I said to no one, and hung up. Three kids, huh? It seemed to me that two were a handful. I was happy for them, though, and it meant becoming an uncle for the third time.

Her insistence on me going to visit Dad confused me. Just be with him? It seemed a waste of time, but if it made her feel better, then I'd do it. I owed her at least that much.

I picked up the book Natalie gave me, and started flipping through it. This volume covered 1853 through 1876. At this time, Brahms was just coming into his own, and had recently been befriended by the Schumanns. As I read through several of the letters, I noticed how Brahms' love shone through. It was a chaste, platonic love, but love, nonetheless. He had felt deep affection for her, being careful not to cause any scandal, and always considerate of her husband's failing health.

Anyone with a heart, though, could tell he had been head-over-heels for her. Just as anyone with ears to listen could tell that Dad had been equally devoted to his Clara. A week had passed since discovering the songs, and I hadn't learned much at all about Clara. Would I ever find out who she was? I had read the songs numerous times, front to back, and played them on the keyboard. Uncle Pietr had suggested that the songs might reveal her identity, but they hadn't.

What those songs had done, though, was tell me a lot about Dad. They had shone a light upon unknown family history. They were also his legacy, a sort of last will and testament. He may have shut me out of his life long ago, but they nonetheless had fallen to me. Blind luck? Fate? Was there a reason why I had found Clara's songs, and I simply hadn't discovered it yet?

Something in the back of my mind nagged at me, as if I had overlooked something. I closed my eyes to concentrate, fo-

247

cusing on what I knew, on what I had learned. A stray, isolated thread lay unattended in the weave that formed this tapestry of Dad's past. If I could find that thread, and follow its course, it might lead me closer to the truth.

I leaned back against the cushions, thinking, replaying the events and conversations from the past week. Dad's episode. The conversation with Gregory. The dinner with Uncle Pietr and Aunt Jane. Talking with Jacoby on his front porch. The arguments with Fanny. I listened for possible neglected clues or details.

A recurring image kept intruding: the memory of Natalie, perched upon her rolling ladder. Despite repeated attempts to dispel it, the picture returned. Why, though? She had absolutely nothing to do with Clara.

But before I could locate that elusive thread, sleep overtook me, and I dreamed of letters, homes, and duets.

# CHAPTER 25

Wednesday morning announced its arrival with an avalanche of thunder, rattling my apartment's windowpanes, and waking me up. It rumbled across the sky like a passing retinue of kettle drums, the reverberations dying off in the distance.

I rolled onto my back, listening to the rain splatter the roof and windows, and sighed. No bike ride today.

A flash of lightning illuminated my bedroom, immediately followed by another crash of thunder, echoing within my ribcage. This one sounded as if it were directly overhead.

I had a feeling today would be one of those days.

The past two days had been perfect: bright blue skies, gentle breezes, no humidity. Both days, I'd biked over twenty-five miles in the morning, followed by Toehead practice for three to four hours. My part in the band was sounding better with each passing day, as we fine-tuned each song's settings, and which effects could be used without ruining the sound.

Lightning lit up my room again, and the resounding thunderclap made it clear no further sleeping would be done. With a groan and a loud yawn, I swung my feet off the edge of the bed and sat up.

I recalled Sunday night's phone call with Fanny. It had been a strange combination of anger, joy, grace, and banter. Things weren't entirely resolved, but the call had ended on a much better note than Thursday's dinner. The tension would soon return, though. Plenty of things remained to be talked about, secrets and histories that needed to be hashed out.

Saturday's barbecue would be the next time we'd be together, but I had no intention of talking about Dad's past, or Clara, there. Nor would I confront Uncle Pietr about Uncle Viktor still owning the old house. That could wait for a private conversation. It would be best just to go to the party, play golf with the guys, smoke a cigar, enjoy a cognac, and leave Dad and Clara at home.

The storm continued to flash and crash, dropping rain in torrents. As I shuffled towards the kitchen, the phone rang.

"Franklin!" It was Ned. "Listen, Joey's canceled practice. His ma's got him doing stuff around the house. Hope it doesn't break your heart."

"Devastated," I replied. "Still on for tomorrow?"

"Hell yeah," and after a few minutes of chatter, we exchanged *Later dude*'s, and hung up.

*Looks like I'm seeing Dad sooner rather than later.*

* * *

The Mellowood entrance doors glided open as I ran up to escape the heavy downpour. The rain hadn't let up, though the lightning and thunder had ended. Imogene huddled behind the counter. Her permanent frown deepened into an exasperated glare upon seeing me come in.

As I signed in, she growled, "Don't cause any problems today."

Yep, she remembered me. If posters of my face had been plastered throughout the office area, warning that I was a known troublemaker, I wouldn't have been shocked.

"I'll do my best, ma'am," I told her.

"Let's pray it's enough," she replied, scowling. Such a ray of pure sunshine.

She buzzed me in, and I headed towards Dad's room. Residents shuffled down the hallway towards me, some led by their aides, others using walkers and canes, a few in wheelchairs. I weaved my way through and past them, offering smiles and uttering frequent 'excuse me's'. A nurse stood at the central station, surveying the scene like a field general. She saw me approach.

"Just in time for the lunch rush," she told me. "You're Ivan's boy, right?"

"Yeah, that's me." I recognized her from my last visit. Estelle.

"I remember you," Estelle said, pointing at me. "No surprises today. Right?"

I held up my hands in a plea of innocence. "No surprises."

"He's still in his room. If you want, you can take him to the cafeteria and eat with him. Hang on." She rifled through her desk, and then handed me an orange ticket. "Here's a voucher, in case you want to join him."

I took it from her. Being with him in his room or in the cafeteria made no difference to me.

The crowd had thinned at this point. Dad's door was open halfway, but I rapped several times before entering.

"Dad? You decent? It's Frank."

Dad sat on the edge of the bed, staring out the window. He didn't acknowledge me. I came to the bed and stood off to his right, within his field of vision. He continued looking out into the courtyard; rainwater streamed down the window, distorting the image beyond. I cleared my throat. No reaction.

"It's lunch time," I said. "You hungry?"

Dad gave a slow nod. He turned his head towards me, and for a split second, an expression that almost resembled recognition flashed in his tired eyes, but it passed as quickly as it appeared.

Dad seemed noticeably more lethargic today compared to my previous visit, as if he were heavily medicated. Fanny had managed a conversation with him on Sunday, or at least an occasional word. It didn't appear that would be happening today. I considered introducing myself as Felix, to see how he'd react, but changed my mind. Misleading him didn't seem right.

His haggard face had been roughly shaved, but his thinning, unruly hair hadn't been combed. He wore clean clothes - a blue golf shirt and tan slacks, with slippers on his feet.

"Well, we can't have you going to the cafeteria looking like you just rolled out of bed," I said, standing up.

His hairbrush lay on the nightstand, and as I reached for it, I quickly glanced at a framed achievement award hanging on the wall nearby. It commemorated the inaugural performance of his first symphony, from 1948. It had hung in his conservatory for decades, and I'd never thought much of it while growing up. I peered at it now, noticing that the ending of his last name had been covered with White Out. What had once been *Stepanov* now read *Stephens*. The change could be seen only if scrutinized up close.

I felt anger and resentment begin to swell, as I thought about what might have been if Dad's pride hadn't destroyed his relationship with Grandpa. So much would have been different for our family if he had never fallen in love with Clara in the first place. Her existence hung over our family like a curse, and I started wishing I had never found those songs. It's said that ignorance is bliss. I believed it, because up until now, knowledge had brought me nothing but strife and aggravation. I turned to look at Dad. He was still staring at the rain coating the window like liquid gauze.

*You sure screwed up, Dad. And you don't even realize it anymore.*

Ignorance was bliss indeed.

I took a deep breath, counted to five, and picked up the brush.

"How will you impress the ladies with your hair all messy, right?" I tried to sound cheery, but anyone nearby would have heard bitterness in my voice.

After brushing his hair, I said, "Much better. C'mon, let's go."

I held out my hand to help him up, and he grabbed it. Still no recognition or reaction. Whatever his eyes saw, his brain failed to register. It seemed his brain's connections and neural pathways were barely functioning, if at all.

*His brain is a houseful of pitch-black rooms, with every light socket empty, with the electricity shut off.*

Taking him by the elbow, I guided him with slow, deliberate steps to the cafeteria. Before reaching the locked security doors at the end of the hallway, we turned right down the side corridor. The community room door stood open, and I sneaked a peek inside as we shuffled past. Against the far wall stood a maple old upright piano. The keys were exposed, the cover slid back into its cavity. It looked like a Baldwin. A brown leather couch stood next to the piano; an elderly woman still wearing her nightgown sat quietly, perhaps asleep. She appeared to be alone in the room. Positioned about were armchairs around low tables; an abandoned, incomplete puzzle covered one tabletop. Dad and I continued by.

The cafeteria reminded me a lot of high school: food was served at one end of the room, a herd of round tables was gathered in the middle, and a squad of tall square wheeled racks near the doorway. The slots were half-filled with trays full of empty dishes, silverware, and partially eaten meals.

The sounds of silverware scraping against the heavy plates, the occasional screech of a chair being dragged across the linoleum, and the noise of food preparation and chatter coming from the kitchen were the only noises in the room. No one spoke, save for one man who was seated by himself, and holding a conversation with an unseen person seated next to him. He made convincing, emphatic points with his fork. I escorted Dad to a table away from him, closer to the food line.

"I'll get our food," I told him as he sat down.

The lunch choices were roast beef and gravy with mashed potatoes, or a version of chicken piccata that looked as if it had been dredged through Quikrete and fried in motor oil. Dad had always been a red meat man, so I chose the roast beef and added green beans, a roll with butter, and a bowl of limp butterscotch pudding. I chose the same for myself. I poured two glasses of water, carried both trays over to our table, and sat.

I attempted small talk during lunch, which resembled a cross between a news report and a monologue, as I added commentary on our food.

"I saw Fanny, Mike, and the kids last week. Everybody's healthy, and the kids are great. Rachel and Justin are taking piano lessons, did you know that?" A bite of roast beef. "What do you think of the beef? Not bad for shoe leather, eh? Anyway, the school laid me off. No money for band programs this year." A forkful of potatoes. "Thank God for gravy, huh? Helps soften the corners on those lumps. Anyway, looking for work. I joined a rock band. Remember Ned Kerrigan? He and some friends have a band, and they've asked me to play keyboards."

At the mention of keyboards, Dad's head ticked to one side. He didn't say anything, but something had registered.

"We have a gig Friday night at Rooster's Rockhouse. It's nothing long-term by any means, just something to make a little cash." An attempt at some green beans. "Wow, the beans are...special. Be easier eating them with a straw. Oh yeah, almost forgot. Pietr and Jane are hosting a barbecue this weekend. They both look good. Pietr said he's going to come see you soon."

Dad had finished the roast beef and potatoes, and had moved onto the beans. I glanced around the room, and caught the eye of a lady sitting at a nearby table with an elderly woman, presumably her mother. She looked to be in her mid-forties, and she smiled at me. I saw sadness in her eyes, or maybe pity. We exchanged the reassuring look people in hopeless situations give one another. I smiled knowingly in return, then looked back at Dad, as he tore his dinner roll in half.

"Other than that, not much else going on," I concluded.

I glanced at the woman again; she had moved closer to her mom, and her left arm was draped across her back, helping her eat. Immediately, an image of Mom appeared in my head, and I became eight years old again, and felt her comforting, consoling hand upon my shoulder.

"You two were made for each other," Mom said.

"I don't know what that means." I laid upon my bed, face turned towards the wall. Her hand rubbed my back.

"It means you are so very alike. Like two peas in a pod."

"I'm not mean like he's mean," I told her. "He's mad I don't play piano anymore, but why should I take lessons when that makes him mad, too?" I wiped my nose with a corner of my pillow-case.

"That's a good question." Her hand stopped moving. "But I think your father is more disappointed than angry. And you can't be mad at him forever."

I blinked away some stray tears. "I can't?"

"No, love." The caressing resumed. "At some point, you'll need to forgive him."

I turned around to face her. "Why? He hasn't said sorry."

She smiled warmly, as if expecting that answer. "If we waited for apologies, no one would ever forgive anybody." Her gaze shifted to the crucifix hung above my bedroom door. "He never would've forgiven us, right?"

I remembered Sister Rita talking in Religion class, telling us that Jesus asked God to forgive those who nailed him to the cross. And they never said sorry or anything.

"What I'm saying, is that forgiveness doesn't excuse the hurtful things. It doesn't mean they were okay. It especially doesn't mean they didn't hurt. It simply means we make room in here," and she tapped me on the chest, "for love to grow."

I scowled a little, and Mom's warm smile returned.

"Forgiveness is very hard. But the more we do it, the easier it gets, little by little. If you can't now, I understand. He understands." She glanced back at the crucifix.

"I don't think I can right now."

"I know. So what should you do?" She gave me an expectant look.

I took a deep breath. "All will be well, in all manner of things all will be well."

Her look changed into a smile, and she stood up. "I'm sorry

you can't join us." She headed to the door.

"Mom?"

"Yes, love?" she replied, stopping in the doorway, turning towards me.

"Did you ever forgive someone when they didn't say sorry?"

She glanced back over her shoulder, into the hallway, perhaps down the stairs, then turned back. "Oh yes. It was the hardest thing I've ever had to do."

I cast a long, thoughtful look at Dad, then placed my hand on his shoulder. We finished our lunch in silence.

As we left the cafeteria, an inspiration struck me. I casually steered him into the community room.

"Let's pop in here for a minute, okay?"

His eyes narrowed a bit as I led him in, but he remained silent as we made our way to the Baldwin. I brought Dad over, and pulled out the stool.

"Come on, sit down," I encouraged him.

He blinked a few times, his face full of confusion. His eyes showed doubt and uncertainty. I hadn't expected this. Last Sunday, he'd complained about his imaginary piano being out for repairs. Now he looked as though he had never seen a piano before.

"Give me a second," I told him, patting him on the shoulder,

Several stacks of green-cushioned chairs, nestled within one another, lined the wall. I grabbed one and placed it to the left of the stool. After sitting down, I motioned for Dad to sit on the stool. He remained standing.

"C'mon, Dad, you know what this is. A piano?" I played a C chord progression: tonic, fourth, back to tonic, fifth, and concluded with the tonic. "Remember?"

He slowly licked his lips, cocking his head a couple degrees. I could tell he struggled to recall, unsure and undecided. It took him several seconds to make up his mind, but he finally sat down, slouched and still uncertain.

I didn't know what to do next, whether to play a song

he'd recognize, or somehow get him to play one. The stack of song books might provide a passable song, but something personal would be better.

Out of the corner of my eye, I noticed several residents standing at the door, curious looks on their faces. My chord progression must have gained their attention. I didn't want Dad to see the gathering audience, lest it make him nervous. I had no idea what would happen should he start to play. Would he react like he had last Sunday? Would he get violent, and hurt himself? Hurt me? Or would it spark memories from better days?

He reached out with a tentative right hand, lightly tapping the white keys with his index and middle fingers. He rubbed his chin and cheeks with his other hand, a tenacious look in his eyes. I recognized that look. Uncle Pietr had described it as his way of working through a problem, sifting, churning. Dad was wrestling with this puzzle, and he needed my help to get the answer.

I started humming a melody in an abstract, nonchalant way, a tune I knew he'd recognize. It was a waltz he'd composed decades ago, titled *The Little Snow Girl*, based on a Russian fable. Fanny had loved this song, and she'd dance around the dining room table as he played, demanding he play it again and again until she could dance no longer.

My humming transitioned into soft singing, loud enough for Dad to hear, yet low enough so the audience wouldn't notice. As I sang, Dad's posture changed. His frail shoulders straightened. He seemed to grow three inches. The determined look in his face softened, and his hand fell from his face, landing at the exact position on the keyboard. With perfectly curved fingers and fluid wrists, Dad accompanied my singing.

The woefully out of tune piano sounded tinny, but the music was spectacular. I closed my eyes, and I saw Fanny twirling about the house, her face beaming with glee. Dad played flawlessly, and soon I stopped singing. I glanced at him, and his face had transformed, as the years and cares of his present life fell away. His eyes were bright with joy, and a broad smile stretched from cheek to cheek. He swayed with the lilting tempo, and his hands bounced across the keys. *The Little Snow Girl* had come back to life after twenty some odd years.

I looked back at the doorway. What had been an audience of maybe four people had grown to ten, perhaps more. Most were residents, along with a couple aides, too. They inched into the room; two residents, a man and a woman, had sat down in nearby armchairs. I turned back to Dad. He showed no sign of stopping anytime.

Then, in the midst of playing, he turned towards me.

"Play with me, Felix."

My heart seemed to turn to lead, and drop onto my spleen. He didn't see me as Felix Mendelssohn, as he had before. He saw me as his son, as his Felix, a nickname he hadn't used in twenty odd years. A lump formed in my throat, but I forced a smile, and shifted my seat closer to the keyboard.

Without missing a beat or misplaying a note, each of his hands jumped up an octave, allowing me room on the bass clef. Dad had originally written the song as a solo piece, meaning that I would have to improvise. That wouldn't be a problem, and perhaps Dad had known that, somewhere deep inside. Were memories of the home parties resurfacing, when I'd performed for his guests, or the time I had played variations of Schumann for Gregory? Those thoughts cycled through my mind; perhaps they returned for him as well.

When the song returned to the main theme, I started to play. It took all of my concentration to hold back the emotion of the moment. We had never played a duet. Ever. Feelings of happiness, remorse, astonishment, and enjoyment coursed through me. At one point, our eyes met. The man looking back at me wasn't the same man who had eaten lunch with me in stoic, unmindful silence. Nor was it the same man from whom I had been estranged for most of my life.

He had become Ivan Stepanov again.

We continued playing for several more minutes until a thick, firm hand clamped down on my shoulder. I suddenly stopped with a crash of discordant notes, which caused Dad to stop as well. I looked up into Estelle's stern face.

"And what do you think you're doing?" she asked. "I had told you, no surprises."

Behind her were close to two dozen people. Many more had entered the room, unbeknown to me, while we had played, taking seats on the couches, or leaning against the walls. They shared expressions of awkwardness and discomfort, knowing I was about to be dressed down. Many cast their gaze at anything other than the three of us at the piano. I looked back at Estelle. She had asked an obvious question, but I couldn't be arrogant or flippant. Not this time.

"I thought Dad might like to play your piano," I told her.

"Well, I'm sorry Mr. Stephens, but you can't just bring your father in here and sit him down without proper permission. There are rules."

Estelle had released my shoulder, and now stood with her hands on her hips.

"Whose permission?" I asked, getting to my feet.

"His physician's, and when he's not here, mine." She jabbed a thumb into her chest. "And I didn't give you no permission to play the piano."

I pointed to my father. "But you saw what it did. You saw his reaction, didn't you?"

Her stony expression told me she wouldn't be persuaded.

"Look at the audience," I continued. "They certainly appreciated it."

"It ain't a question of being appreciated," Estelle said. "It's a question of following the rules, and Ivan doesn't have permission to play the piano."

"But it made a difference!" I looked at Dad, and my shoulders drooped. His blank expression and slumped posture had returned. "You have to believe me, he changed. Playing changed him! You heard how he played, right?"

Estelle folded her arms. She refused to be convinced. "Yeah, I heard him playing, which is why I came in here. No playing!"

"This is bullshit," I said. "Where's his doctor, then? Let me talk to him. I want to show him how this affected Dad."

Estelle shook her head. "His doctor comes in Mondays, and with next week being Labor Day, he won't be back until the following week." She moved over towards Dad. "Now, I'm taking Ivan back to his room, and I ain't going to argue no more!"

She placed her hand across Dad's shoulders. "Let's get you back to your room, Mr. Stephens." As Dad stood, Estelle looked back at me. "I think it's best if you leave now."

Most of the audience were gone, and those who remained exited now, ahead of Estelle. I watched her lead Dad away, and stood by the piano for several more minutes, alone. Then, after slamming the cover closed, I marched to the lobby, scribbled in my sign-out time, and stormed out before Imogene could get in a scolding.

# CHAPTER 26

When I got home from Mellowood, the rain had stopped, and now the sun shone brightly through gaps in the layered patches of white clouds. Steamy wisps rose from the parking lot puddles, disappearing as they rose into the humid air.

The end of my visit with Dad still angered me. Estelle's reaction, though probably perfectly in line with protocol, had seemed over the top and heavy handed. If Dad had been having another episode, that would have been one thing. But the complete opposite had happened.

Playing the piano hadn't cured him, or treated his Alzheimer's, or reversed any of its effects. It had done something, though. Something miraculous, to me as well as to Dad. The piano had acted as a kind of conduit, or a television screen. I'd gotten to watch him as he'd have wanted people to remember him: talented, expressive, and bringing joy to people. We'd shared a few moments together that we never could have when he had been healthy.

Moments he'd probably forgotten the second our duet ended.

I wondered if his final coherent thought, before Alzheimer's consumed him, had filled him with sadness, or maybe anger, realizing the disease would dehumanize him, rob him of the ability to recall faces, conversations, and memories. I was sure he hadn't wanted family and friends to see his memory erased, to watch helplessly while his identity disappeared, while his personality vanished. But it had happened anyway, and we all had to endure it with every visit.

And yet maybe that crappy out-of-tune Baldwin had the power to restore some minimal level of dignity, to provide him a scintilla of purpose in his endless loop of recurring unremembered days and nights. Every time he sat upon the stool, it would be a new experience for him,bringing joy and life to that place of drudgery and monotony. It would splash color across his dull, beige world, one note at a time.

And he'd be happy. Didn't that count for anything?

Estelle didn't seem to think so. She came across as the type of person who followed one rule, and one rule only: enforce the regulations as written, without deviation. I understood that she had her job to do, that she answered to someone above her, and didn't want to jeopardize her position, or put patients at risk. Unfortunately, I wouldn't be able to discuss it with his doctor for nearly two weeks. What if his condition worsened by then and got to the point where the piano made no difference?

I decided to call Fanny and tell her what had happened. I was sure the report had already been written and filed, and being his power of attorney, she'd be included in a review with Mellowood and his doctor. Best to let her know beforehand.

The phone rang several times before Fanny answered.

"Hey Fan, it's me," I replied. "I just got back."

"Do I need to sit down? Was Dad conscious when you left?"

No *Hi Frankie.* Straight to the point.

"He's completely fine," I told her. "Calm, awake, well-fed, and not in restraints. He wasn't very responsive, though. He barely said four words."

*Play with me, Felix.*

"He's been that way since..." she broke off. I knew the rest of the sentence: 'Since the episode.' Maybe she considered it pointless to bring it up, like arguing over a busted old bale of hay. "Anyway, the doctor thinks it's a combination of a couple things, but generally speaking, his prognosis hasn't changed."

'Combination of a couple things' meant sedatives and

straps. Maybe new prescriptions, too. She didn't need to come out and say it.

"I'm glad it went smoothly," Fanny went on, "and I'm sure he recognized you, even if it didn't seem like it."

A compassionate comment, but I suspected she'd said it to comfort herself more than me. And now came the difficult, uncomfortable part.

I rubbed the back of my neck. "Well, I wouldn't say it went entirely smoothly."

"Why?"

It was the shortest 'why' I ever heard her utter. Terse was too long of a description. She was suddenly loaded for bear, and my name was Winnie.

I told her how I'd encouraged Dad to play the piano, describing the scene of our duet, note for note, omitting no details. Fanny didn't interrupt once.

"And once Estelle yelled at me and took Dad to his room, I just up and left, and came home," I concluded.

Fanny remained silent. I couldn't even hear her breathing. After several seconds, she finally spoke in a wavering voice.

"He. . . he played *The Little Snow Girl*? You're not shitting me, are you?"

"I would not lie to you about this."

More silence. Then, "He knew it? From memory?"

"I wouldn't have believed it if I hadn't been sitting right next to him."

"And then. . . then you improvised a duet? Together?"

"That's generally how duets are played," I told her, then paused, searching for the right word. "Incredible fails to adequately describe the experience."

Fanny sniffled, and I heard a long, slow exhale. "I loved that song. I begged him to play it every day. Every damn day." She paused again. "Frankie, if my heart wasn't breaking right now, I'd be screaming at you."

"I didn't mean to break your heart. But I'm glad you're

not screaming."

"But what possessed you? Especially after last time. He might have gone crazy, and then what? The last thing Daddy needs is a second traumatic episode."

She had said Dad didn't need more trauma, but I knew she also meant herself.

"I don't know why. I acted purely on a whim. He's been there six months now, and that's the first time he's played the piano. Right?"

"Yes, I think so, but . . ."

"But why?" I interrupted. "Fanny, if you saw his face, his eyes, his entire being - they all transformed. I don't know how to explain it. I'm not saying the piano cured him or anything, but playing it seemed to . . ."

"It seemed to turn some lights on, in his head," she said, completing my sentence.

"Yeah."

She sniffled again, this one a little longer than the first. "Well, you still did something risky, and Estelle had every right to bark at you," she said. "It could have turned out badly."

"I know. I'm sorry for upsetting you, but I'm not sorry for what I did. I'm sure Mellowood will call you tomorrow and tell you what happened, and I wanted you to hear my side of it - tell you what it did for Dad."

"I appreciate that."

"Plus, I think we should tell the doctor Dad should play every day. Like therapy or something."

"Well, I don't know," Fanny said. "First we need to hear what he says about this before making any demands."

"Fanny, he's our dad. Shouldn't we get a say in his treatment?"

She paused before answering. "What do you mean, 'we?' You've avoided doing anything for Daddy for years, and now suddenly, you're advocating for his treatment? One duet later, and now you care about his well-being?"

I didn't know how to reply. Today had been emotional,

and I hadn't sorted everything out yet. Had I over-reacted?

"Fair enough," I told her. "Maybe I'm coming to the realization, finally, that I haven't been helpful. I haven't been as supportive as I should've been."

"Hmph."

She sounded unconvinced. I was being honest, but maybe it was coming across as condescending and flat.

"Admitting you haven't been helpful is the biggest understatement of the year. I appreciate you want to help out more – finally - but forgive me, Frankie. I doubt your sincerity."

"Expecting a little gratitude is a bridge too far?"

"You have a lot of ground to make up," she said. "I want to believe you, I really do. I desperately want to. But do you think one sentence can make up for everything that's happened between us, between you and Daddy? A sentence starting with 'maybe?' You need to do better than maybe."

"Technically I spoke two sentences."

"Shut up." She heaved a loud sigh, either from exasperation or from exhaustion. Or a combination of both. "All you had to do was just *be* with him. Doing things together doesn't make it more meaningful for him, you know."

"It was totally unplanned. But trust me – this was more than meaningful."

"Well, if you're being straight with me, that you want what's best for Dad, then promise me you won't visit him until after I meet with his doctor. Can you do that?"

"Yeah, I can do that for you."

It seemed a small sacrifice to make. Perhaps she thought I was incapable of larger ones, and was protecting herself against disappointment. This would be one time, though, where I wouldn't let her down.

"Do it for Dad," she added. "Thanks for telling me what happened. I'm relieved it didn't result in another crisis."

"Me too."

She paused. "Oh, one more thing. Mike and I have decided to come to your concert."

"Really? But you hate Ned's band."

"Yes, but if you mess up horribly, I get to mock you."

"Aw, that's awfully sweet of you. I hope to disappoint you."

"We shall see. Listen, I have to go. See you Friday night!" With that, she hung up.

*That went better than expected.*

On a normal Wednesday afternoon in late August, I'd be at Cosgrove, attending meetings, preparing for the new school year, and catching up with fellow teachers. But now, thanks to being fired, I had the freedom to do whatever I wanted. And what I wanted, with the thunderstorm over, was a long bike ride.

\* \* \*

After a thirty-mile ride and a hot shower, I dropped onto the couch, and scowled. The ride had failed to accomplish much of anything, except to tire me out. A nagging feeling persisted at the back of my mind, something I had forgotten. I knew it would come to me sooner or later. People with photographic memories like mine didn't simply forget things, even if they wanted to. Sometimes it took a bit to drag the memory from the storage bin, but it couldn't stay hidden for long. It'd come to me, sooner or later.

At that moment, the sound of rapping upon glass rang through the apartment. Someone was at the door. I got up from the couch, wondering who it could be. Fanny never stopped by unannounced.

I opened the door. The elusive thought suddenly revealed itself, for on the landing stood Natalie.

She was beaming at me. "Hi Frank! Is this a bad time?"

"No, not at all," I said nonchalantly, though my brain raced to understand why she had come. "What brings you by?"

She looked at her feet, and began massaging her fingers,

her pink purse hooked over her wrist. She wore a pair of pink Bermuda shorts and a white tee, covered with a sleeveless turquoise knit sweater. Her hair band matched her shorts.

"Well, I just dropped off Val at Fredonia, and I thought, you know, I'm on Frank's side of town, so why not drop by? Spur of the moment sort of thing, you know?"

"Spur of the moment," I parroted, recalling she had mentioned taking her younger sister to college today. Fredonia was southwest of Buffalo, but Spencerport was more than a slight detour off I-490. My bullshit radar was pinging, but I decided to play along.

"Are you going to invite me in?" she asked.

"Uh, sure," I said, letting her enter. "Welcome to my humble abode."

She glanced around the apartment while I closed the door.

"Can I offer you something to drink? Coke? Water?"

"No thanks," she said, and turned on her heel to face me, but as she did so, the array of compositions on the table grabbed her attention. "What are those? Yours? Did you write those?"

She stepped towards them, but I darted around her, and slammed my hand down. She took a half step backward, giving me a startled look.

"What's the matter?"

"They're not mine," I told her, wondering what she had intended to do or say before being distracted. "But they're private. They're . . . it's difficult to explain."

"I love difficult explanations," she said, smiling.

"Good. Then explain why you're here," I said. "Tell me the real reason, and I'll tell you about the songs. Deal?"

I kept my hand firmly planted down, determined to know the truth. I noticed she hadn't stopped massaging her fingers and knuckles since I answered the door.

"Deal," she said, nodding, as her smile evaporated slowly. "Mind if I sit down?"

I motioned towards the furniture, and Natalie went and sat on the couch, while I took the adjacent armchair. She placed her purse on the coffee table.

"I, uh, hadn't intended to come here," she started. "Not at first, anyway. I originally planned to go straight home from Fredonia. But after our da-." She abruptly stopped. "After our *non-date,* I thought, how could I repay you, or show some sign of my appreciation?"

My heart raced as she talked, its rate increasing with each syllable. Repay me? Show her appreciation? Here, in my apartment? I adjusted my position, trying to appear relaxed, while my insides churned with discomfort.

"So after you left Sunday," she continued, "I decided to give you a present. A small sign of my gratitude. That's why I'm here. It's nothing really."

Natalie picked up her purse, removed a small, rectangular package, wrapped in yellow paper, tied up with a blue ribbon, and offered it to me. I took it, and turned the rigid, wallet-sized box over in my hands. 'It's nothing, really' sounded as honest as 'Spur of the moment.'

"You didn't have to buy me a present," I told her.

"I didn't. Just open it." She inched forward, perched on the very edge of the cushion.

I pulled the ribbon over one corner, and tore off the paper, letting it drop to the floor. It was a gift box from McCurdy's, a hometown department store. I removed the cover. Inside lay an item wrapped in white tissue paper, folded over and held together with tape.

"You spent a lot of time on this," I quipped, peeling off the tape and unraveling the paper.

I held a cassette tape, in a clear plastic case. *Frank's Movie Music, Side A*, in purple ink, was written on the cassette label. I stared at it for a few seconds, took the tape out of its case, and flipped it over. The label on the back said the same, save for *Side B*. Raising my head, I looked at Natalie. Her eyes exuded excitement and glee in equal portions.

"You made me . . ."

"A mixtape!" she exclaimed.

"...of movie music." My voice was as flat as a tabletop. No enthusiasm or enjoyment. I felt confusion and bewilderment. A mixtape most certainly did not qualify as 'It's nothing, really' material.

"Not just any movie music," Natalie said. "I promise, you'll love it." She looked over her shoulder, in the direction of my stereo. "May I play it for you?"

I handed it to her, and placed the carton and cassette case on the coffee table while she scampered to the stereo. She got the tape started, and returned to her seat on the couch. She could barely contain her excitement.

"You'll love this. I just know it. I spent all night Monday and most of yesterday morning making it."

I covered my face with my hands, fingers pressed against my closed eyes, dumbfounded. Why in the world had she made me a mixtape? Of movie music, no less? Did she have any idea what a mixtape represented?

*Is she coming on to me?*

The first tones resounded from the speakers: a sustained double low C, played on double basses, a double bassoon, and an organ. I pulled my fingers away from my eyes slowly, realizing I recognized this music. After four measures, a solitary trumpet pierced the air. I looked at Natalie with gradual astonishment.

While tympani pounded out a measure's worth of energetic octaves, I asked: "Strauss' *Also Sprach Zarathustra?*"

Natalie nodded, her happiness unconstrained. "From *2001: A Space Odyssey!* It's *classical* movie music! Psych!!" And she laughed, not with derision or ridicule, but with pure, clear joy.

I managed a smile, still in uncertain disbelief. "So the songs on this tape are classical pieces used in movies?"

"Uh huh! The playlist is taped on the inside of the cover."

I removed the paper, unfolded it and quickly read it.

I knew every song. Side A included Mozart's *Piano Concerto #21, 2nd movement,* from Elvira Madigan; Strauss' *Blue Danube Waltz,* also from 2001; Wagner's *Ride of the Valkyries* from Apocalypse Now; Mascagni's *Intermezzo from Cavalleria Rusticana* from Raging Bull. The final song was Gershwin's *Rhapsody in Blue,* from Woody Allen's Manhattan. Side B contained the complete soundtrack from Disney's *Fantasia.*

*Rhapsody in Blue.* The power ballad. No way were we getting to *that* song!

"Well?" Natalie asked. "Are you surprised?"

I nodded. "That's one word to describe it. Relieved is another. Reading the label, I thought, wow, what a crazy way to thank me, knowing how I feel about movie music."

I moved over to the stereo and pressed the 'Stop' button. *Zarathustra* was almost over, and I didn't want one of Mozart's most romantic pieces to begin.

"But you got me. If the tape had been all Webber and Williams, it wouldn't be long for the garbage."

"I wouldn't do that to you, Frank," Natalie said, looking up at me, smiling in that winsome way. "I'd tease or trick you, but not insult you. Not today, anyway."

"Fair enough. Thank you. You didn't have to go to all this trouble."

"No trouble at all." She cast a glance to the dining table, and jerked her thumb over her shoulder. "Okay, I've confessed. Those songs?"

I felt she hadn't told me everything, but she had gone through a lot of trouble to make the mixtape. They were personal expressions, not a mere collection of random songs. They took a lot of work: finding the songs, calculating the total running time, arranging the order. I remembered how much time I had spent in my college days making them. So what was Natalie's motive?

*Better to just drop this. She's being as candid as she wants to be.*

"Sure," I said, and I went to get them.

"I'd like a Coke, too, if the offer's still open," she added.

I got us each a can, and arranged Clara's songs in order before returning. Natalie had moved over to the stereo, and was looking at my album collection. She ran her finger across the jacket spines, tilting her head sideways to read the titles.

"You know," she said, without looking up, "for a guy who plays the trumpet, you sure have a lot of records featuring the piano."

"I've a couple Herb Alpert records, you know. And Chuck Mangione."

"And some Chicago, too," she said. "But the other ninety-five percent . . ."

She came back to the couch, sitting adjacent to my chair. As I handed her the Coke, our fingertips brushed, reminding me of when we had played the Gershwin duet. I looked down, away from her face, slightly flustered at the touch, but also at her comment.

Regaining my composure, I said: "Still judging my musical tastes, I see."

"Now don't get defensive," she cooed. "It's merely an observation. I think your taste in music is mostly acceptable. May I see the songs now?"

I handed her the compositions.

"Oh, a waltz! I love waltzes!"

Her eyes scanned the front page, moving from measure to measure completely to the bottom, without saying a word. She pointed to the initials. "Your dad wrote these?"

I nodded. "There are nine of them."

"I don't recognize the waltz," she said, and she pulled out the second piece. "This Romance either. I own all his music, and neither of these are familiar."

"They wouldn't be. They're all unpublished."

"How did you get them?"

"Found them in my attic while clearing it out," I answered. "They were in a carton with a bunch of his old work stuff."

She sifted through the stack, pulled out the sonata, and began browsing from page to page. She stopped at the beginning of the second movement, and began to read the score more deliberately. I sat in silence, drinking my Coke, awaiting her reaction, admiring her music reading ability.

The memory of Natalie upon the rolling ladder returned, that flashback to Sunday evening, when I had fallen asleep on the couch, meditating on that loose, elusive thread. This image had to be significant, but why? What had I seen that afternoon, in her foyer, amongst the shelves?

"This is so beautiful," she breathed. Her eyes seemed to shimmer. "It's so unlike any of his other sonatas. Have you played these yet?"

"All of them," I told her.

Natalie took a deep breath. "The melody here is exquisite. The change from tonic to dominant, the development and exposition, then the recapitulation. It just flows so naturally, so organically. Oh, and the coda..."

She blinked several times, and then closed her eyes. She seemed overwhelmed.

"Yeah, it's something else."

My mind pulsed at a steady cadence, focused on the image of Natalie on the ladder. No. Neither Natalie, nor the ladder. My focus shifted. Something about her books.

"For a contemporary Russian composer, this is so unlike Russian music," Natalie said.

The image in my mind wavered, but I maintained it, working through my mental problem as she talked. I shared this skill with Dad, as Uncle Pietr had noticed.

"I mean, most of his music had that distinctive passion and character. You know what I mean, right?"

I nodded. She immersed herself into the songs more than I had anticipated, while I immersed myself in recollecting her bookshelves.

"You know how you can hear the difference between Rachmaninoff, and Shostakovich, and Kabalevsky, and Stravinsky? Play any of their songs, and you or I could identify them right away. Despite that, they share common elements and structure, too. Plus, you can't separate out the political, cultural, and societal factors that influenced their music. Those aspects differentiate them from, say, French and American composers, for instance. But these songs? They're more similar to Tchaikovsky or Borodin. Even his other compositions."

"They're all like that," I said, looking at her, but also seeing the book jackets, the spines, the titles.

"If you asked me when these were composed, without prompting, I would have guessed late eighteenth century, not the mid twentieth. They're so like Romantic era pieces. Why do you think he never published them?" she asked. "Do you think it's because of their style? Not modern enough?"

I gave a half-shrug. "He can't answer that, unfortunately."

Four shelves of books, and one particular book called out to me. I could feel it.

She leafed through the entire collection, stopping briefly to look over the violin duet.

"These read like love songs." Natalie turned to me. "Maybe these were for your mom?"

The mention of my mom rattled me, just enough to shake my focus and make me fully present.

"I'm not entirely sure," I said slowly.

The impulse to tell her about Clara rose, becoming difficult to resist. On the one hand, the songs represented the passion Dad had felt for Clara, and he deserved his privacy. He had hidden them for a reason. On the other hand, I had already told Uncle Pietr and Aunt Jane about the songs and asked them about Clara. Same with Fanny. So why not ask Natalie, too? A fresh perspective might shine a new light on them.

Just then, she turned towards me. Her hazel eyes glowed with wonderment, and my words caught in my throat. Reading the scores had transformed her in some way.

"Do you remember that scene in *Amadeus*, when Constanze brings Mozart's compositions to Salieri? She gives them to him, asking him if they're any good. As he reads them, he grows more and more amazed at their beauty and originality. He is so overcome with awe, they tumble from his hands, spilling across the floor. He nearly faints. Constanze, fearing the worst, asks 'Is it not good?' Remember his reply?"

I remembered, but said nothing.

"He says to her, 'It is miraculous!' That's how I'm feeling right now. These songs are nothing short of miraculous."

That's not how I would have described Dad's songs, but I understood. Fanny had responded similarly when I played the waltz, not with words but certainly by her emotions. The song had overwhelmed her. Natalie's reaction came only from reading the music; she had yet to hear any of them. Nevertheless, I wouldn't challenge her impression, especially in light of her competence.

"If you want pure genius," I told her, "read the last piece, the duet for piano and violin. I wonder if you'll see what's there."

She picked it up, and settled against the couch cushions. Within moments, she sat erect, and shifted between reading that score, and searching through the other pieces scattered about the coffee table. She sifted the scores until she found the right one, and traced passages and measures with her finger, as if referencing footnotes in a journal.

"This . . .this is amazing," she said, slowly shaking her head. "There are bits and pieces from the other songs included in this duet. It's like a summary, or a collage."

"It's more than that," I told her.

"A synopsis?"

I shook my head. "Think of the first eight songs as scenes of a play. You're watching this beautiful, touching love story. Then, before the final scene, perhaps even before the final act, the playwright comes on stage. A completely unscripted moment, and he says to the audience, *The End.* Full stop. The curtain drops, the house lights go up, and you're left wondering, what was the original ending? How was the play supposed to end?"

Natalie sat still, and I could see understanding in her expression.

"And not just *The End* of that particular performance. It was the final performance, ever." I tapped the score as she held it in her hands. "Dad wrote this song not as the finale, but *instead* of a finale. I think it was unscripted."

Natalie chewed her lower lip, her brow tight and low. "You think he had more to say? That there's more to the story?"

"I think he had wanted to write more, but something happened to change his mind. That's why it contains themes and motifs from all the other pieces. He stopped the play, canceled the ending, and rewrote it. Nothing more would be written because he had nothing left. He gave his everything."

"But why?"

"I don't know, and I'm not sure how to find out."

"These were written for your mom, then," she said. "They must have been. The cancer forced his hand, right?"

I decided then to tell her everything.

"That's possible, I suppose, except for one thing. These were labeled 'For Clara,' and they were written before their marriage."

Natalie did a double take. "What? Who's Clara?"

I shrugged my shoulders. "I haven't found out yet. My sister Fanny has no idea, I've asked one of my uncles, and Dad . . . well, obviously he's in no condition to explain."

I needed to exercise discretion now; showing Natalie the songs was one thing. Telling her about the Communist sympathizer inquiry was something else, and none of her business.

"No one named Clara in my family, either."

"Well, this isn't the sort of music one writes for a great aunt or mother-in-law," Natalie said. "So you think your Dad knew someone else before meeting your mother? Not after?"

I explained how I found them packed with things from

the early 1950's, in a carton that had clearly not been opened since being taped shut. "They're not dated, which doesn't help, but I'm mostly certain these were written earlier than 1951."

"And Clara wasn't his pet name for your mom?"

Shaking my head, I said: "Dad called her Elise. If they were intended for her, why hide them? Why not publish them?"

"Do you think Clara is the woman's real name?"

"I don't know. I'm leaning towards no."

"Quite the interesting mystery you've got on your hands," she said, dropping the score onto the table. "Seems impossible to solve. How do you hope to find out who she is?"

"I have no idea."

"And you're telling me because?" She smiled wryly.

"Because you asked to see the songs, remember?"

"Oh right." She turned a shade of pink slightly paler than her headband. "I've always admired your dad's music, and seeing these songs means a lot. Thank you."

Natalie resumed studying the last piece.

"You know, the technique your dad used in this duet reminds me of something. The elements he included from the other pieces, they're not random or accidental. They have a specific meaning or intent."

"Did you also notice they're written only for the piano?" I asked.

Natalie placed the score on the table, and I pointed to two instances on that page. I flipped the page and pointed out a third one.

Natalie nodded. "This is his swan song, so of course that'd make sense."

"Okay, so that much is established. What does it all mean?"

Natalie tapped her chin with a finger. "It's like trying to read hieroglyphics without the proper cipher. We're missing the cipher."

The scene of Natalie's bookshelves popped back into my

head at that moment. I closed my eyes and leaned back in my chair. The volumes and textbooks vibrated with such clarity, it felt as if I could reach out and pull them off the shelf. Natalie might have said something, but I didn't hear. Her voice sounded distorted, out of tune. My vision narrowed, pinpointing on a specific book.

And then I saw it. A white book with blue text in capital letters on the spine. My eyes shot open, at the same moment I heard Natalie say my name. Then, we said simultaneously:

"Musical cryptograms!"

# CHAPTER 27

I held open the door for Natalie, and followed her into Grandpa Sam's. We waited at the unattended hostess desk.

"Seems pleasant enough," Natalie said quietly.

"Don't let the homey atmosphere fool you," I told her.

"My expectations are sufficiently grounded. You did say this was your favorite local restaurant, so I'm keeping my hopes in check."

The hostess soon arrived. "Thanks for coming to Sam's," she said, smiling. "Hi Frank! Just the two of you?"

"Yep," I said. "Non-smoking please."

She seated us. "Connie will be with you in a moment."

Natalie read the specials sheet tucked inside the menu, then flipped to the salad section, chattering to herself about what to order. I knew what I wanted, so I spent the time mulling over this idea of musical cryptograms, and whether they might be in Clara's songs.

I thought back to the apartment. We had broken into laughter after simultaneously shouting 'Musical cryptograms!'

"Oh my gosh," Natalie had said. "You looked like you had fallen asleep, or were in a trance. I said it twice before you opened your eyes. Were you repeating what I had said, or were you thinking it at the same time?"

"Lucky coincidence," I said. "I remember seeing a book about it in your house. Are you familiar with them?"

She nodded. "My music theory professor loved cryptograms. Thought they were totally awesome. We spent weeks discussing them, identifying them, and they piqued my interest so much I purchased that book. It's fascinating stuff." She glanced at her watch. "You know what, though? I haven't eaten all day practically, and I'm kinda starved. Can we get dinner? Not as a date, of course."

"Of course, not a date," I said. I hadn't eaten since lunch, and I had taken that long bike ride. "I know a good place within walking distance. You'll like it."

A couple minutes later, we were headed to Grandpa Sam's. The humidity had completely abated, and most of the rain had dried up. Only a few puddles remained, scattered here and there along the curbs, or in sidewalk low spots.

"Spencerport is nicer than I had imagined," Natalie commented.

"First time here?" I asked.

"Yup. Never had a reason to come here before now."

She walked with a carefree gait, and I pointed out several historical sites along the way. The canal bridge rose as we crossed Union Street; we spent a couple minutes watching the mast of a canal cruiser float past. We then continued on to the restaurant.

Connie approached our table, her uniform tarred and feathered with brown gravy stains and several smears of mashed potatoes. She placed two glasses of ice water on our table, along with two straws.

"Why, hello Frank! Missed you on Sunday!" she exclaimed. She raised an eyebrow at Natalie and smiled. "Hello there!"

Natalie returned her smile. "Hi."

"I'm Connie's most regular customer," I said to Natalie. "If I fail to show up on my appointed days, she sends out a search and rescue team."

"Oh you!" Connie said with a laugh, her belly shaking. "Now is this your friend who doesn't know anything about music?"

Natalie snapped her head around. If vision had included mass and force, I would've been knocked out of my seat. I shrugged with as much innocence as I could feign.

"So Frank's talked about me, has he?"

Connie looked back and forth between us, her face turning a deep red. "Um, can I take your orders?" she stammered, attempting to recover herself. "And, uh, one bill or two?"

"Two," I said quickly, and we gave our orders – a Teriyaki Chicken salad for Natalie, lasagna for me - and she scooted off, menus in hand.

"I don't know anything about music?" she asked accusingly. "Care to explain?"

"Those weren't my exact words," I said. "What I said was, people with any sense of style or taste don't like *Cats*. Two completely different things."

"Mm hmm." After a quick drink of water, she twirled the straw in her fingers, stirring the ice cubes in deliberate circles. "You know, I can't decide if I'm upset at how you talk about me, or simply flattered you talked about me in the first place."

She turned her gaze towards the nearby window, as if something outside had suddenly caught her attention. It was my turn to be embarrassed. I needed to change the subject and fast.

"Okay," I said, "give me a crash course in cryptograms. I know a little bit, but not much."

"You know what regular cryptograms are, right? They're encrypted texts, where letters, numbers or symbols represent different letters or numbers, but you need the proper cipher to decode them. Once you figure out the cipher, you can translate the text, and solve the riddle."

"Spy messages and espionage, for instance?" I asked.

Natalie nodded. "That's one application, but mainly they're used as mind benders and brain teasers. Like acrostics, for instance. The most common cryptogram is the reversed alphabet, where A stands for Z, B for Y, and so on. Musical cryptograms are similar, simply because the notes have been assigned letter names."

"But there are only seven letters in music notation, A

through G," I said.

"Yes and no," she countered. "Notes are also known as do, re, mi, fa, sol, la, and ti. You know, from *The Sound of Music*?"

"Yes, Maria, I do know, thank you very much," I said with a smile and a hint of mock condescension. "The technical term is solfège, or solfeggio."

"Well look at how smart you are!" she said, smiling. That same winsome look. "As far as the rest of the alphabet, there's one style called 'the French' method, which assigns multiple letters to each note. Let me get a pen."

She rummaged through her purse just as Connie came to the table, leaving a basket of fresh bread. Natalie produced a purple pen, and after grabbing a paper napkin, wrote the seven note names in order across the top.

"The French method continues the alphabet, starting with H, like this," and she wrote an H beneath the A, followed by an I under the B. After writing an N beneath the G, she returned to the start. Under the H, she wrote an O, repeating the pattern until ending with the letter Z in the E-headed column.

"So in this method," I said, "a musical A could represent an H, an O, or a V, as well as a plain A; B also stood for I, P, or W, and so on?"

"Yes. It's simple, but as you can imagine, it makes finding any cryptograms extremely difficult and time-consuming. The 'many-to-one' matching system is cumbersome, but it allows composers to use the entire alphabet."

"Why is it the French method?"

"The French musicologist Jules Écorcheville developed it, prior to World War One. It never really caught on, and hardly anybody uses it now, but it's one of the two most common methods." She grabbed a fresh napkin. "The other is the German method. Bach is the great-grandfather of musical cryptograms, having developed the B-A-C-H motif, and incorporating it into many of his pieces."

"I remember now," I said. "There's a trick, though, of encrypting the H."

"Sort of. B-flat is B, and B-natural is H. His encrypted name is B-flat, A, C, B-natural." She wrote down B♭-A-C-B♮. "Many of his contemporaries incorporated this motif in their works as a kind of tribute to him, showing respect."

"And if I recall correctly, E-flat stood for S, and A-flat stood for AS."

"Just as long as you don't say I have a flat ass," Natalie said, and she nudged me with her elbow. "Know what I mean?"

"What?" It took me a few seconds to get the joke.

*And did she just quote Monty Python?*

Connie returned to our table with a water pitcher. "Care for a refill, kids?" she asked.

She wouldn't be engaging in any more small talk tonight, I could tell. We both said yes, and she left us the pitcher after filling our glasses.

"Here's another German method example," Natalie said, writing out a string of letters. "Whose is this?" She had scrawled D-E♭-C-B♮' in purple.

"D, S, C, H," I mumbled, chewing on a breadstick. "Hang on, I know this one. It's Dmitri Shostakovich."

"Very good! The C is included phonetically, not literally. I think he added it because the Germans spelled his name with a C. Oh, here's one more! It's tricky."

This time she wrote 'E-A-E-D-A.' I thoughtfully munched my bread while working it out.

"French or German method?" I asked.

"Mostly German."

"Mostly German?" I asked. That didn't help much. After racking my brain, I shook my head in defeat. "I've no idea."

"Elmira," Natalie said.

"What? You only wrote five letters."

"I said it was tricky." Using her pen as a pointer, she explained it letter by letter. "E is E. A is la; keep the L. The second E is mi; you know, do-re-mi? D is re; drop the E. Last A is just an A. E-L-MI-R-A."

Now I understood what she meant by *mostly German.*

The composer had also included the solfège system, and I realized now why finding cryptograms could be difficult. Especially when you don't know what to look for.

"Clever, but totally unfair."

"Well, that's Shostakovich for you," Natalie said. "It's in his Tenth Symphony, added as a dedication to his student Elmira Nazirova, whom he loved very much. He used it over ten times. Now that I've given you the basics, let's see how many different versions we can come up with."

She grabbed a napkin and wrote 'CLARA' name across the top in capital letters.

"Let's use the German method," I told her. "Dad hated French composers."

At that moment, Connie came with our meals. Natalie moved the napkins away to make room for our food.

"Can I get you two anything else?" she asked.

I asked for another basket of bread. She gave me a friendly smile, followed by a knowing glance towards Natalie, who wasn't paying attention while arranging the napkin on her lap. I shot her a half-smirk, and as she walked away, Connie's smile expanded into a large grin.

*She's going to talk my ear off next time I come alone.*

"Well, it looks good and smells good, anyway," Natalie said.

"Kinda tough to mess up a salad, isn't it?"

"A person can mess up just about anything, if they're determined enough," she said.

Our eyes locked for a second, and her expression made me think she wasn't merely referring to her dinner. I considered asking for clarification, but decided against it. Some things are better left alone.

She took a bite of her salad, and after swallowing, said: "I'm impressed. Grandpa knows his way around a Teriyaki chicken salad after all."

We came up with various cryptogram possibilities of Clara's name while we ate, and Natalie jotted each one down.

"Here's a thought," she said. "C-La-Re, instead of -Ra. A slight modification, which makes it C-A-D." She tapped the napkin with the pen. "Or maybe . . . gosh, if this is it, your dad is extraordinarily clever."

"What?"

"Okay, it's possible Clara isn't the woman's actual name, right? So what if the C represents Do, and Do are the first two letters of her *real* name? The other two notes might be the initials of her middle and last names. It would be Do, then A.D."

"Possibly," I said, sticking my fork into the remaining piece of lasagna. The cartons of student records sitting in my apartment immediately came to mind. Teachers falling in love with a student wasn't uncommon. Shostakovich did it. Mom had been his student for a short while, and they eventually married. But what about a fellow teacher? Or a violinist?

"Before we get ahead of ourselves, let's focus on the obvious cryptograms first."

"Dorothy, Doris, Donna," Natalie rattled off several names. "Do those ring a bell?"

I raised my eyebrows at her. "Let's not go there. Can we simply focus on Clara, the name?"

"Dominique...ooh, that's a pretty name, don't you think? I think it's pretty."

"Finish your salad," I told her. "Then we'll go back and look through his songs, see if they contain any of these motifs."

Before taking her last bite, she quickly said, "Maybe Doreen?" and tried to suppress a smile while chewing. I gave her a side-eye, and motioned to Connie that we were ready to pay.

Twenty minutes later, I unlocked my apartment door, and Natalie and I walked in.

"Your sister sounds hilarious," Natalie said with laughter in her voice. "And she plays piano as well as you?"

"Heck no!" I answered. "She's good, but she'd admit I'm better."

"Of course she would, to protect your feelings." Natalie headed to the couch, pulling the napkin out of her purse, and dropping it on the coffee table.

"Hey, can I call Eric? I told him I'd be home by four o'clock."

"Sure," I told her.

While she called, I sat in the armchair, picked up the napkin, and read what Natalie had written down. Six possible cryptograms. Despite Dad's talent and cleverness, I had to believe that, if he had used cryptograms, they wouldn't be overly complex. He would've wanted Clara to recognize them without much difficulty. The songs themselves were indicative of his ingenuity and devotion; cryptograms would be icing on the cake. Their own secret language, obscured but not invisible.

Natalie replaced the handset and slid down the couch towards me.

"Eric didn't even notice I hadn't gotten back. Him and that cable TV. I told him I'd be home in an hour." She gathered up the scores into a tidy stack. "I suggest we each pick a score and see who can find a cryptogram first."

"What's the prize for winning?" I asked.

"Depends."

"On?"

"Who loses."

I chose the sonata and she chose the Humoresque, the shortest piece in the group.

I started reading. The sonata was written in E major, in 4/4 time. Traditional format, nothing avant-garde or even remotely modernist. I recognized motifs and ideas lifted from Mozart, Clementi, and early Beethoven, with a dash of Tchaikovsky tossed in. The sonata sang with beauty, brightness, and life.

Two pages into the first movement, and no cryptogram. I had a feeling Natalie did this as a hobby. Looking for hidden messages and secret codes might be a quirky passion of hers. I knew little in comparison, as none of my college professors had covered cryptograms to any great degree. They were uncommon and somewhat eccentric; nothing more than a musical play on words. I had known about Bach's motif, and a couple others Natalie hadn't mentioned, and that was about it.

I knew that ignoring bar lines and clefs was necessary. Cryptograms gave composers the chance to write outside the lines, beyond the measures. Those were prison bars and driving lanes for keeping notes in their places. They were bound by time and meter, forced to obey the rules of musical composition. With a cryptogram, though, the composer could enjoy a breath of freedom, without dismantling the musical constraints that enabled performers and audiences to play, understand, and comprehend the music. Maybe that's why atonality had never really caught on: it was an attempt at a freedom that hadn't been earned, or a destruction of the system that held freedom and restraint in a delicate balance.

"I think I found it!" Natalie exclaimed. She shifted closer to me, and held out the score for me to see.

"May I write on this?" she asked.

"Go ahead, it's a copy."

With her purple pen, she circled the third to last measure. "See, in the left hand? That C-A-D sequence beginning with the quarter note, followed by those sequences of sixteenths? The subsequent quarter notes are important, this A and that D." She circled each quarter note. "The sixteenths are irrelevant, from an encryption standpoint. This sequence appears only here, so maybe this is it. What do you think?"

Her face glowed with elation at her discovery. I took the score, quickly scanned it, and confirmed what she said. I started to believe in our hunch.

"Okay, so maybe you found it. What does it tell me, though?"

"Well, nothing yet. I think it only means something if it's in every song. Once is inconclusive, twice might be coincidental, but nine times would be totally intentional."

"And if it is in each of the songs?"

She shrugged. "It would tell me your dad loved her very much, going to all that trouble."

"But it won't tell me who she is, will it?"

"Frank, I have no idea." She placed her hand on my arm, a gentle gesture meant to assuage me. "I can tell it's pretty important to you, though."

"I mean, if the songs hadn't been clearly marked 'For Clara,' then the cryptograms would be a huge discovery," I told her. "But I already knew these were for her. Cryptograms won't tell me anything I didn't already know."

Natalie patted my arm. "You're frustrated."

"Yeah. But hey, it's something interesting to include in the liner notes should someone record them one day."

"And when you play the album backwards, you'll hear bits of *Clair de Lune* during Romance No. 3, or *Liebestraum* during Duet No. 2," she said, smiling.

I smiled at her attempt to cheer me. "That would be something. Dad had talent, but I don't think he had that much talent. He could probably pull off a palindrome, like Bartok's fifth String Quartet, but I doubt he could add other composers' music in reverse."

Natalie glanced at her watch and stood up. "Oh geez, I should go. I still need to stop at Wegmans on the way home! I wish I could stay and help some more. I've had a lot of fun."

"Me too. And I'll check the other songs. I'll let you know if I find them. Fingers crossed."

She crossed her fingers in solidarity. "I'd appreciate that, thanks."

I opened the door for her as she took out her car keys.

She looked up at me and said, "So it looks like I won our little bet."

"Yeah, congratulations."

"Prize depends on who lost, remember?"

"So that means I choose your prize?"

She nodded, a faint curl of a smile forming at the corners of her mouth, her hazel eyes sparkling.

I hesitated. I had a good idea what Natalie wanted - she wanted me to kiss her. While I enjoyed her company this afternoon, as well as last Sunday, something held me back. I couldn't quite put my finger on it. One thing I knew for certain, I couldn't begin a relationship right now, given my current circumstances. I didn't have a job, I had issues with Fanny to deal with, Dad needed attention, and these songs! These songs had turned my life upside down! Not to mention Friday's concert...

"Well?" she asked, disrupting my thoughts. "My prize?"

My mind spun with jumbled, out of control thoughts, so I blurted out: "So, I'm in a band now, and we're playing Friday night at Rooster's Rockhouse. I'm on keyboards. Would you like to come and hear me play? I mean, *us* play? The band? Um, I think you'd have a fun time."

The words spilled out of my mouth as fast as Rimsky-Korsakov's *Flight of the Bumblebee.*

"That's my prize?"

The surprise in her voice sounded sincere. If she were disappointed or offended, she hid it well. I'm sure she thought my answer had come out of left field, which it had.

"That's your prize."

"You never told me you're in a band!" she said. "That sounds totally fun! I'll be there! Thanks!"

She sounded interested and enthusiastic. I watched her bound down the staircase. Upon reaching the bottom, she turned around and looked up at me.

Smiling sweetly, she said, "Now, is this the same band that Don is in? Because he's left two messages this week about how his band is playing at Rooster's this Friday night, and he's asked me to come."

A deaf person could have heard the teasing in her voice. I felt the blood drain from my face. How could I have forgotten that Don had invited her? Ned had suggested it last week, and Don had said he planned to!

"Uhhh..." was all I could manage.

"I hadn't planned on going, but now I will. See you Friday, Frank!"

She headed to her car, leaving me dazed, without the capacity to say good-bye, or to thank her for the tape, or for dinner. Only one thought ran through my mind:

*I am so screwed.*

* * *

With a loud, long yawn, I pushed myself away from the dining table, stretched my arms wide and flexed all my fingers. All my joints were stiff and cramped. My watch read 11:20. For the past five hours, ever since Natalie had left, I had searched every song for Dad's cryptogram. And I had found the remaining eight. The C-A-D motif was hiding in plain sight throughout, a secret love note concealed within secreted love songs.

The songs lay spread across the table, each one open to the page containing the cryptogram, encircled. No two songs used the exact same permutation, nor was it located in the same part of every song. In several instances, the motif crossed between treble and bass clefs. Dad had taken great pains to not duplicate the effect, and it never appeared forced or out of place. If not for Natalie, I wouldn't have discovered them. She'd be happy to know I found them all.

Unfortunately, I lacked any enthusiasm to tell her. Not due to the lateness of the hour, either. All I felt right now was embarrassment. I dreaded Friday's concert. It would be beyond awkward, and I couldn't do anything about it.

Another large yawn, and I began straightening up the compositions, arranging them in sequence. While doing so, I stopped to compare the cryptograms between two of the songs, one of the romances, and the first waltz. The romance's cryptogram occurred halfway through the piece, and was played by the right hand, while the waltz's appeared in the first ending, also in the right hand. The same motif written in different forms, both songs written in a different key.

My eyes narrowed the longer I looked at each piece. I dropped into my chair, and my eyes darted between the two scores. The more I looked, the more it seemed that another pattern was emerging. A second cryptogram?

Letting go of the romance, I grabbed the Humoresque, which was covered in Natalie's circled notes resembling violet halos. I compared the piece to the waltz, then to the romance. There was no mistaking it.

"Dad, you ingenious bastard," I whispered.

I snatched the pen, and circled the trio of quarter notes immediately following the C-A-D cryptogram in the Humoresque. These, though, weren't located in the bass clef, but in the treble. I proceeded to the romance. Here, the C-A-D cryptogram were the second notes in a progression of augmented seventh chords, all in third position. The subsequent set of chords contained the notes of the second cryptogram, in the same placement within the chord. The notes matched those from the Humoresque, and I circled them.

The waltz's second cryptogram had been a little harder to find. The C-A-D, designated by three eighth notes, appeared in the first ending. The following measure, though, was a second ending, which wasn't played next when the piece was performed. The first ending directed the pianist back to the song's first measure, which contained eighth notes.

And the three eighth notes matched perfectly.

"You sly, ingenious bastard," I said, smiling.

I fished out the napkin Natalie had used at Grandpa Sam's, where she had written C-A-D. Beneath it, in capital letters, I wrote the second cryptogram: 'G-A-E♭'. E-flat meant -es, or the letter S. And if A stood for La, as it did for the "la" in Clara . . .

I wrote out the word *Glass*, and let the pen slip from my fingers.

"I think I just discovered Clara's last name."

# CHAPTER 28

**M**y sweaty palms left a film of perspiration on my steering wheel as I drove to Joey's house. It was Friday evening, and practices were done. The next time I'd be standing at the keyboards, it would be in front of hundreds of drinking, smoking, rock n roll fans. And Fanny. And Natalie.

I had performed in countless concerts. I had given hundreds of recitals and auditions. I'd conducted middle school band for the past four years, where the members barely kept tempo, much less kept their composure, before their classmates and family members. All those experiences, not once had I ever felt as nervous as I did this evening.

My heart pounded like a kettle drum. Blood coursed through my veins with the power of Niagara Falls. It seemed impossible to catch my breath. Despite playing the simplest music I had ever played. Despite not being front and center. All because Fanny and Natalie were going to be there, watching and cheering.

At a stop light, I released the steering wheel. My hands shook. I wiped my palms on my pants, and rolled down the window. The breeze tousled my hair, and I took deep, calming breaths, while playing the set list through my mind.

The last two practices had gone by without any hitches. On Thursday, we'd worked on the transitions between songs, and I'd hit my spots on the mark each time. This morning we'd done two full run throughs, and everything had gone well. Playing in the highest-level ensembles and concert bands throughout high school and college had provided me the skills to seamlessly blend in. Of course, something could still go sideways. Plenty could go wrong during a live show, from technical difficulties to rowdy fans breaking stuff, from sudden illness to power outages. Contingencies could handle most expected problems, but unforeseen things could happen, or an unwise last-minute decision could get made.

Like inviting Natalie. We hadn't spoken since Wednesday. I had been too embarrassed to even tell her that not only had I found all the cryptograms, but that I had found the second one as well. As far as I knew, she still planned to show up. A part of me hoped she'd change her mind, or chicken out.

Why had I invited her anyway? Her Wednesday afternoon visit played over and over in my mind. I knew she liked me; the mixtape proved that. I just didn't know what to do about her. She was an enigma, and she confused me every which way. This would be so much easier if Don weren't in the picture.

Three blasts of a car horn sounded, startling me. Looking up and seeing that the light had turned green, I quickly accelerated through the intersection.

I thought back to this morning's run-through. Ned had given us the details for the concert while we packed the gear. We were scheduled to go on at 9:30, and he wanted us to be at the bar no later than 8:30.

"I know it's earlier than necessary," he had said, "but better safe than sorry."

He had come up to me while I zipped up my keyboard case.

"Dude, you really should have invited Jessica. What's the worst she could've said?"

"Yes?"

I was dead serious. She and I hadn't spoken since my haircut, and I had begun to believe Fanny's theory that I'd broken her heart. I didn't want to find out if she had been right, and I definitely didn't want to find out the morning of the concert.

Not to mention I had already invited Natalie. A guy can only deal with so much drama at one time.

"Well, I get it, dude, I really do," Ned said, slapping me on the back a couple times. "I don't understand, but I get it."

"You and me both, pal," I said.

I had driven home after practice with a lot on my mind.

Now it was nearly 8:00. I turned onto Joey's street, and parked in front of his house. Ned's Impala was pulled up the driveway. I took one last deep breath, hopped out, and headed up the drive. Sounds of Ned and Joey loading gear into the pickup truck came from the backyard. Joey had backed up his truck towards the garage. I heard grunts as they loaded a large amp into the bed.

With as much confidence as I could, I shouted out with raised fist, "Dudes! Let's rock!!"

Ned and Joey stepped out from behind the truck. Ned looked like Meatloaf decked out in Bon Jovi hand-me-downs: black t-shirt under a fringed black leather jacket, covered with silver rivets and zippers, ripped blue jeans, black boots, and a red and white bandanna, wrapped around his head like a pirate skull cap. Joey wore black and white leopard print stretch pants, a white tank, black headband and wristbands, and a pair of white Converses. Their long hair was brushed out and frizzy.

Their mouths fell open. They cast sideways glances at each other, then turned back to me. Joey started laughing.

"What the hell are you wearing?" Ned asked.

I stopped and looked over my outfit: red parachute pants, a tight white tee, a couple gold chains around my neck, dark Ray Bans, and white Keds.

"What? This is my bar outfit."

"Dammit, Frank, this isn't a Wham concert!" Ned exclaimed. "Denise!!" he yelled towards the house.

Denise exited through the back door, wearing a leather skirt, matching leather boots, a cropped jean jacket, and a large black polka-dotted bow in her hair. She did a double take when she saw me.

"Flock of Seagulls in town?" she asked.

"He's George freaking Michael," Ned said. "You gotta help him. People will kill him if he gets on stage looking like that."

"What do you expect me to do?" she asked. "I can barely make you look half decent."

Ned turned to Joey, and punched him on the shoulder to get him to stop laughing. "Dude. He's about your size. Find him something to wear. Denise, fix his face and hair, too. Time is short, people!"

Joey waved for me to follow him. As he approached, I noticed thin black eyeliner drawn beneath his eyes, and dull patches of rouge tinting his cheeks.

"I wish I had a camera," he said, chuckling. "Don won't believe it."

"Make-up?" I asked. "I gotta wear make-up?"

"Let's go, George," Denise said. "I'll pretty you up."

Ten minutes later, I came out of the house completely transformed. Gone were my clothes. Now I wore a torn gray t-shirt, a black leather vest with all the buttons missing, a pair of black jeans with a silver-studded belt, and a pair of black boots a size too large that added two inches to my height. For color, Denise had added two bandannas, one orange and one yellow, loosely tied around my neck. I still had my Ray Bans. My hair, moussed and sprayed, felt spiky and stiff. Denise had drawn eyeliner beneath each eye, and my cheeks were smoothed out with an application of rouge and a daub of powder.

"It's to keep you from looking like Casper the Ghost," she'd said when she rubbed it on. "Bright lights."

Joey disappeared into his garage, just as Ned emerged carrying two snare drums, and saw me leaving the house. "Well, it's an improvement."

"I look like Adam Ant and Cyndi Lauper's love child," I said, being careful not to stumble down the steps. I carried my clothes in a shopping bag. I wanted to wear the Keds, but Joey wouldn't hear of it.

"And I feel like Lurch in these stilts."

Ned smacked me on the shoulder when I reached the truck. "Hey, you want to blend in with the band, or get killed?"

I felt like these boots might kill me anyway.

Joey loaded his bass drum in the truck, and closed the tailgate. "That's it, Ned. Time to go!" He had his drumstick bag in his hand.

Denise and Ned hopped into his Impala, while I stutter-stepped down the driveway towards my car, and tossed the bag in the rear seat.

As Ned backed into the street, he yelled out the window, "It's Toehead time!!"

Joey came to a stop at the bottom of the hill. As I climbed into the passenger seat, my hair scraped the headliner, making an uncomfortable scratching noise.

Joey lived less than ten minutes from Rooster's. At a red light, he reached over and flicked a couple spikes.

"Denise took zero chances. That's not moving anywhere."

I cocked my head to the side. "As long as I can get my old hair back."

Joey laughed. "So. You nervous now?"

I recalled how he had asked me that, after our first practice, and shrugged my shoulders. "The only thing I'm nervous about is someone recognizing me."

No sooner had the words left my mouth, than a lump formed in my throat. Fanny and Natalie would recognize me! I felt sweat trickle down my back, between my shoulder blades.

Joey laughed even louder. "Fat chance, dude! *I* barely recognize you!"

We followed Ned into the bar's rear parking lot. Joey parked his truck as close to the entrance as possible, while Ned slid into a nearby spot. As I got out of the truck, Don and Linda came out of the side entrance. Don's outfit resembled ours, except that his denim jacket's sleeves had been torn off. Soon all four of us stood together, looking like a pale motorcycle gang advertising for Estee Lauder. Denise pulled out a Polaroid camera.

"For the album cover," she joked. We locked arms, and the bulb flashed.

"Dudes," Don said, "you're not gonna believe this, but I called Natalie this afternoon after practice, and she's agreed to come!"

Ned and Joey congratulated him with thumbs up and soft jabs to the shoulder. I felt all the color drain from my face. If not for the rouge, they would've noticed. She accepted his invitation? What sort of game was she playing?

I smiled as honestly as I could, smacked him on the back, and said, "That's fantastic, man! Good for you!"

As Joey dropped the tailgate, Ned grabbed me by the arm. "Welcome to rock 'n roll, dude. This is gonna be something else!"

*No. Kidding.*

\* \* \*

Dragging in the gear and setting up took the better part of an hour. The stage easily accommodated everything with room to spare. My keyboards stood to the left of Joey's kit, next to a stack of amps, behind Don. Ned played stage left. It was the typical classic rock trio arrangement, with the last-minute added bonus of a quasi-unnecessary, rookie keyboardist shoved in the back, more or less out of sight.

After plugging in my keys and checking the connection to the amp, I headed towards Ned as he adjusted his microphone stand. Joey tightened the wing nuts on his cymbal stands, while Don made sure his basses were tuned. Linda and Denise checked the amp hookups.

"I'm set," I yelled to him. Eddie Money's *Take Me Home Tonight* blared over the sound system, combined with the rumble and din of indiscriminate crowd noise. "Anything else?"

Ned grunted as he twisted the pole grip, setting the boom

at the height he wanted. "Grab some beers? They told me the first round is on the house."

A beer sounded good. We exchanged thumbs up signs.

We were twenty minutes from show time. I scanned the room, looking for Natalie or Fanny, but saw neither. The easiest way to find Fanny would be to find Mike: I figured there would be few six-and-a-half foot tall guys in attendance. A dozen or so tables were pushed back from the stage, every seat filled, while the remaining patrons milled about, holding beer bottles and mixed drinks. Some patrons - girls for the most part - danced to Eddie Money. A thick haze of cigarette smoke hovered near the low ceiling, dimming what little light the fluorescent lamp panels cast. Banks of spotlights in black metal housings hung suspended from the ceiling. They were currently off, but soon the house lights would dim, and these would blaze to life. Steel framed columns stood at each stage corner, adorned with similarly sized spotlights, all angled stage-ward.

*Maybe they won't show. Maybe Fanny couldn't get a babysitter. Maybe Natalie changed her mind.*

If they showed up, they'd try to get as close to the stage as possible. Natalie for whatever reason - to make me nervous, or impress Don. Who could tell? Don's announcement outside caught me off guard. I didn't know what to think now.

Fanny would try to distract me, or laugh at me. At first, I imagined feeling mortified at her embarrassing me. However, thinking about it seemed to calm me. It would be so like her to shout something funny, and thinking about that gave me a weird sense of peace. I squatted down and hopped off the three-foot high stage. I twisted and angled my way past mingling drinkers and dancers, gathered in clusters of four and five. A waitress, carrying a tray of empty bottles, drifted past, and I touched her elbow to get her attention.

I held up six fingers and yelled, "Six Miller Lites!" I motioned at the stage. "For the band! On the house, right?"

She nodded, turned, and snaked her way through the

crowd towards the bar.

People brushed past and closed about while I waited for our beer. Van Halen's *Why Can't This Be Love* blared out now, getting the crowd more excited. Several guys sang into their beer bottles like microphones, while their dates danced along. My heart pounded louder in rhythm with the song. I took several deep breaths, feeling the excitement build. I kinda liked it.

I watched customers stream through the entrance, beyond the corner of the long bar. The place would be at capacity soon, and I still hadn't seen the girls. I glanced at Don on stage; as he adjusted his mic's position, with his bass slung over his shoulder, I noticed his eyes searching the crowd.

*He's looking for Natalie, too.*

The waitress came back at last, bearing a tray full of drinks. I grabbed my six beers by their necks, three in each hand. She yelled out "Have a great time!" then weaved her way towards a table to deliver another order.

The larger crowd pressed tighter against the stage, making my way back a little tougher, forcing me to squeeze my way through. The heavy air stank of sweat, smoke, and beer. Three bouncers, all muscles and frowns, wearing bright red logoed t-shirts, had taken their place in front of the stage. One stepped aside as I approached, allowing me to climb back on stage, and distribute the beers around.

Ned took a long swig and then yelled over the strains of Scorpions' *Rock You Like A Hurricane*, "You ready?"

"Hell yeah!" I answered.

I tried to sound confident, but there were beads of sweat breaking out across my forehead. We all clinked bottles. I hoped they didn't notice my shaking hand. Just then, the house lights flashed, and the Scorpions song stopped in mid-chorus. The guys slammed what remained of their beers; I left mine unfinished.

"Time to rock!" Joey yelled out.

Denise and Linda kissed Ned and Joey, and took all the bottles with them before leaving the stage. The incessant hum of patrons' voices morphed into a chorus of hoots and whistles, accentuated with moderate rounds of clapping, just as a feedback howl from a microphone squealed from the sound system. We took our positions.

After the feedback died down, a deep voice rang out while the lights dimmed to near darkness. "Okay music lovers and rock 'n roll fans from across the fruited plain, it's nine-thirty, which means it's time for the number one live show at the number one venue in all of Rochester! Three bands, back to back to back, rock 'n roll, all night long! Are you ready?"

A loud cheer rang out.

"I said, are you ready?" the announcer repeated.

The crowd delivered a louder, more sustained cheer. The excitement was infectious; Don hopped up and down repeatedly, and I shook my hands to keep my wrists loose. Joey spun his drumsticks between his fingers.

"Let me know when you're ready!" the announcer said, and the noise grew into a roar.

"Then give it up for Toehead, making their Rooster's Rockhouse debut!!"

Immediately, all the stage lights switched on, blazing like a dozen fiery suns. The crowd broke out into wild applause, and Ned launched into the opening sequence of Rush's *The Spirit of Radio*.

But in that compressed moment of time between the darkness disbursed by the stage lights, and Ned playing the first note on his Stratocaster, even as the crowd's clamoring overwhelmed nearly every other noise, I heard a strong, distinct, recognizable female voice yell out three words.

"NICE HAIR, FRANKIE!"

# CHAPTER 29

We brought the house down. The bar limited us to two encores despite the crowd wanting more. Everything went right. The transitions, the mechanics, the sound system, the instruments: everything. I hadn't had this much fun for as long as I could remember, and for over an hour, thoughts of Dad, Clara, unemployment, Jessica, Natalie, and Fanny were far removed. Fanny yelling my name a split-second before we began boosted my confidence, and drew me into the moment. All my stress and worry had been wasted effort. The performance became all-encompassing, fueled by adrenaline, driven by the crowd, and energized by our combined enthusiasm and talent. My heart pounded in time with each song, and my ears rang.

Ned had told me I would have the time of my life, and he'd been right.

We bowed for the final time amid the cheers and applause, our arms around each other's waists. My clothes were thoroughly soaked, despite the fact that I'd hardly moved one step the entire show. The other guys were completely drenched, their hair matted and slick, perspiration dripping into their eyes and off their noses. Joey whooped and gave his head a shake, sending drops of sweat everywhere. My hair hadn't collapsed into a sloppy mess of sweat, gel, and hair spray as theirs had, but it still felt like I had biked twenty miles. In ill-fitting boots. I'd have blisters before the night ended.

Denise emerged from offstage and said, "Next act starts in twenty minutes."

Ned nodded, and took a deep breath. "Let's break it down, pack it in, and worry about making it pretty tomorrow. Frank, you're the new kid, so you drag it outside, k?"

"Sounds like a plan," I answered, and got off the stage.

The customers had begun to recede like an ebbing tide, while the bouncers maintained their position. I quickly scanned the dispersing crowd for Natalie, but didn't see her. I didn't notice Fanny or Mike, either. Wherever they were, catching up with them would need to wait.

Five guys emerged from the side hall leading to the parking lot, two carrying guitar cases, while the others pushed carts laden with amps, cables, equipment, and drums. They glanced around the bar as they sauntered in, as if gauging whether the crowd deserved their presence. Their outfits were more outrageous than ours - bigger hair and flashier, wilder clothes. They looked like a knock off version of Poison.

"Kick ass show," the first one told me. "Thanks for warming up the crowd."

"No problem," I said. "Give us a few, and we'll be outta your hair in no time."

"What?" he asked. He dropped his case and teased his platinum blond over-styled hair, a worried look crossing his face. "Something wrong with my hair?"

I gave a short sigh. "No, I said we'll be out . . . you know what? Never mind."

Don handed me his bass guitars. I grabbed them and headed down the corridor to the parking lot. Linda came up behind me, a case in each hand.

"I'm supposed to watch the gear while you bring it out," she told me. "Joey said that's more my speed, whatever that means."

*It means she's busted one or two things in the past.*

Over the next twenty minutes, I hauled the gear out to the parking lot as quickly as the guys had it ready. Joey had relocated his pick-up to a parking spot next to Ned's car. As our equipment came off the stage, the next band's equipment replaced it. At last, the four of us trudged down the corridor with the last of Joey's drums, and my keyboards and stand. Denise carried several coils of cables.

"Okay, so the next thing we buy are some carts," Don quipped, a snare drum in one hand, a cymbal stand in the other.

I brought up the rear, carrying my keyboards, and, upon leaving the building, saw Linda chatting with another girl. Natalie. Time seemed to slow. She wore a black mini skirt and white blouse, covered with a matching black vest, and black high heeled shoes. Her hair looked like Molly Ringwald's in *The Breakfast Club* - wispy long bangs, feathered curls framing her face. She looked nothing like she had at O'Shea's or the Music from the Movies show. She looked fantastic.

And as soon as I saw her, all my fears, doubts, and un-certainties from before the show rushed back. As soon as Don had told us she was coming, I'd known that her presence would create an extremely awkward situation. Now that she stood twenty-five feet away, that time had come.

Don's stride lengthened when he caught sight of her. Ned shot Joey a knowing glance, his mouth stretched into a wry grin, as they loaded drum components into the truck. Joey spared a peek over his shoulder towards Don. At that moment, Natalie noticed Don, and she turned towards him.

"Wow, you came!" he said. I heard more surprise than happiness in his voice.

She smiled, and for a second, I dared to think she was smiling in reaction to his greeting. But I knew better. Natalie looked *towards* him, but not *at* him. Her gaze fixated on me, past him, over his shoulder. Her hazel eyes sparkled. Don came to a sudden stop, and slowly turned around.

I stopped at the same time, still several feet behind him, opening my mouth to speak before he could say something. To call her out for having accepted both our invitations.

I never had the chance.

A familiar voice called out from behind me: "Hey you!"

*Jessica??*

It was my turn to do a one-eighty. Jessica stood at the door, thumbs hooked into the belt loops of her blue jeans. Her face beamed at me, a broad, perfect smile. Standing nearby were Fanny, Mike, and Jessica's older sister Brenda. They must have followed us down the hall, keeping back far enough to not alert me to their presence. Fanny smiled as well, looking as if she had just pulled off a grand deception. They all applauded as I stood there, unsure of what was going on.

I tried to speak, but my mouth had gone dry, and I could manage only a few semi-coherent syllables.

"You're...you came? How...what..." My eyes darted between Jessica's dazzling smile and Fanny's amused look.

Jessica walked towards me, her eyes sparkling. "Fanny invited me. She didn't want me to tell you. So, surprise!!" she exclaimed, raising her arms skyward in dramatic fashion.

She hugged me, and I lowered my keyboard to the pavement to hug her in kind. She wrapped her arms around me, stood on her tiptoes, and kissed me twice on the left cheek. I returned her hug with a few timid, restrained pats on her back. Though she smelled of tobacco and alcohol, I detected the faint aroma of orange blossom and hibiscus.

My eyes narrowed at Fanny. She shrugged, placing one hand upon her chest, and mouthing *Who, me?* while her face shone with mischievous enjoyment.

"Love the hair," Jessica said, lightly poking the porcupine-like spikes. She giggled once. "I mean, it's no Rob Lowe, but it looks kinda cute on you."

I felt a tap on my shoulder, and I turned sideways. Natalie had stepped up behind me. Her smile had disappeared, replaced with a tight-lipped expression.

"Well. This is interesting." Indignation dripped from every syllable.

I swallowed, and could only manage an "Uh..." in response. Natalie stood on one side of me, and Jessica on the other.

Jessica's eyes widened a fraction when she saw Natalie.

"Oh hi!" she squeaked, fingers wiggling in a friendly wave. "I remember you from O'Shea's! Natasha, right?"

"Natalie," she corrected, folding her arms, neither smiling nor waving in response.

Jessica cocked her head and squinted. "Say, aren't you with Don?"

I gave a quick look his way. His expression bordered on bewilderment and irritation, probably heading into full-blown anger territory.

I tried to answer, but Natalie answered first.

"Frank invited me," she said, her left eyebrow slightly arched, her voice a mixture of scorn and smugness.

Jessica's smile vanished in an instant. The back of my neck suddenly felt hot. She looked up into my eyes, and I gave her the most innocent smile I could, hoping to soften the fury that was sweeping across her face.

Before I could offer any defense, she slapped me on the cheek where she had just kissed me. The smack resounded off the cars and walls and pavement like a crack of thunder. My face whipped to the right, and my smile was sent skittering across the lot. Everyone gasped in unison, after which even the universe itself seemed to hold its breath.

"You said there wasn't anyone else!" she spat. "You lied to me! How could you?!"

Jessica made a motion as if to slap me again, and I flinched in response, but she held back, letting her arm fall limp. Tears gathered at the corners of her eyes, and without another word, she turned and marched back into the bar. I watched her leave, unable to find any words. My cheek stung, my ears rang with the echo of the impact, and tiny sparks of pain danced at my vision's periphery. Brenda scowled at me before following her sister inside. Fanny's mouth formed a perfect circle, her eyes bulging, while Mike stood with hands on hips, deep disapproval etched across his face.

Natalie gripped my shoulder firmly, forcing me to turn.

Her face displayed anger and betrayal. As I rubbed my stinging cheek, she suddenly slapped the other one, swiveling my face leftward. Pinpoints of light filled my eyes, and the ringing in my ears intensified. My hair hurt. Everyone gasped again, deeper and louder this time.

"Just a friend, huh?" she asked, each word harsh and bitter. "You are so full of shit."

Natalie stormed away, each step a clipped exclamation mark of hot fury, out of parking lot and towards the main entrance. She brushed past Don and the guys without a single glance.

As her footsteps echoed away, I tried to blink away the pain. Through teary eyes, I noticed Fanny still staring at me, her mouth agape, her face displaying shock and amazement. Mike watched Natalie stalk off, then looked back at me, confused.

Both cheeks burned. I squeezed my eyes shut to beat back the tears. I hadn't envisioned tonight turning out this way. Why did Fanny have to invite Jessica? Why did Natalie have to ignore Don? Why did both end up here, at this moment, in this parking lot, in front of everybody? Things couldn't possibly get any worse.

"So, you and Natalie?" Don asked. "You make a move on her?"

My shoulders dropped, and I sighed heavily.

*Oh crap.*

He had lowered Joey's drum components to the ground beside him. His hands clenched and unclenched to a silent, slow rhythm. His expression wavered between anger and confusion, as if he were trying to decide which emotion was more appropriate. I didn't think confusion would win.

"It's not what it looks like," I said. It hurt to speak.

Ned and Joey remained by the tailgate, most of the gear still on the pavement. They hadn't packed anything since this had begun. Denise and Linda were near the driver's side door, eyes riveted on me. No one spoke.

Don spread his hands. "Yeah? But you invited her? And you knew I invited her too."

"It's kinda complicated," I said. "But I'm gonna just say, she called me, okay? She started all this. And, and you did say she wasn't your type, right? I mean, she treated you like you weren't even standing there. Pretty rude if you ask me."

All delay tactics, which I knew wouldn't deter him.

"But you invited her," he said again. "That's what she said."

Don's sole focus fixated on that singular point of truth. Nothing else mattered. I tried to think of some way to make him see sense, but my mind felt scrambled, uncooperative. The concert noise still droned in my head, and the double slap had exacerbated it. Appeals to logic weren't going to work.

"Yeah, about that," I said. "It just kinda happened. See, she stopped by a couple days ago, and when she left...."

"Whoa whoa whoa!" Don interrupted, holding up one hand.

*Whoops!*

He took a step closer, and I retreated one step.

"She was in your apartment?" His eyes glowered. "What the hell, Frank? You had her OVER?"

I swallowed hard, and ran a hand through my hair.

"Uhhh . . . okay, look. This isn't a good time for this discussion, so how about we . . ."

Don interrupted a second time, coming two steps closer. "How about we discuss this with my fist in your face?"

I backpedaled, as Don's hands formed into fists, his face dark with anger, his lip curled. Joey and Ned swooped in to restrain him. He tried to shake free, but they grabbed him by the arms and shoulders, holding him back. Their expressions shifted between fear and shock, perhaps more out of concern for Don than for me. The veins on Don's neck bulged.

"Screw a buddy's girl behind his back?" he shouted. "What kind of friend are you?"

Ned grimaced at me. "Dude, it's best if you just go. Now."

"Go? You mean, leave?" I asked. Ned nodded, and I looked at Joey. "Really?"

"I ain't driving you, man," Joey said. He stood six inches shorter than Don, and struggled to hold him back.

"What about my keyboards?"

"You got hands," Ned said. "Carry 'em. Or bum a ride. Your call."

"But leave right now?" I asked again in disbelief.

"If you don't want to be picking your teeth up off the ground like Chiclets," Don added, his face red and gnarled with anger, "then yeah, leave. Right now."

I felt a large presence come up beside me, and I quickly looked to my left. Mike cleared his throat.

"Guys, Frank's face has had enough for one night."

"Thanks, bro," I said softly, nudging him with my elbow.

I hadn't realized that he and Fanny had stuck around.

"Shut up, dumbass," he said, looking down at me, zero compassion in his face. "I'm only doing this for Fanny's sake."

"Oh."

Don sized Mike up, took a deep breath, then motioned to Ned and Joey that he had calmed down. They released him, but stayed close at hand. He shook his shoulders, and pointed his finger at me.

"You suck, man. Totally suck."

With that, he shuffled back to the truck, while Ned and Joey accompanied him. Ned looked over his shoulder, shook his head, and turned away.

I grabbed my keyboards, and headed towards Fanny, Mike in tow. I had expected to see a lot more anger in her gaze, but she wore her anger in her stance: perfectly erect, arms crossed tightly against her chest.

I grinned sheepishly and said, "Thanks for saving my ass."

She smirked, and then slapped me on the left cheek. Not as hard as Jessica or Natalie had, but hard enough to rattle my jaw.

"What was that for?" I asked.

Fanny shrugged, the smirk still drawn across her face. "Why should the other girls have all the fun?" She suddenly became serious. "That was for Jessica. Didn't I say you were going to break her heart?"

I looked at my feet. That hadn't been my intent. None of what happened tonight had been my intent. I raised my eyes, meeting Fanny's.

"Yeah, you did," I told her. "I'll have to fix it somehow. But right now, I could use a lift. Can you drop me off at Joey's?"

Mike started to answer, but Fanny grasped his arm, and shook her head.

"We can't. We drove Jessica and Brenda, and I'm sure they'd like to go home now. I'm sorry."

I looked at my feet a second time. Stupid boots with two-inch heels. Joey lived a mile away.

"It's okay," I said. "I get it."

She reached up and patted my shoulder. "For what it's worth, you sounded good up there. We had a lot of fun, and they were smart to not let you sing."

She smiled sweetly, and motioned towards Don and the others. "I hope you can fix that, too. They may be losers, but they're the only friends you've got."

"Gee, thanks Fan. If you said that to make me feel better, it didn't come out the way you meant it to," I said.

Fanny grasped my chin and scrunched my face, making my lips pucker. "You're so cute when you're wrong. I always mean what I say, and I always say what I mean."

She released me and looked up at Mike. "Let's take the girls home."

She grabbed my bandanas, and pulled my head down to kiss me on the cheek, while Mike nodded in his typical brother-in-law way. I knew they were disappointed, but neither believed in kicking a guy when he was down. Their coming to my defense didn't mean they approved what I had done, but I was still grateful they had come. As they went back inside, a raucous roar of applause erupted from within, followed by a rapid-fire sequence of electric guitar power chords. After a couple measures, I recognized the tune: *You've Got Another Thing Coming*, from Judas Priest.

*No kidding.*

I looked back at the others. The guys ignored me, and Denise and Linda stared at me with disapproval, arms crossed. I sighed, and wobbled out of the parking lot, westward to Dewey Avenue.

* * *

The moment Joey had made me put on the shoes, I'd hated them. By the time the show had started, I'd loathed them. And now, as I reached the intersection of Ridge Road and Dewey Ave, less than five hundred feet from the bar, I despised all of humanity, but most especially the fashion designer who'd created these things. Whoever thought male biker boots needed two-inch heels deserved whatever cruel fate befell them.

How did girls do this? Twisting one or both ankles remained a distinct possibility, as well as falling flat on my face, so the twenty-minute walk ended up taking twice as long. It was nearly 11:30 when I limped up to my car. After changing into my clothes and slipping on my Keds, I placed Joey's boots and other items on his rear porch steps.

I then returned to my car, opened the window a couple inches, rested my head against the steering wheel, and closed my eyes.

The slow, deliberate walk back had given me plenty of time to think about everything that had transpired in the parking lot, and I still didn't have a good answer. In the span of ten minutes, I'd pissed off my best friends and most likely gotten myself kicked out of the band, broken Jessica's heart for sure, and incurred Natalie's wrath. She would probably never speak to me again. Add to that the fact that I'd disappointed my sister and ruined everyone's fun night, one could say I'd over-achieved in spectacular fashion.

Numerous variations of 'if only' played out in my head. If only I had been in front of Don instead of behind him, I would have seen Natalie first. If only I had said something witty or smart, instead of stuttering like a fool. If only Fanny hadn't invited Jessica. If only they had waited in the bar instead of fol-lowing us out. If only I hadn't invited Natalie in the first place.

Would she have come if I hadn't invited her? Maybe? Don had said he'd asked her after today's rehearsal, and that she'd said yes. The way she'd blown him off, though, seemed incon-sistent. Totally bogus. Why had she acted that way if she'd really told him she'd come? It didn't make sense.

*The games girls play.*

Then again, maybe Natalie had planned to say some-thing to Don before things got awkward. Perhaps she had meant to greet me first, and then explain things to Don, to smooth things over. Maybe she had prepared a speech, to pre-serve Don's dignity, so he could save face in front of his friends. It was possible, I suppose. A part of me was still convinced she'd made up that elaborate story about the *Music of the Movies* concert tickets, about her 'friend.'

Jessica's appearance, though, had changed everything, and Natalie's plans would've gone out the window as soon as she'd seen her. And Jessica's being there was Fanny's fault. She should have called me and said, "Hey I'm inviting Jessica along, you okay with that?" But she hadn't. Jessica was the innocent lamb led to the slaughter, totally and completely unaware that her emotions were going to get ripped to shreds.

Not that Fanny had known about Natalie being there. But still, Jessica had been there solely because Fanny brought her. How was it my fault she'd come out of the bar at that exact moment? How was it my fault she had acted like we were more than friends?

Plus, she'd overreacted when Natalie said I had invited

her. If she hadn't slapped me, I would've had the chance to explain. Since when do best friends slap one another? And Natalie wasn't 'anyone else.'

"Hell no she's not!" I shouted, smacking my steering wheel.

Across the street, a man walking his dog shouted back, "Shaddup, you drunk!"

I slunk lower in the seat, watching him continue down the sidewalk.

Natalie wasn't 'anyone else.' Not even close. Sure, she'd made me a mixtape, but as a joke. And sure, we'd hung around my dad's childhood home for a bit, and pretended we'd lost her puppy. And maybe we'd played duets together, but so what? So what if we'd looked for cryptograms together, racing to see who could find the first one? That didn't make her 'anyone else.'

I understood why Natalie had been upset, the way Jessica had flung herself at me. I had told Natalie the truth, that we were good friends. But she should have been mad at Jessica, not me. Jessica had hugged and kissed me. I hadn't kissed her in return, had I? No. But once again, I wasn't allowed to defend myself. If Natalie had let me speak, that ugly scene never would have happened. But she'd flown off the handle.

Same with Don. Instead of giving me the opportunity to explain that nothing had happened between us, he'd interrupted. Twice. And then threatened to knock my teeth out. For what? Anyway, Natalie could've at least said 'Hi' to him, and complimented him on the show. If she had, maybe he would have been a little less angry.

Amazing. Everybody had lost their temper, instead of staying calm and rational. All of this could have been avoided if people could have kept their heads.

I started up my car. Flicking on the headlights, I shifted into drive, and pulled away into the street.

Why *hadn't* I invited Jessica? It didn't have anything to do with Natalie, because I'd invited her a couple days ago, a stupid, random spur of the moment thing. Jessica and I had last spoken when she'd cut my hair. I'd joined Toehead the next day. I could have invited her any time, but hadn't. Then again, my life had been crazy since I'd lost my job. When would I have had time? I'd been so busy learning the set, practicing with the guys, dealing with family drama, worrying about being unemployed, thinking about Clara and the songs, and . . . and Natalie. Two non-dates with Natalie.

Come to think of it, I hadn't told Jessica I lost my job, either. I had told the guys, I had told Fanny, and I had told Natalie. I had even told my waitress! But I hadn't told Jessica. Why not?

*You're over-analyzing way too much, dude.*

# CHAPTER 30

With a sudden start, I awoke from a deep sleep and bolted upright, momentarily unsure of my whereabouts. My surroundings came into slow focus, and I recognized my bedroom. Sunshine squeezed through the blinds, leaving narrow strips of light across the bed. I rubbed my eyes, feeling breathless and startled, and collected my thoughts. I squinted at the clock on the dresser. 11:42. Extremely late for me. Work? No, it was a Saturday, and besides, I no longer had a job. Something family related then. My brain cycled through images of family faces. Fanny? Mike? Dad?

Then I remembered. The Labor Day barbecue at Aunt Jane and Uncle Pietr's.

Relieved that I hadn't overslept, I took a deep breath, closed my eyes, and fell back against the mattress. My mouth felt like damp spackle. I tasted stale cigarettes; I had been too exhausted to brush my teeth when I got home. I'd barely had enough energy to trudge up the stairs and stagger into the bedroom. The last thing I remembered was tumbling into bed after getting undressed.

Last night had started with promise, and ended in a disaster. For a moment, I had envisioned joining Toehead permanently, playing gigs all over town. But in an instant, my exhilaration had been shot down by a trifecta of catastrophe: Jessica, Natalie, and Fanny.

I couldn't confront Fanny this afternoon. I knew she wouldn't create a scene in front of the relatives, many of whom we hadn't seen in almost a year. That would be inappropriate and out of character. She never aired dirty laundry with family present. At best she'd shoot me dirty looks, and at worst pull me aside and scold me in private, in which case I planned to explain how she had caused the entire mess.

Anger and frustration began to well up, but I suppressed them. I didn't want to deal with either right now. I sat up again, and swung my legs off the bed. After another yawn, I inspected my feet. Both ankles were red and chafed, and felt worse than they looked. Each big toe sported a nickel sized blister, and my heels felt tender to the touch.

I arched my back, stretched my neck, then headed with a slight limp towards the kitchen. After starting the coffee, I took a long, hot shower, washing away the smoke, the beers, and the sweat. The odors seemed to have a texture, like a thin layer of wax. It felt good to rinse it all off - like shedding old skin. I shampooed twice, figuring two rounds would suffice to expunge the gunk and goo Denise had used.

I stepped out of the shower, and wiped the condensation off the mirror with my towel. When I saw my reflection, my jaw dropped in horror, and I let out a strangled cry of panic.

*  *  *

I stabbed the round, bubblegum pink doorbell with vigorous determination. I could hear the chimes repeat from behind the solid storm door, which was stenciled with an array of bright flowers and fluttery butterflies. My agitation grew with every passing second.

Finally, a woman's irritated voice called out, "Alright already. I'm coming!"

The deadbolt snapped back, and the door opened a crack. The silver door chain pulled taut, and through the gap, a freckled face framed with unruly red curls appeared. Pam eyed me with suspicion.

"Frank?" she asked. "What do you want?"

She released the chain and opened the door all the way.

"And since when do you wear a baseball cap?"

I didn't have time for stupid questions. After pulling the stiff brim further down over my forehead, I gave her a stern look.

"Pam, this is serious. Is Jessica home? I stopped at the salon, and they told me she didn't show up today."

She folded her arms and leaned back, her mouth quickly folding into a condemning accusation. Her body language said everything I needed to know: Jessica had told her about last night.

"You've got a lot of nerve coming here," she snapped. "She's in no mood to talk to you."

She moved to close the door, but in one fluid motion, I flung open the screen door and stuck my foot against the door jamb, preventing her from shutting me out. I was bound and determined to see Jessica.

"This is an emergency," I said through gritted teeth. "I need to see her."

Pam shot me a look that could have peeled paint, but soon relented and let me come in. As she headed up the stairs, she said, "I'll tell her you're here, but that doesn't mean she'll want to see you."

"I'll wait in the living room," I said. "Tell her she's the only one who can help me."

She rolled her eyes and continued on her way. I exhaled through pursed lips, and sat on the futon in their living room. It was folded over a wooden frame, covered with a pink and light blue striped comforter. I squirmed to get comfortable, but there's no good way to sit on a futon.

I heard Pam knock tentatively on the door at the top of the steps, and call Jessica's name. Then, a hushed conversation. Pam's voice sounded pleading, though with less persuasion than I would have preferred; Jessica's responses were nothing more than barely audible murmurs.

My morning's simple plan had changed the moment I'd

looked in the mirror. In a mad dash, I'd thrown on clothes, brushed my teeth, and grabbed a baseball cap from the floor of my closet before flying down the steps to my car. I had made incredible time getting here, even though I'd stopped first at the salon - it had taken me less than half an hour.

The girls' exchange continued for a few more seconds, followed by the sound of Jessica's bedroom door closing. I stood up and prepared myself for the worst, as footsteps came from the stairwell. Pam entered the living room, looking wary.

"She said she'll be down in a couple minutes," she reported, then abruptly left the room, plodding back up the stairs.

Seconds seemed to take minutes, and minutes seemed to take hours. I looked out the large front window that faced the lake. Beachgoers were spread out across the golden sand, some playing in the gentle waves of Lake Ontario. Picnickers ate at picnic tables, or on laid-out blankets, enjoying the warm Saturday afternoon.

I suddenly turned to my left, and Jessica was leaning against the wall at the entryway. She had come downstairs noiselessly. She wore a simple light blue tee and white shorts. Her hair was pulled back into a ponytail, held in place with a scrunchie. Her big eyes seemed smaller somehow. Her face, normally glowing with happiness, looked impassive and dusky, like the sky an hour past sunset.

Her arms were folded, and she held a guarded stance.

"Why are you here, Frank?" She sounded spent. "What's so important?"

"Um, this," I answered, and I removed the ballcap.

Jessica's eyes widened with shock. "What happened to your hair?!" she gasped.

"I'm hoping you could tell me," I said. "I washed it this morning, and something reacted with whatever gunk Denise used."

Jessica approached me, a mixture of fear and amazement on her face. "It's so . . . so clumpy. And orange."

A mirror hung on the wall next to the foyer, and I glanced at my reflection. She was right. In the daylight, the orange seemed to dominate the light browns, yellows, and auburns. None of which were my natural hair color. And 'clumpy' described it well. Little hairy knots dotted my scalp.

She reached out with a tentative hand, and lightly pressed my hair. "It's like . . . like," she paused, unable to come up with a comparison.

"Like furry freeze-dried marshmallows glued to my head," I finished for her. "Can you fix it?"

She withdrew her hand, took a step back, and re-crossed her arms. "Depends."

"On what?"

"On how genuinely, truly sorry you are for your behavior last night."

I bit my lower lip. "Okay. Which means...?"

"Which means shaving your head is one way of fixing your hair, and that's the stage you're at right now."

I grinned, expecting her to respond in kind. When her expression remained serious and somber, my grin vanished.

"Listen," I said, "I get you're angry. And believe me, I'm glad you were there last night. It meant a lot to me."

I paused, hoping for a positive reaction. Her posture didn't change, her face unreadable. I swallowed hard.

*Why is it so hard to tell her what I figured out? Isn't it as obvious to her as it is to me?*

"But here's the thing, Jess. I gave it a lot of thought last night. Do you know what happened after you left?"

She nodded. "Fanny told me. Natalie slapped you, and Don wanted to punch your face, and would have if Mike hadn't stepped in to protect you."

I spread my hands. "So you get how this has been one huge misunderstanding, right?"

"That's it? Just a misunderstanding?"

I shrugged slightly. "Fanny invited you, and if she hadn't, none of this would've happened, and your feelings wouldn't have gotten hurt."

"What?!" Jessica drew in her breath as if to suck all the air out of the room. "You're blaming your *sister*?! Frank, how could you?"

"What?" I asked. "It makes sense to me."

She stepped towards me, and jabbed a perfectly manicured fingernail into my chest. "You just don't get it, do you? My feelings were *already* hurt, because you hadn't invited me!"

She poked me hard in the sternum, a poke for each word after 'because.' The last poke stung with extra emphasis.

"Not only that, you invited *her*. We've been friends forever, and you only met her a couple weeks ago. You never told me you joined their band. You never even told me you got fired. Fanny told me when she invited me."

My eyebrows rose at that revelation. She stepped back again, her bosom rising and falling after a deep breath.

"You say we're best friends, but you never told me about any of this. How do you think I felt when I found out?"

"You looked happy last night," I said.

"Of course I looked happy! A girl learns to put on faces when she needs to. I was happy for you. You'd rather I looked sad and mopey? Don't you understand?"

We stood in silence. Jessica avoided eye contact, instead staring out the window. I tried to make sense of this conversation. I had figured it out last night, but now doubts nagged me. Could I have been wrong?

The word 'her' echoed in my head. Of course Jessica was angry I had invited Natalie. I already knew that. The sting in my cheek from her slap still seemed fresh. I wasn't that stupid. But she was assuming that I had a thing for Natalie, and that I had consciously chosen Natalie over her. That was why we were having this misunderstanding.

"If you're worried that there's something between me and Natalie, I assure you that ... "

"If we're best friends, Frank, why should that bother me?" she interrupted. Her chin quivered, and her eyes blinked rapidly. "Right? We're just friends."

"I'm just saying you don't have to worry about it."

Her cheeks were turning redder, and she slowly shook her head.

*It all made so much sense last night.*

My watch read 1:10, and I needed to leave. I cleared my throat. "I'm in a bit of a hurry. What about my hair?"

"ARE YOU FREAKING KIDDING ME?" Her nostrils were flared, and her eyes flashed. "How can someone so smart be so stupid? Do you really want me using sharp objects close to your neck right now? Do you?"

Her breath quickened, her chest rose and fell rapidly.

"You break my heart, then you have the nerve to come here, expecting me to fix your effed up hair, no apology whatsoever, and in fact, you blame your sister, taking no responsibility for what you did. I'm hurt, embarrassed, pissed off, I feel taken advantage of, and dammit Frank, I still want to love you, but I can't. I can't take it. I can't believe I loved you, and I can't believe I saved myself for you! I wanted you to be the one, but you've turned out to be just like all the rest. So screw you, and screw your screwed up clumpy, orange hair!"

Her body shook, and she pointed an angry finger at the foyer.

"You need to leave!"

I made to respond, to ask her to reconsider, but a twitch of her mouth told me she wouldn't.

Spreading my arms, I asked, "Would a hug help?"

She shrunk away. "Just go."

I replaced my hat, and with slumped shoulders, moved towards the door. Upon reaching the foyer, I turned around, giving her a wistful look. Only her anger restrained her grief. I saw that now.

"Jess, I am so, so sorry. Please forgive me."

Her lips trembled. "Goodbye, Frank."

I let myself out. As the screen door swung shut behind me, her heartrending cries clearly resounded over the muffled pattering of her feet as she raced up the stairs. I reached for the knob, but upon hearing her bedroom door slam heavily from within, I withdrew my hand, and descended the porch stairs, my eyes blurry and clouded.

❊ ❊ ❊

By the time I reached Uncle Pietr's house, the turnaround was lined with half a dozen cars. I recognized Mike and Fanny's distinctive dark blue Plymouth Voyager minivan with wood-grain cladding. I parked behind it.

I readjusted my baseball cap. It had never occurred to me that Jessica wouldn't perform her hair care magic, and fix my grotesquely multi-hued clumpy hair. All we had to do was reach an understanding, and I'd thought I had it all figured out.

I'd thought wrong. I had misinterpreted her tone, and ignored her feelings. The image of her laying in her bed, crying inconsolably, played over and over in my head. I needed to make things right, but I didn't know how. I didn't know if I could. Her goodbye had sounded final, and it had been the most terrible thing I had ever heard. Going there had been a mistake.

Muffled, happy chatter came from the rear of the house, and I heard Fanny's distinctive laugh. I recalled what she told me the other day:

*"This is exactly why you should talk to me about your girl issues. All these years, and you still think you can solve them without me."*

Except I had believed this had been all her fault. I had been angry at her for inviting Jessica behind my back.

Another round of laughter. Time to join the party. I walked around the corner of the house, hearing women's voices babbling, punctuated with an occasional splash and the carefree laughter of children. I let myself in through the iron gate that surrounded the pool.

The crystal blue water shimmered in the sunshine. Several children played in the shallow end; Justin was splashing water with three of his cousins. Fanny sat at a round patio table, in the shade of a green and white striped umbrella, with Rachel on her lap. Aunt Jane sat next to her, and my cousins' wives Molly and Kim sat across from them, their backs to me as I approached. Smoke and steam billowed skyward from two grilles standing close to the house, outside the fence, as two chefs busily attended to them. The aroma of German sausage and barbecued chicken wafted its way across the backyard.

Justin saw me first.

"Uncle Frank!" he exclaimed, hoisting himself out of the pool.

He splashed across the bricks as he ran towards me, leaving wet footprints in his wake. Upon hearing his shout, Rachel squirmed off of Fanny's lap and scampered my way. Justin met me first, giving me a wet hug, and then Rachel grabbed my leg. She wore a slightly damp, bright yellow bathing suit.

"Hey monkeys!" I said, placing my hands on their shoulders, giving each a squeeze. "Are you behaving?"

They both nodded. Molly and Kim turned in their chairs to see, while Fanny rose and headed towards me. Aunt Jane waved, as did my other cousins, who were in the pool.

"Hello, everyone! Sorry I'm late."

"Pietr and the boys teed off at 11:30," Aunt Jane called out. "We were going to call, but Fanny said you might not be in the mood to play?"

Her tone sounded as if she hadn't quite accepted Fanny's explanation.

*Golf with the guys! That's what I forgot!*

I simply shrugged and said, "I overslept, that's all."

Justin tugged at my shirt. "Can you come swim with us? Please?"

"Forgot my bathing suit, pal. Sorry!"

After a disappointing 'Awww,' he dashed back to play with his cousins. Rachel hung close as Fanny reached me.

"Baseball cap?" she asked, one eyebrow raised. "That's new. So you just overslept, huh?"

"Scout's honor," I told her, hand raised in mock salute.

"But you were never a scout."

As she leaned in to kiss me on the cheek, she stopped and pulled up short. "This won't hurt, will it?"

The pain from last night's slapfest had gone. I chuckled and said no.

"Oh, too bad." As we exchanged a kiss, she whispered in my ear: "You've spared me. I forgot how boring our cousins are."

When we reached the table, I gave a peck to Aunt Jane, and greeted Molly and Kim. The chair next to Fanny was vacant. I sat down, and we filled the next fifteen minutes with small talk. Pitchers of lemonade and iced tea stood on the table, next to a platter of glasses. I would've liked something stronger, but that would have to wait until the golfers returned and the food was served.

"Be a dear, and refill mine, would you?" Aunt Jane asked, offering her glass. As I poured, she said, "It's a shame you missed the golf, Frank. It meant the second foursome was short a man."

I wondered what she meant. Her two sons and two sons-in-law would've played as one foursome, leaving Uncle Pietr to play with Mike. If I had been here, we would have comprised a threesome.

"I don't understand," I said. "Who's the other golfer?"

"Why, Viktor of course!" she said, as if surprised at my question. "He drove up from Pennsylvania last night. Alice couldn't come, unfortunately. Something to do with a birthing cow, I think he said."

"Uncle Viktor's here? That's great!" I said. "I haven't seen him since Mom's funeral. Gosh. I haven't been to the farm in at least fifteen years."

Molly chirped. "We took the kids down a couple years ago. Hasn't changed a bit."

For the next ten minutes, we shared memories of trips and weekend stays. During the conversation, I thought of questions to ask Uncle Viktor. I hadn't intended to discuss the house on Barrington today, but with Uncle Viktor here, the perfect opportunity had presented itself.

Fanny pinched my elbow, perhaps a bit harder than she had intended. I pulled it away sharply, glaring back. She smiled, and through her grin, said, "Let's go chat."

She rose from her seat, and said to the others, "Would you excuse us a moment? A brief family confab. Ivan."

The others nodded with sympathetic looks on their faces. Mentioning Dad made for a graceful exit.

"How about that bench by the front door?" I suggested.

Fanny nodded, and as we walked, she yelled back to Rachel and Justin, "I'll be back in a minute, kids! Going to talk with Uncle Frank!"

"Is this about last night?" I whispered.

She took my arm. "No, I need investment advice," she answered, her husky voice heavy with snark. She was still smiling; she probably didn't want any of the family to see us arguing.

"Buy high, sell low."

"If that's your advice, it's no wonder you suck at relationships," she quickly replied.

We walked the rest of the way in silence. I figured she'd tell me what had happened during their drive home the night before. I wondered if I should preempt her, and tell her I wished she hadn't invited Jessica at all, before she had the chance to recount every painful detail of the conversation.

*Best to wait to see what she has to say, and go from there.*

The cement bench stood across from the front door beneath the portico, flanked by two concrete urns filled with ferns and flowers. We sat down in the shade of a tall elm, whose shadow stretched across the lawn. Its leaves were just beginning to shift from green to yellow.

Fanny took a deep breath. "You were in rare form last

night, buddy. I have never seen you act that douche-y before. You can be a jerk at times, and you've certainly been a jerk to Dad, but last night? All I can say is, wow. Oscar-worthy performance. You invited another guy's girlfriend?"

"It's not like that. Natalie is not Don's girlfriend."

"Don thinks she is, or wants her to be, based on his reaction." She held up her hand as I opened my mouth. "Stuff it. I know what you're about to say, but we aren't talking about Natalie's actions, and she isn't here to explain herself. You're responsible for your actions, and regardless of her feelings for Don, you shouldn't have invited her. You made a bad call. You jumped in where you had no business jumping."

She had known what I'd been about to say.

"I'm not defending her actions, by the way," Fanny added. "Blowing Don off in front of everybody was pretty bitchy. But like I said, you screwed up big time. She obviously likes you, and you made it sound like your date . . . I mean, *non-date*, had been mutually enjoyable. You know, Mozarting her Chopin and all that."

"There's something about her I haven't figured out yet."

"Well, you might not get the chance now," she said. "I mean, it looked like she slapped you harder than Jessica did. But listen, we all make mistakes. The hard thing is knowing which ones define a person, and which ones are lapses of good judgment and common sense. You gotta figure that out."

"Yeah." I heaved a sigh. "How can you tell, though? Say Mike says something that really pisses you off. How do you know if he made an honest mistake, or if he was being a jerk?"

Fanny smiled kindly at me. "By how quickly he apologizes, and tries to make up for it. It's not all that complicated."

I swallowed, and looked away, wanting to focus on anything other than Fanny at that moment. I settled on the elm tree, its branches rustling from a slight gust of wind.

"Oh."

She rubbed her hand across my back, somewhat spontaneously, from shoulder to shoulder, like Mom used to do after I had argued with Dad. Mom didn't necessarily take sides, she just hated seeing me upset. She must have done the same for Fanny.

"If Mike gave me a lame excuse, or tried to justify his behavior, it meant he was just being a jerk. Sure, we argue like most couples do, and sometimes over stupid stuff. But I know his heart. And we don't let stuff fester. Which is why it's so important that you apologize to Jessica as soon as you can. She was so upset last night, you have no idea. But trust me, after all these years, she knows your heart."

She paused for a moment.

"And can I give you another piece of advice?"

"I guess so."

"You don't need to be her protector anymore. She's outgrown being Tommy's baby sister. You did a great job filling his shoes, but that's not what she needs. She's no longer a little girl. It's time to shit or get off the pot. Know what I mean?"

I knew what she meant. I'd known it since last week, back in her salon. If I was honest with myself, I'd known it for years.

"Because the last thing you want," she went on, "is Jessica thinking you're a big, fat, thoughtless jerk."

I closed my eyes, slumped my shoulders, and let my head droop. Fanny immediately removed her hand, and I felt her tense up beside me.

"What?" she asked. "Oh Frank. What did you do?"

I pressed the heels of my palms against my eyes, an elbow propped on each knee, and grimaced.

"She already thinks I'm a big, fat, thoughtless jerk. With clumpy orange hair."

"What. Did. You. Do."

"I should probably go back to her house and apologize again."

"Go back?" Fanny asked. "You went there this morning?"

I pointed to my hat. "My hair's a mess, so I went to see her, hoping she'd fix it."

Fanny reached up to remove my cap, but I slammed my hand down on it to prevent her.

"No way. Trust me, it's not pretty. Anyway, I said the wrong thing, and when I left, she was crying."

Fanny folded her arms, her face full of admonishment. "What wrong thing?"

"I'd rather not say. She called me a jerk, said she doesn't love me, and then kicked me out. She didn't accept my apology. I have to fix this."

I got to my feet, but Fanny snatched my shirttail, and yanked me back down.

"You can't leave the party!" she said, her posture suddenly erect. "Aunt Jane arranged this barbecue because of you! If you leave me with the Stepford Wives," she spat out, jerking her thumb towards the house, "then as God as my witness, you will wish Don had punched you in the nose last night!"

I knew she was serious, but so was my problem.

"But Jessica. I gotta make things right. Apologize as soon as I can. That's what you said." I hoped she heard the concern in my voice.

"Don't you dare throw my words back at me!" she said, pointing an angry finger. "Jessica isn't your only problem. If you were to leave twenty minutes after arriving - arriving late, I might add - what excuse would you give Aunt Jane? You've made this bed, you lie in it."

I gritted my teeth. Fanny was right. I couldn't just up and leave.

"Fine."

"Oh, stop feeling sorry for yourself. You screwed up, so own it. Be a man about it."

She stood up and brushed off her butt, scattering flat flower petals upon the grass.

"Next time you see Jessica, be super-duper sorry, hat in hand. No excuses." She paused. "Speaking of hat in hand...."

She snatched my cap.

"Give me that!" I demanded through clenched teeth, my

hand grasping for the hat. I lurched towards her, but she took several steps backwards on the grass, staying just out of reach. She laughed once or twice, but then her laughter caught in her throat, and horror washed across her face. She quickly jammed the hat back on my head.

"For the love of Pete!! What . . . what happened?"

"I warned you it wasn't pretty," I growled, adjusting the hat.

"Frank, leprosy isn't pretty. Mick Jagger isn't pretty. That," and she pointed at my head, "is hideous. Nightmarish. Have you considered shampoo?"

"Shampoo *caused* it. Some weird chemical reaction, which is why I went to see Jessica."

"Whatever you do, keep that on, lest you scar the children for life." She took a deep breath. "We should go back. They're probably wondering what's taking so long. And don't worry, I won't tell them you're a horrible human being. Let them figure that out on their own."

"You're all heart, Fanny."

"It's why you love me," she said, wrapping an arm around my waist and squeezing. "And why I love you. Your cluelessness is an endless source of entertainment."

"You're welcome?"

We headed back, but when we reached the corner of the house, I stopped.

"I've got something else to tell you. It's about Dad's songs."

I explained how I'd found the pair of musical cryptograms in each piece.

"Frank, that's amazing! But what do they mean? You still don't know if Clara's her real name. 'Glass' could be her last name, but it might mean something else completely."

"I know. But it's another indication they were intended for someone else. Why else would Dad have gone through all that trouble?"

"Because he was a moody, melodramatic Russian composer?"

I smirked at her. "Listen, I know those songs don't exactly make you happy, and that you'd rather I forget about them. But I feel I'm so close to figuring this out."

Fanny wrinkled her nose, and sighed. "In all honesty, I think I've come to terms with them. I'm sure there's a reason why you were meant to find them, I just can't see it yet. Whatever it is, I'm hoping it's for the better."

"Not a lucky coincidence then?"

"I don't believe in coincidence," she said quickly. "Believe it or not, when we found the boxes, my first instinct was to pitch them. Since Dad and Mom hadn't bothered to ID them, I figured they were unimportant. Mike convinced me to save them, and something inside me told me he was right, so I agreed with him, on the condition that they be given to you."

We resumed our stroll back to the party.

"Where'd you get the idea about the cryptograms, anyway?" she asked.

"Oh, yeah." I stammered, and started nibbling on my lower lip.

Fanny tsked, gave a short gasp, and stopped in her tracks. "Don't tell me. Natalie?"

"We came up with the idea at the same time," I said, trying to look innocent.

Realization spread across her face. "When you admitted Natalie had been at your place! Boy, Don was pissed. What in the world were you thinking?"

I quickly explained how Natalie had stopped by after taking her sister to college, and how I had shown her the compositions.

"It was all her, Fanny. I never invited her over, and Don's mind immediately went to thinking we had sex. We had dinner, we looked at the songs, and that's it. In fact, I found the second cryptogram after she left."

I inhaled deeply, realizing I had been speaking in fourth gear, and on a single breath. Omitting the part about the mixtape seemed wise.

"I believe you, but it's Don you have to convince," she said. "Hoo boy, she's got it bad for you. I see why she slapped you. They're both your problem, and I'm staying out of that mud pit. I mean, I'll grab a popcorn and watch with great amusement as you make it worse, but I'm not getting involved. I'm solely concerned about Jessica."

I considered agreeing with her, but instead said nothing until we rejoined the others.

# CHAPTER 31

Shortly after we rejoined the others, the golfers returned, a little bit sunburned and a little bit buzzed. Mike and two of the cousins were enjoying Uncle Pietr's cigars. Aunt Jane looked restless, curious to know why mine and Fanny's absence had lasted so long, but now that everyone was finally present and just about ready to eat, her curiosity would have to remain unsatisfied. I found it amusing.

Uncle Pietr came up to me, and clapped me on the shoulder as I stood to greet him. "We waited as long as we could, Frank. The starter said, tee off or no golf. What happened?"

"Forgot to set my alarm," I confessed. "Sorry I missed it."

Behind Uncle Pietr stood a man who practically could have been his twin, though he looked slightly older and more weatherbeaten.

"Uncle Viktor, so great to see you!" I reached out to shake his hand, which he ignored and instead nearly crushed me in a bear hug.

"Little Frankie," he said, his voice gruff with cigar, beer, and age. I would never outgrow that name with him. "You look good. How are you?"

"Fine," I said. "It's been a long time."

After rounds of greetings and a quick recap of how everyone had played – Mike, the natural athlete, had won with a miracle chip-in birdie on the 9th hole - Whitney stepped onto the patio and announced that lunch was ready. The moms herded kids from the pool and wrapped them in thick multi-colored towels, and the rest of us made our way towards the patio sliding doors. Fanny ruffled Justin's hair with an orange towel while his teeth chattered, and Rachel stood patiently, cocooned in a Care Bears towel, only her face showing. Mike whisked her up as effortlessly as a feather pillow.

"Let's go eat, Monkeyface," he told her, and I smiled. Mike adopted the nickname I had given her.

I turned around and saw Uncle Viktor standing behind me, watching Mike carry Rachel to the house.

"She is princess of the family, nyet?" he asked, with a broad smile.

"Her royal highness is the queen, actually," I replied, as we followed Mike to the door. "Uncle Viktor, I'm glad you came. I have a couple things I'd like to ask you during dinner, if that's okay."

"Da, and I may have one or two things to tell you," he said. "When Pietr invited me, he said you had a conversation about Ivan. You are curious about family history."

"You could say that."

We stepped into the dining room. A buffet had been set up on the long table. Aunt Jane stood at the far end and tapped the side of her glass with a spoon, getting everybody's attention.

"Once you serve yourselves," she announced, "please return to the patio. It's much too nice to be eating indoors. Enjoy, everyone!"

Mike lowered Rachel to the floor, and grabbed several plates. He handed one to Fanny, another to Justin, and they joined the cousins and their families at the buffet.

"You are the last to marry," Uncle Viktor said, as we stepped into the back of the line. "Pietr's and my children, married. Fanny, married. Only you are left."

A knot formed in my gut. "Someone's gotta be last," I said.

"Is there someone special?" he asked, a twinkle in his eye.

Viktor considered himself the village matchmaker, town gossip, and market busybody, simultaneously. There were no questions too awkward, no observations too uncomfortable. The last time we had spoken, ironically, had been in the buffet line at Mom's funeral luncheon.

*"Little Frankie, you did a good job reading at church."*

*He dropped a spoonful of mostacholi on his plate, and we shuffled down the line.*

*"Thanks." I spooned some green beans onto my plate.*

*"And the priest gave good sermon. Seems like a good man. Beautiful prayers at grave site, too. I saw a pretty girl standing next to you in the cemetery. Someone special?"*

*"That's Jessica. We're just good friends."*

*"Good friends make good spouses. Alice was my best friend, you know."*

*"You don't say. Jessica's 15. Aunt Alice, though. A great woman."*

*"Da, the greatest. Have I ever told you the story of how we met? We were 15 at the time..."*

*The story lasted until we reached the end of the buffet.*

"Not really, no," I answered him, but that wasn't true.

The memory reminded me that Jessica had been more than just a good friend when Mom had died. Her experience with having lost Tommy had helped me get through my grief. She had been my rock. Come to think of it, she'd attended most of my important events: concerts, graduations, award ceremonies. She'd always been there for me, without me having to ask.

By the time I returned outside, the cousins and their kids occupied three tables. Fanny and her family sat at the remaining table, with enough seats for me, Uncle Pietr and Aunt Jane, and Uncle Viktor. I hadn't wanted to sit with Fanny and the uncles, though. Not with the questions I planned to ask. We'd be talking about the house on Barrington and the inheritance, which would then lead to Fanny getting upset in front of the family. It looked like I hadn't any other choice.

Uncle Viktor came up next to me and cleared his throat, startling me somewhat.

"You waiting for a bus?" he asked, smiling. "Let's sit with

Fanny and the queen, nyet?"

He headed towards their table, and as I followed, the knot in my stomach tightened a little bit more.

＊ ＊ ＊

At first, we engaged in light conversation. Pietr and Aunt Jane joined us shortly after I had sat down. I sat as far from Fanny as possible, Viktor to my left, and Pietr to my right. Fanny sat between Justin and Rachel, contending with their picky eating habits, while Mike, Uncle Viktor, and Uncle Pietr regaled us with highlights from their round of golf.

The other tables were boisterous. Children shrieked and whooped amid stern shouts and warnings to settle down, and eat their lunch. Compared to them, Justin and Rachel were angelic.

At one point, Aunt Jane touched Pietr on the arm. "It's so nice hearing the pleasant sounds of children at the house, isn't it?"

She smiled as she said it, but it seemed forced, and I saw embarrassment in her eyes. I was sure she was worrying about her neighbors' opinions.

Viktor chortled. "Roosters make pleasant sounds," he said. "This sounds more like foxes in hen house."

"Pietr, I should say something to them," Aunt Jane said.

"My love," he said, "enjoy the day. Time enough to complain tomorrow."

And that was that. Aunt Jane spent most of the meal informing us in great detail about how the Christmas gala plans were coming along, though she was still struggling to land entertainment for the evening.

"It's just one disappointment after another," she groaned. "I'm absolutely at wits' end!"

Uncle Viktor nodded towards me. "What work do you do now, little Frankie? Last time I was here, you were still in college."

"As of last Wednesday, I taught middle school band. Just got laid off."

Out of the corner of my eye, I saw Fanny mimic playing a keyboard, but I wouldn't be mentioning the band, especially since Toehead had now probably returned to being a trio.

Jane and Pietr's forks fell to their plate nearly at once, rattling about.

"You didn't mention this when you were here last week!" Pietr exclaimed.

"You poor thing!" Jane added.

"It happened the next day," I told them. "Budget cuts." I slashed the air with my knife for effect. "It's a state-wide thing."

"Whatever will you do?" Jane asked. She looked horrified. "How will you live?"

"Well, I have some money saved up, and I do get a severance. I'm thinking about offering lessons. I can teach most instruments."

Justin looked at Fanny. "Can Uncle Frank be my teacher? Please?"

"Mine too!" Rachel chimed in.

Fanny shushed them. "Eat your food, you two. Uncle Frank isn't serious, I'm sure. Right?"

She shot me a when-Hell-freezes-over type of look. I shrugged in reply and grinned. I knew she'd never hire me. Neither of us wanted to inflict our childhood disasters on her kids.

"Perhaps you come down to my farm, nyet?" Viktor suggested. "Pay is not good, but the rent is free."

I couldn't tell if he was serious, but working on a dairy farm didn't appeal to me. Besides, moving away had never been a consideration, unemployed or not. Fanny meant too much to me to leave, plus she was having another baby, and I couldn't leave Dad. Plus I had friends here...

*Used to have friends.*

Moving would be a simple way to avoid dealing with

those problems, that was for sure. I wouldn't have to face Don or Natalie. However, it would also mean leaving Jessica, and I couldn't do that to her, not without trying to make amends, without asking for forgiveness.

Like Fanny had said, I had screwed up, so I needed to own it.

I half-laughed at his offer. "I appreciate it, but I'm a late to bed, late to rise sorta guy."

"So are my cows!" he said with a smile, and everyone laughed.

Viktor spent the rest of lunch talking about Aunt Alice, the farm, and how their kids were faring. He used more tact in his telling compared to Aunt Jane, omitting personal issues and private troubles. Today was a happy day, a fun family day. For the time being, anyway.

Several white-coated servers emerged from the house, and began clearing our dishes, while one circled the table, re-filling our water glasses. The troupe of servers finished at our table, and as they swarmed to the next one, Justin and Rachel asked to be excused. Mike announced he was going to get a Heineken, and asked if anybody else wanted one. Everyone but Aunt Jane said yes, and Fanny asked for a Coke instead.

As Mike left, and the kids clambered off their seats and went to collect their cousins, Viktor turned to me and asked, "Little Frankie, you wanted to ask me something about Ivan and father. Was it about the will, the house, or something else?"

Fanny came to immediate attention, sitting straight up. "Excuse me, but what did you just say? What's this about Dad and Grandpa? And a will? Frank, what is he talking about?"

*Oh boy. The shit's about to hit the Fan.*

Everyone turned to face her, and looking at each person, she said, "I would like to speak with Frank privately, if you don't mind. Frank, inside."

She stood up, but I remained seated.

"Frank, come on. In the house." She had raised her voice,

and her face reddened.

To this day, I'm not sure what possessed me at that moment. Something inside empowered me to overcome my usual tactic of conflict avoidance. Maybe it was her tone of voice, or her presumption that I'd automatically fall in line and obey. Or maybe I had had enough. I could see her growing angrier, while my heart pounded like Tchaikovsky's cannons. But this was important to me, and I had to stand my ground, whatever the consequences.

I looked up at her as she stood across the table, her arms folded tight against her chest.

"We already had our private chat," I calmly said, "Right now, I want to talk with Uncle Viktor. You can either sit and listen, or you can go sit at one of the other tables. Your call."

It didn't sound like my own voice. Nonetheless, I liked the way it sounded.

Fanny blinked several times, and opened her mouth, but no words came forth. Everyone at our table stared at her. Mike remained several feet away, unmoving, carrying four beers and a Coke. For several seconds, no one spoke. Time seemed to stop, until a caterer dropped a spoon, which clattered upon the patio. Fanny closed her mouth, swallowed, and slowly sat back down. She seemed to wither under everybody's gaze, and as time resumed its normal flow, her eyes narrowed at me for just a second, before looking away. Mike offered the Coke to her, and she snatched it from between his fingers.

*Whoa.*

"We'll discuss this later?" she asked, though it might have been intended as a declaration. She pulled her knees up against her chest, heels on the front lip of her chair, and twisted off the bottle cap.

"I promise."

Mike winked at me, almost imperceptibly, while handing me a Heineken. Fanny didn't see it. It didn't come across as an 'Atta boy.' Mike never acted that way. He loved and respected Fanny with every fiber of his being, so he wasn't saying, 'Good for you for putting her in her place.' He meant something deeper, as if to say, 'You did the right thing for the right reason in the right way.' I felt reassured, somehow. If Mike was cool with what I'd just done, then it must have been okay.

Aunt Jane cleared her throat. "I think I'll see how Whitney and the catering staff are managing inside," and she excused herself demurely.

After Mike handed out everyone else's beer, he sat down next to Fanny, and Uncle Viktor repeated his questions.

"So. What is on your mind?"

"I'm not sure where to start," I said. The confrontation with Fanny had delayed my train of thought while still in the station, and I needed a second to get it moving again.

"Uncle Pietr gave me the address to the old house, and I went there the other day," I said, omitting any mention of Natalie. Uncle Pietr stirred a bit in his chair. "And I learned you still own it."

The two brothers exchanged glances. I couldn't see Pietr's expression, but Viktor looked surprised.

"How did you come to find out?" he asked.

"An old guy from the neighborhood saw me, and said a man named Vic Steppenoff rents it out. Maybe you didn't know, but it's currently vacant, and the yard service hasn't been by in a few weeks."

"As matter of fact, I do know," he said. "I intended to stop by tomorrow, to check on things before returning to Pennsylvania on Monday."

"I'd like to go with you," I said, "and see inside."

Fanny slid her feet off her chair, and leaned forward. "Daddy's childhood house is still around? It hadn't burned down?"

I nodded to her. "It's a beautiful house."

She looked at Pietr, then Viktor. "Why would Daddy lie to us about this?"

Neither man answered. Viktor focused on his beer, while Pietr chewed his lip. I decided to answer for them.

"Fan, it's a long story, and it involves Dad's inquiry, it involves Grandpa, and in one way or another, I'm convinced it involves Clara."

I could tell by her face that questions were forming in her mind, and if she started asking them, we'd be here for a while. Before she could speak, I continued.

"There's a lot about Dad's life we were never told, but right now isn't the time or place to get into it."

I indicated the other three tables; Fanny looked that way, and I saw that she got my point. The cousins didn't need to know about this. She leaned back in her chair, and grabbed Mike's hand. I looked back at Viktor.

"How about it?" I asked. "Can I meet you there tomorrow?"

He grimly nodded. "Da. What time?"

"Three o'clock," Fanny answered. "I wanna go too, after my regular visit with Daddy."

We all exchanged looks, and as a group, nodded in agreement.

"What else is on your mind?" Viktor asked.

"My other questions can wait until tomorrow."

I downed my beer. Tomorrow would be a long time coming, but I got what I wanted: getting inside the house.

"I hope to remember answers," Viktor said, a slight smile on his face. He looked past me to Pietr. "You have playing cards?"

"Da. Why?"

"Party is too serious. Fanny looks like she's trying to lay egg like my chickens. It is time for some fun, nyet? Get two decks of cards, and we play Durak. I'll get the others to play too."

I perked up, and glanced at Fanny and Mike, still holding hands. Her face appeared serious and brooding, but I saw the corners of her mouth soften a bit. Pietr went to get a deck of cards, while Viktor headed to the cousins' tables. Mike appeared a little confused.

I said to Mike, "Durak is Russian for fool. Remember playing two Christmases ago?"

"Oh yeah," he said. "I remember losing."

"Fanny, you in?"

Lines deepened across her forehead, and she crimpled her mouth. She squeezed Mike's hand, and stood up.

"I think I'll sit out, and watch the kids. But thanks. Just one game, honey, and then we should head home."

Mike nodded, and Fanny came around the table towards me. She patted my shoulder a couple of times as she passed by, then walked on to where Justin and Rachel were drawing with pastel chalks on the patio with their cousins.

Mike said, "Thanks for not tossing her a bowling ball."

I turned around to face him. "I thought I had."

"You almost did."

Viktor came back to our table and sat down.

"Some of the cousins will play," he told me, slapping me on the knee. "We'll have a tournament, best of five, and winners play each other."

"Only one game for me," Mike interjected.

Viktor rolled his eyes. "It will take one game for you to remember how to play!"

Pietr returned to our table carrying two decks of cards, and the cousins joined us. The ones not playing continued chatting, or joined Fanny, or swam with the children.

One game turned into two games, and two games turned into four. Pietr produced more cigars, and laughter flowed like cold Heinekens. Mike had just started dealing the fifth game when Fanny approached our table.

"Mike? The kids are beat, and if we leave now, we might make it to the 590 before they turn into pools of whiny mush. Keys please?" she asked, her hand outstretched.

"Good timing," I said. "Mike just lost, and was just about to deal the second game."

"Uh huh. Sure, second game," she said, rolling her eyes. "I'm not a *durak*. This is your fifth game, and Mike hasn't won a single one."

We all chuckled. She was right. Mike fished the keys out of his pocket and handed them to her. She hugged the uncles, smiled and said goodbye to the cousins.

"Aunt Jane is in her office," Pietr told her. "The afternoon heat doesn't agree with her."

"We'll cut through the house, then, and say goodbye" she said. "Thank you so much for hosting. It was great seeing everybody."

Most of the cousins took that opportunity to also say good-bye. Once they had gone, me, one cousin, Pietr, and Viktor were left at the table.

"I've been meaning to ask you all day," Uncle Pietr said. "Why are you wearing that hat?"

Viktor said with a laugh. *"Shapku s duraka ne snimayut."*

"What's that mean?" I asked him. My Russian was far too limited to translate that.

Pietr broke out in laughter. "'*One should not take the hat away from a fool.*' It means you deal."

# CHAPTER 32

The barbecue ended an hour after Fanny left. Once goodbyes were exchanged, and thanks lavished upon Uncle Pietr and Aunt Jane, and having reluctantly accepted a tin foil catering tray full of leftovers - "I don't want you to starve!" Aunt Jane pleaded – I was finally able to leave. It was around seven o'clock by the time I made it home.

I noticed the blinking message light as soon as I walked in the door, emitting a recurring pattern of three red flashes. Never before had dread surged through me as it did right now, seeing that red light. The knot I'd felt in my gut earlier returned - tighter, larger, and more uncomfortable. The party had been a welcome distraction from the storms in my life, but heavy black clouds still hung low overhead, ready to drop a torrential downpour of Biblical proportions.

Fanny had told me to man up and own it. Easy for her to say; she wasn't the one having to deal with it. Then again, she'd been dealing with her own issues. Maybe I shouldn't complain, especially since I'd done this to myself.

I couldn't go back and undo any of it. And while ignoring the problems and disasters seemed like an easier course of action, I knew it wouldn't solve anything. Keeping things uncomplicated had always been my philosophy. But life had suddenly become complicated, and sticking to that philosophy would probably make things worse. Running away from problems, or shutting people out, wasn't going to work.

Taking a deep breath, I went back to the living room, stared at the red light flashing its portents of doom, and with grim resolve, pressed Play. I sat down on the arm of the couch to listen.

"Hi Frank. It's Natalie. I'm . . . I'm not sure why I'm call-ing, to be honest. I'm over being mad, I think. Well, as soon as I think I am, I get all mad again. I feel like you lied to me about Jessica. I feel . . .I don't know. I've never slapped anyone before. I thought you were different. I had hoped you would have called by now, but maybe you won't call at all. Maybe I shouldn't have called. And now I feel stupid for leaving this message. Bye."

Her voice sounded angry, confused, and discouraged. Mistrust laced every word, as if she was using a tentative foot to test thin ice, uncertain that her weight would be supported, afraid the wrong step would send her crashing through into frigid waters. My feelings were equally unsettled. Both of our behaviors disappointed me, and I regretted putting her in that position. Fanny was right - I'd no business doing what I'd done. But beyond an apology, what else could I say?

"Franklin, Ned. Dude, I got your cash for last night. I'll come out Sunday around noon and drop it off, save you a trip. And your keyboard stand. If you're there, cool. If not, I'll uh, slide it under your door or something. Not the stand though. That's too big to fit under the door. Later."

The next message was five seconds of dead air, followed by the click of the receiver being replaced.

I erased the messages. My instincts told me that Jessica had made that final call. Natalie didn't seem the type of girl to do that. She would have talked; she couldn't help herself. Jes-sica calling me probably meant one of two things: either she was considering accepting my apology, or she had called to say good-bye forever. The fact she'd hung up without saying anything made me fear it was the latter. It wasn't like her to say good-bye over an answering machine. The ball was in my court.

I needed music, to clear my head and settle things down before I called anybody. The two new Beethoven albums leaned against the stereo. I had listened to both already, but which one for right now? Concerto No. 3 in C-minor, or Concerto No. 4 in

G-Major?

*Minor is dreary, major is cheery. Concerto No. 4.*

\* \* \*

Halfway through the third movement, the phone rang, disturbing my reverie. At first, I considered screening the call, but I decided that hiding behind my technology would be the coward's way.

I picked up the receiver. "Hello?"

"Oh. Frank. You're . . . home."

Natalie. Hearing her voice filled me with a vague sense of relief. Of all the people I had pissed off, Natalie was the only one I felt ready to talk to. Our relationship wasn't completely destroyed, perhaps because it was the newest. Like a coffee mug with a cracked handle, maybe all it needed was a couple of spots of crazy glue to repair it. My friendships with Jessica and Don, in comparison, lay shattered into pieces large and small.

"Well, yeah, this is my home, where I live," I said, trying to come across as lighthearted.

"You weren't home earlier, is what I meant." She sounded tired and serious.

"Family thing," I said, leaning back. This wouldn't be a lighthearted conversation. "I got your message."

A beat. "Oh."

Did that pause mean she didn't believe me? Or was it a sign of annoyance over the fact that I hadn't returned her call? Did it matter one way or the other? I didn't want to let semantics and second guesses add more confusion. Cut to the chase.

"I've done a lot of thinking since last night," I said.

"Me too," she answered. "You first," she quickly added.

That was only fair. After all, I owed her the phone call.

"First of all, I shouldn't have invited you to the concert. That was a mistake. I knew Don had invited you, yet I invited you anyway. So, I'm sorry."

Several seconds of silence. "Shouldn't you be saying that to Don?"

"Excuse me?"

"Inviting me betrayed him, not me. You're apologizing to the wrong person. You're apologizing to me for the wrong thing."

I removed my ballcap. It suddenly felt tight around the temples.

"But if I hadn't invited you, you might not have come, and none of last night would've happened. I put you in an awkward position."

More seconds of silence passed. "You're really not good at this, are you, Frank."

"Um . . ."

"Maybe you should think some more tonight," she said. "After you get it figured out, call me."

"What? Wait!" I spoke. "Don't go."

A few more seconds of silence. "I'm still here."

"Can I try again? I mean, I really did think a lot about this last night. Lord knows I had plenty of time. And maybe I reached some wrong conclusions, but I realized I made mistakes. And yeah, I do suck at this. Big time. So can I get one last chance?"

"It doesn't have to be a last chance," she said. "Unless you want it to be."

I swallowed. "Okay."

I took a deep breath, exhaled through whistled lips, and closed my eyes, recalling last night's events. When Natalie had slapped me, she'd said I had lied to her about Jessica being more than a friend. In her message, she'd sounded hurt and disappointed. That I hadn't apologized. But I couldn't apologize for the way Jessica had acted. I couldn't apologize for the friendship we shared.

And a lot had happened since Friday night, stuff that needed processing. What if Jessica and I were no longer friends? Or what if, by some sort of miracle, we became more than friends?

She'd said I apologized for the wrong thing, just now. What had she wanted me to apologize for?

And then I remembered the expression on her face, as she stood in the doorway of my apartment last Wednesday, waiting for me to decide. How she had looked up to me, her eyes full of expectation and hope. There were plenty of reasons why it would have been the wrong thing to do, despite the fact she believed it would've been right. Maybe that was what she wanted to hear.

"Frank?" Her voice broke the silence.

"Yeah, still here." I paused. "Natalie, I'm so sorry."

"For what?"

"For not kissing you."

"Oh, at your apartment!" Her surprise sounded genuine. "Not the apology I expected."

"But?"

"What?"

"Whenever someone says 'Not the apology I expected,' it's always followed by a *but*."

She let out a short, stifled, chuckle. "I suppose you're right."

*Right about the apology, or about her unfinished sentence?*

Natalie continued. "I've been thinking a lot about that day. I had so much fun, with dinner, and reading your dad's songs together, finding the cryptogram. Oh, and giving you the mixtape! It made me sad when it ended. Then you invited me to the concert, I was so excited. It meant I'd be seeing you again. It told me you wanted to see me, too."

She hesitated, perhaps to collect her thoughts, or choose her words. She was right, though. At the time, I had wanted to see her again, but if I could relive that moment, I'd do things differently. I heard her exhale once, then begin again.

"But there was Don, too, and I . . . I handled that so badly. I really did. Seeing you walk out of the bar made me so happy. Nothing else existed at that moment. It was as if everyone else had disappeared. I treated Don horribly."

I said nothing.

"And then when Jessica showed up, I didn't know what to think. I guess I didn't think at all. I got so angry, convinced you had lied to me about her, about being just friends. When she threw herself at you, and kissed you, I lost it. I didn't give you the benefit of the doubt, and that was wrong of me. I'm so sorry I slapped you."

I blinked several times, not expecting this at all. "You're apologizing to me?"

"Yes."

"Then what were you expecting me to be sorry for?" I asked.

"I expected you to apologize for having lied about your relationship with Jessica. My anger would've been justified. But you weren't lying. I hear it in your voice." I heard a soft sniffle through the phone. "I hope you can forgive me."

"I think so," I said. "But one thing puzzles me. Why did you accept Don's invitation, after you accepted mine?"

She paused for several seconds, and finally said, "What are you talking about?"

"Before the show, Don told us he called you earlier in the afternoon, and you told him you'd come."

"He said that? Frank, I was at the florist. I never spoke with him."

*Why that son of a . . .*

"Eleven to six, Monday through Friday . . .," I said.

". . . and every other Saturday. Exactly. He had left messages, but I never returned them."

That changed things.

"Will you still forgive me?" she asked.

I closed my eyes and thought for a second before answering. "Natalie, my head is in a weird place right now, and I need time to figure stuff out. Jessica probably doesn't want to be friends with me anymore because of what I did and how I acted. But we've been friends a long, long time, and I want to make things right, if she'll let me. Know what I mean?"

"I think I do. Now."

"Along with all the other stuff going wrong in my life. I guess what I'm saying is, before I can decide anything, I gotta fix things. I hope you can understand."

"Frank, I'm not asking for a commitment," she said. "Only that you accept my apology." She held a beat, then added, "Please."

I knew her apology was sincere. She'd admitted that her behavior had been out of line. At the same time, I didn't want her to assume my forgiveness meant things were good. Regardless of whether either of us hoped it might be the case. Still, she was right. Forgiving her didn't mean making a commitment. It meant applying the glue.

Sighing deeply, I said "Apology accepted. It's just that I need some time."

"Take all the time you need," she said, a smile in her voice. It sounded wistful, if not relieved. "If you need anything, just call. Thank you, Frank. I'm glad you picked up."

"I am too," I said. "Good night, Natalie."

"Bye."

I hung up, and immediately dialed again. After three rings, the phone was answered.

"Denise, this is Frank. I need your help, right now!!"

After five minutes of deflection, coercion, and a fair bit of cajoling, I hung up, grabbed my keys, and dashed out.

Twenty minutes later, I burst back into my apartment, carrying a Wegman's bag. I hurried into the bathroom, and dumped its contents into the sink. Plastic bottles of various hair care products spilled out, tumbling and bouncing about the porcelain. I quickly got undressed, turned on the shower, and gathered up the bottles.

I emerged from my bathroom ten minutes later, one towel around my waist, while I used a second one to vigorously dry my hair. Entering my bedroom, I flicked on the light, and faced the bureau mirror, eyes closed. I slowly opened one eye, and then the other, my face screwed into a tight wince.

The marshmallow clumps were gone, and the multicolored streaks were washed out. Denise's advice had been spot on. My hair felt normal again.

It would have been nice, though, if she had told me my hair would turn blond.

# CHAPTER 33

I replaced the handset in its cradle and frowned. Two calls to Jessica before noon on a Sunday, each with the same result – her answering machine. The same thing had happened last night. I considered going to see her, but it seemed too soon. If she wouldn't pick up the phone, she sure as hell wouldn't let me in.

With a loud sigh, I plopped down in the armchair, and picked up Volume 1 of Schumann and Brahms' letters, flipping open to a random page. As soon as I saw Natalie's margin notes, I slammed the book shut and tossed it back onto the table. Nope, didn't want to be reminded of her either at the moment. I sank into self-pity.

Just then, the rapped-out rhythm of *Shave and a Haircut* came from the door. Ned Kerrigan's signature mark of arrival. I crossed the room, tapped out *Two Bits* in reply, then opened the door.

Ned's eyes popped, and he took a half step backwards. "Dude! What happened?"

"Denise's remedy," I said, running my hand through my hair.

"You look like Ricky Schroeder had a fight with puberty and lost."

"Ha ha. Come on in, dude."

He handed an envelope to me as he entered; he held my keyboard stand in the other.

"Here's your cut from Friday night. Fifty bucks."

Inside were two twenties and a ten. Getting paid felt good, but something more important than money needed to be discussed. I slipped the bills into my pocket, while Ned set the stand down next to the door.

"So, how's Don? Still pissed?"

I wanted to hear about what had happened after I had been told to leave, before telling him Don had lied about talking to Natalie. Had he fessed up to the guys?

"Pfft, no. I mean, he was for a while, but he settled down after a buncha brews."

"Huh."

Ned leaned against the table, and shoved his hands into his pockets. "Don't get me wrong, it was good you left. He would've clocked you if you stuck around." He smirked. "Lucky for you Drago saved your butt."

His latest nickname for Mike. There was a vague resemblance.

"After loading the truck, we went back in, listened to the other bands. We were way better, by the way. We talked about what happened, and concluded that while you were a huge bonehead, Natalie acted like a bitch. And everyone knows bitch is worse than bonehead."

"That was it?" My jaw clenched. "Don said nothing else?"

Ned nodded and shrugged. "Pretty much, yeah."

I took a deep breath. "That's interesting because I found out Don never spoke with her. He never invited her."

Ned's eyes widened, and his mouth fell agape. "Seriously? How do you know?"

I told him about my conversation with Natalie last night.

"She's not the bad guy here, Ned. She didn't blow off Don. It only looked like it because he lied to us."

"No. Way. You believe her?"

"Yes. She starts work at 11:00, and Don said he spoke with her after our practice which ended when, 1:30?" I shrugged. "Don tried to save face by threatening to pound mine."

"So if she hadn't shown..."

"Don would've said he got stood up, making her look

bad."

"What a loser! Wait till I tell Joey! We'll totally bust his chops."

I grabbed him by the arm. "Don't. Wait until after I talk with him. He owes me an apology."

Ned gave a casual shrug. "Does this mean you want to quit the band?"

"Quit? You mean you haven't kicked me out?"

He *pfft*'d again. "What? Of course not? Listen, just because you acted like a total bonehead by inviting Natalie doesn't mean we're kicking you out. This stuff happens in bands all the time. You played great, you didn't screw up, and you didn't break anything. That's all we really care about."

It was a strange logic, but it apparently made sense to him. Whether or not I remained part of the band was left to me.

"We'll see how things stand after I talk to Don."

"Sounds fair, dude. But next time, don't invite any girls. Just to be safe."

❊ ❊ ❊

I pulled into the drive on Barrington a little before three o'clock. A silver Ford pickup with Pennsylvania plates was parked close to the house. Fanny hadn't arrived yet. I saw Viktor and Pietr surveying the overgrown lilac bushes on the far side of the yard. I took a deep breath, stepped out of the car, and headed their way. They turned around as I called out to them.

"*Bozhe!*" Pietr exclaimed. "I see why you wear hat yesterday!"

"This is actually an improvement," I said. When a quizzical look crossed his face, I added. "Don't ask."

I looked up at the house, bathed in bright sunlight. Though it showed its age here and there, it looked more beautiful being fully illuminated.

"You must have had quite the childhood, growing up here," I said.

"We had a good life," Pietr said. "For many years."

"Come," Viktor said. "It is too warm. Let's go inside and I'll turn on the AC."

As he headed towards the front door, he reached into his pocket and pulled out a key ring. He ascended the concrete steps beneath the stone arch, with Pietr close behind. Viktor unlocked the heavy, wooden door, and it swung inward silently. I remained at the foot of the steps for several extra seconds, my hand resting against the bricks. When I'd come here last week, it had been on a whim, to see what the house looked like. To see if it really existed as Pietr said.

Now I stood beneath the open doorway Dad walked through one final time, having turned his back on his father. I had been told my entire life this house didn't exist, and I would soon be crossing the threshold. Viktor turned, and seeing that I hadn't followed them up the short flight of steps, raised an eyebrow.

"You coming in or not?"

"I think I'll wait for Fanny. It seems right that way."

Pietr and Viktor shared a glance, looked back at me, and shrugged. Viktor slowly closed the door, and I sat on the front steps, waiting for Fanny to arrive.

Several moments later, Fanny's van made the long approach at a slow, deliberate speed, and parked behind my car. I stood up so she would see me, and stepped to the drive. She hadn't gotten out yet. I saw her through the windshield - her hands were gripping the steering wheel. The maple trees' reflection in the glass obscured her face. She let go of the wheel, unbuckled her seatbelt, and haltingly opened the door.

She still had on her church clothes - floral skirt, light pink blouse, moderate heels. She looked guarded, almost cautious. Her pace was purposeful, not her normal carefree, quick walk. Her hands were clasped at her waist, and her vision was fixated on the house. I couldn't tell if she'd noticed me yet. I guessed at the thoughts and questions that must have been racing through her mind while she drove here. I expected her to be annoyed at me, for not telling her about the home, and perhaps at Uncle Pietr, too, for never saying a word all these years. I suspected she felt strong resentment towards Dad most of all, for having lied to us.

She hadn't phoned me since the barbecue to discuss this. Approaching me was either quiet, pensive Fanny, or calm before the storm Fanny. Given her recent stress levels, I prepared myself for the latter.

As she came around Viktor's truck, she saw me standing on the short sidewalk between the drive and the stairs. Her eyes were puffy; she had been crying.

"Hey," I said, coming forward to embrace her. She let me, and gripped my shoulders more tightly than she had in recent memory. She shuddered in my arms, her head pressed against my shoulder, face turned away.

"You okay?" I asked.

"I managed to keep it together until I got to Barrington," she said. "I had to stop halfway down the street because I couldn't see, and needed to blow my nose. And I also cried during Mass. And for a bit last night. Other than that, I'm peachy."

She let go of me, and looked at my face.

"No hat. And blond. Huh. You've achieved full dork."

"Full dork is cool," I said. "Did you see Dad?"

Fanny took a deep breath and ran a hand through her hair.

"Yes. I asked why he had told us the house had burned down. No reaction, no response."

She glanced up and about the entranceway and upper story of the house, squinting in the sunshine.

"Wow, it's so beautiful. Pietr and Viktor inside?"

I nodded and asked, "You ready for this?"

"No, but I have plenty of Kleenex in my purse."

"Before we go in, I want to apologize for how this got

sprung on you. You were blindsided."

She gave my chest a single smack with an open palm. "I was, and you should. I know why you didn't want to tell me, but a warning would've been nice."

And then she smiled warmly, and her eyes mellowed.

"I guess I owe you an apology as well. Mike tried to tell me to tell you I'd invited Jessica, but I didn't listen. I'm sorry it blew up in your face. Literally."

We hugged. There was no need to say anything else about the matter.

Taking a deep breath, she said, "Let's go in. Despite my feelings right now, I do want to do this."

We climbed the steps and let ourselves in. I wondered if Fanny was holding her breath when I opened the door. I knew I was.

We stepped into a large foyer. The dark hardwood floors contrasted with white-painted walls, which were edged with crown moldings stained the same as the floor. A wide staircase hugged the wall in the far-right corner, rising four steps to a landing before turning and ascending to the upstairs. A low couch sat against the wall beneath a window, at the bottom of the steps. The bay window included a built-in seat, covered with upholstered cushions. A doorway directly across from the entry led deeper into the home. On our left stood a closed pair of doors with leaded glass panels.

Footsteps sounded from the upstairs, overlaid with a muffled conversation in Russian. The steps and voices approached the staircase. Fanny reached out and grasped my hand. Tears had gathered at the corners of her eyes.

"Why did Daddy lie to us, Frankie?" she whispered.

I squeezed her hand. "Because when he moved out, the house vanished. Up in smoke. Poof, gone."

"I don't understand."

Viktor and Pietr's conversation stopped when they reached the landing, seeing us hand in hand near the entry. We exchanged greetings.

"Ah, Fanny," Viktor said, "coming here is emotional, nyet?"

"You could say that," she said, daubing her eyes with the back of her hand, and looked between both men. "Now. It's just the four of us, no cousins, no Aunt Jane. Tell me why Daddy lied."

"Da." Viktor took her by the hand, led her to the bay window seat, and they sat down together. Pietr took the bench near the bottom of the stairs. I leaned against the banister's newel post.

Viktor told her everything, starting with their estrangement. How Grandpa had disowned him, how Dad had changed his name and been written out of the will. How Viktor had ended up with the house when Grandpa died, and how he and Pietr had been given half of everything else.

"Ivan said he never wanted to talk about father again, so we honored his wish," Viktor said. "For thirty-five years, we raise our families, work our jobs, and live our lives. But we all live two lives, nyet? Before, and after."

Fanny looked at each of us in turn. "Daddy said none of this to me. When I became his power of attorney, he told me nothing. I thought he trusted me."

"Ivan was...is a proud man," Pietr said. "You always knew this."

Fanny bit her lip and turned to look out the window. I watched her arms slowly fold across her waist.

"If he didn't want us to know," she said, turning to look at Pietr, "then why did you tell Frank about the house? And the will?"

"You must understand," Pietr started, "Ivan told neither of us about the inquiry. When Frank told me, pieces began to fall into place. We had both believed Ivan's and father's disagreement was over his marriage to Louise, and his conversion to Catholicism. At the time, it seemed the only reasonable explanation, nyet? Frank's story changed our opinions. It was an even more powerful and likely explanation for why things happened."

"That doesn't answer my question," she said. Her arms drew tighter around herself.

Pietr nodded. "I know. I'm getting there. We thought the door to Ivan's past would always be closed. Viktor and I kept our promise to never open it, and Ivan kept his word as well. These songs, though . . . the door is open now. Frank has good reasons to find out who this Clara woman is. He deserves to know - you both do – about Ivan. Perhaps all of us deserve to know. The songs changed everything."

"Not everything," I said, and they turned to face me. "You told me about Dad and Grandpa's problems, and told me about this house. You wanted me to see it. But you hadn't told me everything about our family history. How come you didn't tell me he," at which I pointed to Uncle Viktor, "still owned it?"

Viktor and Pietr exchanged a glance.

"Is there something in this house you don't want me to find?" I asked.

"You told Frank about the house, thinking he wouldn't bother trying to find out who owned it?" Fanny asked. "You obviously don't know him very well. Frank may be stupid at times . . ." She gave me a sympathetic look. "Sorry Frank, but you know it's true. And now you have the hair to match."

She looked back at Pietr. "But he's also determined and stubborn. Once an idea gets in his head, he doesn't let go. He's insufferable like that. I mean, look at how much he's learned since finding those songs a couple weeks ago!"

"I would have found out eventually," I said.

"You are very much like Ivan," Pietr said. "Yes, I should have known."

"So what is it you didn't want me to discover?" I asked him. "Or rather, what is it you *didn't* want to tell me?"

Viktor sighed heavily, and patted Fanny on her leg. "You are not the only person in the room with stupid brother, da?"

She managed a little smile. "Da."

Viktor stood up. "Frank, I have something for you."

My heart skipped a beat. "Okay?"

"When Father died, and the house came to me, I cleaned and fixed it up, thinking it would be best to sell. But I decided to keep it, and rent out rooms. Make extra money in case the farm has a bad year. Anyway, I found some of Ivan's things that had been left behind. He took little with him when he moved out, and father . . . well, he did not care to save Ivan's things."

"It's true," Pietr said. "Soon after Ivan moved out, most of Ivan's belongings were thrown away."

A sick feeling grew in my stomach, that some of those belongings might have been irreplaceable and valuable. Perhaps the final clues I imagined. Hope clashed with despair.

"Most," Viktor said, "but not all. Come with me. We go to Ivan's old room."

Pietr and Fanny stood up, and the three of us followed Viktor towards the staircase. As I stepped aside, I cast a glance through the panes of the closed side door. Beyond stood an upright piano. I touched Fanny's arm to get her attention, and pointed towards the piano. She gasped.

"Uncle Viktor," I said, "excuse me, but is that Dad's piano?"

Viktor had taken two steps, and looked to where I pointed. "It belonged to Mother. Ivan played it every day. I didn't have the heart to sell it. "

I felt myself drawn to it. "May I look at it?" I asked. "Perhaps play it? A chord or two is all."

He gestured with no hesitation, and I opened the doors, stepping into the room.

"This had been the parlor," Pietr explained upon walking in. "Mother played on Sundays for friends, and Ivan practiced the other days of the week. He spent more time here than anywhere else, it seemed."

The piano seemed to be carved from solid maple. Its cover was closed, and the bench was missing. The brass pedals lacked polish, but beyond that, the piano seemed to be in excellent shape. I lifted the cover, and it hinged open noiselessly.

The keys gleamed in the afternoon light. None were chipped, though many in the mid-range looked worn with use, the ivory discolored through repeated playing. "H. Wolfframm," in capital letters with gold ink, was printed on the inside of the cover.

"Wow, a Wolfframm," I said. "Probably built in the late 1800's."

I extended my hand and positioned my fingers above the keys, lowering them so they just touched their surface. My fingertips comfortably settled into the depressions, and I inhaled quickly. My grandmother, whom I had never met, had once played this. Dad had played this piano, perhaps composed his older pieces here. I shifted my hand to a different key, and began to play Clara's Humoresque.

The piano had a rich sound, its tone full and expansive, its pitch pure. The keys' response was firm but yielding. I played several measures and abruptly stopped, and turned to Viktor.

"You've been getting this tuned?" I asked.

He shrugged. "Twice a year for thirty years. I kept it in good repair. In our mother's memory." He paused. "And Ivan's."

"That's one of her songs, isn't it?" Fanny asked, and I nodded at her. She spotted an armchair near the front window. "I think I better sit down."

"Wait a moment," Uncle Pietr said, and, going through a wide doorway on the adjacent wall, returned carrying a dining table chair. "This might help you be more comfortable."

I took it from him, and adjusted my distance. After resetting my hands, I played. The Humoresque was lively, light, and full of joy. It bounced like a heart in the presence of love itself. The playful melody resonated without being overwhelming. When the notes played *Clara Glass*, the song seemed to whisper her name, and only I had the privilege of hearing it.

At the song's conclusion, as the final chord faded away into breath, I dropped my hands in my lap. Viktor and Pietr clapped politely, while Fanny discreetly wiped her eyes.

"Whoever Clara is, Ivan cared much for her," Viktor said.

Fanny stood up, placed a hand upon my back, and forced a smile. "That piece was more stunning than the waltz. I'm not sure I can bear to hear the others."

Pietr cleared his throat. "Shall we go upstairs? We can take the rear staircase, in the kitchen through the pantry. Frank, would you take the chair?"

I would have liked to spend the rest of the afternoon playing, but we weren't here for that. After picking up the chair, we followed Uncle Pietr into the dining room. The sparsely furnished room held a round table in the center that seated four. Two additional chairs flanked the pantry door. A modest buffet stood against one wall, opposite a large box window with a built-in seat. Sunlight filtered through gauzy lace curtains.

"I took the original furniture to Pennsylvania," Viktor said, as we passed through the room towards the other door. I replaced the chair in the empty slot at the table.

We passed through a pantry and into a bright, spacious kitchen. Modern appliances were placed around the room's perimeter. A narrow flight of steps in the corner led upwards. Based on its location, I guessed that it ran parallel to the main staircase. Large alternating white and light blue tiles covered the floor. A doorway off the back led to a large eating area and sitting room, with two doors opening to the patio, where Natalie and I had been the other evening.

"I added the sunroom and patio twenty years ago," Viktor explained. "It faces west, so not as good for breakfast time, but makes for pleasant evening dining, nyet?"

The afternoon sun filtered through the lowered blinds, shedding just enough light to reveal a circular table surrounded by chairs, and several cushioned couches with wicker frames.

Viktor said, "Good. Old tenant had the sense to close the blinds. No need for curious folk to get funny ideas, spying on empty house."

I felt myself starting to blush. I spied several rags and

hand towels lying next to the sink, and began to fold them.

"You've managed to keep the house in fantastic shape, Uncle Vik," Fanny said.

"Fortunately, I had a good tenant for many years. He moved out at the end of July, and I have had no luck finding a new one. Can't let just any *durak* move in."

"What you need," Fanny said, "is a resident caretaker, to take care of the property and to keep their eye on things. Someone who needs a job. Perhaps someone you know and trust might be interested."

After a short moment of silence, Viktor exclaimed "Oh! Little Frankie?"

At the sound of my name, I whirled, holding the last unfolded dish towel in my hand. They all looked at me with anticipation. Viktor stood in the sunroom doorway, Pietr had taken a seat upon the steps, and Fanny, leaning against the refrigerator, grinned.

"Run that by me again?" I asked. "Resident caretaker?"

"Fanny makes good suggestion," Viktor said.

"And you'd pay me?"

"Something for us to think about," he said. "It seems like a good idea. Think now, talk later."

The thought of living here hadn't entered my mind. But Fanny's idea made sense. I'd have something to do while I was laid off. Plus I'd get to live rent free, and have access to a real piano. Sure, I'd have actual responsibilities, and living arrangements would need to be ironed out when a new tenant came around. What about the commute once the school rehired me? I'd hate it, sure, but I could manage. Totally worth it. Then again, I'd never owned a house before. What about minor home repairs? I could change a light bulb and run a vacuum. But fix a toilet? Switch out one of those things in the electrical box? What were they called?

"Frank!" Fanny was calling. She waited at the foot of the stairs. "You've fallen into a thought hole again! Pietr and Viktor have already gone up. C'mon."

"Sorry," I said, "and thanks for suggesting me."

"You're welcome, but don't get ahead of yourself. I can tell you're already mentally moving your stuff in."

We headed upstairs, where Viktor and Pietr waited in the hallway.

"There were once four bedrooms upstairs," Viktor said. "Two in front, one in back, and one right here." He indicated a closed door behind him. "Also only one bathroom. When I added the sunroom, I changed Pietr's old bedroom into a second bathroom."

"Our parents slept in the rear bedroom," Pietr added. "Ivan's room is this way."

Two closed doors faced us on the open landing. Pietr headed towards the left one, and opened the door to let Fanny and me enter.

The bare twelve-foot square room had the same hardwood floors as the rest of the house. The front window was identical to the bay window in the room directly beneath us, with no built-in seat. Maroon drapes framed the window, held back with a looped, corded gold sash. White lace curtains hung nearly to the floor. An opaque, oval glass light fixture lay squat against the ceiling. A closet door stood shut on the wall to our right.

Fanny had gripped my hand before stepping inside, and she showed no sign of letting go.

"This room has been empty for a long time," Viktor explained. "Tenants use it for storage. Most times they use the main bedroom that faces the backyard."

Standing where Dad had slept, studied, and imagined his music felt incredible. I pictured where his bed might have been, and perhaps a desk and chair, a dresser over next to the closet. This had been his room since he'd immigrated from Russia, through grade school, high school, and college. He'd returned here after his Navy service, and stayed here during his early years at Prescott. Until that fateful day.

Viktor adjusted one of the drapes in the bay window.

"After Ivan moved out, Father kept the bedroom locked. Two weeks later, he had the furniture removed. Donated all his clothing. In one month, it was as if Ivan never lived here at all."

"Daddy never came back to get his things?" Fanny asked.

Viktor slowly shook his head. "He left in summer of 1951, with clothes on his back. Perhaps some personal things. Mother was heartbroken, of course, but what could she say?"

"And Dad never explained why?" I asked.

"We assumed Louise was the reason," Pietr answered. "They married some months later."

"And Father never spoke of it," Viktor added.

Fanny cleared her throat. "Didn't you ever think to ask? 'Dad, why are you so mad at Ivan?' 'Dad, how come Ivan and Louise don't come for Christmas?' 'Dad, when are you gonna stop being a douche?'"

I gave her hand a hard squeeze. Pietr grunted, and swiped a stray clump of dust with his shoe, while Viktor idly adjusted the curtains.

"I'll take that as a no," she said.

Pietr rubbed his chin, and said gruffly, "When you were young, Fanny, did you question Ivan's reasons? Did you demand explanations for his decisions? I doubt it. And if you had, were his answers ever to your satisfaction?"

She looked down, and I recalled her telling me about how Dad had disregarded her requests to reconcile with me. And his response to her when questioned about having changed his name. I wondered if those same memories were crossing her mind. She had called him a stubborn old mule, after all.

Before the silence became too awkward, I broke it. "Uncle Viktor, you said you found some of Dad's things that Grandpa didn't know about, or had overlooked? Things Dad might have hidden?"

"Da," he said, nodding. "Except, Ivan didn't hide them. Mother did."

Fanny and I exchanged surprised looks. Pietr appeared shocked as well.

"Viktor, you only told me you had found some of his things. How do you know Mother hid them?"

"Where they were hidden. When I knocked down the kitchen wall to build the sunroom, I found three boxes in the dead space of a corner cupboard. Ivan would not have put them there. Mother saved them, probably hid them when Father was at work." He moved towards the door, back into the hallway. "Let me show you other rooms, da?"

We left the room in single file, with Uncle Pietr closing the door behind him. As Viktor led on, he continued his tale.

"Perhaps Mother hoped Ivan and Father would reconcile. Or that she could somehow get them to Ivan. But she died soon after Ivan left, and hadn't told anybody. Father died several years later. I did not see them when getting the house ready. Who would think to look in a dark corner, da?"

"Did you open them?" I asked.

"And why didn't you give them to Daddy?" Fanny asked.

We reached the rear bedroom, its double door closed. The house no longer interested me. I needed to know what was in those boxes.

"I opened one," Viktor said, "and saw right away they belonged to Ivan. I did not look at the other two, and no, before you ask, I did not read his things."

"Was it music?" I asked. I may have sounded more urgent than I intended.

"There may have been music sheets. I closed the box back up and removed them."

Fanny repeated her question, adding, "You had plenty of opportunities."

Viktor made a thoughtful face. "Since moving out, Ivan changed his name, he never spoke to Father, and he never spoke of old family things. He visited us in Pennsylvania, came to my boys' weddings, but we never discussed this. He kept that door closed, nyet? It would be wrong for me to open it."

"You could have given them to him at Mom's funeral," she told him.

"That would've been inappropriate," Pietr said. "A slap in Ivan's face during his time of grief."

"Well, now that I have power of attorney, I want them," Fanny said. "Nothing is stopping you from giving them to me now. Not honor, not dignity, not anything."

"Fanny, if it's all the same to you," I interjected, "I'd like them." I turned to Uncle Viktor. "Where are they?"

"They are at the farm."

# CHAPTER 34

After saying goodbye to our uncles, Fanny and I headed back to our cars. Her mood had changed since we'd arrived an hour ago - instead of being tearful, she had grown irritated. I struggled to match her quick march-like pace down the driveway, each step clipped with measured determination.

"We have one weird family," she said. "I don't get this family honor, dignity, and integrity stuff, do you?"

"Kinda."

"Care to explain it to me? I mean, I understand why Grandpa got involved in the inquiry, given his position at Prescott. And I can see why Daddy got angry. If he'd planned to accept the inquiry's decision, in order to protect Clara, only to have Grandpa pull the rug out from under him, then it makes some sense."

"Right so far."

"So, what am I missing?"

We had stopped at my car, and I dug out my keys.

"Dad was willing to sacrifice his career for Clara's sake, but Grandpa's decision to protect his reputation and the company took that away from him. Each thought they were doing the right thing for the right reasons. Or maybe Grandpa knew about Clara and didn't care. Regardless, Dad felt pretty disrespected. He did what he felt he had to do."

"All for a woman."

"All for love," I corrected her.

"And screwed our family out of an inheritance, and created this gaping hole in our family history. They," at which she pointed back to the house, "kept it all secret, knowing Daddy was lying to us."

"But they didn't know about the inquiry."

"I'm talking about the fight, the will, and the house! Those lies!" Fanny chewed her lip. "Do you think Mom knew any of this?"

I shrugged. "Don't know. If she had, it would mean she had known about Clara, and that's unlikely. I'm sure she knew about Dad and Grandpa's falling out, despite not ever meeting him. Who knows what Dad told her, though."

"She never met Grandpa?" Fanny asked.

"That's what Uncle Pietr told me. As far as the inheritance, I'm sure she knew. The house? Dad probably told her it had burned, just like he told us."

Fanny shook her head. "Dad was one determined stubborn man. Makes me feel terrible for Mom."

"What do you mean?"

"All those years, she wrongly believed she was responsible for Dad and Grandpa's falling out. Being Catholic, Dad's conversion, disrupting the family dynamic. And Dad knew it. He allowed Mom to believe that throughout their entire marriage."

I hadn't considered that. A part of me wanted to believe that Dad had eventually told her the truth, and that it had become their own secret from everyone else. There'd be no way of ever finding out.

"You holding up okay?" I asked her.

Fanny made a face, as if unsure how to answer. "I think so. Better now than when I got here, believe it or not. I felt even worse yesterday. Emotion explosion. Poor Mike, he's borne the brunt of it. On the one hand, seeing the house, there's this sense of closure. On the other hand, though. . . I don't know."

"Disappointment?"

"Yeah. I'm either angrily disappointed, or disappointedly angry. It's like believing in Santa as a kid, only to become upset and disillusioned when you discover he's not real. A part of you is pissed you've been lied to all those years. This is like that."

"Wait. There isn't a Santa Claus?"

"Or an Easter Bunny. Sorry, kid." She punched me playfully on the shoulder. "Normally I'm a 'quick to forgive' kind of person, and I try to give the benefit of the doubt, but this whole thing..."

She looked back at the house, and her eyes darkened, and her face seemed to cloud over.

"Frankie, I hate being lied to. And today I learned just how dishonest Daddy has been. Not out of malice, or cruelty, but out of pride. It just seems so stupid. But that's not even the worst of it."

"What is?"

"What hurts my heart most is, he hurt Mom the worst of all. It's going to take me some time to forgive him."

"Secrets, lies, and promises. They suck."

"Amen, brother."

"Maybe the only silver lining out of this is the possibility I end up living here," I said.

"That would be good for you, once you work out the details down in Pennsylvania."

After telling us he'd brought the three boxes to his Pennsylvania farm, Viktor had encouraged me to come tomorrow and collect them. His farm was just south of the New York state line, a little more than a two-hour drive.

Fanny looked up at me. "What do you think you'll find in those boxes?"

"I have no idea," I answered. "I'm hoping for more than just secrets and promises. Speaking of which, I need to ask you something. Are you keeping anything else from me?"

Fanny's eyes narrowed. "Regarding?"

"Dad. He didn't want you to ask me if I wanted the house, remember? I had to drag it out of you. I'm wondering if you're keeping more from me, having power of attorney and all."

She winced, only for a second, either because I had struck a nerve, or because she felt offended. I expected her to either cross her arms, or sock me in the shoulder again, this time with more conviction. Instead, her face softened, and she hugged me tightly.

"Oh Frankie, not now."

I returned her hug, realizing Dad had made other conditions, binding her to secrecy. And whether she wished to prevent hurt feelings, or ward off an angry outburst, Fanny decided to hold to her promise. To keep that door closed. For now.

Rather than push against the door, I simply held her close.

She stepped away, the smile on her face betrayed by a pensive look in her eyes. She kissed me on the cheek, and tousled my hair.

"Dork." Her smile broadened momentarily, then her face turned serious, tinged with hope. "Jessica?"

I spread my hands. "I've called three times, no answer. Maybe I'll try again tonight."

"Give her more time," she said. "At least wait until after you get back from Pennsylvania. And the other one?"

She meant Natalie. I considered recounting the details of our phone call, but decided it could wait.

"We spoke last night. Not gonna say it's good, but it's better. I'll tell you about it some other time."

"Fair enough. Drive safely tomorrow, okay? Call me when you get home."

She got into her van, and waved goodbye through the windshield. I watched until she reached the street and headed towards East Avenue.

I took a long look at the house, glad I had walked through it, while also disappointed at what might have been. Fanny had a sense of closure seeing it. I felt like I had lost two homes in a single month. A huge part of our family history had ended here in 1951, leaving behind pain, unlived memories, and three old cartons that might hold all the answers.

\* \* \*

The drive to Pennsylvania went smoothly; I had left early to avoid holiday traffic. On the passenger seat lay a Triple-A road map, folded open to show the town of Mansfield. Scribbled directions to Uncle Viktor's farm on a piece of loose leaf were paperclipped to the back of the map.

After two hours, I reached the town of Lawrenceville, just inside Pennsylvania. The cassette player stopped, so I flipped the tape over, and Strauss' *Also Sprach Zarathustra* began to play. I'd be at Uncle Viktor's farm in about twenty minutes.

Mists rose from the tree-topped mountains as the sun continued to rise. Route 15 wound through the Allegheny Mountains, leapfrogging the Tioga River several times as the river curled its way through the valley. Giant steel utility towers carried power lines up and over the hills. Small homesteads pressed tightly together in the valleys, with a few cattle farms carved into the hillsides, creating a patchwork of green and gold fields amid the forested slopes. I rolled down my window, letting in the fresh, crisp, country air.

Several minutes later, on a country road outside Mansfield, I spied a barn-shaped mailbox with the name 'Stephens' stenciled on its side standing at the entrance of the farm. Affixed to the mailbox's top was a stamped metallic cow, painted white with black splotches. I'd made it.

With a deep breath, I turned into the long, dusty dirt driveway. Memories of those long ago summer visits flashed by: milking cows in the dairy barn, gathering eggs from the hen houses, swimming in the fishpond, playing in the woods with my older cousins Alexei and Yuri.

I parked next to Viktor's truck, on a bare patch of lawn between the farmhouse and firetruck-red barn. Their house reminded me of the Waltons' farmhouse, but smaller. The barn didn't seem as large now as it had when I was a kid. The sliding door stood open, and the strong aromas of straw and hay intermixed with manure wafted through the air. An orange and white cat sat in the doorway, washing its paw.

The squeak of rusty hinges broke the silence. I walked around Viktor's truck, heading towards the porch, where he stood on the wide wooden steps.

"Little Frankie, you made good time!" he said, descending the steps to greet me, a smile stretched across his face. "I just finished feeding the chickens and stealing their eggs. Alice is scrambling the harvest, and frying some bacon. Come!"

He enveloped me in another bear hug.

"Sounds delicious," I said. "Coffee too I hope."

"This is a farm," Viktor said. "Farms run on coffee."

He led me inside, the front door opening immediately into a spacious living room. I quickly glanced around the room while heading towards the kitchen. It had been ten years since my last visit, for Yuri's wedding, and very little had changed. The wallpaper was a little more faded, the furniture a little more worn, and the carpeting a little more threadbare. The passage of time had shown its hand, but in many ways, the farmhouse seemed to have been untouched.

"Alice! Little Frankie is here!"

From the kitchen I heard her yell "Frankie, get in here and give me a kiss hello!"

Aunt Alice was whisking eggs near the stove when I entered the kitchen.

"Hi Aunt Alice," I said, and she presented her cheek for a kiss, which I dutifully provided, leaning down to reach her. She stood all of 5'3, stout and solid. Her black hair, streaked with silver, was tied back in a bun. The effects of farm labor showed in the lines of her face, though her blue eyes sparkled with clear vitality. Her white and red checkered apron was splattered with grease and dusted with flour.

"It made me so happy when Viktor called last night to tell me you were coming," she said. "It's a shame you can't stay long."

"Just a pop in visit," I told her.

"Sit down, and I pour you coffee," Viktor said, pointing to the table in the nook off the kitchen.

I sat down as instructed, and updated Alice with a condensed version of my life since Mom's funeral, which was the last time we'd seen each other. Throughout a hearty breakfast and several cups of coffee, I filled her in on Dad, Fanny, Mike and the kids, careful to leave out the pregnancy. Alice leaned back in her chair, and sighed.

"Fanny needs to visit so I can love on those children," she said. "I hope you invited her, Viktor."

"Of course."

"And poor Ivan," she added. Her eyes turned a darker shade of blue. "So sad."

Viktor refilled my cup. "Enough family talk. Let us discuss caretaker, da? I have given this much thought."

For the next twenty minutes, we spoke while Alice cleaned up from breakfast. In the end, we negotiated a deal, sealed with an exuberant handshake that left my fingers aching. When my lease expired at year's end, I would officially move in, and Viktor would pay me to maintain the grounds, and keep the home in good shape while he advertised for new tenants.

"And of course, you live there even after tenants move in. To keep eye on things."

The arrangements sounded fair to me. A modest income, free housing, and access to a well-cared for piano. He would return to Rochester in a few weeks to go over all of my responsibilities in detail.

After one last coffee, Viktor said to me, "Let's go up to the attic."

He and Aunt Alice exchanged a glance, a glance which told me she knew why I'd come. I followed him up the stairs, a step or two behind. His pace seemed slower than it had when he'd showed Fanny and me the old house yesterday.

"You never looked through those boxes?" I asked him. "You've had them for so long."

He shook his head. "I was tempted, at first. I opened one, remember, when I found them. But not after. They were his secrets, his past."

"So why did you keep them? Why not just throw them away?"

"In case Ivan opened the door."

We reached the upstairs hallway, and he turned to face me.

"You must think our ways are strange. Odd customs. All these questions from you and Fanny. But to us, they are not strange or odd. They are old customs, old ways of living, with honor. With respect. So many things in the world have changed, nyet? Old things get torn down to make way for new things. Just because something is old, does not mean it is bad. And just because something is new, does not mean it is better."

"But these secrets have hurt people," I told him. "They've hurt me, Fanny, maybe Mom most of all. Fanny is so upset, you have no idea."

He shifted his weight from one foot to the other. "Da," he said softly.

"So how can you say it's living with honor? When you come down to it, what's the difference between keeping a secret and telling a lie?"

He remained silent for several seconds, but it seemed longer, and I didn't know if he would answer. Finally, he looked at me with a certainty I hadn't seen in a long time.

"Lies would have killed us in Russia, secrets saved us in America. That is the difference."

I shook my head. "That may have been true seventy years ago, but it seems to me that Dad told a lot of lies to keep his secrets."

"Perhaps you think so because you don't know the whole truth," he said. "Perhaps you never will. You search for this Clara woman, da? You may still not find her today."

"I know. But I have to try."

"And if you find the truth? What then?"

"Then I'll have a choice to make, won't I? But at least I'll have that option."

He gave a slow nod, then said, "Let us get boxes, da?"

We reached the end of the hall, and he opened the attic door. Shoe boxes, small cartons, a few odds and ends, and several short stacks of National Geographic magazines lined each side of the staircase. At the top of the steps, Viktor pulled an overhead shoestring, and two bare light bulbs suspended on black wires turned on.

"This way," he said, heading towards a dormer facing rearward.

My pulse quickened as he led me to a rectangular-shaped sheet-covered arrangement, which was about chest high. Viktor slowly pulled away the sheet to keep the dust from scattering everywhere. Three large wooden luggage trunks had been stacked underneath, and they were weathered and scored with age.

"They are in the top trunk," Viktor said.

My hands suddenly grew sweaty. We lowered it to the floor. Viktor undid the two clasps, and opened the lid. I swallowed, sure the lump in my throat was my stomach, ready to lurch out of my mouth.

Packed inside were three square rigid boxes, slightly larger than a department store garment gift box, and twice as deep. I carefully lifted the topmost box out, and set it on top of the nearby trunk. I removed the remaining two, placing them on top of the first. They were in good condition, despite their age.

Viktor lowered the trunk lid, and flicked the clasps closed.

"Take them downstairs," he said, "where the light is better."

After replacing the trunk and sheet, we left the attic. I carried the three boxes as if they were gifts of gold, frankincense, and myrrh for the baby Jesus. Viktor showed me into the dining room, and I placed them on the table, exhaling a long, anxious breath. Alice emerged from the kitchen, drying her hands with a towel. Seeing the cartons, she gave Viktor a concerned look. His face remained impassive.

"Why are you both so worried?" I asked. "This is pretty exciting for me, yet you both look like I'm about to exhume the dead."

Alice sighed, draping the towel over her shoulder. "Maybe you are, Frank."

Her comment rattled me somewhat. "You know what's in them?"

She shook her head, and hesitated before answering. "Sometimes, the past is best left in the past. We've lived all these years without knowing about this Clara person, and things were fine. Ever since you found those songs..." Her voice drifted off.

"Ever since I found those songs," I continued, "I've discovered things weren't as fine as everyone thought." I placed my hands on the top carton, fingers gripping the cover. "If it helps, I can leave and open these at home."

Viktor waved his hand. "No, this is okay."

He gave Alice a pleading look, and she slowly retreated into the kitchen.

"This business upsets your aunt," he said to me. "She and Louise were very close, and she is afraid this Clara woman . . . I tell her Ivan never cheated on her, but still she worries."

I wanted to believe Dad had been faithful, too. I sympathized with Alice's concerns, but discovering Clara's identity was the only way to allay everybody's fears.

I removed the lid, and peered inside. Viktor leaned forward to look as well. Two items were stacked one on top the other: a bundle of letter-size postage envelopes tied with brown sisal twine, and beneath it a package wrapped in brown paper, the sort butchers wrap cuts of meat in, tied with similar twine. I removed the bundle of envelopes, and flipped through them, counting at least fifteen. The postage stamps were Finnish; the postmarks read *Par Avion* and *Suomi Finland*, and they were dated 1950 and 1951. Each was addressed to Ivan Stepanov, Prescott Conservatory of Musical Studies, Rochester NY

14613 USA.

Had I found letters Clara had written Dad? Were these them? Of course she would have mailed them to the school, rather than to the house.

But from Finland? It seemed so improbable.

"Louise was Finnish," Viktor said. He pointed to the postmark. "Hanko. Her hometown."

"And Dad studied in Helsinki for a year after World War Two," I added. My heart raced.

Mom's nationality and hometown were no secret, but I had considered it a mere coincidence. Had he met Clara in Finland? I put down the letters and untied the larger package, unwrapping the brittle, brown paper covered with postage and postmarks.

Inside was a collection of sheet music, roughly written and very rudimentary. I immediately recognized Dad's handwriting. These resembled the rough drafts of his compositions packed in the unmarked cartons sitting in my apartment. But these weren't just any compositions. I recognized the topmost song.

*Waltz, Opus 1, Number 1.*

Clara's songs.

My shaking hands held the marked up and edited original scores. Notation and symbols were scattered up and down the margins, in different color inks, hallmarks of his editing. These were Dad's working manuscripts. There was no title, but there didn't need to be. I knew this song. I knew all these songs. I couldn't believe my eyes. Or my good fortune.

"I need to sit down," I said, pulling out the chair. "Uncle Viktor, these are the original drafts of Clara's songs."

"Then it is good I saved boxes, nyet?"

"Good? It's fantastic!"

I leafed through several scores, pausing to look at one of the Romances, looking for the cryptograms Natalie and I had found. They were there, both of them, the black notes circled in blue ink. Russian text, written with red in Dad's handwriting, filled the space between staves. My heart skipped a beat.

Suddenly, I sat upright and leaned forward, peering at the page. Something looked wrong, looked out of place.

"What is it?" Viktor asked.

"This is Dad's handwriting, see?" I said, pointing to various places where he had written notes and corrections.

"Da, I recognize it."

"So, who wrote this here? And over here?" I asked, pointing to two examples of a different handwriting. "It's not even Russian."

Alice had returned to the dining room, and now stood behind me, looking over my shoulder.

"That's Finnish," Viktor said.

"It's Louise's handwriting," Alice added.

I snatched the wrapping paper, and read it more closely. The postage and postmarks were Finnish, addressed to Dad via Prescott. The handwriting was identical.

*To Dad? From Mom? From Finland?*

I fell against the back of the chair. Mom had co-written Dad's songs? For Clara?

"But she was in Rochester," I said. "Wasn't she?"

Neither Viktor nor Alice responded. They both stepped away from the table, moving closer to the kitchen entrance. Their expressions remained stoic, but I sensed they knew something.

Were the letters from her too? I undid the twine, and studied several envelopes. They were arranged chronologically, the latest one postmarked *Elo 7 1951*. Mom had taught Fanny and me some basic Finnish. Elo, an abbreviation for August. The earliest letter was postmarked *Tuoko 15 1950*. May 15th.

The handwriting on the envelopes and manuscripts matched.

"Why was Mom in Finland?" I asked, looking at them both.

"Perhaps the letters say why," Viktor replied softly. I noticed that Alice had grabbed his forearm. A question flashed through my mind – did she know?

My pulse quickened, and I felt sweat collect along the back of my neck. I decided to read the last one. The envelope had been cleanly slit open using a letter opener. I carefully removed the letter, a sheet of medium weight stationery folded in half, yellowing at the corners and along the edges. A stenciled delicate ivy design edged the perimeter, the ink slightly faded.

The letter was in English, the penmanship precise and feminine. My hand shook, as I read it in silence.

*My dearest Ivan,*

*I purchased a ticket, departing from Hanko on September 11, arriving in New York City September 17. I shall arrange passage by train once I reach the United States. My family does not know, otherwise they will stop me from returning. They have done so once already. I leave so much behind. And do not worry about papers - I've taken care of that at great expense.*

*Only a few more weeks, my love, and we shall be together, this ghastly, horrific experience behind us forever. Our new life will begin, filled with joy, happiness, and music. Prescott has rejected my appeal for readmission. So be it. That life is behind me now. I know you struggle to remain there, but remain you must, for no other reason than to be a staunch reminder of what they've done.*

*The songs are exquisite and beyond beautiful. I hope the packet reached you safely, and I pray my suggestions and ideas are of use. Your skill amazes me. I am in tears as I write this, thinking of how deep and abiding this tribute shall be upon its completion, even if only for our ears alone.*

*Stay steadfast, my love. We are not guilty of the greater sin. We shall be together soon, and all shall be well. All shall be well, and all manner of things shall be well.*

*Yours in love,*

*Louise*

*All shall be well, and all manner of things shall be well.* How many times had she said that? She'd told me some saint had said it, but she had quoted it so often that it had lost any and all significance to me. It occurred to me now just how significant those words had been to her.

And what did she mean by *ghastly, horrific experience*? The inquiry? Or something else? What did *We are not guilty of the greater sin* mean? And the songs, *a deep and abiding tribute*? I stared at the remaining letters on the table, not wanting to read them, yet knowing I would have to. But not here, not now.

I quickly refolded the letter, and slid it back into its envelope.

"What did the letter say?" Alice asked. Her face seemed paler, despite the room being bathed in sunlight.

"I'm not entirely sure," I answered, though my heart - and that final sentence of encouragement to Dad - told me otherwise.

"I have to go." I stood up, collecting the letters and manuscripts, and putting them back in the carton.

"You are not opening the others?" Viktor asked.

"Yes, but not here," I said, replacing the cover.

This needed to be done on my own, or perhaps with Fanny. Not here, though, and not in their presence. I suddenly understood who Clara was. I had found her.

And everything had changed.

# CHAPTER 35

R ather than directly going to Fanny's house from Viktor's, I had returned to my apartment, and called her.

"I'm back," I'd said.

"And?"

"And how much beer do you have?"

"I'm pregnant, remember?" A beat. "Are you okay? You sound exhausted."

"Lotta driving," I'd said, but that was a partial reason. "Listen, I think it'd be better if it's just the two of us when I come over. Can you kick Mike and the kids out?"

She'd paused, and her voice became softer and more serious. "I'll send them to his parents. Come at six."

I had spent the rest of the afternoon reading and rereading Mom's letters. Everything about Clara, about Dad and Mom, about the inquiry, about the songs – it had all fallen into place.

I pulled into Fanny's driveway a little after six, and I wasn't looking forward to telling her. Overcoming the apprehension took some time; I remained in the car a full ten minutes after turning off the engine. Finally, I got out, grabbed the boxes off the passenger seat, and headed straight into Fanny and Mike's backyard. Turning the corner, I saw her sitting at the patio table, idly twirling a bottle of pop. An open bottle of Genny Twelve Horse waited for me at the neighboring chair, a clear invitation. She jerked her head up as I approached.

"Frankie," she said, rising.

I placed the boxes on the table, and gave her a long,

tender hug. She pulled away, her arms still around my waist, her face stretched thin. I imagined mine looked similar. She glanced down at the boxes.

"You learned who Clara is."

I nodded, looking at the boxes. "It's all there. No more secrets."

Sitting down, I reached towards Fanny with both hands. She put hers in mine, and I squeezed them.

"First of all, Clara's not who I thought. She's a real person, and it's her real name, not a nickname or anything like that. She's just not . . ." I clamped my mouth shut. There would be no easy way to do this.

"How do you know? What did you find?"

"Letters. Songs. The bottom two boxes are notes and rough drafts for some of his compositions from the 40's. The top box, though..."

I opened it and removed the letters, now bound with a large rubber band, no longer in their envelopes. I handed the packet to her, and I spoke without giving her time to ask anything.

"Mom wrote them when she was in Finland, between 1950 and 1951. I've arranged them oldest to newest. I think you should read them."

"I don't understand," she said, taking them. Her eyes, wide and distracted, darted between me and the letters in her hand. "Why was Mom in Finland? This makes no sense."

"Okay. Bear with me here." I took a long swig. "We know Mom started her grad work at Prescott in 1949, right? We both thought that was when they first met."

"Mom told us their courtship started in the summer of 1950." She blinked several times. "After she had dropped out."

"Yeah, I know. However, one of these letters mentions that they first met in 1947, in Helsinki. She was enrolled at the Sibelius Academy while Dad was there, and he convinced her to apply to Prescott."

Fanny swallowed hard, her gaze riveted on the letters. "They were already in love when Mom got to Prescott. But . . .but fraternizing with students was prohibited!"

"Let me finish, okay? You're getting ahead of yourself." I took a deep breath to gather myself. "Yes, Prescott had a strict policy against fraternization, which Dad and Mom ignored. They dated quietly for more than a year, one thing led to another . . . and he got her pregnant."

Fanny gasped.

"They tried to keep it secret," I continued, "but the school found out anyway. They held that inquiry, and in order to protect Mom's reputation, the administration cooked up the communist sympathizer charge. That's when Grandpa got involved, at which point everything went to hell."

Fanny squeezed her eyes shut, and let the letters fall from her hands. "What happened to Mom?"

"Prescott expelled her, ordered her to sail back to Finland, and to remain in the custody of her parents. That's why she 'dropped out.' Dad objected, of course. He was prepared to admit to being a sympathizer, if it meant she could stay. They wanted to marry. Grandpa quashed the inquiry, but Mom's expulsion was upheld. Dad kept his job, and a scandal was avoided.

"Grandpa wouldn't let them marry?"

"No. Mom tried to return so they could marry, and she finally did in September of 1951, and they got married right away. Dad lived at home to save money for a house. I can't imagine how he managed to stand living there all that time."

"Stubbornness and defiance," Fanny said. "I still don't understand why Grandpa didn't simply let them marry."

I shrugged my shoulders. "Maybe he didn't want the publicity of an out of wedlock grandchild, or the school didn't want the scandal of a teacher behaving improperly. They thought it better to make the . . . problem go away."

Fanny scowled. "Do the letters say when she got pregnant?"

"She spoke of a Valentine's Day date, so probably then."

Fanny heaved a drawn-out sigh. "So, she went to Finland and had the baby in..." she counted on her fingers, "...November. November 1950."

She sat to attention, as if poked in the back or stung by a bee.

"Clara is our older sister!"

"Yes, and no," I said, recalling Mom's words in her final letter: '...this ghastly, horrific experience behind us forever.' I took a deep breath, and gathered myself.

"There was a baby girl, whom she named Clara Lasinen Stepanov. Mom's maiden name. It's 'glass' in English. I should've known."

Fanny's face drained of color, her whole body slumped, and one hand fell across her stomach.

"Stillborn?" she asked, her voice barely audible, as if saying it too loudly might make it true.

I removed a letter from the packet, dated Kesäkuu 9 1950. June 9th.

"It'd be better to hear it in Mom's words." I cleared my throat.

*"Ivan, my love -*

*"It is over. I have been compelled against my will, and it is done. The illness I contracted aboard The Finland Star on the return sail home delayed the procedure for three weeks.*

*"I am bereft, and miss you dearly. There are no words. How shall I ever forgive the evil done against us? Yet that is what I must do. And you as well. Please find it in your heart to do so. If not for your own sake, then for mine.*

*"We shall be together again, my love. I know it in my heart. I hope your heart believes the same. All shall be well, and all manner of things shall be well.*

*"The nurse told me our child is a girl. I have named her Clara Lasinen Stepanov.*

*"Promise me you shall never forget her. I never shall.*

*"With all my broken heart, forever yours - Louise"*

My voice broke numerous times as I read. I held out the

letter for Fanny to take, but she didn't reach for it. Her eyes were too blurred to focus on the letter or anything else. The corners of her mouth quivered. She wiped her wet cheeks with the back of her hand, and forced herself to stand, leaning upon the table for help. As I got to my feet, Fanny fell into my arms, and her body shook with heavy sobs as I held her.

She whispered through tears and gulping breaths as she clung to me.

"The songs, they're his promise."

I stroked her hair, and began to cry. We wept for ourselves, for Dad and Mom, for Clara, and against all the secrets, lies, and promises come to light, in the enduring brilliance of his memorial in song.

# EPILOGUE

*June 1995*

I parked my maroon Dodge Caravan halfway up the drive at 181 Augustine Street. Before opening the door, I turned to my passengers and said, "Let me make sure they're okay with this before you get out, alright?"

Some things had changed. The giant elm near the street no longer towered above the yard. Only a weathered, flat stump remained. The landscaping had been updated. The scraggly bushes which had once surrounded the porch had been replaced with a Japanese maple and an assortment of fragrant perennials and colorful annuals. The concrete sidewalk to the front porch had been changed to decorative bricks. The clapboard siding had been updated with yellow vinyl siding and white trim.

I rang the doorbell, and a middle-aged woman came to the screen, holding a blue and white striped dish towel. She wasn't the person who had bought the house nine years ago.

"May I help you?" she asked.

"Hi," I said, in a cheerful voice. "You don't know me, but I used to live here, back in the 60s and 70s." I indicated the minivan. "We were in the neighborhood, and I wanted to show my kids where I grew up. I hope I'm not imposing."

The woman smiled. "Not at all! You don't mean to come in, do ya? I'm in the middle of cleaning, that's all."

I shook my head. "A walk in the backyard would be enough."

"That'd be fine!"

I waved to the van for everyone to come over. The rear door slid open, and two children jumped out: a young boy and a younger girl. The passenger door swung open as well. Soon we were all gathered at the base of the steps.

"Cute family you got there. Hi, I'm Judy. Judy Weathers."

After they all said hello, I introduced them.

"This is my son Lewis, my daughter Jenny . . ."

"I'm four!" she announced, and Judy smiled.

". . . and my wife Jessica."

"Pleasure meeting you all," she said. "You seem to be pretty far along there, miss."

Jessica beamed. "Due in August."

Judy turned back to me. "And you are?"

"I'm Frank. Frank Stepanov."

# THE END

# ACKNOWLEDGEMENTS

This is where I thank all the people who made Clara possible.

First off, a heartfelt thank you to my wife, Mindy - for being understanding and patient throughout this process. You inspired me to write a better story, gave me time and space to explore it, and the freedom to bring it across the finish line. I am forever grateful.

A huge thank you to Mary Dundas and Rebecca French who read through the roughest-of-the-rough draft, chapter by chapter, and survived. Phew, that was a lot of words! You encouraged and motivated me to carry on until the end, and discover Clara's identity. I can't thank the two of you enough.

Thanks to my awesome beta readers - you know who you are! Your questions and feedback in real time were a fantastic help. A special shout out to Mark Schaad who meticulously fact-checked every song, movie, and Rochester reference for accuracy. Here's a Scooby Snack for ya!

A round of thanks to Brendan Hodge for a crash course on Russian history and names, as well as sound advice navigating the self-publishing process.

A special thank you to Stacia Humby for illustrating the beautiful cover - it came out more wonderful than I had imagined. You are an amazing, talented artist!

A *super* big thank you to my editor, Rose Judge. Finding you was pure providence. There aren't enough words to express my gratitude at your relentless determination to make Clara shine and sing (even if there were enough words, you'd edit out most of them, anyway!). Thanks for fixing my verb tenses, for curbing my prolific use of semi-colons, and letting me win the occasional battle. And now you know all about mixtapes! I look forward to our next collaboration!

Finally, and most importantly - all my thanks and praise to almighty God. Because at the end of the day, it all comes down to Grace.